# Pascal's Spring

Peter Holdroyd

NVP Publications

Published by NVP Publications
Norwich
www.nvppublications.uk

This book is a work of fiction, and except in the case of historical fact, any resemblance to actual persons, living or dead, is purely coincidental

ISBN-13: 978-0-9933409-5-6

i

# DEDICATION

To my wonderful and supportive wife, Dee.

**The burden of work for the East Anglian town of** Breydon's small CID team, headed by DI George Pascal, usually light, is about to become a whole lot busier.

The problems begin with the discovery of a young man who is found unconscious with a serious head wound on a quayside in one of the small fishing harbours on the Norfolk coast, and the disappearance of a teenage girl.

The team's investigations lead them to become involved with abduction, murder, arson and sex-trafficking, to say nothing of the embezzlement of a substantial sum which was meant to pay for a supply of drugs. And drug dealers are unforgiving of that sort of thing...

Other books by Peter Holdroyd

Brain Fever

The Silent Years

Leaving it all Behind

# CHAPTER 1

Danny Bakker sat between two young Latvian girls who were chatting across him excitedly in their own language. Like the other girls in the crowded cabin, their expressions were of hope and good humour. Obviously, then, he thought, nobody'd yet told them what was in store for them when they got to England. A sour smile twisted his lips at the idea.

He'd been told by Mr van Ruys back in Amsterdam, that the boat was taking over a cargo and he could hitch a lift to England. He'd expected a cabin full of heroin, cocaine and cannabis, but instead found it to contain around fifteen females. He wasn't involved much in the trafficking side of his employer's business. The shy looks he was getting from some of the girls made him wonder if the fringe benefits wouldn't be better than those he got as van Ruys's enforcer against those who failed to complete their side of their contracts – mainly by failing to pay for drugs.

The engines changed pitch, becoming quieter, and the cruiser's motion through the North Sea changed. The cabin door opened and one of the two Germans crewing the vessel, reached in and flicked off the cabin light.

'You shut up now!' he told the girls. 'Otherwise we will be heard and you could spend the rest of your lives in prison.' He looked at Danny. 'Keep them quiet, eh, Danny.'

'It will be my pleasure,' Danny told him. His smile didn't reflect in his eyes.

'No rough stuff, no bruising,' said Kurt, shutting the cabin door.

The girls stopped talking. Those either side of Danny moved back, glancing at him uncertainly in the gloom. It was the first time, he supposed, they'd been given cause to consider him as anything other than someone like them, seeking to enter the United Kingdom below the radar of the Immigration Service.

The only light now was from the moon, glinting from the surface of the sea and slanting dimly in through the portholes. The girls, mostly in their teens, and young at that, gazed at him silently, and with a hint of fear he found exciting.

He didn't normally travel to the UK this way, even on his clandestine visits, but on this occasion, Mr van Ruys, his boss, had told him he could ride shotgun on the voyage, keeping the cargo safe, whilst achieving his objective of slipping into England unnoticed.

Twenty minutes later, the boat gently nudged a quay heading. The Master of the vessel opened the cabin door, put his finger to his lips, and beckoned Danny outside.

He was glad to leave the stifling and claustrophobic confines of the cabin and breathed the fresh air appreciatively while taking in the situation on the quay. Three men stood between the boat and a plain white Ford Transit, which was parked with its rear doors open. The crewman had moored the boat and he and the Master began offloading the girls onto the quay. The three men waiting there hurried the girls into the back of the van.

Danny stood a little apart, on the foredeck of the boat, scanning the area. His attention was caught by a movement. Someone was watching from behind an old sea container a few metres away. He leapt down from the boat and keeping the van between himself and the watcher, circled round, until he was beside the container. A two-foot length of rusting steel tube caught his eye. He picked it up silently, and slipped, on rubber-soled shoes, along the side of the container.

At the last moment, his foot skidded on some gravel and his quarry turned and saw him. Danny only had time to register that he was a young man before he began to run. Danny caught up with him and brought the tube down on the man's head. He heard the skull crack and watched as the body tumbled to the ground and blood spread silently across the concrete. He stood there for a moment, looking for signs of life. There were none.

Behind him, he heard the van engine start up. He turned in time to see it pull away. The cruiser was already turning away from the quay and heading out of the tiny harbour. Danny swore under his breath: he'd expected to travel in the van into Breydon, and now he'd have to find another means of transport. In Norfolk, at two in the morning, there weren't many options.

He threw the tube down in disgust against the old rusted fence which was supposed to keep people off the quayside. The clatter as it hit the ground was loud in the silence of the night, echoing off the nearby cliffs. He cursed his carelessness, and scanned the row of old fishermen's cottages facing the quay from the other side of the road for any signs that anyone had noticed. The occupants seemed to be heavy sleepers. Nothing moved except a cat, intent on prey he couldn't see. After a moment, he moved – cat-like himself – along the quay to the old rusty gates, wedged open, and headed out, along Fish Dock Road, towards the market square of Hartley-Over-Sands.

*

'Is he still alive?'

Detective Inspector George Pascal reached the small group of people led by a doctor in orange overalls who were gathered around the supine body of a young man.

The doctor held the head steady while the Air Ambulance's paramedic fitted a neck brace. He spared Pascal a glance.

'He's unconscious, as you can see. Looks as if he's been here some time: his head wound has stopped bleeding.' He paused while they strapped the young man's head firmly to prevent it moving.

Pascal could see matted hair, stuck together with dried blood. The stain on the concrete quayside beneath the young man's head was also dry. In his seventeen years with the police, he had seen the bloody outcome of many acts of violence, and they never ceased to make him angry.

'It's quite a nasty injury,' said the doctor.

'Deliberate?'

The doctor nodded. 'Oh yes. He was belted with something substantial. There's an obvious compression fracture of his skull. One reason we have to get him into hospital a.s.a.p.'

Pascal thanked him, and turned to John Walker, the detective constable standing at his shoulder.

'Have a look round and see if there's anything that might have been used to hit him with.' He studied the unconscious man. 'He doesn't look very old. Late teens, I'd guess.'

'Yeah. If this was Breydon, I'd be thinking in terms of a gang fight or a drunken brawl outside a nightclub, but in Hartley-over-Sands? There's a couple of pubs this side of the market place, but they're rarely any trouble.'

'As long as you don't count the toms who buy their gin-and-tonics between customers at the one in Fish Dock Road.'

'They're a bit long in the tooth these days, sir,' said Walker, his eyes scanning the surrounding area. 'There's only two of them, left over from when we used to have a trawler fleet to speak of. Ah!'

He strode across the quay to the broken fence. Pascal followed, in time to see him stop beside a length of rusty scaffolding tube, one end stained with what looked like blood.

'Have we got a bag big enough for that?' asked Walker.

'No, but there's a roll of cling-film in the boot of the car for just such emergencies.'

While Walker went to retrieve the plastic wrapping, Pascal watched the medics gently sliding the young man, now firmly strapped to a stretcher, into the cargo bay of the helicopter. Moments later, the rotors began to turn again and the aircraft lifted off.

Uniformed police finished cordoning-off the quay with blue and white plastic tape and making sure the crime scene was not contaminated further by curious onlookers. Pascal wished his new sergeant had arrived yesterday: he could have used the extra pair of hands to help Walker look for any more clues.

\*

They'd done it this time! Julia Fox was furious with her parents. All she'd asked was that they let her go camping with David over the Easter weekend. It wasn't a lot to ask, but they'd refused. Point blank, just like that. Just like they'd always done when she wanted to taste adventure. When, she asked herself, would they realise she was no longer a little girl but a seventeen-year-old young woman, perfectly capable of controlling what happened to her and looking out for herself.

She'd shut herself in her room after their row, and cranked up the volume on her music player because she knew they'd hate the thump-thump-thump of the bass if she didn't silence it by plugging in headphones. She lay on her bed and extended her fulmination to cover her boyfriend – *so called!* – who had been supposed to meet her last night and support her request this morning. He'd not turned up for either event, and she wondered if he'd been nobbled by her parents, who occasionally displayed uncanny prescience about her schemes.

Her eye fell on a photograph of her Godmother. Now *there* was a woman who would understand the fact that Julia was a young adult. Sara must be forty, she calculated, but you'd never guess it from the way she looked or behaved. At one time, she and her mother had been best friends, but they'd drifted apart and hadn't seen each other for some time. Sara had never taken her role as godparent seriously, and never visited the Foxes these days. Julia had been ten when her mother introduced Sara to her, and Julia had felt an instant connection, a feeling that they shared a perfect understanding. Since then, she and Sara had kept in contact by email and SMS. Sara was exciting, fascinating Julia with her determination not to let the fact that she was married cramp her flirtatious style. She would leave the young Julia open-mouthed with her tales of secret lovers and romantic trysts, and had latterly introduced Julia to an internet chat room she used.

Uncle Jared, Sara's husband, was a bit of a dry old stick, but that, Julia supposed, was probably because he spent his days doing things with investments and concentrated on making pots of dosh – which Sara enjoyed spending. She was not like Julia's mother, Cathy. Where *she* was boringly cautious and conservative, Sara's life was really cool.

It wasn't until she noticed the suitcase on top of her wardrobe that the idea of inviting herself to stay with Sara and Jared occurred to her. Brilliant! she thought, standing on her bed to reach it. Quickly and quietly, she packed it with enough clothes to last her a week.

She hesitated at the last minute. Even while she inspected her appearance in the long mirror on her wardrobe door, hitching her skirt up another inch, she felt nervous of going out without telling her parents. She smoothed the blouse against her stomach, and was satisfied with the way it pulled taut over her breasts. Sara would realise she was a woman, not a girl. Julia's resolve strengthened, she opened her bedroom door quietly and slipped downstairs. Her mum and dad were still arguing in the front room when she pulled the door softly shut behind her.

Her decision was to change her life.

*

Sara knew little of what her husband did for a living, which kept him secluded in his office off the hallway of their home for many evenings, leaving her to amuse herself in her own way. She only knew that it generated a sizable income which enabled her to do the things she liked. More often than not, and almost always in recent months, she'd been going out alone while he stayed at home.

She arrived home from a quick trip to her favourite boutique. He was waiting for her.

'Will you be going out tonight?' he asked.

She paused in the process of unpacking one of several large plastic carriers. 'Yes.'

'Why don't I go with you?' he suggested.

'Because I don't want you to.'

He looked at her under his eyebrows. 'I am your husband, you know.'

She scoffed. 'Jared, you spend all your waking hours in your office. You don't want me anymore. You haven't come near me for weeks. I like to be with men who actually like me.'

'I don't just like you, Sara, I love you.'

She yawned theatrically, putting a hand in front of her mouth before turning to him. 'It's obvious you've forgotten what it means to love a girl.' She peered at him sideways. 'Unless the truth is you've found someone else and are burning up your energy on her instead of me?'

He shook his head.

'Because if you have another girl, just bring her along one night and we can have a threesome,' Sara continued. 'I expect you'd like that.'

'There's no other woman. You're all I ever wanted.'

She scoffed again. 'I see you used the past tense.'

'I've never wanted another woman, and I've never been unfaithful – and nor do I want to be,' he assured her.

She put down the lacy teddy she was holding and led him into the lounge, walking into the centre of the thick-pile carpet. She pulled off her top, to reveal her firm breasts. For a moment she posed, her feet apart and her hands on her hips, before unzipping her skirt and letting it fall to the ground. A moment later, her panties joined it.

Wearing only high-heeled shoes, an amethyst necklace and a wristwatch, she took another step towards him.

'If it's true you love only me, here I am. Show me.'

He covered his face with his hands. She noticed no physiological response from him, as she had expected. There was contempt in her voice.

'Fuck you, Jared Martin!'

*

Once, Jared would have found it hard to keep his hands off her. She'd always known which of his buttons to press. Even six months ago, when he'd become aware that his sexual powers were failing, he could still give a good account of himself, satisfying her needs. But a year ago, his need for more money than his business activities normally generated had increasingly manifested itself in the loss of libido, until around six months earlier, when he had been forced to acknowledge his sexual dysfunctionality.

The stress had stemmed from the moment he'd begun to steal from his clients. One in particular, whom he suspected of making his money from drugs and prostitution. There was some salving of conscience, he felt, in taking money from a man who made big profits from such illicit activity. Nevertheless, the stress had worsened.

Most of the money had gone to keep Sara happy, with her frequent shopping trips and purchases of Designer clothing. But a significant proportion had gone into a secret offshore fund where he'd allowed it to accumulate until he'd had enough to buy a luxurious villa on the Caribbean island of Aruba.

He'd been sufficiently prudent so that there had always been enough left to transfer his client's money to another offshore account, from where it should have disappeared, though Jared had used his skills to discover that the money made its way to a particular account in Holland belonging to a Willem van Ruys.

Then, just before a payment of £50,000 was due, the stock market had suddenly crashed, wiping forty per cent off the value of his portfolio. He had been simply unable to make the payment, and now he feared the consequence.

The question in his mind was, if he was to cut and run to Aruba, should he take Sara with him? Events like the show she had just put on tended to dissuade him from doing so. He figured, at moments like these, that he'd be better off alone. He accepted that he was no use to any sexually demanding female. His wife's taunts about his lack of manliness only piled on the agony, making his own anxieties even worse.

And there was the little matter of what Sara got up to when she went out alone. She came home as often as not smelling like a two-quid whore, and looking not much better. He had no doubt she was picking up men, and probably doing it at *The Kitty Klub*, which, though she didn't know it, was ironical. His drug-dealing and girl-running client was the owner.

*

The doorbell rang. Jared answered it while Sara finished putting her clothes on.

He found a smiling Julia on the step.

'Hi, Jared, mind if I come in?' she asked cheerfully, stepping past him carrying her suitcase. Sara stepped into the hallway and smiled at the girl.

'Why, Julia! What a surprise.'

Julia dropped the suitcase, hugged her godmother and kissed her on the cheek.

'Hi, Auntie. Here I am.'

Sara frowned. 'Were we expecting you?'

Julia's cheerful mien faltered. 'Didn't you get my email?'

'Um, no. When did you send it?'

'This morning. Look, can we go and sit down?'

'Of course, dear. I'll tell you what: we'll take your case up to the guest room. I can check I've cleared my last man-friend out at the same time. Tell you what,' she added as she picked up the suitcase, 'if he's still there, I'll let you borrow him.'

'Would I want your men, Auntie?' asked Julia, sensing that this was a game.

'My men are all hand-picked for size, dear. And I've told you before, cut the Auntie bit: I'm not your aunt, so call me Sara.'

Julia nodded through her giggle at the double entendre.

In the guest room, Sara watched as Julia opened her case and revealed her best party dress.

'Wow,' she said, 'I bet that has the men drooling all over you.'

It was a stereotypical 'little black number', in fine yarn, which fitted her precisely and made her look years older than her age. Three or four, anyway.

'I don't know. I've not worn it before.'

'We'll have to see if I can think of a place you could wear it.'

*

Downstairs, Jared could hear the two women chatting and laughing in the spare bedroom. A guest was the last thing he wanted. Life was complicated enough. Sara had mentioned once or twice that she and Julia had kept in contact even after she and Julia's mother had slowly drifted apart through their vastly different lifestyles. He had not seen any harm in it, and in any case, there would have been nothing he could have done if he'd thought for a moment that the correspondence might be undesirable.

He went into his office, off the hallway, and checked the FTSE 100 in vain for any signs of stock market recovery. He began to go through his shareholdings, looking for any good news.

*

'Perhaps we should go out tonight?'

Julia's face lit up. 'Where?' she asked.

Sara grinned at the girl's enthusiasm. She understood precisely her niece's desire to be treated as an adult. Well, she knew just the place.

'How'd you like to go to a very grown up night-club where there are lots of men?'

'Wow! That sounds great.' Julia hesitated. 'I – I have a boyfriend, but – hey! – I'm on holiday and he's not with me.'

Jared, sat on the other side of the tea-table, was stony-faced.

'That's my girl,' said Sara. 'What the eye doesn't see, the heart doesn't grieve over, as I always say,' she added, glancing at Jared. 'What're one or two more notches on your bedpost if your boyfriend doesn't find out?'

Julia giggled again. 'Oh, Auntie – Sara, I mean – I haven't any notches on my bedpost yet.'

Sara looked at her speculatively. 'Really? Well time you got a few. What are you saving it for?'

Julia blushed prettily. 'I guess, for the man I marry.'

Sara turned away to hide a cynical smile. 'Well in that case, my dear, I'll think of somewhere else we can go where there won't be so much temptation – and opportunity.' She turned back and saw the frown on Julia's face she'd expected to see.

Julia touched her arm anxiously. 'No, you're right, why should I? I mean, I might never marry.'

'I don't think you need to be *so* pessimistic, Julia. We'll get ready to go out around nine – and don't mind Jared, if he seems quiet; he's been quite dismal lately.'

Jared stood up and went out of the room towards his office.

Sara leaned closer to Julia and whispered in a confidential tone, 'I think it's something to do with his business affairs.' She grinned wickedly. 'His affairs and mine run along quite different tracks, as you'll see.'

Julia stared at her. 'Do you have affairs, Aunt— Sara?'

Sara tapped the side of her nose with s slim and finely-manicured finger, and grinned. 'Maybe I'll tell you one day, when I think you're up to knowing.'

*

11

She slipped quickly from the room, closing the door. So Julia was a virgin, was she. She'd be the first one through the front door of *The Kitty Klub* for quite some time.

Sara Martin had been popular with men since the age of fourteen. A poetry student from the local university, six years older than she, caught her eye and took her virginity whilst reciting something Byronesque in her ear. A precocious girl, with great presence of mind, she'd taken herself off to the family-planning clinic and arranged for contraceptive measures to be taken. Once assured that she couldn't become pregnant, she had encouraged the poet to wax lyrical many more times, until he discovered her age. He promptly stopped having anything more to do with her, but there had been plenty of others keen to take his place.

Eleven years later, Jared Martin had swept her off her feet. Not short of money, and with prospects, his other attractions for her were his looks and his insatiable appetite for her body. She'd married him without hesitation when he'd asked, and the marriage had lasted fifteen years.

Three years earlier, she'd been on a friend's hen-night visit to *The Kitty Klub,* a nightclub. She'd quickly been fascinated by Derrick Jackson, who owned it, and spent much of that night being the charming host to the women. He'd paid particular attention to her, and she was flattered. He was tall and blond, sturdy and had Nordic blue eyes that seemed to be staring right into her. She'd experienced a frisson of sexual excitement, knowing that Jared would disapprove. The knowledge only encouraged her to flirt even more boldly, and she'd happily gone with him through the building to a part she'd never seen before, which he said was a private club called *Kittens*. There, in a back room which contained a bed covered in a purple silk sheet, they'd had sex. Afterwards, he'd offered her a line of coke, and then another.

Sara recognised within herself that she needed a lot of sex, and Derrick Jackson had begun to provide her with opportunities to take on strangers in his very private members' club at the rear of *The Kitty Klub*. As Jared's libido and his ability to satisfy her had declined, she had sought compensations at *Kittens*, where Derrick encouraged her to have sex with any of the men present in exchange for more coke, though suggesting that she use another name. She chose Vivien, or Viv, simply because she liked it. The more men she fucked, the more coke he gave her. He never offered her money, though she was aware the other girls were prostitutes. She was convinced he regarded her in some way as superior to them.

Occasionally Derrick asked her to fuck some man she found revolting, but he made up for it by offering her extra lines. She'd also tried smoking heroin, but on the whole didn't like it: it made her feel sick and she liked to feel good about her body, not wretched. And for every revolting punter, better ones soon came along.

*

Detective Constable Douglas Frimley pushed aside the papers strewn over his desk at Breydon Police Station until he found an unused piece of notepaper. With his other hand, he pressed the telephone received firmly to his ear.

'When was the last time you saw your daughter, Mrs Fox?'

'This morning,' said the distressed woman on the other end of the line. 'We had a row. She wanted to go camping with her boyfriend over the holiday. We – her father and I – wouldn't let her. She's only seventeen.'

'And you've no idea where she might have gone?'

'She never tells me anything, you know. She's at that age. Oh—!' Cathy Fox broke off.

Frimley heard her blowing her nose. She sounded tearful. 'I'll get someone round to see you as soon as possible. Can I have your address again?'

He finished making a note of the call and went across the corridor into Pascal's office.

Pascal was picking at his computer keyboard, one finger at a time. He looked up when Frimley came in.

'Douglas! Just the man!'

Frimley recognised the tone, and began to back away from Pascal's desk.

'Surely not, sir,' he said.

Pascal's eyes focussed on the note in Frimley's hand. 'What have you got there, Douglas?'

Frimley cleared his throat. 'Just had a Mrs Cathy Fox on the phone, sir. Her 17-year-old daughter Julia's gone missing.'

Frimley passed over the note. 'I was thinking, sir, Hartley isn't that big, doesn't experience much crime, and suddenly two incidents come along together.'

'The last thing I seem to recall coming to notice up there was when someone wrote something extremely rude and anatomically impossible in purple paint on the harbour wall,' said Pascal. 'Didn't go down well with the Parish Council or the visitors, if I remember correctly. While you're here,' he continued, 'make sure whoever's at the hospital keeping an eye on the young man in question keeps people away from him. Parents can visit, nobody else. I want to know who he is as soon as possible. Okay?'

'Understood, sir. I'll get on it.'

'Good. John and I will go round to see this Mrs Fox.'

Frimley was gone before Pascal could nobble him to type in whatever he was doing so slowly.

As Frimley resumed his seat, Pascal appeared at the door.

'John, we're back to Hartley. Distressed woman to see. That's your sort of thing isn't it?'

Walker shrugged, cleared the solitaire game off his workstation screen, and followed Pascal down the corridor.

## CHAPTER 2

'You'd best sit down,' Andrew Fox told them, indicating the settee next to the chair occupied by his wife.

Pascal thanked him and turned his attention to Cathy Fox, who was sobbing into a handkerchief held to her face by both hands.

'Tell me about the last time you saw Julia,' he asked.

'This morning, at breakfast,' said Andrew.

'What makes you think she's gone missing? It's not that long ago.'

'Her suitcase and some of her clothes are missing,' replied Cathy, 'including her new dress.'

'Hmm.' Pascal stroked his chin. 'Do you have any idea where she might have gone?'

'I've telephoned her friends, and they haven't seen her.'

'Boyfriend?'

Cathy shrugged. 'David – David Ellis.'

'How long has Julia known David?'

Cathy dabbed her eyes. 'They've been at the same schools all their lives. They've only been seeing each other since Christmas.'

Walker leaned forward, his notebook open. 'Can you tell me what Julia was wearing when she went out?'

'Just a skirt and a top. Black. Low-heeled shoes. Just ordinary stuff girls wear these days.'

'Did she have a coat?'

'Oh, yes. Grey and black, coarse woven check, wool. It has a fringed edging all round the collar and cuffs.'

Walker nodded. 'I think I know the sort. Popular with girls of her age. The other thing we need is a recent photograph, if you have one.'

She stood up. 'Yes. There's one on the sideboard in the other room.'

'Mind if I come with you, Mrs Fox?' asked Pascal.

She shook her head and he followed her out of the lounge into the dining room.

There was a French-polished square wooden draw-leaf table in the centre of the floor, and a sideboard against the far wall. Three black-and-white photographs rested on it, behind a scattering of ceramic figurines and *objets d'art*. One was of Andrew and Cathy Fox on their wedding day, one of a baby in the arms of a woman – shot over the woman's right shoulder. Her head was turned towards the child, on whom the picture was focussed.

The third photograph was obviously of more recent date, and Pascal guessed it was a school portrait. The girl who smiled out of the picture had her hair tied up in a po-ny-tail. Even teeth showed where her lips were parted, and the smile carried through to her eyes.

Cathy Fox picked up the picture and for a moment held it close to her cheek. She pointed at the baby in the other photograph.

'That was our son, Ian.' She looked at Pascal as fresh tears filled her eyes. 'He died... ' She brushed the tears away with her hand. 'It was a cot death. I – I found him one morning. I thought at first he was sleeping, but he was so still. His eyes were closed and he looked so peaceful. But when I touched him, he was cold.'

More tears rolled down her cheeks. Pascal waited pa-tiently until she was ready to go on. She pulled a well-crumpled tissue out of her sleeve and passed him the pho-tograph of Julia while she dabbed her eyes and blew her nose.

'Thank you,' he said. 'We'll do everything possible to get Julia back,' he added, feeling the need to comfort and reassure her. 'I promise. Mind if I take this photograph?' he asked.

She shrugged. He slipped it out of the frame

Andrew Fox appeared in the doorway and glanced at Pascal before coming into the room and taking his wife in his arms. He turned to look at Pascal over her shoulder.

'Cathy's never got over losing Ian,' he said. 'Please – please! – find Julia. We couldn't bear to lose another child.'

Pascal, who was not unaffected by Cathy Fox's grief, nodded. 'It's far too soon to be even thinking about losing her. She's seventeen, she's missing, possibly with her boy-friend. She wouldn't be the first girl of her age to go AWOL. We'll check everywhere we can think of, locally, in Breydon, and elsewhere in the county. It's far too soon to fear the worst.'

Andrew Fox nodded and held his wife close. He turned so he was speaking into her hair. 'You heard that, sweet-heart? Come on, let's go back in the other room.' He turned back to Pascal. 'Is there anything else we can help you with?'

'Do you mind if DC Walker takes a look round, at Julia's room?'

Andrew shook his head and turned to Walker. 'No, go ahead. It's at the top of the stairs on the right.'

Walker nodded and went upstairs. Pascal followed the Foxes back into the lounge. Cathy seemed to have recov-ered her composure by the time she sat down.

'I'll need a list of Julia's friends, and where she went to school. Now, can you tell me anything else about Julia's boyfriend?'

'David's a nice lad; young man, I suppose I should say. His mother and I met at mother-and-baby group when both he and Julia were still in push-chairs.'

She pulled a fresh tissue from a box on a side-table near her and blew her nose again before continuing. The room smelt faintly of lavender-scented beeswax, Pascal noticed. The dining room furniture was undoubtedly fifty years old or more, but solidly-built and obviously cared for.

'What does David look like?' he asked when she was finished with the tissue.

'He's nice and tall. Slim.'

'About six feet, I'd say,' interjected her husband.

'Dark hair, dark eyes. He's very gentle, too,' added Mrs Fox.

'So you've never thought he was any kind of threat or danger to Julia?'

'No!' they both said in unison.

'Absolutely not,' added Andrew Fox.

'No. He's... he's an ideal first boyfriend,' said his wife.

Pascal tilted his head interrogatively.

'I mean he would never do anything to hurt Julia. He's considerate of her,' she explained, 'and to be honest, he puts up with a lot of her moods.'

Pascal asked for David's address. Walker came back into the room and stood by the door.

Pascal got up. 'Well, thanks for your help. We'd better go, the sooner to get this photograph circulated – you don't mind if I take it, do you? We'll look after it and you can have it back as soon as it's copied.'

Andrew nodded. 'Thanks. What do we do now? Shall we go out and look for her?'

'I'd say not,' said Pascal. 'It's best you stay near your telephone. As soon as we have any news, we'll call you.' He looked again at Cathy Fox. 'And don't forget what I said. We'll find her.'

They returned to the car.

'Find anything interesting upstairs?' asked Pascal.

'Nothing that stood out,' Walker replied. 'Just your average teenage girl's room. Music system, laptop computer, tablet, posters of footballers on the wall.'

'We might have to take a look at the laptop. Did it have internet access?'

'Which teenager doesn't?'

*

'Mrs Ellis? DI George Pascal, Breydon CID.'

Pascal introduced Walker and explained why they were there. Marion Ellis confirmed that her son had been out all night, but had been less inclined to call the police as she reasoned it was not so strange that a young man of seventeen might do so.

'Julia's parents are concerned,' Pascal explained. 'If she's with David, then there's probably nothing to worry us, but not contacting them is not like Julia at all.'

Mrs Ellis nodded. 'I don't know where he is. He's been out all night – but at seventeen, I suppose that's something to be expected.'

'Is it likely he's with Julia?'

She shrugged. 'They seem attached at the hip at present, so it wouldn't surprise me.'

'Does he have a mobile phone, and is it likely he's got it with him?' asked Walker.

'Yes.'

'Will you let me have the number.'

She gave it to him. He keyed it into his own phone. After a moment, he spoke.

'David, this is Detective Constable John Walker. When you get this message, please call me.' He added his own mobile number and closed the connection. He shrugged. 'Switched off.'

'So we won't be able to trace it,' said Pascal. 'I wonder, do you have a recent photograph of your son?' he asked Marion Ellis.

She frowned and went to a bureau from which she took a black-and-white school portrait similar to the one of Julia in Pascal's pocket. She looked up into his eyes, seeking an answer to her question.

Pascal held the photograph so Walker could see it over his shoulder. The two policemen glanced at each other.

'We don't know exactly what happened,' explained Pascal gently, 'but it seems there was an incident on the quayside sometime during the night. A young man was found there, early this morning, seriously injured. He wasn't carrying any form of identification.'

Mrs Ellis's face drained of colour.

Pascal took a deep, steadying breath. 'I'm sorry to have to tell you, Mrs Ellis, but the young man looks very like your son.'

She covered her face with her hands for a moment and swallowed. 'Are you sure?'

'Sure enough to ask you to go to the hospital to see if he is David. But first, do you know of anyone who might dislike your son enough to have hurt him?'

Mrs Ellis was struggling to control her feelings. Biting her lip, she shook her head.

'The only person I know who might... When he stopped going out with Jennifer Manners, before Christmas, well, I think she was very surprised: she's very attractive, and she knows it. I don't know why David went off her – maybe he saw her for the rather vain and shallow creature she is – but I think it certainly put her nose out of joint.' She covered her face with her hands briefly. 'Tell me what happened.'

'The young man found on the quayside had been hit on the head. We don't know why, nor who did it.'

'Oh, God!'

Pascal nodded sympathetically. 'Is there a Mr Ellis?'

'My husband was in the army. He was killed in the Middle East. I want to go to the hospital.' She stood up, Pascal following suit.

'I understand,' he said. 'Can you tell me where Jennifer Manners lives?'

'No. I'm sorry. I need to go.'

'We can take you.'

She thanked him for the offer, but decided to take her own car the twenty-four miles to the general hospital where the young man had been taken. Pascal and Walker returned to their car to study the photographs of David and Julia.

'We'll find out where the Manners girl lives and talk to her.' He put the photographs in an evidence envelope and fastened his seat belt. 'I doubt if she's got anything to do with this, but she's the only person with the slightest motive I've heard about so far.'

Walker nodded and started the engine.

Back at the police station in Breydon, they made arrangements for the photographs to be copied, and that of Julia Fox to be distributed to every police officer in Norfolk.

\*

Jared Dale Martin was frightened. He'd opened the door of his elegant Georgian house on the ridge above the town of Breydon to find himself facing a man in his mid-twenties with a thin, mean face, who spoke with a Dutch accent.

'Mr Martin?' he asked. 'Mr van Ruys sent me. I'm Danny Bakker.'

Martin felt a cold chill invade his stomach. He'd only recently discovered that Willem van Ruys was the man behind the Dutch nominee company he paid large sums into at regular intervals, on behalf of a client.

'Y-you'd better come in.'

He led Bakker into the lounge and offered him a drink. Bakker pointedly looked at his watch.

'You start early, Mr Martin,' he said. 'Too early for me.'

Martin nodded and crossed the room to the bar built across one corner of it and half-filled a tumbler with whisky. He stayed behind the counter: it felt safer. He was a pen-pusher, good with numbers, a man who understood the complexities of the world of finance. In front of him, Danny Bakker might as well have been an extra-terrestrial: there was no doubt in Martin's mind that Bakker was a man of violence, and he dreaded being hurt.

Bakker came to stand opposite him, leaning against the counter.

'Mr van Ruys's money?'

'I – I haven't got it,' stammered Martin.

Bakker put his head on one side. 'Why is that, Mr Martin? Mr Jackson pays you, you pay Mr van Ruys. It has been this way for many years. Why suddenly is there this difficulty?'

Martin attempted an air of superiority. 'I'm afraid it's the stock market. Maybe you haven't noticed, but it's been dropping like a stone these last few weeks.'

Bakker nodded. 'Ah, yes, but that has nothing to do with what you owe Mr van Ruys.'

'Well, it does, actually,' said Martin, feeling some of his courage return. 'You see, the money Mr Jackson gives to me – less, of course, my commission – is invested through nominees in the stock market. Unfortunately, with the crash in the value of securities, it isn't worth what it was.'

'How much less?'

'Well, the Footsie – that's the London Financial Times Share index – has dropped by forty per cent.'

Bakker smiled at him humourlessly. 'It has indeed – but that's from its December peak, so it has fallen forty per cent over three months. Mr Jackson gave you the money for Mr van Ruys three weeks ago, and the market had nearly bottomed out by then, so selling prices now should not be significantly below buying prices then. Is that not correct, Mr Martin?'

Martin realised that Bakker was not someone he could bluff. He felt fear begin to loosen his bowels. His confidence evaporated.

'Well, it might seem so, if you're not familiar with the process,' he said, trying to sound more confident than he felt.

'Explain to me why investments bought in the last three weeks should be worth so much less if they were realised now.'

Martin remembered his drink, and swallowed half the whisky at one gulp. It caught in his throat and made him cough. To his horror, he saw droplets of scotch spray

Bakker's smart grey suit. While he gasped for breath, he watched as the Dutchman brushed the droplets off the fabric with deliberate movements of his hands before looking up at him.

Bakker's hand darted across the counter and grabbed Martin's shirt, close to the throat, pulling him across the surface until his face was only inches away from Bakker's.

'You've had your opportunity, Mr Martin,' he hissed, 'and we both know you are talking bullshit. Now I will tell you: you will give me the fifty thousand due to Mr van Ruys or suffer the consequences. You have one week.'

Martin attempted to nod but movement of his head was restricted. Worse, the Dutchman's cologne, a particularly flowery scent, was getting up his nose and he dreaded the idea that he might be about to sneeze in his face.

'There – there's no need for any violence, Mr Bakker,' he managed to say at last, 'after all, I've been reliably passing on Mr Jackson's payments for years. Surely my credit's good for something? I just need a little time,' he added, thinking he also needed a small miracle, too.

Bakker released him. 'It is only because you have served us well in the past that I am giving you time to pay,' he said. 'Rely on it: I will take measures to encourage you.'

Martin felt his hair stand on end.

Bakker moved away from the bar, towards the door. 'Don't bother to show me out.'

As the front door slammed, Martin finally sneezed. He slid to the floor behind the bar counter and wished he was a million miles away – or at least safe in Aruba. He knew instinctively that Danny Bakker was a thug, and probably, given that he was an enforcer for van Ruys, a killer. Whatever he was, nothing was more certain than that he was someone to be feared, and avoided if possible.

He'd guessed that something like this might happen, that he would be called to account for failing to pay the Dutch their money. He told himself that if he was going to retire to the Caribbean, he should go now. He'd never meant to get involved with a criminal like Jackson: he'd trained as an accountant, but discovered a flair for making money on the stock markets. His wife, Sara, had dragged him into town one evening and insisted on going to the then new venue, *The Kitty Klub,* after their meal.

The place was owned by Derrick Jackson. He'd shown a marked interest in Sara the moment she walked in. Martin watched her preening and displaying herself, which gave him a sour taste in his mouth. At the same time, he couldn't resist the opportunity Jackson gave him to talk about his business success. It had not been surprising when the club owner contacted him a few days later to ask if he could transfer some funds to Holland in a way which couldn't be traced back.

\*

Breydon Police Station was a monument to unremarkable 1960s architecture, built from yellow faced bricks, with ground floor windows protected by white-painted steel bars. A ramp for wheelchairs and prams zigzagged its way to the public entrance, beside a short flight of three steps in pseudo marble. Inside the front door was a small waiting area, just a couple of seats facing a glass-doored enquiry counter. Beside the counter was a door to the offices normally beyond the public's gaze. It was to this door that Pascal marched on Easter Saturday morning. His stubby forefinger punched out the code on the combination lock and passed through, going up the stairs two at a time to his office on the first floor. Walker had gone directly to the police canteen, looking for lunch.

Pascal saw Frimley at the coffee machine in the corridor.

'Get one for me, will you, Douglas,' he called as he entered his small airless office. He only had time to drop the photographs of Julia Fox and David Ellis on his cluttered desk and hang his old raincoat on the hat stand before Frimley shuffled in, carefully carrying three cardboard cups of hot coffee by the fingertips.

'I'd have been happy with just the one, constable,' said Pascal.

'Yes, sir, that's all I bought you, sir. The other cup is for Alison.'

'Who?'

'Alison Collins, sir. Acting Detective Sergeant. Transferred in from Norwich to help out with the missing girl, sir.'

Pascal took the coffee and stared at Frimley. 'You know her? She any good?'

'I've only just met her. I believe she comes highly recommended by the ACC.'

'Save us from another high-flyer, long on telling others what to do, and short on any real experience,' muttered Pascal.

There was a knock at the open door. Pascal looked round and saw a tall blonde woman in a charcoal-grey suit in the doorway. Before he could speak, he was struck forcibly by a pair of ice blue eyes set in a pale face, and red lips. His mouth dropped open.

'Acting DS Alison Collins, sir,' said the Vision.

Pascal closed his jaws with an audible snap.

'Ah! Uh! Welcome to Breydon CID. Take a seat, why don't you. I think Douglas has made you a coffee already.'

'Thank you sir.' She lowered her long form gracefully into the chair opposite Pascal's desk. The gas lift had broken some time before, and Pascal was in no hurry to have the chair replaced as it put even the Chief Constable below his eye line on the odd occasion he popped over from County HQ to talk to "the team at Breydon", as he phrased it. On this occasion, however, Pascal studied the fluidity of Alison Collins's curves as she folded herself gracefully into the chair, slanting her legs because the seat was so much closer to the floor than her knees. Both men were silent as she sat, awed by the elegant way she rearranged her limbs. She glanced at both of them as she took her coffee from Frimley's hand. With a slight shake of her head, a small smile stole into her pale cheeks.

Pascal was the first to break the tableau. 'Yes, right. Well, thank you, DC Frimley.'

Frimley shrugged and left the room, taking a last lingering look at his new colleague.

'So tell me, Alison, what have you been doing since you joined the Force?'

'I've been working in Norwich and at County HQ over the last couple of years, since I came out of training,' she told him. 'Beat bobby in the south of the city, though only for three months, then they took me indoors and sat me in front of a computer.'

Pascal worked his way past precarious piles of paper stacked on the floor near his desk and sat down.

'You've only had three months of real front-line policing?'

'Yes, sir.' She met his gaze levelly as if daring him to say it was hardly enough.

'And how long were you stuck in front of a computer?'

'Twenty-one months, give or take a bit.'

Pascal glanced at the computer monitor on his desk. It was, as usual, not switched on.

'What can you do with a computer that takes twenty-one months?'

'Analysis and research, sir. It helps with profiling.'

'You were a profiler?'

'I was *the* profiler for a long time. They've got a couple more now I've just finished training.'

He leaned back and re-evaluated his first impression of her.

'Did you join the police from another job?' he asked.

She shook her head. 'No, I came in as a direct entrant from university.'

Pascal pursed his lips. 'You're being fast-tracked?' he asked. To be made Acting DS in such a short span of time was extremely exceptional. He wondered if she had some special 'pull' on the higher management – particularly the ACC, if he was the one who'd "highly recommended" her, as Frimley had said.

She nodded. 'Hope you don't think that means I won't be doing my best in this team.'

'I should hope so, Alison,' he said, crossing his fingers below the desk, out of her sight. A thought occurred to him. 'You came straight in and within three months you became our first profiler?'

She glanced down, and the faint blush spread to her cheeks again, he noticed.

'I think nobody else would do it, so they gave the new job to the new officer.'

Pascal had been around long enough to know the powers-that-be didn't work that way. They'd give any job to the officer best equipped in their opinion to do it, including a new one. He decided not to contradict her statement, nor to ask just what she'd done at university. Part of him was naturally curious, but the other part thought it best if he didn't find out in case it prejudiced his decisions in respect of her. He knew enough now to employ her skills to the best advantage.

'Right. Anything you want to ask me?'

She looked up. 'Where do I sit and what do you want me to work on?'

He stood up and watched as Alison gracefully unbent herself out of the chair. When he allowed himself to breathe again, her subtle scent filled his head.

'We have workstations, Alison, as well as hot and cold running water and flush toilets. You'll like it here, in the rural fastness, away from the hustle and bustle of Norwich.' He picked up the photographs of Julia Fox and David Ellis and followed her into the CID office.

'Look, you can sit there.' He pointed. 'There's a computer and it's brand new. And we have enough hustle and bustle of our own to keep us off the streets – in a manner of speaking. Speaking of Manners...' He sat at the unused workstation and passed her the photographs. 'I want you to oversee the search for Julia Fox. Douglas has a note of the phone-calls, and these are photographs of her and David Ellis. He's in the hospital, unconscious. I've sent a bobby down there so hopefully you'll hear as soon as he wakes up. He can probably tell us what happened to Julia. Meantime, she's the one I'm most worried about.'

'How old are they, sir?' she asked.

He told her what he and Walker had learned.

She considered the matter for a moment. 'I think we need to carry out some door-to-door enquiries at Hartley, especially the places overlooking the quayside. And I think we need to conduct a search of the immediate area.'

Pascal nodded. 'Do it. Give it twenty-four hours before going to the media, but you could get the police helicopter involved. And I'd like you and Walker to talk to Jennifer Manners. I suspect she needs eliminating from the enquiry, but in fact she's the only person we've found so far to have a smidgen of a reason to want to hit David over the head.'

'Right, sir.'

'I'd better go and fill the DCI in,' said Pascal, getting up and leaving the room. Collins reached for the phone.

*

Sara was beginning to find Julia's innocent jabber irritating. It was quite obvious the kid was not as mature as she looked. She'd give her that, she thought: she has a nice bod. Good, straight legs, but not always quite sure how to show them off to best advantage.

When she'd finished pampering herself in Sara's bathroom – helping herself to some of her expensive toiletries in the process – she'd put on some lacy underwear beneath the little black dress, and a pair of high-heeled sandals. In the lounge, having a long drink at Jared's bar, Sara had deliberately draped herself half on, half off, a bar stool, so Julia could see how, from a particular angle, it was possible to see up her skirt. Sara touched a finger to her lips in a warning gesture.

'Only if you really fancy the man,' she said.

Julia nodded.

Half an hour later, Sara parked her car and led Julia into
*The Kitten Klub.*

# CHAPTER 3

If Julia thought it odd that Sara should be going to a night-club without her husband, she didn't let it bother her. In the meantime, Sara was being nice.

'Let me fix your eye-shadow,' she said, crouching beside Julia who was sitting at her dressing-table. With a few deft strokes of a pair of brushes, she gave Julia's eyes a soft and luminous appearance which she saw at once was a considerable improvement on her usual effort. Sara moved on to tweak Julia's curls into a style which, while reflecting her youth and vitality, also gave her the look of the girl-about-town she wanted.

Julia had the brief thought that Sara was going to a lot of trouble for her, considering she'd arrived unexpectedly. Her email had not turned up until later.

Then it was time to go.

The leisure district of Breydon was much larger than anything Hartley-over-Sands had to offer. There were cinemas and themed bars, open paved areas dotted with trees in small flower beds, and in one corner stood a large building which contained one of the town's two night-clubs, *The Kitty Klub*. Sara, who was wearing a typical short skirt and close-fitting top, led the way in through the double doors, past a large, shaven-headed doorman.

'New visitor tonight, Ernest,' she said to him, smiling.

Julia was aware of his glance sweeping her. He nodded approvingly.

'She'll be a welcome addition,' he said.

Inside, the large room had been carefully illuminated, some areas being brightly lit, and others kept low. The dance-floor, with its flashing disco lights, was full of people who mostly looked older than Julia, gyrating to the thumping beat of the music being played by a DJ, operating from a small platform some twelve feet above the arena, surrounded by his kit.

At the far side of the room a long bar counter ran, turning towards the other small room behind it, set with tables and chairs and apparently meant for those who wanted a rest from the energies and noise of the main part of the club. Bar stools stood in front of the counter, and Sara led the way to these.

'Good place to be seen,' she said softly to Julia. 'What'll you have to drink?'

Julia thought hard for a moment, wanting to say the right thing, that would fit with her new, sophisticated image.

'Uh, vodka and orange, please.'

The girl behind the bar took the order. She looked Julia over and smiled politely.

Glancing at Sara, she raised an eyebrow. Sara nodded briefly. The girl pushed Sara's glass twice against the bottle in the optic, added ice and took the crown cap off a bottle of orange juice. After pouring a splash of orange juice into the vodka, she passed glass and bottle to Sara.

'Orange juice for me, too,' said Sara. The girl poured one on ice and passed it to her.

Julia sipped her drink. The strong liquor hit the back of her throat. She fought the reflex to gag and managed to swallow the mouthful in a ladylike manner. Sara was watching her.

'Take a couple of breaths. It helps,' she said.

Julia did so, feeling the urge to cough recede.

Sara looked over her shoulder. 'Let me introduce you to a friend of mine.'

Julia turned as a tall, well-built man with a fresh complexion and scraped back blond hair approached them. He wore a black dinner jacket and bow tie. Sara said he was the owner, Derrick Jackson.

He smiled at Julia, who was again aware of a man's searching glance. It pleased her that they found her attractive.

'Let me get you another of those,' he said, indicating her drink. He glanced at the bartender, who quickly provided another vodka and orange.

'Thank you,' said Julia shyly. She could already feel the effects of the first beginning to spread through her blood. She had no idea if she could get through a second glass without getting drunk. Still, she wasn't letting that stop her. She wanted to charm him.

He turned to Sara. 'Julia's a niece? Daughter?'

Sara shook her head. 'No. Uh, God-daughter.'

He leaned back and stared at her in surprise.

'I didn't think you were particularly religious, Sara?'

'Julia's mother and I were friends at College. When Julia was born, she asked me to stand as her Godmother.' She glanced at Julia and shrugged. 'I've been totally remiss, I'm afraid. The only things Julia might have learned from me are not godly ones.'

He grinned. 'I'm relieved to hear that.' He turned to Julia. 'Paragons of virtue can be such bores, don't you think?'

She nodded, feeling very sophisticated, being appealed to; very adult. 'Oh, yes.'

'Being good is nowhere like as much fun as being bad.'

She nodded again and giggled. It annoyed her, because it made her sound to her own ears very little-girlish, but he didn't seem to notice.

'Sara here,' he said, 'is a very bad woman. She could teach you a lot.'

Julia grinned uncertainly at her Godmother.

Sara arched one eyebrow. 'Of course not. Derrick is pulling your leg.' She grinned at him. 'I do what I want to do, don't I, dear?'

He wrinkled his nose. 'Quite often, I believe.'

Julia was suddenly aware of a sub-text going on between the other two, and wondered what it was about.

Derrick was watching someone over Sara's shoulder. Julia followed his look and saw a man enter through the main door. He was tall, dark, and rakish, and glanced their way. She saw Sara look at him and raise her eyebrow again, and once more, Julia was aware of some hidden communication.

Sara turned to her. 'Would you mind very much if I abandoned you for a while. I'm sure Derrick will look after you – won't you, dear?'

He grinned at Julia. 'I expect so.' He glanced up at Sara. 'I could show her around, or we could dance with the trogs,' he added softly, turning to encompass the dance-floor, which was beginning to heave with bodies.

Julia did not want to be a "trog", whatever that was: she had caught the note of contempt in his voice.

'I'd like to look round,' she said, wondering what there was to see that couldn't be seen from where they were perched.

'Let's have another drink first,' he said. 'You can bring it with you.'

\*

In the discreetly-hidden back rooms of *The Kitty Klub*, known as *Kittens*, the party was beginning to warm up. The music was up-tempo but not loud. In the low-lit room with its faded flock wallpaper and smoky atmosphere, young girls were moving among the seats, chatting to the men, most of whom were middle-aged, some even elderly, smiling and occasionally leaning forward to kiss them. Hands slid up the smartly-pressed creases of expensive trousers, and from time to time a man and a girl would leave the room through a rear door and reappear twenty minutes later, the man, at least, looking ruffled.

The rakish man had handed over his "entrance fee" at the door, which included the cost of a couple of lines of cocaine and however many girls he could get through in the night. He rubbed the crystals that had not gone up his nose across his gums, and washed his mouth with a malt whisky he'd bought from the bar. Settling in a leather arm-chair, he surveyed the women.

Across the room, he saw a woman he'd never tried – probably, if he were truthful, because she was a little older than the rest, and he liked the younger ones. He watched as she found a line of cocaine abandoned by its owner, and in a practised move, snorted it through a small gold tube she took from her clutch bag. She pinched her nose after-wards, no doubt waiting for the familiar tingle, then scanned the room much as he had.

His attention was taken when three young women closed in on him. They all had the look he recognised, the dry skin and glittering eyes which were signs of heroin ad-diction. Sometimes, he thought it was a shame that such pretty girls had developed a drug habit to the point where they needed to resort to prostitution to feed it. He shrugged such considerations away as two of the girls perched on the chair arms, while the third sat on his knees.

He was aware of the older woman watching. She moved until she was fully in his line of vision. She rested one hand on her hip and raked the girls with her stare.

'Go and find someone you can handle and leave the re-al man in this room to the expert.'

She smiled into his eyes. The girls shrugged, not want-ing the hassle, and left the man to the older woman.

She turned her attention back to the man. 'Hi,' she said, 'I'm Vivien. Viv. Welcome to *Kittens*. I've seen you here before, but somehow we've never got it together. What's your name?'

'John,' said the man, looking at her curiously. 'So you're Viv. I hope you can deliver what your reputation promises. A three-way is a dream fantasy for any man, and I think you've just lost me the opportunity.'

'I'll make it up to you. Let me dance a little.'

Viv began to gyrate her hips in time with the music, watching his face. Suddenly she stopped, slipped her hands up her short dress and hooked her fingers into her panties. She wriggled teasingly as she slid them down her long legs in a practised way. Stepping one leg clear of them, she leaned back against a nearby table, using her hands to support her, and lifted the other, her panties dangling from the pointed toe of her stiletto shoe and held them out so he could take them. She watched with satisfaction as he took the opportunity to glance up her leg as he removed the flimsy lingerie from her foot. He tucked the panties in the top pocket of his suit, while she began to dance again suggestively, closer and closer to his knees. She straddled his legs and leant forward to place her hands on his shoulders. She finally settled on his lap, rubbing herself against him until she felt his arousal. She unzipped him, slid her hand inside his trousers, and squeezed his erection encouragingly.

'Shall we go and get better acquainted?' she suggested.

They got to their feet. He allowed her to lead him across the floor, past other couples, some engaged in discreet coitus, through the door leading to a number of private rooms on either side of a short corridor. Each was furnished with a bed, a washbasin and were dimly-lit. Hidden in the shadowy corners of the ceiling were a couple of cameras recording the activities in each room, providing footage which could be used to shake down local business leaders or councillors, should they avail themselves of the services offered by *Kittens*.

\*

Julia was finding Derrick's attention flattering. When a young man nearer to her age had come close, eyeing her up, Derrick curtly dismissed him.

'If you're looking for a girl for the night, you know where to go, son,' he said, jerking his head towards the rear of the premises. 'Julia here,' he patted her knees, 'needs a real man.'

His touch made her skin tingle. She watched as the young man scowled and walked away, turning her attention back to Derrick and shifting uncomfortably on the stool.

'What real man is that?' she asked coyly.

He grinned at her in a way that made her heart pound. 'It's for you to judge, of course, but it could be me.'

'Wh-what would I do with a real man?'

His expression was one of bland innocence. 'Anything you want.' He stared at her lips as he spoke, and she suddenly knew he was going to kiss her.

Her heart pounded again and she felt blood pumping round her body. She squirmed on the stool again, one leg stretched down until the tip of her shoe made contact with the floor. Slowly he leaned towards her and she waited for the contact. At the last minute, she felt the warmth of his hand on the inside of her right knee. As tingles shot up her leg, making her gasp, his lips pressed against hers and she automatically opened her mouth to allow his tongue access.

She held her breath as long as she could, while his hand slowly advanced up her leg, and his tongue explored her mouth. She wanted him to touch her breasts and pushed them towards him. Finally she had to breathe, a process which was made ragged when his other hand did at last touch her sensitive nipples.

She broke the kiss when she could stand his tantalising touch no longer. She sat, half on and half off the stool, simply waiting for him to tell her what to do. For a moment he gazed at her, then helping her down off the stool, he held her close and led her across the floor, to the room behind the bar, and across that through the long wall-hangings which concealed the door to the bordello.

Beyond it was a large room, filled with upholstered chairs and settees, and tables which were waited on by young women wearing clothing which barely covered them. There were men in the chairs, and women perched on their laps. Julia gasped as she saw that one man was laying back as far as he could in an easy chair with his trousers open. One girl was kissing him while another had his erect penis in her hand and was licking the tip of it.

Derrick led the way through another door, which led into a corridor. Several doors opened off it, and he ushered her into one of the rooms.

She still had her vodka and orange in her hand, and sipped from it. That it didn't taste quite the same as the previous ones she put down to the fact that she was feeling quite giddy. Slowly the room she was in, which contained nothing but a bed covered in a purple satin sheet, began to spin and she felt Derrick's comfortable and strong arms lower her to the mattress.

One of the last impressions she had before she passed out was that another man had come into the room and was taking photographs. She was only dimly aware when her dress was taken off and her panties removed, and when both men in the room with her took turns at ejaculating just inside her vagina while the other photographed the moments in close up. Afterwards, Derrick held her still while the other man injected her with a small quantity of brown stuff, into a vein on her thigh. Almost at once, she felt dreamy and slept.

*

Sara was in the main room of *Kittens*, watching a crowd of young vigorous punters, when Derrick returned to her side.

'Where's Julia?' she asked.

'Sleeping it off.'

'Sleeping what off?' she asked, suspicious of his uninformative answer.

'We gave her a little relaxer, so she could enjoy her first experience better.'

Sara, who had been perching on one of the bar stools again, stood up, fury gathering in her face.

'What first fucking experience?'

'Actually, it was her first and second. And Paul and I got it on film. Well, a memory card, I suppose it is these days.' His voice was calm and unperturbed by her obvious anger.

'You bastard, Derrick! She's my God-daughter – I told you! How the hell do I explain this to her parents?'

He grinned and beckoned the bartender over, ordering a whisky. 'You'd only have to do that if she wanted to go home.'

She glared at him. 'What do you mean? Of course she'll want to go home.'

'Not today.'

'No, but after the holiday. Some time next week.'

'By then, she probably won't want to leave her new friend.'

Sara stared at him. 'Oh, god! Don't tell me you've dosed her up on heroin?'

'Only a little, so far. Paul will give her more as she's able to take it.'

'Are you going to put her to work here?'

'Of course. We were careful not to break her hymen. We can get a lot of money for that. I hear there are a few Middle-Eastern members who can and will pay big money for the right to be first.'

She sat down again, at a loss.

'What am I supposed to tell her parents when they ask me where she is?'

He sipped his drink. 'I should deny ever having seen her.' He fumbled in his jacket pocket. 'Did you see to our dear friend, John?'

'What do you think! Of course.'

'Okay, okay. I'm just asking. Here.' He withdrew a small plastic deal bag containing crystals of cocaine. 'These are for you, my best girl.'

Sara's eyes fixed on the package and she took it from him quickly, putting it into her small clutch bag. She looked up and met his gaze, ignoring the cynical glint she saw there. 'Thanks, Derrick,' she said softly, her anger dissipated at the promise of the drug. 'And thanks for saying I'm your best girl.'

She stood up and pressed her body against him, running her fingers through his fine fair hair.

'You know, you're very handsome,' she said.

His lips curved into a smile which didn't reach his eyes. 'I always look better from the other side of a coke snort,' he said.

She undulated gently against him. 'Deej,' she breathed in his ear.

'Fuck off – Viv! How's your beloved husband these days?'

She frowned. 'Don't call me that out here. Drifted away from me.'

'You don't give a toss really. And you from him?'

'You know me, Derrick, I like sex. He seems to have forgotten what his Willie's for.'

'I'm sure he still keeps you in food, shelter and clothing. What more does a girl want?'

She stopped flirting. 'Respect,' she said after a moment. 'He doesn't respect me any more.'

Derrick raised a sceptical eyebrow. He pointed at a couple of men in business suits who were staring about the place like first-timers.

'How about you give them a good time before you go home?'

*

Jared was particularly unpleasant when she arrived back at the house at almost three o'clock in the morning.

The place was in darkness as she slipped her key into the lock and turned it. Switching on the hall light, she caught sight of herself in the long mirror set into an antique hat-stand just inside the door. Her mascara had run – probably when she'd found herself in the ladies' toilet half an hour previously, feeling sore, lonely and depressed.

She kicked her shoes off and padded upstairs in bare feet, heading for the bathroom with the intention of showering away the residues of her activities. Something made her look up the stairwell, to see Jared watching her from the landing.

'I thought you'd be in bed,' she said.

'I was.' He studied her, the corners of his mouth turned down. 'You look a mess, Sara.'

'Fuck off!'

'You disgust me!'

She stared at him, fulminating. It really was the last straw, she told herself. She took an instant decision to move out: Derrick would find her a place to live – he'd probably invite her to stay with him.

His enquiry cut across her thoughts.

'Where's Julia?'

She stared at him. The coke swirling around in her bloodstream had pushed the memory of her God-daughter out of her conscious mind. She gripped her head as the recollection of her conversation with Derrick flooded back.

'Oh, bugger!' The expletive was mostly directed at herself. She saw Jared staring at her over the banister.

'Don't tell me you left her there?'

'She was sleeping it off,' she mumbled.

'What?'

She frowned at him and set off to climb the last few steps. 'If anybody asks, you'd better keep your trap shut. She never came here: we know nothing.' She paused in the bathroom doorway. 'I'll clear her stuff out of the guest room first thing in the morning. Now go back to bed and let me get a bath.'

He was staring at her in shocked disbelief. 'You've left your God-daughter, Julia, in the clutches of Derrick Jackson? Are you mad?'

In reply, she slammed the bathroom door and leaned against it, slowly slipping down until she sat on the floor. Oh, Christ! she thought, I have. I really have. Oh, shit!

The thing was, after doing the business suits – and yes, it had been their first time in *Kittens* – there'd been a couple of lines of coke, and then she'd felt really good and unstoppable. There'd been other men keen to have her, and she'd ended up with a stag party who'd fucked her for what seemed like hours in every orifice, and a few places that weren't, like her armpits. And the whole thing had been punctuated with more coke they bought for her. She'd forgotten, simply forgotten, about Julia.

Could life get any worse?

## CHAPTER 4

Walker was late again. Douglas Frimley had at least mentioned he would be, this being the most important day in the Christian calendar, and his being a member of Breydon's Parish Church choir and reading the epistle. After he arrived, Pascal sat himself at the spare workstation and sighed, looking theatrically at his watch. It was the fourth time in two weeks.

Collins occupied the seat opposite Frimley. She had a small official notebook on the desk, and she loaded a CD-ROM into her computer. Frimley asked her what she was doing.

'I designed a relational database which I thought might help with investigative work, so I'm loading it on here in the hope it might be useful.'

Pascal looked up. 'Very soon, Alison – perhaps sooner than you think,' he said. Collins and Frimley looked at him.

'And where is our colleague and valued team member?' he asked, indicating Walker's chair.

John Walker entered the room at that moment and shuffled behind Collins to his workstation in the corner. He smiled up at Pascal, opposite him.

'Sorry I'm a bit late, sir. Heavy night.'

Pascal looked dour. 'You should go steady on these dates of yours,' he said. 'You're not as young as you used to be.' He glanced over Collins' shoulder to read the status board.

'Any progress?

'Nothing helpful, sir,' she replied.

'I want you to interview the harbour-master at Hartley. I take it they've got one.'

'It's not approved for international arrivals; it was a fishing port until ten years or so ago, since when it's declined. Practically nothing arrives there these days.'

'Well, see what you can find out. Take DC Walker with you. He looks as if he needs the fresh air.' His gaze caught Walker's eye. 'Okay?'

Walker's expression relaxed. 'Okay, sir.' He sniffed.

'Need a tissue, John?' asked Pascal, pushing a box towards him.

'Thanks, sir,' said Walker, blowing his nose ostentatiously.

'Nothing from the house-to-house enquiries?' Pascal asked Collins.

She shook her head. 'Not yet, sir.

\*

Collins drove to Hartley, and parked beside the quay. A couple of small inshore fishing boats were moored up, their bottoms resting on the mud which remained in the harbour after the tide had receded. Other than that, there was no sign of maritime activity.

She looked at the spot where David Ellis's body had been found. The concrete was still stained with his blood, though someone had made an effort to scrub it clean. She got out of the car and walked to the spot, near the old container. Walker got out slowly and came up behind her.

'David was found here?' she asked, pointing at the bloodstain, roughly half way between the quay heading and the container.

'Uh-huh.'

'Did you read the report from the CSI?'

'Uh-huh.'

'The blood spatter pattern made him think David was moving towards the container when he was struck.'

'Yes,' said Walker.

'Do you think it's an odd direction for him to be taking?' she asked, not expecting an answer. She took the few paces necessary to reach the container and studied it. It's metallic grey sides were covered in dust.

'Frankly, no,' said Walker, 'what makes you think so?'

Collins wrinkled her brow. 'It's just that I think anything interesting here would be going on at the quay. So something made him go away from whatever was happening here. We know from the medics that his injuries were probably inflicted quite few hours before he was found, so we're talking about the middle of the night. What happened here then?'

Walker shrugged but didn't press the matter.

'Where's the harbour-master live?' she asked.

'Overlooking the harbour.'

'Should be handy to see all the comings and goings.'

'The old bloke who does it's an unpaid volunteer. Parish Councillor. Depends whether he was in when we think anything might have arrived,' Walker said.

He led the way along the row of old cottages facing the sea and separated from it by the quay. He stopped outside a house painted in white lime wash, with a yellow door and matching window frame. A yellow window box filled with early geraniums and fuchsias promised a summer display of eye-catching scarlet.

Collins knocked on the yellow door. A man in his sixties opened it. His tan, she saw, was of a kind to make one underestimate his age, though the silver-fringed tonsure of his head corrected the image.

Collins held out her ID and introduced herself and Walker.

'I understand you're Harbour-Master?'

He stood a little straighter. 'I am,' he said. 'Arthur Gathercole.'

'I wondered if you could think back to the night before they found the injured lad on the quay,' she said.

'Aye?'

She thought a look of alarm had briefly flitted across his face.

'What shipping was in the harbour that night?'

'Would you like to come in and we can have a look at my book?'

'Yes, please.'

'I'll wait out here,' said Walker.

'Okay,' replied Collins as she followed Gathercole into the small living room.

It was dark enough to need the lights on to read by. The walls were lime washed and the ceiling so low she felt the constant need to duck her head . A small fire burned in the grate of a small cast-iron range, down the sides of which were strips of horse brasses, and the room smelled of smoke and soot. Brightly polished brass lamps hung from the ceiling beams here and there, though a centrally-positioned electric lamp was providing the illumination. At the rear of the room, furthest from the fire, was a dining table covered with a light maroon coloured thick chenille cloth.

Gathercole opened a large landscape-format book which lay on it and flipped through the pages to the last one containing entries.

'I record all arrivals and departures in here,' he said, 'and collect the fees for the Port and Haven Commissioners.'

'And what do you have for Thursday night, Friday morning?' asked Collins. Again, she was aware of something in his attitude. His eyes stayed on the book while he pointed.

'No boats in.' He turned towards her but kept his eyes lowered. 'That's not unusual.' At last he met her gaze, but looked away again almost at once.

She had the strong suspicion that he was lying. She looked round the room. The place was quite tidy, but there was no evidence of a woman's presence, so she supposed he kept the place clean himself, or maybe had a cleaner in occasionally. Her eye was caught by a small crucifix on the sideboard, next to a photograph of a woman in her thirties wearing a full-skirted dress, perched on a wall.

She went over to look at it.

'Who's this, Mr Gathercole?'

He closed his book and stepped towards her.

'That was Danuta. My wife. Died five years ago. It's an old photograph.'

'She was very pretty.'

'She was beautiful. Her father was in the Free Polish Air-force during the war.'

Collins pointed at the crucifix. 'She was Catholic, then?'

Gathercole took the small ornament into his hands and rubbed it lightly, as if cherishing it. He nodded.

'Yes. This was hers.' His eyes closed as if he was re-membering.

'While you're holding that,' said Collins, 'tell me again whether there was a boat in harbour on Thursday night.'

He opened his eyes and stared at her, then looked down at the icon in his hands. He swallowed.

'I'm sorry,' he said quietly. 'There was a boat. Someone came to see me just as the tide was beginning to rise and suggested I have a night out at the Fishermen's Arms. He gave me a lot of money not to be here until after high tide.'

'Did you see the boat?'

He shook his head, tears beginning to track down his cheeks. He still stared at the figure of the crucified Christ. 'I'm sorry,' he said again, as if he was speaking to the im-age, before he looked up into Collins's eyes. 'I'm so sorry. I came home sooner than I should. A large cabin cruiser was just leaving the harbour. It had no lights on. I didn't get its name.'

Collins nodded. 'Did you see any vehicles on the quay-side, or heading away from it?'

He shook his head again, then stopped as if he'd just remembered something else..

'There was a van, driving up Fish Dock Road. That had no lights on either.'

She nodded again, sensing he'd told her everything now. 'Well, thank you for your help, Mr Gathercole. In future you need to make your book entries more contemporaneously, and not put it off.'

She watched relief flood his features.

'I will, I promise,' he said.

Outside, she found that Walker was on the quayside. She nodded towards the car, and Walker followed her to it. She slid into the passenger seat and waited until he was seated beside her.

'Find out anything?' he asked.

She summarised what Arthur Gathercole told her.

'I'm going to ring the Port and Haven Commissioners at Great Yarmouth,' she told him, taking her phone out of her bag. 'I reckon it's possible the boat that left here just after high tide might have gone round the coast and moored up at Yarmouth. It's the nearest proper mooring for a gin palace. They wouldn't take on fuel here, if their purpose was clandestine, assuming they needed some, so Yarmouth would be the obvious place.'

She keyed in the number from the phone's memory and learned that the only vessel which had come into the river at Yarmouth very early on Friday morning had come up from the south, not the north as it would have if it had travelled the shortest route from Hartley on the north coast. The vessel had refuelled and its two-man crew had restocked with food before it had cast off not long after first light. The Port Authority had the boats registered details and undertook to find them and provide them to the police.

\*

Collins sat in the broken chair in Pascal's office, leaving Walker standing by the door. Pascal was becoming acclimatised to the effect she had on him physically, and doing his best to ignore the residual interest.

'I take it I'd have heard already if the girl had been found?'

'Uh-huh. No such luck, I'm afraid,' said Collins, before telling him about her conversation with the Harbour-master and Yarmouth Port and Haven Commissioners.

Pascal screwed up his face in an effort to remember something. 'Isn't there a CCTV system in Hartley?'

'I'll check, but I don't think there's a municipal one,' Collins replied. 'There might be private ones – outside banks and other shops,' she added.

'Douglas is good at checking things like that. If anyone has any video of the quayside or Fish Dock Road, let's see if a van turns up on them at around the right time.'

'Yes, sir.'

'If that doesn't get us anywhere,' he said, 'we shall have to involve the media.'

Frimley was dispatched to Hartley on a mission to lo-cate, and if possible acquire, any security camera footage which might contain images that would help identify the van.

*

Julia Fox woke in a small room. It had a high window she was not tall enough to see out of, a single bed covered with a thin mattress and a coarse blanket, a bucket and a small washbasin. A chair and small table completed the furnishings. Her head was spinning and she felt sick. She swung her legs off the bed onto the floor, which was cov-ered with a threadbare carpet, and made her way cautiously to the door. It was locked.

The place had a damp smell, faintly redolent of sewage. Old wallpaper hung down in places, partly obscuring words – they looked as if they might be names – in foreign languages, scribbled over the faded pattern. She could hear the sounds of people coming and going outside the room door. Suddenly, the nausea grew too much to resist and she lurched towards the bucket, spilling the contents of her stomach into it to the accompaniment of hoarse grunts.

Afterward, her forehead feeling clammy and cold, she lay on the mattress. Her wristwatch had gone, and the light coming through the window gave her no clues what time it was. All she knew was that it was daylight outside, so it must be the following morning, she reasoned.

She slowly began to feel hungry and thirsty, and the headache receded. She got to her feet again and went to the door.

'Hello!' she shouted, rattling the handle, 'hello! Help!'

She thumped again, with her fist this time. She put her ear to the door and thought she could hear someone crying, but a long way off. The sound, added to her own misery and fear, brought tears to her own eyes. She laid back on the bed, pulling the blanket over her and wished she was back home.

Back on the bed, she hugged herself for comfort and curled up. Time slipped by and she slept.

She woke up when she heard a key turn in the lock. The door opened and a man appeared, carrying a tray of hot food. She thought she recognised him, but her memories were hazy and unpleasant. He was probably thirty, she thought, and his face was stubbly, with red spots beside his nose and in his beard. His gaze was watchful as he put the tray down on a small side table.

'Sit up,' he told her.

She obeyed, wrinkling her nose at the smell of his sweat mixed with something she'd last noticed when she'd been with David and he'd got so worked up he'd come in his pants.

'Where am I? Why am I here? Who are you?' she demanded, trying hard to keep the tremor out of her voice.

'Call me Paul. We met last night, and now you're with us.'

'Who?'

'The other girls here have to work off big debts for getting them here. Plus, they'll soon have expensive habits. I'm afraid they're going to be working to clear what they owe. They won't of course, but it doesn't do to give them no hope.'

'What about me?'

'You're here because... well, Derrick and I discovered you're a virgin. As such you can be profitable.'

She stared at him. 'You can't mean it!'

'Try me. And in the meantime, you're going to get an expensive little habit as well. Makes you more controllable.'

'What are you talking about?'

He glanced at the tray. The aroma from the food made her mouth water in anticipation, but for the first time, she noticed a loaded syringe beside the foil plate. He reached over and picked it up.

'My parents'll miss me. They'll tell the police.'

He grinned without humour. 'They'll find nothing. Now here's lesson one.'

With his free hand he gripped her chin hard.

'Keep still or this'll hurt,' he told her. She watched, feeling helpless as he lifted the skirt of her little black dress up to bare her thighs, then stuck the needle in and pressed the plunger.

She tried to push him away. 'What the hell are you doing!'

He was stronger than she was and let go her chin long enough to smack her open-handed on the side of her head which made her ears ring.

A moment later she felt warmth and languor begin to spread through her body.

'Your new best friend,' he replied, pulling the needle out and watching her eyes.

'Time for a little training,' he said when he thought she was far enough gone. He dropped his trousers and pushed her down on the bed.

Fifteen minutes later, nursing bruised arms and thighs, though still technically a virgin, she got to eat the food, which was now cold. She no longer cared.

Some time later – it was still daylight, though it seemed to be getting darker, the key turned in the lock again and Julia gazed up at the man again. She was still feeling the previous hit. There was no tray this time: he simply held another loaded syringe. She was groggy and couldn't defend herself from him. She lay still, her mind somehow disconnected while he injected her thigh with half the contents of the syringe.

He smiled. 'That's my girl. We'll soon have you out of here.'

She blinked at him. 'I can go home?'

'Don't be stupid. You won't leave here until your expensive little habit has become indispensable, and you have to work off the debt.'

'What is it you give me?'

'Heroin.'

'But I don't want any more heroin.'

He smiled again. 'Are you sure? Let's see how you feel about it after a little more.'

He picked up the syringe, pinched the flesh of her thigh and drove the needle in.

'We won't go for a vein until you really, really want it,' he said, pushing the plunger home.

Tears fell down her face.

'You'll be ready to leave here when you can't live without this stuff. Then you're ours.'

He removed the needle from her leg and left the room. She felt total detachment from reality steal across her, and slipped down sideways onto the thin pillow. Sometime during the hours that followed, she dreamed that someone came into the room. It smelled like Paul. She felt the prick of a needle in her thigh again and slipped into unconsciousness.

It was dark when she woke up and felt hungry. She felt dirty and needed the latrine bucket. Afterwards, she tried to wash herself without soap or towel. She was cold and shivering. She banged on the door.

'Hey! What about some food!' she called as loudly as she could.

She banged again, but there was no response.

She had no idea how much time passed before she heard the key turn in the lock and Paul appeared with a tray bearing a steaming foil dish. There was also another syringe.

He grinned at her. 'Here!' He thrust the foil plate at her. 'Now, eat.' He gave her a plastic teaspoon.

While she pushed the food into her mouth as fast as possible, he lifted her dress and injected her with the contents of the syringe. He watched as her interest in the food waned and her eyelids started to droop.

'I'll have to cut the dosage down a bit. Can't have you gauching out in front of the customers.'

'What's "gauching out"?' she asked sleepily.

'H is a depressant. It depresses all your body's systems. Give you too much all at once and you go to sleep. Much more, and you stop breathing.'

She felt his hand roam over her body, but she didn't care.

'We want you awake enough to be able to take care of the punters properly. You only have to need heroin, and ask us for it. When you start doing that, that's when you can go to work.'

'Work?'

'You're going to be working in a private members' club. All the members are men, and you and the other girls will be letting them fuck you. Keep them happy, and you'll keep Derrick happy. The longer you do that, the longer it'll be before you start to work the streets.'

'What do you mean?'

'When you're no more use round here, that's what you'll do. When you want more H and have to do anything to afford it.' He shrugged unfeelingly. 'And, of course, you'll still be paying over a percentage of your earnings to cover our present investment.'

She felt relaxed and comfortable. Julia's eyes closed.

He caught the foil dish as she released her grip on it. He put it on the table and left the room, not bothering this time to lock the door.

\*

The weather on Easter Day was not pleasant. Sara had woken up late and discovered that Jared was not in the house. After his comments last night when she'd at last returned home, she was glad. She realised she needed to make a decision: she couldn't go on living this way. Jared had been good to her for a long time, but now he was boring. Most importantly, he wasn't functioning in the department she considered essential.

She packed a pair of suitcases with her favourite things, scribbled a note to Jared saying she'd gone, and half an hour later turned up on Derrick Jackson's doorstep. It was raining, the water soaking her hair and running down her neck.

He stared at her. 'What do you want?'

She smiled back, with just a hint of uncertainty.

'Hi, Deej. I've left Jared. Will you put me up for a night?'

He stared at her. 'Where do you think I might do that?'

She shrugged. 'I don't know. Your home?'

He shook his head and thought for a moment. 'Wait here.'

He shut the door. She felt cold water run down her back. The door opened again. Derrick held out a key.

'83 Columbine Road. Room four. Best I can offer.'

He shut the door again.

Sara swallowed. It was, she knew, a former guest house he now owned, where he housed the working girls. She hoped it would be just until he found her somewhere better. She put the key in her pocket, picked up her cases and made her way back to her car.

\*

'Mr van Ruys wants his money.'

'I've already paid: gave the cash to our usual contact. I don't know why he wouldn't have paid you.'

'I've been to see him. Says he's lost it on the stock market.'

'Maybe he has.'

'Mr van Ruys still has to be paid.'

'Not my problem as I see it. Go and have a word with Jared Martin.'

'I've done that. I need to make him believe I mean my threats.'

'Hmm. Well, I'm not telling you this, of course, but you could try making an example of his wife.'

'How much of an example? I'm curious what you'll sanction.'

'That's up to you.'

'Where do I find her?'

'83 Columbine Road, room four.'

*

Around ten o'clock, Walker glanced along the street behind him before stepping smartly into *The Kitty Klub*. He nodded at Ernest, one of the security guards, who recognised him and led the way beyond the island bar into the less-used rear of the premises and towards the far wall, which was covered with curtains.

Walker had his hand in his pocket and counted out three twenty-pound notes which he placed in Ernest's hand as the latter pushed through the curtains and opened a door into *The Kitty Klub's* secret sister. Walker thought of *Kittens* as a private gentlemen's club, but it had more in common with the Hell-Fire Club than with the honourable institutions of Boodle's or White's. Derrick Jackson glanced up as Walker entered and smiled at him. He crossed the room from his table, holding out his hand in welcome.

'John! Good to see you again.'

'Evening, Derrick,' said Walker, allowing his eyes to become accustomed to the dim lighting. Girls in revealing underwear moved between the tables which were occupied by men of Walker's age and older. At one end of the long room was a low stage where three girls were gyrating around gleaming chrome-plated poles in time with disco music set at such a level that those sitting further away from them could hold conversations without having to shout.

Walker liked the look of them. His eyes alighted on a trio who fitted the bill. Barely-developed bodies, barely covered. He swallowed as his imagination came into play.

'Think they'd keep your mind off the daily drudgery, do you, John?' asked Jackson, following Walker's glance. Walker was startled: he'd forgotten the man was so close to him.

He glanced round and grinned. 'I reckon so.'

'Need a little something to get your motor running?' asked Jackson.

Walker turned towards him and nodded. 'A couple of lines of toot if you please.' He handed over two twenties which disappeared into Jackson's pocket.

Jackson tipped the crystalline contents of a plastic bag from one pocket of his white jacket onto a mirror on the table. Walker used his credit card to break up the sugar-like crystals as small as possible and arrange them in two lines, then rolled up another twenty-pound note and used it to inhale a line of the drug up each nostril. Afterwards, he sniffed hard and pinched the sides of his nose to encourage the drug into his bloodstream.

He'd avoided the temptation to 'do' crack cocaine, because he didn't want to be such a slave to the stuff that he could no longer do his job. It was difficult enough affording his cravings for both the girls and the drug, and he knew if he lost his job, then life would be over. He nodded thanks to Jackson and walked over to a large overstuffed leather easy chair, beckoning one of the three nymphets to join him.

When he got her in the back room, she was obviously starting to come down from whatever she was on, and he didn't enjoy the sex as much as he'd expected. When he'd finished, he stripped off the condom and left her to tidy herself up while he returned to the main room.

Viv had arrived, he noticed. He might like his girls young, but Viv brought a lot of experience to the game. She wore a tantalising scarlet basque. He smiled at her.

'Can I buy you a drink?' he asked.

'I'll have a dry Martini,' she said, smiling at Jackson. He produced the drink, and a whisky for Walker.

'On the house, John,' he said.

'Thanks.' He raised his glass to her. 'Cheers.'

'What have you been up to then, John?' she asked.

'This and that,' he said.

She looked amused and pursed her lips, glancing pointedly at the door to the back rooms. 'And a bit of the other?'

'I guess so. Could have been better.' He took her arm lightly and guided her to a table. He didn't want Jackson to hear him criticize one of the girls as he suspected she would be punished if he thought she'd fallen short of the standard of service he expected.

He sat on one of the upright leather chairs, Viv in the easy chair next to it. She lay back and lifted her legs across his thighs, raising the cocktail glass to her scarlet lips. He studied her immaculate maquillage, her dark eyes shaped into oriental almonds by the black lining around them and the dark shadow on their lids. Her lips had a natural pout, and careful application of highlight and shadow to her cheeks brought out the structure of her face.

Her hair was bobbed, black and shiny. His eyes slid down her long throat to the inviting swell of her breasts in the low-cut, figure-hugging basque, and finally to her long, shapely, black nylon-clad legs terminated in scarlet high-heeled shoes.

As he watched, she loosened one of her shoes, so it hung only by her toes, and dragged her heel back across his thighs, allowing it to press gently on his crotch until his growing arousal made it uncomfortable. She watched him, cat-like, over the rim of her glass. He allowed the hand not holding his whisky to slide along her leg towards her sex, where the gusset of the basque was fastened by poppers.

'You were very good last time we met,' she said huskily.

He nodded. 'So were you.'

'Good. I'm glad you think so,' she replied, draining her glass. 'Want to try it again?' She allowed the fingers of her other hand to slip down her belly until the tips were pressed against her in an unmistakable invitation.

He felt his erection pressing against his trousers and figured he was probably up to it again if he took things slowly. And Viv probably knew enough tricks to make sure he got the most out of fucking her. He nodded and finished the whisky.

## Chapter 5

Frimley stretched and leaned back in his chair. The clock on the office wall showed the time to be nearly eleven. Pascal had left. The street-lamps illuminated the market place outside the window. It had been a long day, he thought as he felt and heard his stiffened joints crack. Opposite him, there was no sign of Collins behind the screens which divided off the four workstations. He stood up and saw that she had fallen asleep, her head resting on her arms, on the desk surface. He allowed himself a small smile. It was the usual effect he had on women. He wished he had Walker's ease and conversation with them.

He crossed the room to take his anorak from the coat pegs behind the door. She stirred and lifted her head to gaze at him through sleep-filled eyes.

'Oh, it's you, Douglas. I must have nodded off.'

'I guess,' he said. 'Still, I got a result from two of the cameras.'

She woke up properly. 'What?'

'There's a bank in the market place at Hartley. One of their cameras takes a wide shot of the area, and it's possible to see a white panel van come out of Fish Dock Road, across the square and leave past the camera on the Breydon road.'

'Dare I ask: any sign of the index mark?'

He shook his head. 'Not from that camera.'

She caught the inference and tilted her head slightly. 'There's another? You said you'd got results from two cameras?'

'Yes.' He grinned with a hint of triumph which made her smile. 'You know the pub in Fish Dock Road?'

'Not intimately, but I know there's one there. Bit spit-and-sawdust by all accounts. Just locals and ex-fishermen.'

'That about sums it up, except that the landlord has had CCTV fitted recently. There's a couple of old toms, as the DI calls them, who frequent the place, but the landlord doesn't want them doing business on the premises – or outside. Reckons it'll give the place a bad name, if it didn't already have one.'

She smiled.

He continued, 'Anyway, seems he's invested a hundred quid in a couple of web-cams which are mounted outside in order to record any "misbehaviour" by these two women. They happen to cover the street, and there are a couple of street lights which are more than adequate for the cameras.'

'So?' she asked, with growing excitement.

'The van's index mark, or at least part of it, is clearly visible.'

'Great! Have you tried cleaning the image up?'

'No. I thought I might have to put it to the CSIs.'

She shook her head. 'I'll have a look at it tomorrow. Look at the time. Let me buy you a drink at The Swan. You've earned it.'

The Swan was less than five minutes' walk from the police station, and was a popular haunt of officers whose working day had finished. Frimley and Collins jogged the short distance and quickly reached the warmth and comfort of the bar.

'What do you want, Douglas?' Collins asked, getting her purse from her handbag.

She brought his pint of bitter and her own spritzer to the table he'd occupied by the window overlooking the main shopping area of Breydon.

'Do you live in town?' she asked.

'Yes. There are some apartment blocks the other side of the market place. DC Walker lives at the far end from me.' He didn't know why he'd brought his colleague into the conversation. 'What about you?' he asked.

'I commute from Norwich at present, but I want to find a place closer to here.'

'Bit of a retrograde step, isn't it?' he asked, 'you'll be moving on soon, back to the hurly-burly.'

She tilted her head again. 'Why do you think that?'

'Come on, Sergeant!'

'Call me Alison. We're off duty. And I still want to know why you think that.'

He grinned at her and looked down at his beer. 'Okay – Alison. Anybody can tell you're going places. Two years since you started proper police work and a DS already—'

'Acting DS.'

'I feel sure you'll be made up substantively as soon as the powers-that-be reasonably can. You'll be CC one day, and probably of a much bigger force than this.'

She looked deep into his eyes. Frimley felt he was drowning in hers.

'You're talking bullshit, Douglas. Have you never heard of the "Glass Ceiling"?'

He nodded. 'Yes, but it's beginning to break. There are already a few female CCs about. Attitudes are much more enlightened than they were just a few years ago.'

She looked down into her glass. 'I don't know whether I want that.' She glanced up at him and he thought she looked lost. 'I want a home life. Husband, children; the usual things. I don't think I could do that properly *and* have the kind of high-flying future you think I'll have.'

Frimley felt his heart ache for a moment. It was an un-usual sensation. He lifted his glass and swallowed several mouthfuls of beer while he recovered. Collins raised her own glass to her lips and sipped.

'I thought women were good at multi-tasking? "You can have it all", they tell you in the magazines.'

'I don't think I'm that good,' she replied, shaking her head and smiling. 'And I'm not sure I want to be.'

'You'd give up your career for a husband and family?'

'I can't answer that,' she said. 'What about you? Is there a Mrs Frimley and two-point-four little Frimleys somewhere in the background?'

He smiled at her. 'All right. We'll change the subject. Yes, there is a Mrs Frimley and she has two children.'

'Oh,' said Collins, slightly surprised.

It was Frimley's turn to tilt his head and raise his eyebrows in enquiry.

'I, uh, it's just that I thought you were single.'

He grinned. 'I thought that'd surprise you.' He sipped his beer. 'But you're right. They're my sister-in-law, nephew and niece.'

Collins laughed. 'Oh, okay, you caught me out.' The smile disappeared. 'So, no girlfriend?'

'I'm far too boring,' he told her. 'Always have been. I'm too geeky for most of the women I've ever fancied. I last about five minutes with them, until they find out I enjoy programming in Pascal. Oh!' he put his fingers to his lips and laughed. 'No pun intended.'

She laughed. 'I learned to program in that language.'

'You did computer science?'

'Don't look so surprised! I got my degree in it.'

Frimley could not disguise his curiosity about a colleague who had similar interests to his own. He and Collins stared at each other.

'I – I don't suppose you'd like to come round to my apartment and continue this conversation?' he said, then shook his head. 'No, it won't do to mingle with a colleague...'

She stared at him, her pale complexion warmed to a light pink.

'That should be my line, Douglas, but you'll note I'm not using it. Is it far?'

He shook his head, surprised. 'No. Quarter of a mile. It's another quarter of a mile upwards, but hopefully the lift is still working.'

'You have a computer at home?'

'Of course... '

They drained their glasses and walked out of The Swan deep in conversation about procedures and variables.

\*

Pascal had not gone home. He visited the hospital to see how David Ellis was. He found him still unconscious. Beside the bed, Marion Ellis was asleep in the chair provided for visitors. Someone had provided her with a blanket. The main overhead lights were off, illumination being provided by a wall-lamp. Pascal stood at the foot of the bed and watched mother and son, the steady rise and fall of their chests beneath their respective coverings.

He became aware that Mrs Ellis's eyes had opened. She sat up straighter and pushed the blanket down onto her lap.

'Any news?' she asked quietly. 'Have you caught whoever did this?' She gestured at David's inert body, his head swathed in bandages.

'Not yet,' he said. 'We've made some progress today, and we'll keep going. There's a missing girl as well. Every day we don't find her is another day of torture for her parents.'

'I suppose I should phone them,' she said.

'Can't see it would do any harm,' replied Pascal. 'Any developments here?'

He nodded towards David.

She shook her head. 'He's still alive. He had surgery to men his skull. The doctors say there's every chance he'll recover. They say a coma is the brain's way of repairing itself, so they're not unduly worried.' She leaned over the bed and rested her hand on her son's arm.

'They say his autonomic systems are still working well, so they're not concerned that he'll stop breathing or anything. The only thing that does worry them, I gather, is if there's a blood clot on his brain. They check quite often to make sure there are no signs of one. And I think the alarms would tell them.' She indicated the array of cabling which connected points on David's body to the monitor screen on the far side of the bed.

Pascal noted that heart-rate, blood pressure and respiration all looked to be steady. How closely the readings were to 'normal', he had no idea, but took their regularity as a good sign.

He looked back at Mrs Ellis, amazed that in this day and age when public histrionics seemed to be the norm, she was containing her anxieties and doing all she could – just being there – for her son. If there was any justice in this world, thought Pascal, the boy would recover fully.

'Well, I'd better catch up on some sleep,' he said. 'Long day tomorrow.'

They were all long days when a big case was live. He had a Press Conference lined up.

'Goodnight, Mr Pascal,' Mrs Ellis said. 'And thank you for coming by.'

'We all have our fingers crossed for David,' he said, and left her to her vigil.

*

In the back office of *The Kitty Klub*, Derrick Jackson finished watching the local television news. He picked up the telephone on his desk.

'Paul? Have you seen the TV?'

He listened. 'Well, they've put out an appeal for that girl.' He listened. 'Which girl? The one we acquired from Viv. I had a bad feeling about it as soon as we'd done it. You know how I prefer to plan things. She just seemed like too good an opportunity to miss.'

There was another pause while he listened. 'We'll just have to be careful. Change her image. Get her hair cut, turn her blonde, give her a tan – whatever it takes. They've put out a good photo of her, so we need to do what we can to make her unrecognisable. Yes, even by her own mother – not that *she's* likely to be visiting *Kittens*. In the meantime, make sure the girl stays indoors and hidden.'

He hung up. It was probably just as well it took about three weeks to get the girls hooked enough to be let loose on the punters. In a fortnight, when Julia and the rest of the new girls were ready, the heat might have died down. Not that it was likely too many members of *Kittens* would be either alert enough to recognise her, or public-spirited enough to mention her whereabouts to the police, but you never knew.

\*

Frimley knocked on Pascal's door.

'What have you got?' asked Pascal, waving the DC to the broken chair.

Frimley ignored the invitation and stood, leaning forward on the desk.

'The van, sir. I think I've traced the keeper.'

'You think?' asked Pascal, but he was grinning.

'Ernest Miller. He's got form. I managed to clean up the image of the licence plate. Look.'

Frimley laid a Criminal Records Office printout taken off the Police National Computer in front of his chief.

'Mostly violence against the person. One drunk-and-disorderly. Last offence two years ago, assault occasioning actual bodily harm to a sixteen-year-old outside *The Kitty Klub*.'

Pascal stared at him, but Frimley had said his piece.

'You'll have to tell me, Douglas. What's *The Kitty Klub* and where is it?'

'Sorry, sir. It's a night club in Breydon. Just the other side of the Old Market Square.'

'Where all those theme bars and the cinema are?'

'Yes. Have you never been?'

'Don't have time.'

Frimley looked at him askance. 'Where do you take your girlfriends?'

Pascal gazed at him balefully. 'Don't have time for them, either. Anyway, I wouldn't necessarily take them to the pictures. It was something I last did in my teens, mainly because it was the only sort of date I could afford.'

'Well, anyway, *The Kitty Klub* is down there.'

'Has this Ernest fellow got a home address?'

'There's one on his CRO, but it's two years old.'

'Let's go and visit it, Douglas,' said Pascal.

Less than twenty minutes later, they were parked at the kerb outside the last known address of Ernest Miller. It was a street of old, small Victorian terrace houses, with small front gardens not much deeper than a couple of ten-inch flower pots. The house had an air of neglect about it, Pascal decided as he knocked on the door. There were no signs of movement from within, but the curtain of the adjacent house twitched. A moment later, the neighbouring front door opened and a thin woman with long, unkempt hair, holding a toddler in her bony arms stepped out.

'You looking for Ernest?' she asked.

Both Pascal and Frimley showed her their ID cards. 'Yes,' replied Pascal, 'do you know where he is?'

The woman's face had closed up as she saw the police identity cards. 'Why?'

'We're making enquiries about a van we believe he owns. Do you know if he owns a van, uh, Mrs... ?' He let the question tail off.

'Seaman,' she said. 'Jean Seaman.'

'How well do you know Mr Miller, Mrs Seaman?'

'Only as a neighbour,' she explained quickly.

Pascal had seen the track marks on her arms. 'Of course. Now, do you know if he owns a van?'

'Might do,' she said.

'And do you know where we can find him?'

'He works at *The Kitty Klub,* in the town centre. Bouncer or something.'

Pascal smiled at her. 'Thank you, Mrs Seaman. We'll see if we can find him there. Just one thing,' he added as she turned to go indoors. She faced him again.

'What?'

'What time does he usually get home from work – just in case we miss him at the club?'

'Middle of the night. Early morning. It varies.'

He nodded. 'Thank you.'

She watched as they returned to their car and Frimley drove them back towards the Old Market Square.

*The Kitty Klub* opened its bar at lunchtime, but the bulk of its business was done in the evening when the club proper opened and the disco began. Pascal had not had occasion to step into the gloomy interior before. His eyes gradually adjusted to the lighting scheme which illuminated the important places, like the bar, while keeping everywhere else in mysterious shadow. Behind the counter, a young man polished glasses. Pascal and Frimley approached him and Pascal explained their wish to speak to Miller.

'He's behind you,' said the barman, pointing between them with his glass-cloth.

They turned as a large, broad-shouldered man with a shaven head came across the room. He was wearing a dark suit and a prominent Bluetooth earpiece was fixed to his ear.

'Can I help you gentlemen?' he asked.

Pascal and Frimley identified themselves.

Frimley asked if he still owned the panel van he'd identified from the CCTV footage. Pascal noticed that Miller's face tightened and his gaze became wary.

'Why do you want to know?'

'It's a simple enough question, Mr Miller. Do you still own that van?'

Miller stared at him a moment before nodding. 'Yes. Why do you want to know?'

'Were you driving it last Thursday evening?'

For a moment, a look of alarm flashed across Miller's eyes. 'Some of the time.'

Pascal smiled thinly. 'I wonder if you would be kind enough to let me see your licence and insurance.'

'Why?'

'There is a complaint that the vehicle had defective lights,' said Frimley.

Pascal continued, 'When you say you were driving the vehicle "some of the time", do you mean some of the time you were driving it, and some of the time it was parked, or do you mean that someone else drove some of the time, you shared the driving?'

Miller's head switched from one to the other.

'I'll 'ave ter get me documents.'

'I'll have you served with a Notice to Produce. Well, Mr Miller?' prompted Pascal.

'I was the only one driving.'

'What were you doing in Hartley late on Thursday evening?'

Miller licked his lips. 'Delivering some stuff for a friend.'

'I'll need the friend's name and address, Mr Miller,' said Pascal, as Frimley stared intently at the insurance certificate.

Miller stared at the wall. 'Can't remember,' he muttered.

Pascal's face adopted an expression of concern. 'Are you feeling all right, Mr Miller? Sudden loss of memory can be caused by stress. Are you stressed? Was it anything we said – or are you worried about telling us who your friend is? Would he be angry with you if you told us?'

'Are you all right, Ernest?'

At the sound of the new voice, all three men turned to see the club's owner had entered the bar from his office.

'They're police, Mr Jackson,' said Miller, looking relieved.

Jackson smiled at Frimley and Pascal. 'Can I answer your questions at all?' he enquired.

'I don't think so, sir,' said Pascal, 'unless you were with Mr Miller in Hartley on Thursday evening.'

Jackson tilted his head enquiringly at Miller. 'I don't know: *was* I with you in Hartley last Thursday evening? Were *you* in Hartley last Thursday evening?'

Miller nodded, dropping his eyes to the floor in the manner of a naughty schoolboy.

'And what were you doing?' pressed Jackson.

Miller stared at him, then at the police officers. 'I was d-del-delivering the— '

Jackson nodded. 'Packages. From the fishing boat. I remember.' He smiled at the police. 'It was a late consignment of sea-food which Ernest collected for me. Is there anything else, Inspector?'

'*Detective* Inspector,' corrected Pascal. He turned to Miller. 'Where did you deliver these, uh, packages?'

Miller glanced briefly at Jackson. 'To the kitchens here at the club.'

Frimley tilted his head. 'You do food here?'

'Bar snacks, Detective Constable.'

'Where're your staff's certificates in food hygiene?' asked Frimley.

Jackson stared at him glassily. 'I don't know. I'll make sure that they display what they have, if that's the requirement.'

'Very good sir,' said Frimley. 'And have the public health people given the place the once-over recently?'

Jackson allowed his anger to show. 'Look! I've had enough. This has nothing to do with your stated purpose. You know where, when and why our van was where it was on Thursday. So we've answered all your *pertinent* questions. If you don't mind, we're busy.'

Miller nodded and made to turn away.

'Just one thing, Mr Miller.'

Miller stopped and turned back to them. 'What, *Detective* Inspector?'

'Where do you keep the van? Where is it now?'

Miller swallowed. 'There's a garage at the back of the club.'

'Mind if we take a look?' asked Pascal.

Miller shrugged. Behind him, standing by the door to his office, Jackson pressed his lips together.

'Show us,' Pascal said.

Miller pointedly avoided looking at Jackson, and led the way out of the club and down Wickham Street, the access road beside it. At the end, on the right, just in front of the wall which closed the street off, was a garage roller door. Beside it was a small personal door which Miller unlocked. Pascal and Frimley stepped over the threshold behind him, ducking to avoid hitting their heads on the low aperture.

A dirty white panel van was parked in the space behind the roller door. Pascal's nose twitched at the smell which assailed his nostrils. He turned to Frimley whose own nose was wrinkling.

'Bleach,' he said quietly.

Miller opened the back of the van and the smell was suddenly stronger. Pascal stared at the spotless interior, then at Miller in time to see a smile appear on his lips. He'd known all along that the van was clean. Bleach killed and removed virtually all forensic traces. Pascal forced himself to be polite.

'Thanks, Mr Miller. Unusual to find a van so clean.'

'When one is transporting foodstuffs, one can't be too careful,' said Miller sanctimoniously.

Pascal turned away and led Frimley out into the street. They walked in silence back to their car.

*

Jared Martin was growing increasingly desperate. He knew he shouldn't complain that van Ruys had sent his emissary to collect the fifty-K due – he'd expected it, as soon as he'd seen the stock market begin to drop like a stone, just after transmitting half a million dollars, give or take, to Aruba and Abel Scarman.

Abel had taken him under his wing when he'd visited the island during a trip to the United States. It was a curious amalgam of Dutch and American: a Dutch dependency on America's doorstep, so much so that a huge part of the airport terminal was given over to US Immigration and Homeland Security checks, so travellers to the USA were effectively given – or refused – permission to land there before they even left the island.

Sara had left, apparently for good, and he had no idea where she was, though her note said something about staying with "Deej". Well, good luck to her! The way she'd started behaving in the days before she left, he could easily believe she'd been working off her nymphomania on other men, and it made him feel sick. Still, Martin was reluctant to disappear without making an effort to get her back. On the other hand, the property Scarman had purchased for him on Aruba was his Little Secret, and he wasn't sure, if he told Sara about it (assuming he could find her), that it would remain a secret. The last thing Martin wanted was to have Bakker or anyone else from his past life, turning up in his intended new one.

He went into his office, off the hallway of his home, and logged onto the internet, wondering about the best way to get to Aruba without being too obvious.

After an hour's research, he decided that his best option might be to travel to Paris and fly from there. It would be a somewhat convoluted journey, since Air France was allied with KLM, the Dutch flag operator, and the flight from Paris went via Amsterdam. Still, he thought, it was better to do that than fly from the local airport to Amsterdam and board the flight there: too much risk that Bakker would find out – or the police, for that matter.

\*

In what had once been the residents' lounge, when 83 Columbine Road had been a proper guest-house, Derrick Jackson was waiting when Paul Unwin, the man who broke the girls in and got them hooked on heroin, returned from Julia's room.

'Ah, Paul! How's the girl?' he asked.

'Coming round,' said Unwin. 'She will need training to give the appearance at least that she enjoys a fuck, because at the minute she just lets you get on with it, barely notices when you're doing it.'

'That'll change when we cut the dosage. Does she mainline yet?'

'No, I'm injecting her thighs. I've told her I'll only give it to her in a vein when she asks for it. It'll be a good test.'

'Yes. Think she'll be up for it soon?'

'Give it a couple of weeks. It takes time to build up dependency and get her in a pliable frame of mind. I can't give her too much at once, she flakes out, and in any case, it's easy to OD on this stuff.'

'Don't want any accidents, or having to explain bodies to the police,' said Jackson, horrified at the thought of the trouble an accidental overdose would create. 'How are the other girls taking to it?'

'Much like Julia. They should all be ready in a couple of weeks. At the moment, they need cleaning up and as I said, a bit of training, but we'll be on schedule.'

'Get Sara to sort Julia out.'

Unwin pursed his lips. 'You sure?'

Derrick shrugged. 'Maybe she'll see a reflection of herself. Maybe, if she does, it'll encourage her to take herself off.'

Unwin scratched his head. 'She ain't like the others, is she? I mean, it's obvious she's older, but... She don't do it because she *has* to, do she?'

Jackson's lip curled. 'She has to, all right, just not for the same reasons the others have. She enjoys fucking the punters.' His nose wrinkled. 'And she seems to think I fancy her. Christ! As if I would, when I know where she's been – and who she's been with. I wish she'd sling her hook, go back to her husband or preferably move far away and never come back.'

Unwin shrugged. 'Some of the punters like her.'

'Some of 'em are desperate,' Jackson replied acerbically. 'I keep pushing her onto the really rough ones in the hope she'll take herself off, but she just goes and does it and comes back for more.'

'You could stop letting her do coke.'

Jackson appeared to consider that. 'Yeah, I could. Maybe I should. I'm too soft-hearted, that's my trouble. Besides, I don't want her getting it anywhere else. It might get out that she's using, and that could be bad news for us. And it's only a line or two a night.'

'It's your funeral, Derrick.'

'Thank you for the sympathy, Paul.' He turned away. 'If only it was hers!'

*

'Do you know what this is?' asked Detective Chief Inspector Julian Steel when Pascal was seated in front of him with a cup of coffee. He pushed the paper over his desk.

It was not the way Pascal would have preferred to start a new day. The paper was a photocopy, attached to a memo from HR. Pascal had to make an effort to remember that 'Human Resources' was the new buzzword for Personnel. What had been wrong with the previous term? he wondered. But the heading of the photocopied sheet focussed his mind.

He pursed his lips. 'Not good news is it.'

'No.' Steel's lips were so pursed Pascal thought he'd been sucking lemons.

'What'll happen?'

'It's a breach of the disciplinary rules. It's probably a breach of them for me to be showing you this, but you work with him and know him better than anybody else.' He leaned across the desk on his elbows. 'I want to know: how seriously shall I take this?'

Pascal shrugged. 'It says here he owes the bank more than ten thousand pounds.' He shook his head regretfully. 'I don't see how you can't treat it seriously.'

'Will you have a word with him.'

Pascal realised Steel was trying to delegate the unpleas-antness.

'If he's to be suspended, I think you'll have to do that, sir,' he said.

'Let's try and avoid that, George. Have a word with Walker and see what he has to say for himself. How could he get into this much debt?'

'I'll ask him, sir. Shall I show him the Attachment of Earnings Order?'

'Uh...' Steel looked as if he was about to push it to-wards Pascal, but changed his mind at the last minute. 'I think I'd better hang on to it.'

Pascal stood up and drained his coffee. 'I'd better go and find him. I assume this has top priority.'

'Yes, please, George. And if you can't sort it out, you'll have to come back to me and I'll have to do it officially, by the book.'

Pascal lifted an eyebrow as he turned and left Steel's of-fice. By the book indeed! he thought. If he was worried about what the book said, he'd have seen Walker himself and suspended him there and then, instead of asking Pas-cal to try to find some way round it.

He phoned Walker's mobile from his desk. 'Can you get back here as soon as possible, John. I need a word as soon as you're in the building.'

'Okay, sir. Anything wrong?'

'No. I just need to talk to you fairly urgently.'

'Right sir.'

He hung up.

Twenty-five minutes later, Walker entered Pascal's of-fice.

\*

'Shut the door will you, John.'

'What's up, sir?' asked Walker, sitting on the broken chair, sensing that the brown stuff was about to hit the fan.

Pascal touched the tips of his fingers lightly against each other. 'The boss has just shown me an Attachment of

Earnings Order which your bank has obtained. It's for recovery of a debt of £10,000. He thinks you should be suspended. I think you should be suspended. Any reason you can think of why you shouldn't be?'

The blood left Walker's face. He licked his lips and rubbed his chin.

'I've got a few problems,' he said at last.

'That's undeniable, John,' said Pascal, 'so what are you doing about it?'

Walker swallowed. 'What I can.'

Pascal sat back and waited.

It wasn't quite what Walker had been expecting, but it was bad enough. It made him jittery as he tried to work out how to explain the debt. The unpalatable truth was that it had gone into the pockets of Derrick Jackson over a number of years. He sniffed, and pulled a handkerchief out of his pocket in time to catch a sneeze, turning away as he did so and spending some time mopping at his nose afterwards.

'You all right, John? Got a nosebleed?' Pascal asked, concerned.

Walker shook his head. 'It's nothing.' He dabbed again at his nose before putting the handkerchief away. His nose felt very sore and sensitive to the touch.

'So what are we going to do about you?' Pascal continued. 'I don't want to suspend you – or, more accurately, have to watch while Julian does – but you know the rules about getting into debt. It makes you vulnerable. You know that some of our criminals are not above exploiting the situation.'

'Yes, sir.'

Pascal seemed to be studying him. Walker sniffed again.

Pascal frowned. 'Got a cold, or something?'

Walker swallowed again and stared at him. 'Maybe a touch of 'flu.'

The frown had not left Pascal's face. 'Tell you what, John. Go home, sick. You've got the flu. You keep your warrant card and pay, for the time being. Use the time to figure out how you're going to sort out your finances. If you can come back to work in a week or two with a plan, we'll see if Julian can be talked out of suspending you.'

'Not much chance of that, sir.'

'We'll see, won't we. According to this order, they'll be taking over five hundred pounds a month from your pay to recover the overdraft. I guess what I'm saying is, what can you do to repay it faster? This Order goes on for years.'

'I suppose I could sell my apartment.'

'Where would you live?'

'I don't know. Somewhere cheaper.'

Pascal nodded. 'You take a couple of weeks to think about it, and I'll try to keep Julian off your back. This Order will be put into effect, though, so expect a smaller pay packet at the end of the month.'

'Yes sir. What are you going to tell the others?'

'Just that you're sick and not feeling up to visitors. You need to keep away from your colleagues, you know how good they are at working things out from a few clues.'

'Yes, sir. Thanks,' said Walker, rising to his feet.

'One more thing, John,' said Pascal. Walker waited for him to continue. 'I need to know how you got into such financial straits.'

Walker sat down again and glanced into the DI's face. There was no way he could tell Pascal the truth.

'I made an investment in a business. It went bad,' he said, and shrugged.

'What sort of business was that?' asked Pascal.

'Uh, it was a share in a racehorse.' Walker was making it up as he went along. He hated being unprepared, and knew the signs which Pascal would be reading, which gave such *ad hoc* lies away. 'You know: the best thing since sliced bread, and when they actually get to race it, it's rubbish.'

'And what happened to the horse?'

'Knacker's.'

'Ah. Shame. Presumably, not insured?'

Walker shook his head. 'Wouldn't be in this position if I had been.'

Pascal gazed at him consideringly. 'You make a better copper than a businessman.'

Walker allowed a small grin to twist his lips. 'I won't be doing it again.'

'Glad to hear it,' said Pascal dismissively.

Walker stood up. He sniffed again as he left the room, closing the door. One thing seemed in his favour: there was no-one else around. He slipped out of the police station unnoticed.

He crossed the road without looking back. He'd known this was likely to happen. He was theoretically on sick leave, but it was only an excuse: suspension by another name. Whatever you called it, it wasn't nice.

He'd wanted to be a copper since his mum had been mugged in the street and a beat bobby had not only come to her immediate rescue, but he'd tracked down the mugger and got him into court. It gave Walker a real aim in life, and things had been going well for him until he'd been dragged into *The Kitty Klub* one evening when he was with a group of friends on a stag night.

At some point during the evening, the man whose stag it was paid for them to get into *Kittens,* where Walker had been tempted by the negotiable affections of the women, and encouraged to try a line of coke and "see the difference" it made. After that, he couldn't keep away: he enjoyed both the girls, who always seemed young and fresh and willing, and the coke. One line led to two, and two led to three.

He hadn't realised how much this lifestyle was costing until he'd had a letter from his bank inviting him to come in for a talk about his overdraft. And now the overdraft had grown until the bank had felt it necessary to do something about getting its money back. His own attempts to repay it had amounted only to token gestures, and the bank were plainly after something much more substantial.

The prospect of losing five hundred a month from his salary was one he didn't want to contemplate.

He let himself into his flat. The breakfast dishes still adorned the sink, but otherwise it wasn't in too bad a state. It was just as well, because he couldn't face housework. He slumped on his old settee and turned on the television, more for company than out of interest. Some garrulous woman was persuading members of the audience to share confidences about their private troubles with her and a few thousand viewers. They must be mad, thought Walker, quite certain that he would never share his private troubles with anyone, whatever the inducement.

He reached beside the settee and found a bottle of cheap whisky. It was barely the middle of the morning, but he figured he deserved a mouthful or two. It deadened thought, which was a good thing, he figured. The fiery heat of the liquor washed through him. He swigged again from the bottle, then put it down. He fell asleep and didn't hear two utility bills printed in red drop through the letterbox.

## Chapter 6

Danny Bakker was feeling the need to do something. He had a job to complete, and he needed to get on with it. He'd given Jared Martin time to come up with the money he owed Mr van Ruys, but a little encouragement would do no harm.

He formulated a two-stage plan. Already he had in mind threatening Martin's wife, but he felt he needed an interim measure. Something more direct, that wouldn't kill Martin, but would put the fear of God into him. This was the only point at which Danny felt his life had something in common with his Maker's, and on the whole he felt satisfied and didn't pursue the connection further.

Danny had used fire as a frightener in the past, and it seemed like a good idea to use it again. It was simple and straightforward, and left few clues.

Now he had decided, he wanted to begin implementing the plan at once. The sooner it was done, the sooner he could move on to Martin's wife. He would enjoy dealing with her.

In a way, it would be a pity if firing Martin's house caused him to pay up: maybe, thought Danny, he would take his pleasure with Sara Martin in either case.

Looking like any other smart young man, in a grey business suit and carrying a briefcase, he entered High Ridge Avenue, Breydon, an hour later, with a spring in his step. He hoped he radiated an air of nonchalance which would have been quite unremarkable by anyone observing him. His eyes, however, were watchful.

The street was empty. The houses were among the oldest in town, and the place exuded an almost palpable gentility which Danny fully intended to destroy in the next few minutes. The corner of his mouth turned down with scorn when he recalled how scared Martin had been of him. Well, thought Danny, he hadn't even begun to be scary.

He hoped people would think he was an insurance agent, or someone selling double glazing, if they saw him mount the steps to Martin's front door. Danny had been along the street a couple of times, and once along the service road which ran behind the gardens at the rear. He knew the windows were modern, with uPVC frames, and close up, he realised that the door, too, was uPVC, cleverly designed to look like the timber door it no doubt replaced. Above it, a fanlight in stained glass harked back to the house's origins as Victorian period mock-Georgian.

He heard the doorbell ring, but there was no response. After a quick look round at the empty street, he squatted and peered through the letterbox. There were no signs of life in the house. He rang again, but the house gave every impression of being empty.

Danny put his briefcase on the ground and opened it. A whisky half-bottle and a rag stood in the bottom. When he opened the bottle, petrol vapour filled his nostrils. He dampened one end of the rag with the petrol and took a cheap disposable lighter from his pocket.

Glancing round again, Bakker checked the street once more, then poured the petrol through the letterbox. Quickly, he pushed the dry end of the rag through after it, leaving just the petrol-soaked corner sticking out. With one hand, he held open the letterbox flap, sparked up the lighter. The rag burst into flame and fell away inside the hallway.

He held the letterbox lid open and peered through until he saw flames rising past it from the hall floor. That would remind Martin that their business was not finished, he thought, smiling thinly. He packed the empty bottle away in his briefcase and closed it with a snap. He lifted the letterbox once more – it was already beginning to feel hot –

and took one last glance through it. He stood up, scanned the street, which was still empty, and walked away without a backward glance. Behind him, a smoke alarm burst into life.

He needed to wash his hands to get rid of the smell of petrol. At the corner of the street there was still no sign of the fire. He wondered how far it would burn before someone noticed and called the fire brigade.

*

Getting a cup of coffee from the vending machine at the end of the corridor was a process which required tact, diplomacy, and a modicum of understanding of the neuroses afflicting the microprocessor at its heart. Pascal put his money into the slot and waited for the machine to respond. When nothing happened, he smacked it, open-handedly, on its side. The impact made the plumbing rattle, but did not result instantly in the production of coffee.

As he was gearing up to kick it, the door at the top of the staircase opened and the grey-haired sergeant from the Control Room, Claude Henslow, stepped into the corridor. The moment Pascal turned to see who it was, the machine burst into life, sliding a cup so vigorously forward that it overshot its mark and fell on the floor. As Pascal made a dive for it, a stream of hot water was ejected, splashing his hands. While holding the cup in the aperture on the front of the machine to catch what remained of the water, he reached across to the adjacent sink and ran cold water from its tap. He held his free hand in the stream. As soon as the hot water stopped, he held the other under the icy flow.

'Hello, sir,' said the uniformed sergeant cheerfully, 'still measuring yourself against the technology?' He peered into Pascal's cup, barely half full of brown liquid.

'And not exactly on top of it,' muttered Pascal. 'Where are the staff when you need them?'

'Oh, absolutely. Maybe you should stop sending them out on cases so they can be around to work the machine.'

'One of these days,' said Pascal, eyeing the paper in the sergeant's hand, 'I will get one of those nice little filter machines.'

'You could always use a kettle and a jar of instant like ordinary mortals.'

'Hmm. What have you got there?' asked Pascal, leading the way back to his office.

'Call from the Fire Service. House fire at...' he peered at the paper, '... 17 High Ridge Avenue.'

'Yes?'

'Home of someone called Martin. Jared Martin and wife Sara.'

Pascal frowned. 'Yes. So what?'

'They think it's arson.'

'What gives them that idea?'

'Years of professional training and a big burn mark just inside the letterbox.'

Pascal stared at the sergeant. 'And it's burning now?'

'As we speak.'

Pascal stood up. 'I'd better get down there.'

'I don't suppose you'll be able to put it out.'

'If I have enough of this alleged coffee...'

'Don't pursue that thought!' Henslow grinned.

'No, but when the brigade have – put it out, I mean – I might have a quick firkle through the remains. Looking for evidence, you know.'

'Of the cause of the blaze?'

'What else?'

'I'd have thought that was mostly a CSI job.'

'It is – but you know how much I enjoy sticking my nose into other peoples' business.'

He was half-way out of the door when the sergeant called after him.

'Mind if I have this coffee if you don't want it, George?'

Pascal ignored him and dragged his phone from his pocket. He called Frimley and told him to meet at the Martins' home.

High Ridge Avenue was cordoned off at both ends, uniformed constables restricting access to the scene. Two fire tenders filled the road and hoses snaked from a hydrant to the pump and from the pump to the front door of the house.

Pascal parked his car and made his way to the Martins' house. The Incident Commander, his white helmet making him stand out from the others, approached.

Pascal recognised him from earlier similar meetings. 'Hello, Harry,' he said, shaking the man's hand, 'what's afoot?'

'Still twelve inches last time I looked, George.'

'You tell me that every time I see you.'

'You ask me the same question: you put 'em up – I knock 'em down.'

'Right – so what's happened here? I can see the front door's a mess. How'd it start?'

As Pascal stared at the front door, off its hinges and badly charred, its surface bubbled and discoloured, the fire officer cleared his throat.

'Beginning with the good news: the fire's out. The guys you can see going in and out of the place are just making sure the place is safe for you to poke around in.'

'They've not had a chance to discover the cause yet?'

Harry, standing shoulder to shoulder with Pascal, looked down at him. 'I didn't say that.'

'No, no. Quite. So how'd it start?'

Harry folded his arms and rolled his eyes. 'To my untutored eye—'

'Don't come the old soldier,' Pascal interrupted. 'You used to teach these blokes how to do the job. How'd it start? I bet you've had a look.'

Harry frowned and pointed at the long, thin triangular stain on the door, from letterbox at its apex to the ground. 'Petrol through the letterbox.'

Pascal slapped him lightly between the shoulder-blades.

'That's what I wanted, Harry. The expert opinion.'

Frimley joined them from the other end of the street. Pascal turned to him.

'Douglas! We can add a case of arson to our workload.'

Frimley scanned the damage. 'What's one more case, sir.'

Pascal shrugged. 'Best we get a CSI in to have a look.' He turned back to Harry while Frimley got on the phone.

'I don't suppose any of your people have come across whatever was used to carry the petrol?'

Harry shook his head. 'Not that they've mentioned.' He rubbed his chin, easing the strap which held his helmet in place. 'I don't think it was necessarily very big.'

'The container?'

'Yes. The pool effect you get in these cases – on the floor where the accelerant gathers and the fire begins – gives some idea of the volume of material. I'm pretty sure this was simply petrol – easily obtained – and the pool wasn't very big, so you're not looking at more than a couple of cupfuls.'

Pascal looked thoughtful. 'It wouldn't be brought here in cups.'

'No. Any kind of container that would hold that sort of quantity.'

'And not left at the scene.'

'Not that we've found.'

'I'll see if I can get some uniforms to have a look round.'

He took out his mobile phone and rang the police station. With more uniformed officers promised, he began to walk along the street from the burnt property, looking for any suitable discarded container. Frimley began looking in the opposite direction. The CSI van and a minibus full of uniformed officers arrived more or less together and for a while, Pascal was involved in bringing them up to speed on the situation.

As the house was cordoned off behind a blue tape, Frimley went with Jimmy Tasker, the Senior Crime Scene

Investigator, as far as the door of the house and left him to begin his examination, resuming his search for the container.

The search of the street took an hour and was unproductive. Pascal had to accept that the arsonist had taken the container away with him. Or her. He set the uniformed men and women to call at all the houses in the street to see if anyone had seen anything from behind their net curtains. A sign on a lamp-post advised that it was a 'Neighbourhood Watch Area', so there was a faint possibility at least that someone had been watching the neighbourhood.

Frimley joined him. 'You want me on the door-to-doors as well, sir?'

Pascal sighed. 'No, Douglas.' He hesitated. 'Except for number 14. That's who made the triple-nine call. Let's pay them a visit. Uniform can do the rest of the street. I'll just tell Claude – I see he's got out of the office for once.'

After speaking to Sergeant Henslow, Pascal and Frimley crossed the road. The even-numbered houses in High Ridge Avenue had, for the most part, stood there for almost two centuries. The area had been chosen by the wealthier merchants of the day for the ostentatious display of their means and consequence, and occupied a ridge of higher land to the south of the town. Each home had acquired a generous allocation of land, and that translated into long carriage drives to their front doors. Victorian aspirants had come along later and built houses facing them, the odd-numbered ones, which copied the earlier style, but featured mod-cons such as electric light, running water, and mains drainage. They had much less land and consequently shorter gardens, all at the rear.

Pascal and Frimley trudged up the drive to the front door of number 14. A quarter of an hour later, they returned to the road, no further forward. The occupier had been in his garden and heard the smoke detector of number 17 shrieking. Intending nothing more than to complain about the noise, he'd been astonished to see flames through the fanlight above the front door, which presumably had broken with the heat. He'd phoned the fire brigade immediately. He'd seen no signs of anyone trapped in the building, and after the fire appliances arrived, he'd returned to his garden and lit a bonfire.

'Let's go and see what Jimmy's been up to,' said Pascal.

They crossed the road again and went up to the open doorway of number 17. Tasker was in the hallway beyond.

'Jimmy! Can we come in?' asked Pascal.

'If you stick to the walk-boards, George,' said Tasker, pointing at wooden blocks laid along the left side of the hall to prevent any forensic evidence on the floor from being damaged or compromised. Frimley waited on the step as there wasn't room for all of them in the hallway together. Pascal stood on the walk-boards. Even with the door open, the smell of petrol, soot and melted plastic filled the air.

'Anything of interest actually inside the house, Jimmy?' asked Pascal.

'Not that I've found – connected to the arson.' Tasker's response sounded guarded.

'And what have you found that *isn't* connected to the arson?'

Tasker stood up to straighten his limbs and ease his back. He held out a small evidence envelope with his gloved hand. There was a clear plastic window in it.

'What's in here?' asked the detective.

'White powder. It field tests positive for cocaine,' replied Tasker.

'Oh!' Pascal spoke slowly, his lips forming a pronounced circle. 'Oh.' He turned to Frimley. 'You hear that, Douglas? Coke.'

Frimley was noting the fact in his pocket book. 'Yes, sir.'

'Wonder if that might be connected to the reason for the arson?' said Pascal. He looked at Tasker. 'I reckon we need to look upstairs in the bedrooms and bathrooms.'

'Need a warrant to go beyond the immediate area of the fire, George,' said the investigator. 'Technically, Mr and Mrs Martin are victims, not suspects.'

'Hmm.' Pascal thought a moment. 'Anything else likely to be of interest?'

'No. And for what it's worth, I think you'd be lucky to get a warrant on the basis of a few milligrams of cocaine.'

'Where was it?'

Tasker pointed to an area about a foot in front of the first step of the staircase.

'So it was probably on someone's clothes and fell off as they were taking off their coat?' Pascal speculated.

Tasker nodded and pointed to the right-hand wall. 'It fits with the coat-rack being there.'

The sound of a raised voice outside drew the attention of both detectives. A Constable was keeping a man carrying a computer bag over his shoulder at bay.

'But it's my house!' cried the man.

Pascal glanced at the coats hanging from the rack and turned so his body shielded them from view outside. He quickly felt through the pockets of the garments which were both male and female, without finding any more suspicious substances. He turned back and went to the door.

'Mr Martin?' asked Pascal, gesturing to the Constable to allow the man under the tape.

'Yes. It's my house. What's happened?'

Pascal barred his way. 'Wait here, Mr Martin, we can't go in until the Crime Scene Investigator has finished.'

Martin stared at him. 'Crime Scene— !'

'Of course,' said Pascal. 'The fire didn't start itself.'

The colour seemed to drain from Martin's face. For a moment, Pascal thought he was going to be sick.

'Are you all right?' he asked. 'I suppose you don't have much of this sort of arson in High Ridge Avenue?'

Martin shook his head, licking his lips. 'No. What do you mean by "this sort"?'

Pascal pointed at the ruined door. 'Somebody poured petrol through the letterbox and set it alight. Now that method doesn't guarantee the place will burn down, because – as you can see – even when there's no-one home, very often the fire brigade can prevent serious damage. That's not to say it isn't a successful method sometimes, but to do the job properly and more surely, an arsonist would have to set things up better. Petrol through the letterbox is quite often sheer mischief or a warning. It's a bit... unsophisticated, if you see what I mean.'

Martin nodded. He kept glancing at the door and looking at the rest of the house as if to check it really wasn't damaged.

'Is there a rear entrance?' asked Pascal.

'Yes. Round the back.'

Pascal looked at him askance. 'I suppose that would have occurred to me eventually.' He glanced at Frimley, rolling his eyes, unseen by Martin. 'Mind if we go round there? I'd like to talk to you about matters.' He indicated the smoke-blackened hallway.

Martin shrugged. 'If you want. What's to say?'

'Let's get indoors so we can talk without the whole street and half the fire brigade being able to hear.'

Martin led Pascal and Frimley along the street and round the corner into the narrow service road, walking back parallel to the Avenue, until he reached the gate in the high wall guarding his property.

The houses on the odd-numbered side of the street were constructed on a slope. The door in the rear walls, off the gardens, led into cellars which had once been the kitchen. A narrow stairway led up into the hallway, where they emerged beneath the staircase. Jimmy Tasker was beginning to put his equipment away.

'You finished, Jimmy?' Pascal asked.

'Here, yes. I'll take the door away for more tests.'

'Okay.' Pascal turned to Martin. 'As you heard, the door is going to the lab. The doorway will be boarded up until you get another, but it's going to be a matter of using the back door until then.'

Martin took them into the lounge and offered them a drink. There was a bar across one corner of the room. Both declined, but watched as Martin himself poured a large measure of whisky and added a little soda from the siphon on the bar counter. He drank half the glass before sitting opposite the two detectives.

'Now, what do you want to talk about?'

Pascal had been studying photographs displayed on the walls. 'I take it from these and the coats in the hallway that there is a Mrs Martin?'

Martin nodded. 'Yes. But she's not here.'

He seemed to stop himself from saying more. Pascal prompted him.

'Is she away on business? On holiday?'

'What has this to do with the fire?' demanded Martin.

'Just trying to get the circumstances sorted out in my head,' Pascal explained. 'So where is your wife?'

Martin suddenly looked haggard. His shoulders slumped. 'She's moved out.'

Pascal saw what he took to be despair in the man's face. 'Permanently? '

'I think so.'

'Do you know why?'

'This has nothing to do with the fire, has it? No way!'

'Yes, it does. I need to know who has access to the house, and I also want to find out if someone doesn't like you. It sounds as if your wife might come into both those categories.'

Martin studied his hands, his fingers interlaced and clenched.

'We had an argument over... over sex,' he said hesitant-ly.

Pascal waited. 'What was the nature of the disagree-ment?'

Martin lifted his eyes to Pascal's, and glanced at Frimley sitting beside him on the settee.

'I'm having a spot of trouble at the minute. My libido is... largely gone.'

'So you and your wife don't make love very often?' asked Pascal gently.

Martin shook his head, not meeting Pascal's eyes. 'No.'

'How long has the situation gone on?'

'A few months. You have to understand, Detective Inspector, that my wife enjoys sex. A great deal of sex.' He paused. 'And she wasn't getting any from me. I couldn't.'

'And that made her decide to leave?'

'She was very patient. Didn't go as soon as she might have done. I, uh, think she found someone else.'

'When did you last hear from her?'

'The day she left. We'd had a terrible row the night before. She came in around three in the morning, looking terrible.'

'Terrible?'

'Her makeup was smudged. Her hair was untidy. I don't know! And she was in a foul mood.' He looked down at his hands again. 'Frankly, I told her she disgusted me. The smell...'

'What smell?'

'She smelt of... sex.'

He stood up and paced up and down the room. 'To be honest, Mr Pascal, she looked as if she'd serviced the entire male membership of a rugby club, to put it crudely. It is not a thought I enjoy having about my wife, but it conveys how I felt when I saw her.'

'I think I understand, Mr Martin,' said Pascal with some sympathy. 'Do you know where she went?'

'She left me a note saying something about staying with a man she called Deej.'

'Do you know any more about him?'

Martin shook his head, still staring at the carpet. 'I wish I knew more. I'd like my wife back.'

'One last question, Mr Martin,' said Pascal, 'is there anyone else who might be wishing you harm at this time?'

Martin kept his eyes on his glass as he drained it. 'No.'

'Are you certain?' Pascal studied him closely.

Martin put the glass down on the counter. 'Quite certain.' He turned and met Pascal's gaze.

The detectives left through the cellar and garden. Once outside and some distance from the property Frimley glanced round at his DI.

'Think he was lying about something, sir.'

'Yes. So do I. I think he was lying about there being nobody else who might be wishing him harm.'

'Yes, sir.'

'Yes, and one other thing.'

## CHAPTER 7

It was Thursday before Julia finally succumbed. As Unwin approached her with the dripping syringe, she held up her hands to stop him.

'Let me,' she said.

He handed it over without a word. She pulled her skirt up and rested the needle against her thigh, which was starting to look bruised.

'You should try somewhere else,' he said. 'Bruises don't look good. Round here, they'll all know what you're doing.'

She looked up. 'Where, then?'

'A lot of the girls put it into their feet. Plenty of veins to get at. If that's what you want,' he added.

'What's the difference?' she asked.

'You get more of a rush.'

She lifted her right foot onto the bed and studied the veins faintly visible through her pale skin.

'In there?'

'Any one you like,' he said.

She pressed the needle into the blood vessel.

'Just half now, half later,' he said. 'You draw a bit of blood into the syringe, to mix it first, then in it goes.'

Her hand trembling slightly, Julia did as he said, watching her blood swirl into the brownish mixture in the syringe as she pulled the plunger out, before pressing it in and expelling half of the volume back into her bloodstream. She had barely pulled the needle out before she felt the effect. She didn't realise she'd dropped the syringe and allowed her head to fall back on the mattress. She watched Unwin through slitted eyes, vaguely expecting him to drop his trousers and climb on her, but he simply sat on the

91

edge of the bed and watched her. He leaned over and gently slapped her cheeks.

'That's my girl,' he said, and smiled.

She thought he was being quite nice.

'Now, this time, before you get the other half, you have to get me hard and encourage me to fuck you. And that means you have to be nice. Try and think what a man wants from a woman, and give it to him.'

She kept trying to drift off to sleep, but every time she did, Unwin slapped her face again. They were only light slaps, they stung but didn't leave marks.

All right, she thought, what he wants is sex. She forced herself to sit up. It took a lot of concentration.

'Don't forget to smile, girl. Look as if you're pleased to see me,' he said.

She smiled, and crossed her arms to opposite sides of her top, pulling it up and over her head. She saw him staring at her breasts. She reached behind and unfastened her bra. She expected him to lean forward and kiss them, but he simply watched, glancing up at her eyes occasionally.

'Smile,' he reminded her, 'and come over here to put your tit in my mouth.'

She knelt on the mattress and did as he asked. He licked and sucked on her nipples.

'Now, slide your hands up my legs and unfasten my jeans.'

She did so.

'Now get my cock out.'

He waited while she complied.

'And now kiss it, and lick it.'

While she was doing this, he rested a hand on the back of her head.

'Now open your mouth and suck on it. Like a lollipop. And be gentle,' he added, winding a skein of her hair round his hand so he could pull her head away if she was tempted to use her teeth on him.

She bobbed her head up and down for a while until he was ready for the next step.

'Okay, you can get off now. Put a condom on.' He dug one out from his trousers' pocket. She tore the pack open and unrolled it on him.

'Take your panties off and open your legs.'

He watched her.

'Now you take my cock, very gently, and you lead it to your cunt. Keep your knees apart and bent a bit so you present a better angle.'

She watched dispassionately as she pulled him closer, until she felt him at her entrance. He smiled at her.

'That's a good girl. For the time being, that's where we stop. The Boss is negotiating a price for your cherry. So get on your knees.' A moment later, she felt him apply some lubricant gel to her anus, and swab his penis around the small puckered hole.

'Now a little shove, and you'll find we're in business,' he told her.

She hunched her hips up towards him and felt him slip inside her. The pain wasn't too bad, thanks to the gel and the analgesic effect of the heroin. He began to thrust himself in and out, and she rocked her hips, and waited for him to finish.

Unwin drove one last time into her and she felt him pulsing deep inside. He waited for a moment, then pulled himself out. After he'd removed the condom and thrown it in the bucket which was slowly filling up in the corner of the room, he dressed himself again and held out the syringe.

'Here. You've earned this,' he said.

She took it quickly and pulled her right foot close enough to reach, but he put his hand on hers.

'You want to alternate. You don't want bruises or track-marks.'

She swapped over and quickly inserted the needle into a vein on her left foot, sucking blood into the syringe before pressing it all into her bloodstream. The hit affected her almost at once. This was good – he'd leave her this time to enjoy it. He picked up the syringe and gazed down at her with something like satisfaction.

'I think you can start the payback process soon. I'll send Viv to you with some new clothes. Those old ones stink.'

She said nothing, but just before he left, she remembered to smile.

\*

Later – she had no idea how long she'd been laying there while the hit wore off – the door opened. She expected another visit from her jailer, and was surprised when Sara, looking sexy and smart, came in, with clothes over one arm and a carrier bag in the other hand.

'Sara!' she exclaimed. 'Can I go home now?'

Her Godmother looked at her dully.

'No, dear. Derrick owns you now and you have to do as he says. Paul says you've developed a heroin habit – '

'One he's given me!'

'Yes, well, they have to do that to keep all you girls in order.'

Julia blinked. 'You – you *know* about what goes on here, don't you?'

'Of course. But it's different for me. You see, I'm Derrick's *best* girl, the one he didn't have to get on heroin. I just happen to like sex a lot, and I'm not getting any at home.'

She picked up Julia's top. 'I've left Jared, you know. We had a row. Put your clothes on and come with me.'

She waited until Julia put her bra on, then handed her the top before leading the way out of the room and along the corridor.

Before leaving, Julia looked round the room. There was nothing of hers remaining. She followed Sara.

It was the first time Julia had seen any other part of the house. She discovered they appeared to be in the attic. The floor was bare boards, the walls filthy, the plaster cracked. Julia followed Sara to the end of the corridor and down a narrow staircase. They went along the next landing to a door on which a number four was painted. Sara unlocked it with a key she kept round her neck on a piece of string, and led the way inside.

It was larger than the room Julia had been in, and there was a proper toilet and a shower unit in the corner. Sara put the clothes down on the bed and turned to her.

'First off, strip and get in the shower. There's some shampoo and gel in there, so clean yourself up. Afterwards, they want you to go blonde and tanned, so we have a lot to do.'

Julia stripped off. It was funny, she thought, a week ago she would have been horribly embarrassed to strip in front of anyone else, but now she found she didn't care. Her clothes hit the floor and she turned.

She pointed at the toilet. 'Do you mind?'

Sara looked her up and down. 'If you make it filthy, you clean it,' she said, turning away to look out of the window. Julia flushed the toilet when she'd finished and got into the shower.

The water was warm and wonderful. The jets stung her skin. She put her head under the spray and felt her hair soak. The shampoo was gently scented and contained conditioner, and she slowly and with thoroughness washed her hair and rinsed it clean. Then she rubbed shower gel all over, the scent rising in the steam, and it was heaven to feel so clean when she rinsed away the last of the filth.

She opened the door of the cubicle. Sara stood there, holding out a clean, dry towel. Julia rubbed herself dry. Sara passed her a new thong, followed by a bra, and pointed her at the chemicals arranged round the washbasin, which included the chemicals to bleach and colour her hair and a light tan stain. When they'd finished, Julia completed dressing with a skirt and T-shirt. Sara sat her in front of a small dressing table and brushed her hair.

'Deej wants you to have this cut,' she said.

'Why?'

'Well, for a start, round here you do what Deej wants. That's Mr Jackson to you, and you'd better show him respect. Look at it this way, if you have a load of blokes shooting off all over you, the less hair you have to wash the easier life will be.'

Julia stared at her through the mirror.

'Is – is that likely to happen?'

Sara stopped brushing and sat on her bed. Julia swung round to face her.

'What do you think?' asked Sara.

Julia shrugged.

'Well, dear, when Derrick, or Deej as *I* call him, decides you're ready to work, there'll be a little party. You and the other girls who came in last week will be the star attractions.'

'Wh-what?'

Sara shook her head, looking exasperated. 'They'll be fucking you all night, dear. The way you look, you'll be the most popular girl on the mattress.'

Julia stared at her. There was no more avoiding it. This was no temporary hitch, a nightmare which would soon end. She was to be a prostitute and the heroin was to make her compliant. The admission to herself of what she'd been trying to shut away since being taken made her feel suddenly very sick. She made a dash for the toilet.

When she'd finished retching, she felt terrible – and it wasn't just the vomiting. There was shame, too, but also a growing need for the calm and comfort of another shot of heroin. Her head began to ache and her skin feel clammy. She looked round pathetically at Sara.

'I need another hit of heroin, Auntie.'

'I'm not your aunt!' snapped Sara, 'And round here I'm known as Viv! Paul decides whether you get one, and what you have to do to earn it.'

'You don't understand, I want one *now*!'

'You heard me. Now clean that bowl and rinse your mouth out.'

Julia, feeling quite wretched, cleaned the bowl with the brush kept behind it. When she glanced at Sara, she saw the older woman's lack of concern, and realised that, ultimately, she was on her own. She had somehow to survive.

*

Friday. Sara lay on the single bed. Ever since she'd arrived, six days ago, she'd hoped that Derrick would come to her, somehow prove that she was his special woman. The room was not so bad, she thought, though you could hear the girls either side through the thin walls, rabbiting away in their own language, or the occasional toilet flush.

She got up and paced restlessly. She wasn't going to stay in her room all day. She was a free agent: she could come and go as she pleased. Besides she needed some money for food. She thought she might browse some of the shops which sold good quality underwear and buy some new stockings since they seemed to last no time at all at *Kittens*. She spent her evenings there, and might have sex two or three times with men she fancied. Derrick, she recalled with a shudder, nearly always made her fuck some of his older clients in exchange for an extra line of coke. Well, not exactly *make her* fuck them, but it was worth the small feeling of disgust she often experienced for the reward, so she never declined. She *could* have, of course, if she'd wanted to. But she didn't.

She glanced out of the window. A young man, mid to late twenties, with short dark hair, in what she thought was called a crew-cut, was staring up impassively at her window from across the street. She blinked and looked again. Yes, definitely, he was staring at her.

She dressed for town and let herself out of the building. It was a short walk to the shops. Once or twice she thought she saw the young man following her, but she couldn't be sure. After a while, she no longer noticed him.

In the lingerie shop, she found underwear she couldn't resist and placed it in a basket. At the checkout, she presented her credit card and was surprised and embarrassed when the sales assistant told her the card had been cancelled and that she'd been asked to keep it. Sara felt her cheeks burning and abandoned the basket and its contents while she headed for the door. She still had her cash card and she took it to an ATM outside her bank. The machine swallowed the card and refused to return it. She went into the branch and waited for a cashier to become free.

'Your cash machine has swallowed my cash card,' she explained, 'and there seems to be a problem with my credit card.'

The teller checked her computer screen before glancing up at Sara.

'Your account has been closed, Mrs Martin.' She stared at the screen again. 'It was a joint account with your husband, I see, and he closed it yesterday. He paid off the credit card and closed that, too.'

Sara stared at her. 'The bastard!' she muttered.

The teller shrugged and smiled sympathetically. 'Sorry.'

'What about our savings account?'

The girl looked at her screen. 'Sorry. All the accounts you shared with Mr Jared Martin have been closed.'

Sara stared. 'Oh hell!'

The teller watched her nervously.

'Thanks.' Sara turned and left the building.

You bastard, Jared! she thought. She had a small amount of cash in her handbag, not enough for a taxi home, and it was too far to walk in high-heels. She'd tap Deej for a loan – hell, make it a gift: she'd earned it – this evening, and sort out Jared first thing in the morning. She fumed inwardly and, after finding enough change to buy a sandwich, walked slowly back to Columbine Road.

*

*Kittens* was busy when she arrived that evening, and her attempts to get close to Derrick Jackson were thwarted by people slipping him money for product, and sometimes the younger girls simply taking a breather by his side. When she had gotten close, he'd barely smiled at her.

'There's someone special here tonight, Viv,' he said. 'I want you to be nice to him: give him a treat. Anything he wants.'

'Not tonight, Deej,' she'd said. 'Tonight is for you. Let's go in the back, I've something to show you.' She took his wrist in one hand and rubbed the other over his groin. She smiled tantalisingly. 'Find out what you've been missing,' she added in a whisper.

He smiled at her thinly: not quite the delighted look she expected, and brushed her hand away.

'Too busy, tonight, Sara,' he said, further disconcerting her by the use of her real name. 'Here. Be happy.'

He pulled a small plastic bag from his pocket and shook some of the white crystalline contents on to a mirror beside him.

'Very good, fresh in.'

She tried to look grateful, but felt chagrined that he had turned down her suggestion. Keeping her eyes averted, she pulled out the little gold tube she carried in her clutch bag and rummaged for a credit card to break up the crystals and form them into lines before she remembered she no longer had it. She used one of Jared's old business cards instead.

He watched her snort the powder, the smile gone from his lips.

'Now come and meet Gordon. He was a valuable investor when I was starting out, and I want you to treat him well.'

Part of her mind registered that this sounded more like a command than a request and she bridled somewhat, but she let the moment pass. Besides, with her nose full of his coke and the familiar *frisson* starting up in her brain, she thought it would be churlish to complain. She looked for the punter Derrick might mean, but all the ones who caught her gaze were geezers in their fifties and sixties. There was one old bloke who might have been in his eighties. When he smiled at her and rubbed his groin suggestively, she felt repugnance and scowled at him.

'There you go, Viv!' said Derrick in her ear. 'Give him what he wants.' He pushed her forward with a hand firmly applied to her rump.

As she reached him, the punter reached out a gnarled, bony hand and slipped it between her bare legs, pushing up under her skirt and grinning.

She swallowed and glanced round at Derrick, hoping he'd take pity on her and tell her to see someone else but he was simply standing in his customary place, watching her, frowning, and clearly expecting her to get it on with the old geezer. She tried a smile, as the old man's fingers pulled aside the thong she was wearing and insinuated themselves inside her. She brushed at his hands as she leaned down.

'Not too fast, eh,' she said. 'We need to get to know each other a little bit.'

She expected him to stop. Instead, he jammed his fingers as far into her as he could, and his smile disappeared.

'Shut up! Get my cock out and sit on it!'

She stared at him. He jabbed her again, making her wince.

'Hurry up!' he insisted.

She glanced pitifully at Derrick before turning back and complying with the man's demand. She normally took men out to the back rooms, and she simply dreaded to think what the sight of her impaled on the old geezer's erection in full view of everyone else would do to her reputation. She took a foil-wrapped condom from her bag with one hand and bit on one end of the package. As she was about to tear it open, she caught sight of the old man's head, shaking.

'Nah! My old todger don't need a raincoat.'

She allowed herself a small smile of relief: obviously, he couldn't come. His stiffness was probably Viagra-induced. She put the condom packet bag in her bag, straddled him until she felt the tip of his cock against her opening and gently lowered herself down. She was gratified to see, as she did so, that he gritted his teeth in something like ecstasy. She gently slid up and down, expecting him at some time to tell her he'd had enough.

A small crowd of the younger girls and some punters were making their interest and amusement apparent. She felt a blush stealing into her cheeks and she quickened her movements. She felt him begin to thrust beneath her and figured it wouldn't be long now – he'd exhaust himself quickly and then she could bring this ludicrous pantomime to an end.

Suddenly, he closed his eyes and jammed himself up against her. A moment later she felt him pulse within her, the familiar slickness of their combined juices begin to wet her buttocks. She stared at him until he relaxed, before trying to stand up. He grabbed her hips.

'Nah! You just sit there a moment, m'dear,' he said. 'I like to give him a soak after one of these outings – he don't get 'em that often, so we make the most o' the times we do.' Sara lowered herself back down on his shrinking flesh, feeling her gorge rise at the very idea that he'd come in her. It felt like bucketsful. The bastard! She was about to get up again when she felt a hand on her shoulder, pressing her down, and she turned to find Derrick by her side.

'That all right for you, Gordon? I said she'd be good.'

Gordon put a hand in his pocket and brought out a wallet.

'You'll not mind if I give the girl a tip, will you?'

Derrick shrugged.

Sara wondered how much it would be. She could use the money. He shut the wallet suddenly and pushed his face as close to hers as he could reach.

'"Contraceptives should be used on every conceivable occasion", to quote Spike Milligan. That's a tip.' He uttered a crack of laughter.

Derrick grinned and removed his hand. Sara stood up, determinedly this time. Gordon's cock flopped wetly against his peeled-back trousers.

'You gonna clean it and put it away for me like a good girl?' he asked plaintively.

Sara felt stuff beginning to run in cold trails down her thighs. She shook her head, turned and almost ran across the room to the toilet. Behind her, there was a small round of applause and some laughter. In the privacy of a cubicle, while she cleaned herself, she felt hot tears stain her cheeks. The evening had not worked out as she'd planned.

If only it had been Derrick... Another time, maybe she should be more subtle. If she'd managed to get some coke earlier, she'd have felt more confident dealing with him, and wouldn't have had to take it when he offered. She caught her thought: no she hadn't *had* to have the coke. She wasn't dependent. Really! She wasn't!

She wept again.

When she returned from the toilets, she was surprised to see the man she'd seen in the street outside her room earlier. He wore new blue Levi's, and an open-necked shirt. He carried his jacket slung over one shoulder, and was talking to Derrick. Sara watched from a distance until she caught his eyes on her. Her first impression was that they were cold, light blue eyes, set in an inexpressive face. She felt a ripple of fear insinuate itself down her spine.

Derrick turned towards her. 'Viv, this is Danny. He's a visitor from Holland, and I'd like him to enjoy his stay.'

Danny was smiling at her now, though his eyes remained cold and watchful. He held out his hand. She noticed his fingers were long, the nails clean and trimmed. When he took hers, she felt the strength of his grip. Male strength and power usually had an aphrodisiac effect on her, but there was something about Danny's which fright-ened her.

'Hello, Viv,' he said. 'Derrick says you're really very good, and might, given the right incentive, be persuaded to spend an evening in my company – somewhere other than here?'

He put his hand into his hip pocket and dragged out a fat roll of banknotes which he held out for her. Sara glanced at Derrick, but he'd moved away. She gently took the notes from Danny's hand.

'What do you want to do?' she asked.

'Take me for a little drive,' he replied. 'I like the coast at night. It's wild and windy, and tonight the stars are out.'

'Are you for real? You want me to drive you up to the coast? And then what?'

He shrugged. 'We'll see what impulse occurs,' he said.

It was a long time since she'd had sex in the back of a car. She supposed that would be the "impulse" he'd have. She slipped the banknotes into her bag.

'Now?' she asked.

He nodded. 'Let's not hang around.'

'I'll get my coat.'

'I'll wait by the door.'

An hour later, they were parked on firm ground a hun-dred metres back from the edge of a notoriously unstable cliff. Periodically, she knew, the tide washed away large chunks of earth onto the beach, and also periodically, houses which had once been hundreds of yards from the sea, tumbled to destruction on the shore.

Danny had not said much on the journey from Brey-don. She pulled the handbrake on and switched off the engine, turning to him.

'What would you like to do now?' She glanced at the inviting space in the back of the Mercedes.

He grinned. 'You would like sex in the back?'

She shrugged. 'If it's what you want.'

'I can do what I want with you, can I?'

'You've paid for the privilege.'

He nodded, then leaned towards her, his right hand gripping the back of her neck. Before she could move, he clamped his left hand, encased in a soft latex glove, over her face. She couldn't breathe. In the gloom, the last things she saw were his blazing eyes and moonlight glinting on his teeth as he smiled.

# CHAPTER 8

Half-past six on a Saturday morning. The beach was still wet from the receding tide, which had left its usual deposit of flotsam and weed along the high water mark. Two cocker spaniels ran here and there, examining the detritus, sniffing, and pawing at broken shells. Norman Chappell strolled along in their wake, taking pleasure from the early sunshine breaking through the clouds of the night before. There had been another cliff fall, he noticed: nothing new along this bit of coast.

A salt-laden north-easterly breeze was blowing the cellophane wrapper from a cigarette packet over the beach. The younger dog was chasing it, leaping and snapping his jaws together in an attempt to capture it, moving further up the beach towards the base of the cliffs and the mound of fresh earth which marked the site of the fall. A new scent filled its sensitive nostrils: leaving the cellophane, the dog investigated. At the mound of fallen earth, it clambered up onto a broad, flat ledge, and scrabbled at the sandy surface.

Metal and plastic, red and amber, became visible. The dog sniffed around it, caught another scent, uttered a short, sharp urgent yip, which brought its master from the smooth part of the beach to scramble over the loose pieces of rock and soil to see what the dog had found. A few times in the past, the dog had turned up something he'd been able to sell for a few pounds. His hopes of this being in a similar vein were dashed when he recognised part of the tail-light cluster of a car, buried beneath the collapsed cliff.

With his bare hands, he began to brush dirt and clear the smaller rocks from the side of the car. The interior became visible through the restricted view offered by the rear offside quarter light. The inside surface of the glass was blackened and scorched. At about the same time his nose identified the pungent smell of petrol, his eyes caught sight of a black shape occupying the driver's seat. It was difficult to see at such a sharp angle to his right, but as he recognised a charred head, he felt his gorge rise, and he staggered back, down the loose slope, scattering stones and earth until, at a point some fifteen yards from the wreck, he heaved up the contents of his stomach.

*

Pascal was still on his way to the police station when Norman Chappell's telephone call was received through the 999 service and passed to Frimley in the CID office. He grabbed his coat, and headed for the stairs, meeting Pascal as he reached the ground floor.

'Where's the fire?' Pascal asked.

'On the beach, sir. Body found in a burned-out car. Triple nine call a few minutes ago. Found by a man walking his dogs.'

He kept walking as he spoke. Pascal turned on his heel and followed him through the rear door of the building into the car park.

It took half an hour to reach the coast. Pascal and Frimley spotted a group of marked police cars close to a new scar in the cliff, where a fresh fall of earth had taken place, and parked next to them. They cautiously approached the new area of instability, where the salt-laden wind hit them, before finding an uneven pathway and slithering down the seaward side on to the beach. A collection of figures and an area bounded by blue-and-white scene-of-crime tape, billowing in the breeze, identified the spot. A civilian, holding two frisking spaniels on leashes, and a uniformed police officer, were standing together, at a little distance from the scene. Pascal walked towards them, nodding to the constable.

'What happened here?' he asked.

Chappell explained, and added that he'd had to clamber back to the landward side of the coastal dune in order to get a signal for his mobile phone.

'Thanks very much for your help, Mr Chappell, it can't have been a pleasant experience,' nodded Pascal. 'What time did you find the body?'

'Probably around half-past six. I left the house just after six, and we'd been walking along the beach for a while. So I guess around half-past.'

'Thanks. If the constable has taken your details, I won't keep you. I expect you'd like to get on your way.'

Chappell nodded and swallowed. 'I would.'

'We'd appreciate it if you'd come to Breydon Police Station later today so we can get your story down in writing.'

'I hope you find out what happened here,' said Chappell as he turned to go.

'Do our best.'

Pascal preceded Frimley past the other group of constables, who were watching them. They ducked under the tape, which cracked and clattered in the breeze, and stared at the scene. Someone had scraped more of the loose earth from the side windows. The car had come to rest on its wheels, with its nearside tucked fairly close to the cliff, and parallel to it. The mixture of rock and earth that had given way under its weight had formed a platform on the beach on which the car rested, with lighter sand and scree tumbling down on top of it to bury the remains. A little more material, Pascal thought, and the car would not have been found until the next high tide washed its covering away.

Frimley had gone to where the front of the car lay still buried. He sniffed. 'Sarge?'

Pascal looked up.

'There's a smell of petrol.'

'Yes, okay. Best warn people about it.' There was no telling what damage the fall might have done to the car's fuel system.

While Frimley went to speak to the small knot of uniformed officers, Pascal peered through the rear quarter light, and twisted his head as much as possible to see the body occupying the driving seat. There was much blackening of the inside of the vehicle, and it had clearly been on fire – probably saved from further destruction by the cliff fall's shutting off the supply of oxygen. He managed to focus on the corpse's skull. It was blackened and almost hairless. The body seemed to be twisted in the seat, but his restricted angle of view and the sooty murk on the inside of the glass prevented Pascal seeing clearly. He stood back and turned to see where his constable was.

Frimley was talking to a new arrival on the scene. Senior CSI, Jimmy Tasker, was wriggling into a pair of paper overalls. As he turned, he saw Pascal and waved. A few minutes later, the Forensic Medical Examiner arrived on site and waited patiently while the CSI cleared her access to the corpse.

Frimley stared towards the wrecked car. 'I'll get the index number and check DVLA. And I'd like to see what the FME thinks after she's had a look at the situation, so I'll be along soon.'

'I'll be in the caff.'

Pascal set off along the beach as far as the track up the cliff. He struggled up, wading against the tide of soft sand which seemed determined to sweep him back down onto the beach. At the top, Norman Chappell was standing with his dogs. He was staring down at the knot of people standing by the taped-off area, and glanced round as Pascal reached him.

'Poor sod,' he said.

'Yes,' Pascal replied.

'Any closer to finding out who it was?'

'Not yet. There's a doctor taking a look at the body now, so we should be a bit wiser when she's finished. You say you left home just after six this morning?'

'Yes. I'm an early riser. I've always had dogs to look after, and you need to up early for them.'

Pascal bent and petted the older dog, which was sniffing his ankles. The other joined them, its tail swishing from side to side, not wishing to be left out. He squatted so he could tickle their ears and rake his nails gently down their spines.

'I don't suppose you heard or saw anything during the night?'

'No, sorry,' said Chappell. 'I get so much fresh air and exercise I sleep like a log.'

'Must have been a shock to find the body,' he said.

Chappell nodded. 'Put me in mind of the morning I found my wife. She'd died in her sleep, though: not like this one.'

'It's possible this was just an accident,' said Pascal.

'Let's hope so,' said Chappell lugubriously.

'We'll see you later to get a statement.'

'Yes, okay. Good luck.' He paused. 'Just one thing.'

Pascal straightened up. 'Yes?'

'The body: was it male or female?'

Pascal screwed up his lips. 'I'm not altogether sure.'

Chappell nodded sadly and turned away, calling the dogs to heel.

Pascal walked as briskly as the loose sand underfoot would let him, down to the approach road.

Not far along was the café Pascal intended to visit. By its location and the lack of local custom, he had no trouble deducing that it was targeted mainly at the tourist trade. The owner, it seemed, had become aware of the burst of activity on her doorstep, and the possibility of extra takings had lured her into opening up for full English breakfasts and mugs of hot strong tea and coffee. Pascal was delighted to take advantage of the offer. Choosing tea to accompany his plateful, he sat next to the window, from where he could look up the path to the top of the dune. He saw Frimley striding towards him and called across to the proprietor to supply another mug of tea.

She put it on the counter as Frimley entered the café. Pascal pointed at it, and the detective constable nodded in acknowledgement as he placed his breakfast order at the small counter. Seating himself opposite Pascal, Frimley opened his notebook.

'The vehicle is registered to a Sara Rebecca Martin. Dr Ferrari said the body is female, but that's as far as she's committing herself until she's had a bit more time.'

'Never heard of her. She live local?' asked Pascal between sips of the hot brew.

Frimley glanced up, puzzled. 'It's the same doctor as we had on the last killing.'

Pascal frowned. 'Not the doctor, the corpse.' He recalled Jane Ferrari well.

'Oh. Mrs Martin's from Breydon. You remember the bloke we saw after the letterbox fire? I guess she's the missing wife.'

Pascal studied his breakfast speculatively. 'Chief suspect for the arson. Well, after we've seen to the welfare of the inner man, we can go round and find out where the husband was last night. Don't want to be too early when you've got potentially depressing news. Assuming he didn't do it, of course.'

'Yes, sir.'

Two breakfasts arrived, Pascal's cholesterol-laden one and Frimley's healthier scrambled egg on toast. For a while, they ate in silence. At last, with clean plates and empty mugs before them, Pascal leaned back in his chair and stretched.

'Right, then, Douglas, let's go and solve this one. You never know, by some stroke of good fortune, we could be back in the nick by eleven.'

Frimley lifted a sceptical eyebrow. Pascal wondered if he could see that his tongue was jammed firmly in his cheek.

*

The front door of 17 High Ridge Avenue was still absent, the doorway covered by an ugly piece of unpainted board. Pascal and Frimley went round to the rear entrance and knocked on the cellar door. After a few minutes, Jared Martin opened it.

'Yes?' he demanded.

'You remember us from last Tuesday, do you sir, when we spoke about the letterbox fire?' asked Pascal.

'Oh. Yes, sorry,' said Martin. He seemed relieved to see them. 'You'd better come in.' He led the way up to the lounge.

'How can I help you?' he asked after they were seated.

'Is your wife Sara Rebecca Martin, sir?' asked Pascal.

'Yes. I thought I told you.'

'Has she been home since we last spoke?'

'No.'

'And have you seen her or found out where she is since then?'

'No. Why?'

'Does she own a car – a beige coloured Mercedes?'

'Yes. Why?' Martin repeated.

Pascal took a deep breath. 'I'm sorry to have to tell you, Mr Martin, but we found a body in your wife's car this morning. We can't be certain of its identity, or even whether it is of a man or a woman, but I think you need to prepare yourself for the worst news."

Martin stared at him. 'Are you telling me my wife's dead?'

'We can't be certain,' said Pascal, 'but one of the things we need to do is collect something with her DNA on it. I also need to know the name of her dentist.'

Martin's mouth fell open. 'Why can't I see her? Why won't a photograph do? I have one of those.' He stood up, clearly agitated.

Pascal remained seated and gestured with his hand that Martin should sit down again. 'I'm afraid it isn't possible to identify the body from a photograph; you see there was a fire—'

'Oh, God!' groaned Martin.

'That's why we need her DNA and the name of her dentist.' Pascal sat back. 'I'm sorry, Mr Martin.'

Martin said nothing. He appeared to be struggling to come to terms with the news. Frimley stood up.

'Mr Martin? Could I take a look at your wife's things in the bedroom and bathroom?'

'Yes, yes. Go ahead - upstairs.' Martin took him into the hallway and pointed at the door. He came back into the room and sat down again. Pascal leaned forward again.

'I'm sorry to bring you such unwelcome news, Mr Martin. Do you want us to contact anyone for you?'

'No, no thanks. I'll do it myself.'

'I was wondering, do you know anyone who might have wanted her dead?'

'No.'

Pascal studied his eyes. 'How did you feel about her, Mr Martin? After all, you told us your wife had left you the day someone set fire to your home. I don't suppose she was *your* favourite person?'

Martin looked shocked. 'I'd never kill my wife. I know we have argued, but I've always loved her. Everyone argues with their wife or husband, but rarely resorts to murder to settle matters.'

'Indeed not,' Pascal agreed, 'otherwise we wouldn't be able to move for bodies. So you're denying you had anything to do with her death? Didn't ask anyone else to kill her for you?'

'Mr Pascal!' Martin exclaimed, standing up, 'That's outrageous.'

'Sorry but I had to ask. Do you have any children?'

'No' replied Martin, calmer. 'Some people would call it a selfish choice, but neither of us wanted kids interfering with our lifestyles.'

Pascal stood up as Frimley came back into the room, and shook Martin's hand. 'Thank you very much for your co-operation, sir. I hope we'll have some news – about the car at least – later today. In the meantime, I'll ask one of our Family Liaison Officers to come round, if you don't mind.'

Martin shook his head. 'No, please don't. I'd rather not have anyone with me.'

'I'll have to tell them, anyway, but I'll pass that message on.'

Outside, Frimley drew a small plain paper evidence bag from his pocket.

'Found Mrs Martin's hairbrush. Got a few hairs forensics should be able to extract DNA from.'

'Anything else of interest?'

'Not that I saw, sir,' said Frimley.

'Let's drop your package off and go for a coffee.'

\*

Martin watched them go from the window overlooking his garden. He felt sad about Sara and a little frightened. He was almost certain his wife's murder was intended as a further warning that the Enforcer and his boss, van Ruys, were not messing about. He kept remembering the image of his wife in this room, stripping off as he'd last seen her, her dark eyes challenging him, and his own failure to meet that challenge.

At the same time, he was certain that van Ruys's Enforcer would come after him any day now. He looked around the room. There were things he would be sorry to leave behind, but nothing that couldn't be replaced. Even Sara was replaceable, once he got his powers back, when the heat came off. Yes, he decided, it was time to go.

He packed a single suitcase with clothes and a sheaf of documents from the filing cabinet in his study. It took him fifteen minutes to remove the hard drives from his desktop computer and pack them. He used the laptop to email Abel Scarman in Aruba and tell him he was on his way, then packed the laptop in its travelling bag. He had over six thousand pounds in sterling, most of which went in a body belt, the rest in his pocket for use. It was untraceable cash, in fives, tens and twenties.

He'd already worked out his escape route, which began with a cross-channel trip on the Eurostar to Paris, then Air France from Charles de Gaulle airport, via Amsterdam, to Aruba. It was his intention to pay cash for the tickets.

As evening approached, he decided to add one more sector to his journey and in the first instance travel to Southend, from where it was a short hop across the Thames to Ashford and the train. His theory was that if you wanted to escape, you did it slowly, so as not to raise dust your pursuers could see from a distance. And the more sectors in the journey and different kinds of transport, the better.

Very early on Sunday morning, he left Breydon, and drove carefully south.

\*

Later that day, Pascal assembled his team in the CID office and stood in front of the status board behind Collins. It seemed odd without Walker.

'We have the dead body of a person we believe to be Sara Rebecca Martin, found badly burned in her car at the foot of, and largely covered by, the cliffs south-east of Hartley-over-Sands. PM is later today, Alison and I will cover it.'

Collins and Frimley were making notes.

'Douglas, I want you to organise a fingertip search of the cliff-top and beach. Take some uniforms with you. There was a strong smell of petrol round the car, which didn't all come from the vehicle's fuel tank. Someone used petrol to set fire to the Martins' home. Might be a connection.'

'Okay, sir.'

'Alison, anything new on the Julia Fox and David Ellis case?'

'Nothing you don't know about, sir,' she replied. 'The Press Conference wasn't particularly helpful. At the moment, we're stymied, I think.'

'Miller's van was seen in Hartley on the night Julia Fox disappeared. As we all know, it had been cleaned out with bleach by the time Douglas and I found it, garaged at the back of *The Kitty Klub,* so the chances are there'll be no forensics. I'd like CCTV checked for Breydon centre, to see what time it arrived there, on the night of Maundy Thursday or early Good Friday. We're getting a new DC from Norwich to sit in for John. Not sure when he's arriving. Now, any questions?'

*

'First stop, the morgue. We need COD, TOD and positive ID of the body,' said Pascal later as he climbed into the passenger seat of the Mondeo beside Collins.

'Yes, sir.'

In the morgue at the county hospital, Collins and Pascal, in surgical gowns, approached the remains thought to be of Sara Martin with Dr Jane Ferrari, wearing green scrubs and gloves. The corpse had been stripped of clothing, and was marked by a large U-shaped scar running from under each arm down and across the lower abdomen.

'Are you ready for this?' Ferrari asked them.

Collins nodded. She held a notebook in one hand and a pen in the other.

Pascal muttered, 'Go on.' It was not an environment or a task he enjoyed.

Ferrari switched on the microphone suspended above the examination table and began to record her findings.

'The body is that of an adult female aged around forty. It has been partly damaged by fire, the parts mainly affected being the head, most of the right side of the face, right arm, and right side of the torso, over some three-quarters of its width, to the pelvic region.'

She studied the less burned left side of the body. The legs were untouched by flame.

'There's a strong smell,' the doctor continued, 'that together with the pattern of burning, suggests that someone poured petrol on her from the right side, targeting her head mainly, but taking in the right side of her chest and torso down to the waist. Her legs are mostly intact, with a small amount of fire damage across the pelvic region. She was found in the driving seat of the car, so I'd say someone standing outside the car opened the door and doused her with petrol – probably less than a litre – fairly hastily, ignited it and encouraged the car to roll over the edge of the cliff. Only it didn't go over the edge. As it neared the edge, the cliff gave way and the car went down as if on an elevator. We're obliged to the loose stuff which came down afterwards and buried the car for cutting off the oxygen supply to the fire before more damage was done.'

She stood back and looked up at Pascal. 'My guess – and it's only a guess – is that it was meant to look as if she'd driven over the cliff, crashed onto the beach and the car caught fire from the impact. Your CSI, Jimmy Tasker, will probably have his own ideas, but that's what I think.'

Pascal nodded. 'I'll see what he says, but I can't argue with your reasoning. I take it from that that you're pretty sure it's a murder?'

'Yes. I checked her internal organs and stomach contents, and apart from high levels of cocaine in her blood, she was fit and healthy. There was some damage to her septum, probably from the coke.'

'Septum?'

'It's the gristle that keeps your nostrils apart,' Ferrari explained. 'Heavy users of cocaine find it eats away the

septum – of course, cocaine being a very good local anaesthetic, they don't feel it happening.'

'So the chances are she was a heavy regular user of
coke?'

'Yes. Not much doubt there.'

'Did you check for sexual activity.'

Ferrari glanced at him. 'Of course. When you look for a
reason for her to be where she was, sex is a reasonable
guess. '

Pascal nodded. 'It was the only reason I could think
why she'd be up there on that bit of coast at night. It's very
quiet and isolated.'

'Yes,' nodded Ferrari. 'I'd certainly want to be somewhere out of the way if I was, uh, intending to have sex in
the back of a car.' He saw a blush bloom in her cheeks.

'Hmm. Quite,' he said, not meeting her eyes.

'Vaginas do a good job of protecting sperm deposited
in them.' She glanced up at him across the body, to where
he stood by the head. 'She undoubtedly had unprotected
sex shortly before she was killed, and going by the marks
around the area, it was probably fairly rough.'

'Not enough to kill her, though.'

'Rough sex, in the sense we usually mean it, doesn't
usually kill fit and healthy women,' said Ferrari.

Pascal nodded, wondering what Dr Ferrari usually
meant by "rough sex".

'DNA?' he asked.

'Still awaiting the analysis. I'll let you know as soon as
the results are through.'

'Thanks,' said Pascal. 'How about COD and TOD?'

'In reverse order, time of death is very difficult to establish because of the fire. Best I can offer is that her
wristwatch was broken and stopped working at one-
eighteen, presumably in the morning.'

'That's the best evidence?' he asked.

'Let's say there is nothing I've found yet that would
cause me to doubt that as the time she died.'

'Okay. And cause?'

'There's no evidence of smoke inhalation in her lungs, no defence marks, no sign she tried to get out of the car. She wasn't tied down – didn't even have her seat belt on – so I conclude that she was killed before the fire.'

She moved nearer to the head and beckoned Pascal and Collins to look. She pointed around the left eye which was less damaged than the right one and moved an illuminated magnifier into position so Pascal could look through it.

'These little speckles are called petechiae.'

The flame damage looked worse through the magnifier, and Pascal moved aside after a quick glance to allow Collins to see.

'And the significance is?' he asked.

'They're symptomatic of asphyxiation,' explained Ferrari. She waited until Collins stepped back and turned off the powerful light in the magnifier. 'There are no marks on the throat, so I conclude she wasn't strangled.'

'Someone put a pillow over her face?' asked Collins.

'Not a pillow. There are no fibres, and I think she would have inhaled some or at least got some in her mouth if any kind of fabric had been used. The material of choice these days for killing people without weapons is plastic. A bag or plastic or latex or vinyl gloves.'

'Surgical gloves?'

'As used by many in the medical profession,' said Ferrari, 'but available to the general public to buy.'

'Any clues which sort?'

Ferrari smiled at him. 'You're such a good detective, chasing down all the questions. Yes. The killer wore a latex glove.'

Pascal smiled. 'Is this what you call keeping the best till last?'

'I always do, George,' said Ferrari, in a tone he could have sworn sounded more friendly than professional. He glanced sharply into her eyes, which glinted with mischief.

He found himself grinning, caught sight of Collins, and realised she'd noticed.

'I said there were no fibres in her mouth – but there was a tiny piece of latex. Since they don't make shopping bags from latex, I conclude it came from a glove. There's a little bruising round the back of her head which suggests the killer held her head while he suffocated her.'

'Nice person,' muttered Pascal.

'That's about all I can tell you for now, Detective Inspector.' Ferrari hesitated. 'I'll be in touch when the other results come in,' she added.

'Thanks, Doctor,' he said.

'My name's Jane,' she told him as he followed Collins out of the room.

*

After the post mortem, Pascal and Collins stopped off at the cafe in the main foyer.

'Chases away the taste and smell of the place,' said Pascal, stirring a cappuccino.

Collins seemed quietly amused.

'Do you like Dr Ferrari, sir?'

'You mean as a person, or a professionally?'

'Romantically, I suppose.'

Pascal stared at her over the edge of his cup as he sipped, the foam coating his top lip.

'No. Tell you the truth, I find her a bit – just a wee bit – frightening. You heard her talk about rough sex, as if it was something she enjoyed?'

'Do you not enjoy it, sir?'

Pascal raised an eyebrow. 'That, DS Collins, is between me and my psychiatrist.' He took another sip of his coffee. 'Professionally is another matter.'

'Oh, yes?'

'Professionally, I think she's excellent. Don't think we could find anyone to improve on her.'

Collins flipped through the pages of notes she'd made.

'I wonder what Jimmy made of the car?'

'Let's go and ask him.'

On the way to visit the CSI, Pascal phoned ahead to make sure he would be in.

It was always a surprising place, Pascal thought as they entered the building. It seemed full of smells, a mixture of cordite, bleach, disinfectant, and less identifiable ones. They changed as the two police officers walked along the corridor past different laboratories until they reached the Senior CSI's office. Tasker was at his desk, word-processing a report on his computer terminal. He glanced up and waved them towards a couple of chairs on the oth-er side of his desk.

Pascal and Collins waited a few moments while Tasker reached a point where he could break off. He sat back and rested his elbows on the desk.

'Let me guess,' he grinned, 'you want to know about the arson in High Ridge Avenue and the murder on the north coast.'

'If you feel you've kept the information to yourself long enough,' said Pascal. 'You know, let the tension rise, get the audience sitting on the edge of their seats, et cetera, et cetera.'

'Yeah. That's about it,' said Tasker, still grinning. 'We want our customers to really appreciate our efforts. And might I say,' he added, 'I always appreciate the standard of badinage when it's you wanting something. It's why I pick your cases, given the choice.'

Pascal sighed. 'So, the pleasantries out of the way, what can you tell me?'

Tasker put his fingertips together. 'The arson was start-ed by petrol through the letterbox, ignited by a burning cloth being shoved through afterwards on top of the liq-uid. Acted like a wick. The door, which is through there,' he nodded towards a laboratory door across the corridor, 'was blistered and burned. The one useful thing I got off it was a thumb-print from a left thumb, I'm guessing, on the left underside of the letterbox flap. It's not a place you'd get a thumb-print from normal use, but exactly where you'd get one if you lifted the flap with your left hand in order to peer through and see what was going on inside. In fact there are several prints, suggesting the flap was lifted two or three times, but fortunately, the last print is clear.'

'Whose is it?' asked Pascal.

Tasker shook his head. 'Nobody we've got on file.' He leaned forward. 'But the really interesting news is that the same thumb was used to close the driver's door on the car on the beach.'

'Ah!' exclaimed Pascal. 'I wondered if the two things might be linked – just because they both used petrol. The print on the car is much more conclusive.'

'It will be, when you find out whose it is.'

'Anything else about the murder?'

'When the killer – let's assume the print is the killer's – closed the door, he used a certain amount of force, enough to scrape a few skin cells off. We can analyse the DNA from such small samples these days, so we'll be getting the result of that back shortly.'

'Is it possible that the killer is left-handed?' asked Collins.

'It's possible, but I tend to think you use your dominant hand for the more important task, if you can. I think our killer would be pouring petrol and throwing in matches or handkerchiefs with his right hand, and using his left in a supporting role, as you might put it, lifting flaps, closing doors. So if I had to guess, I'd say our killer is right-handed.'

'And male?'

'Ah, no, Detective Sergeant. Not necessarily. There's no clues as to gender at this moment, though my feeling is getting the woman to drive to the cliff top and then kill her in the way it was done is more likely to be the work of a man than a woman.' He grinned at her. 'That's not to say a woman couldn't have done it, and to be quite honest I'm not prepared to stick my neck out one way or the other, outside this room.'

Collins nodded.

'DC Frimley dropped off some DNA samples of Sara Martin earlier today,' said Pascal.

'Yes. I'm having them processed now, and we should be able to confirm if the body is her within a day or so.'

## CHAPTER 9

John Walker needed to get out. He had stayed home most days after Pascal dismissed him. He knocked back two generous slugs of whisky and pulled a pair of jeans and a T-shirt on, and slipped into his trainers. A glance in the mirror at his unkempt hair and four days' growth of beard drove him into the small bathroom of his one-bedroomed flat. Five minutes later, looking far from his usual suave self, he dragged a fleece on and went into the town centre.

He stopped at a cash dispenser and debated whether to risk his card being 'swallowed' by the machine. There was an available balance of fifty pounds which would have to last him for three weeks. He punched the button to withdraw twenty.

With the money in his pocket, and no clear idea in his head how he was going to survive three weeks with only fifty pounds, he strolled aimlessly into the pedestrian precinct where *The Kitty Klub* was located. He was feeling lonely and guilt-stricken, and nothing seemed to matter any more except the need to survive.

The first of the following month would be a problem, too, because he had to make a minimum payment of £500 off his credit card, and with his wages being reduced by a similar amount as the bank clawed back the money it was owed, he was going to find it difficult to manage on what was left of his salary.

He was so deep in such considerations that he didn't notice Derrick Jackson until he tapped him on his arm.

'John! You're looking far too pensive this fine evening. Come in the club and let me get you a drink.'

Walker's first inclination was to refuse.

'On the house,' Jackson added.

Walker shrugged, smiled and thanked the man. Jackson led the way to the bar. The place was about half-full of young people on the dance floor and round the edges. Ernest Miller was behind the bar counter chatting to the barman. Jackson moved himself and Walker to a dimly-lit area where there was only one other customer, his face in shadow.

'What'll you have, Detective Constable?'

Walker looked up sharply at Jackson's use of his rank.

'You know I'm a cop?'

Jackson grinned. 'Of course. It's not a secret, is it?'

There was, in Walker's mind, no "of course" about it, and whilst it wasn't exactly a secret, it was something he didn't bandy around in *The Kitty Klub* or *Kittens*. He shrugged.

'Not on duty now?'

Walker shook his head. 'On leave for a couple of weeks. Have to take some before I lose it.'

Jackson placed a half-full tumbler of Scotch by Walker's elbow, and raised another to his lips.

'Cheers.'

'Slàinte mhór.'

Jackson studied Walker surreptitiously while he sipped his Scotch. Walker was aware of the fact and wondered what was going through his host's mind.

'Will you be joining us again on Friday?' asked Jackson.

Walker would have loved to. He enjoyed his weekly fix of cocaine and sex, and in the recent past had increased the frequency of his visits to the club. But the twenty pounds in his pocket, even when added to the other thirty the bank were prepared to offer him, would not have bought his admission to the club, let alone a couple of lines of coke. He shook his head.

'Think I might have to take a rain check this week, Derrick,' he said. 'Maybe next week, too. Until I get back to work.' He swallowed, keeping his eyes on the table. 'It may be some time.'

He felt Jackson's eyes on the top of his head. He was beginning to think it had been a bad idea to enter the club with Jackson. He swallowed a large mouthful of the amber liquid and prepared to leave, when Jackson spoke again.

'John, you've been a member for a long time. People would miss you if you weren't here. Is there anything I can do to change your mind? How about if I waive the admission fee?'

Walker glanced up. It was tempting, but a small voice in his head was trying to warn him that accepting a benefit from Derrick Jackson would be frowned upon by Pascal and the DCI – if they ever found out about it. On the other hand, he was suspended in all but name. And it would just be the once. Somehow, he would find the money for a couple of lines of coke. He grinned.

'It would be churlish to refuse, put that way,' he said. 'I'll see you on Friday.'

'Good man,' smiled Jackson as Walker drained his glass. 'Is there anything else I can help with? I'd like to think we could be friends after all this time.'

Walker was feeling nervous about giving in to temptation, and shook his head. 'No, I'm fine, thanks, Derrick. I'll see you Friday – and thanks.'

'No need for thanks,' said Jackson.

Walker finished his drink and went back out into the street.

\*

Jackson stared after him, speculatively.

A noise made him turn round. The shadowed figure came over to the table at which Jackson was sitting. He recognised Danny Bakker.

'Christ!' he exclaimed, 'How long have you been there?'

'A while,' said Bakker. 'So he's a cop?' he asked, nodding towards the door through which Walker had left.

'Yeah,' replied Jackson, 'but he's never been a problem. I don't imagine he talks about what he does here to anyone, especially those at work.'

Bakker studied Jackson speculatively. 'He's on the payroll?'

'He hasn't been.'

Bakker tilted his head slightly. 'Maybe you should think about it. A cop in your pocket could be useful.'

Jackson shrugged. 'I'll think about it.' He stood up. 'I've been meaning to ask: do you know where Viv – Sara Martin – is? She seems to be missing from the guest house, but her stuff is still there.'

'Why ask me?'

'Because you were the one who wanted a means of threatening her husband and I gave you her address.'

Bakker grinned tightly and tapped the side of his nose with a long forefinger.

'Probably best you don't know.'

Jackson stared at him hard, while the implications slowly filled his brain. He moved until his lips were close to Bakker's ear and spoke in a low voice.

'What-the-fuck have you done with her?'

Bakker turned to face him. 'The bitch is dead.'

His voice was cold, unemotional, his expression bland. He seemed to be defying Jackson to argue the matter, but the mixture of anger and fear he felt overcame any reluctance in this respect.

'You fucking idiot! We'll have the police swarming all over us as soon as they trace her here.'

Two spots of crimson coloured Bakker's cheeks and Jackson saw the muscles of his jaw clench. For a moment he thought the Dutchman was going to hit him and moved his feet into a defensive stance. Bakker looked down at them, consideringly, before a cold vicious smile twisted his lips.

'Perhaps the sooner you get your friendly copper on the payroll, the better.'

Jackson stared after him as he turned and walked towards the exit.

Bakker looked round. 'Send me a girl, to the hotel.'

'Why the hell should I?' demanded Jackson.

'Because it will keep me happy – and that's very much in your interests.'

'It'll cost you at this time of day,' grumbled Jackson.

Bakker strode back towards him, his hand closing like a vice round Jackson's wrist. 'Don't be stupid.'

'No, you're right,' said Jackson, rubbing his wrist after Bakker released it. 'To quote our policeman, it would be churlish of me to charge.'

'Yes. Talking of money, where is Jared Martin?'

'I've no idea.'

'He's keeping a very low profile. Never in when I call.'

'Are you thinking he's done a runner?'

'I don't know. It's possible. I shall have another look at his house when I've finished with the girl.'

Jackson nodded.

Bakker grinned. 'Make sure she's pretty.' He turned and walked outside. Jackson scowled after him before picking up the telephone at the end of the bar.

\*

Danny Bakker enjoyed the girl. Her screams excited him and he kept slapping and punching her until he came. It didn't bother him that he'd hurt her – after all, what did girls like her expect? But as his rational mind reasserted itself, he realised it would be a good idea to get out without being seen. He gripped her jaw painfully.

'You say nothing to anyone about tonight. Understand? Or I will find you and kill you. But first I will peel the skin off your face.' He slipped his knife out of the little scabbard he kept strapped to an ankle and waved it slowly in front of her frightened eyes. 'You understand?'

She nodded, swallowing.

He got off her and went into the bathroom to flush away the condom. He checked his appearance and washed the blood off his hands, then packed his toilet bag in his brief case. Back in the bedroom, the girl was showing signs of getting out of the bed. He strode across the room and hit her hard on the back of the neck with the edge of his hand. She fell back, unconscious. He felt for a pulse in her throat, dressed himself, and removed all traces of his presence before picking up his briefcase – his only baggage – and letting himself out of the room.

He slipped down the fire staircase and out through the emergency doors into the night.

He made his way on foot to High Ridge Avenue and strolled past Martin's house until he was satisfied no-one was watching him. His lip curled at the sight of the board covering the front doorway. He kept his pace casual and made his way round to the rear of the house. It took him only a few seconds to pick the lock on the cellar door and let himself in.

He listened but heard nothing. Taking a small torch from his pocket, he found the steps which led up into the house. Opening the door at the top he listened again, but he was fairly sure the place was empty. The hallway, where he found himself, was black with soot and stank of the fire. He guessed the electrical power had been switched off. He risked a flick of the light-switch in the hall and proved his suspicion correct.

He found the door into Martin's office. It was difficult to open because the intumescent strip set in each of its edges, designed to keep smoke out, had expanded in the heat, he imagined. He barged it open with his shoulder. In the silence after the noise of opening the door, he listened but heard no signs that anyone had heard and responded to it. He gripped the torch between his teeth before stepping into the room.

A single small window admitted light from the street lamps. He drew the curtains and began to search for any hint where Jared Martin might have gone. Martin's computer stood there, but without power it was useless to him. He grunted disgustedly at it.

The telephone caught his eye. He picked up the handset but found that. too. was dead.

Frustrated, he took another look round the office, until he noticed an Air France brochure from which a couple of pages had been roughly torn. He wondered what information had been on them. The flights listed in the rest of the brochure were all long-haul from Charles de Gaulle airport just outside Paris.

He slowly pulled his mobile phone from his pocket and opened the back. He kept the phone switched off most of the time as a precaution against the authorities being able to trace it. Another precaution he took was to have a selection of SIM cards from different suppliers in different countries. He opened his wallet and removed a small SIM, which he used to replace the one in the phone. From memory – another precaution, not saving any numbers on the card – he dialled Willem van Ruys in Amsterdam.

The connection made, Bakker continued in his native language.

'Martin has disappeared. I think he may have left the country.'

'Where?' demanded van Ruys.

'I don't know. The best clue I have is an Air France brochure with some pages missing. They're all long-haul flights from Charles de Gaulle, Paris.'

'How did he get away? And where's my money?' van Ruys's voice alternated between gravelly and whining. The whining was quite misleading, thought Bakker, as it made him sound as frail and elderly as he looked. At least the gravelly voice made him sound like the bullying, sadistic bastard he really was.

'I guess he got frightened after I killed his wife.'

'What!' Nothing whiny about that tone of voice, Bakker thought, moving the earpiece away from his head. van

Ruys sounded furious. A thin line of sweat broke out on Bakker's brow.

'I wanted him to know my threats were serious. It seemed like a good idea. Besides, I got the feeling from our customer that he'd be glad not to have her around.'

'What had *she* to do with *him*?'

'She was one of his whores. Enjoyed too much coke, I think.'

'You're a fool! The British police aren't stupid. How long will it take before they discover her connection to his club? If they haven't already. The last thing we want is them sniffing about.'

'I think Jackson has just put a copper on the payroll, so he should be fairly safe.'

'I suppose you've never heard of double agents? I remember stories my father told me about the war. Holland seemed full of them then. I'm always suspicious of people like this copper on the payroll: what if he's undercover? Still working for them, spying on Jackson?'

'It's his problem. Maybe I could solve it for him for a few pounds. A job on the side.'

'While you're working for me, you don't do jobs on the side,' said van Ruys, gravelly-voiced again.

'Of course not, Mr van Ruys,' said Bakker in as placatory tone as he could manage. 'I was wondering...'

'Yes?'

'If you have any contacts in Air France? It could be useful finding out what flight Martin is on, and where it's going.'

'You're sure he's flying Air France from Paris?'

'Not certain, but the brochure he left lying around is all from there.'

'I'll see what I can find out. Call me again – and not in the middle of the night. And tell Jackson, I still want my money.'

'Yes, Mr van Ruys. Thank you.'

Bakker closed the connection with relief and let the air out of his lungs slowly.

*

Pascal was in his office early the next morning. When Frimley's telephone rang, he went through into the still-empty general office and answered the call.

'CID. DI Pascal.'

'Control room here, sir,' said the voice of Sergeant Claude Henslow. 'Just had a triple nine call from the Weston Arms. Girl found badly beaten up in one of their rooms. Told them not to touch anything and that we'd be along a.s.a.p. Sent the area car already to keep the lid on.'

'Thanks Claude, I'll get over there now.'

As he reached the door to the car park at the rear of the building, Alison Collins was just arriving.

'Alison! Drive us over to the Weston Arms will you,' he said, tossing her the keys of Mondeo.

On the way, he told her what little he knew.

They found the girl in the security office, behind Reception, wrapped in a blanket and being given a cup of tea. A woman, who identified herself as the hotel's deputy manager, was with her.

The police officers sat down. Pascal let Collins take the lead, figuring she'd seem less of a threat to the girl, who seemed terrified. She had a split lip which she dabbed at with a tissue, and her right eye was gradually closing. Her face was blackened with bruising. As Pascal watched, the girl reached out to put her cup on the desk and in doing so, the blanket was pushed far enough open for Pascal and Collins to see that the bruises covered much of her body.

Collins formally identified herself and Pascal to the girl. She stared at them, her breath catching in her throat.

'We need to know what happened,' said Collins gently, ' who did this to you. Can we start with your name?'

The girl raised her head with seeming effort and stared at Collins listlessly.

'Dora,' she said.

'And where do you live?'

Dora looked from Collins to Pascal and back. 'In a big house. In town.'

Her voice was strongly accented.

'Where are you from? What is your accent?'

'Look! I'm all right. Can I go now?'

Pascal leaned forwards. 'We need the answers to some questions. Now, where do you come from?'

The girl stared at him, plucking at her arms with torn nails. She scratched at her leg. Pascal saw the needle marks.

'How long is it since you last injected?' Collins asked.

The girl glanced at the clock on the wall. 'Last night. I need to go now.'

'How long have you been using heroin?'

'Two, three months. More.'

'Where do you come from?'

The girl looked at her tiredly. 'I am from Latvia. A small village near Jelgava.'

'And what are you doing in Norfolk?'

She looked down at her hands and remained silent.

'Did you come here to be a prostitute?' asked Pascal.

The girl stared at him sullenly. 'I was going to be a secretary.'

'Why the change of career?'

'There was no secretary job. This only one which offered. Owe a lot.'

'Who gave you the heroin?'

'A man at the house.'

'What's his name?'

'I not say. He gives me food and heroin. He make me fuck.'

Pascal swallowed. He hated men who preyed on women and children. If he ever got his hands on this man...

'This big house you're staying at, tell me about it,' said Collins. Her expression, Pascal noticed, was as grim as his own.

The girl yawned and rubbed her legs where the needle marks were. She shrugged. 'I don't know.'

Pascal suspected she was feeling withdrawal symptoms.

'Is it in Breydon?'

'Yes. Short distance to *Kittens*.'

'*Kittens?*' asked Pascal.

'Where we work. It is club, I think.'

Pascal glanced at Collins, who shook her head. Apparently, she hadn't heard of it either. He turned his attention back to the girl. She yawned again, and sniffed. It reminded him of Walker. Yawning and sniffing were early withdrawal symptoms arising from a growing need for another hit.

'What's the house like?'

'It is big. Many rooms.'

'And the only people you see there are other girls working at *Kittens?*'

She nodded and rubbed her arms. 'And Paul.'

'Paul?'

The girl bit her lip, aware she'd made a slip. Her pallid face flushed.

'Is mistake. Didn't mean to say.'

Pascal nodded. 'But now that you have, Paul is the man who gives you heroin?'

'Yes,' she replied crossly. 'And I need some.'

'I'll get the FME over,' announced Collins. 'Wait here, I won't be a moment.' She left Pascal and the girl with the deputy manager.

Pascal nodded. 'So, now, Dora, tell me about last night. You were here with a man?'

She nodded. 'Man sent me.'

Pascal was becoming confused. 'A man. Paul? Or someone else? The man who rented the room?'

'Not Paul. Man who own club.'

'*Kittens?*'

'Yes.'

A frown had appeared as she'd been talking. ' I not feel well. I need to see Paul,' she said with a hint of truculence, rubbing hard at her arms and thighs.

Pascal nodded. 'I understand. DS Collins is asking a doctor to come and examine you. The doctor will be able to give you something.'

He could see she was losing her concentration. Her gaze was beginning to rove around the room, and she seemed less and less interested in her answers. Maybe, he thought, it was time to move on.

'The man you were with here, last night, do you know his name?'

'He told me to call him Dutchman.'

The hotel's deputy manager, who had been sitting quietly in the far corner of the room cleared her throat. Pascal looked round.

'The room was booked by a Danny Bakker, a Dutch national according to his passport,' she said. 'I have his registration card.' She held the document out so Pascal could take it. 'We've not seen him since last night.'

Collins came back into the room. He showed her the card. 'We'll get the local ports and airports to keep a look-out for this person and have him detained.'

She nodded.

'And I'll have the room checked over for fingerprints and any other evidence of identity.'

'Dr Ferrari is coming over straight away, and one of the DCs on Vice who's dealt with rape victims,' said Collins.

The girl was watching and listening hard. She shook her head. 'No, no! I not raped. There is no problem. Just let me go.'

'That may be true,' said Pascal, 'but you have undoubtedly been assaulted. I don't treat assaults lightly. And I'd like to know how it happened, so tell me.'

The girl covered her face with her hands. Pascal waited silently. She drew a ragged breath.

'We just had sex. He liked it a bit rough.'

'Did he use a condom?'

The girl shrugged. 'I wanted him to, but he just hit me. The more he hit me the more he... ' She struggled for words.

'Got excited?' prompted Collins.

The girl nodded. 'Yes. It turned him on. I don't know if he was using a condom. I – I couldn't see very well.'

Pascal was leaning his elbow on a filing cabinet and stared at the girl. He found himself thinking what he'd like to do to Bakker if he ever laid hands on the him.

Collins continued, her voice deliberately gentle and soothing. 'If you had unprotected sex, the doctor might be able to obtain a sample of semen, and if you're worried about pregnancy, she can supply you with a couple of tablets which will make sure you aren't. And she can check you out for any damage he might have done.'

The girl shrugged.

'Good. Then as soon as she arrives, we'll get on with it. Just one thing,' she added. The girl looked up. 'What's your real name? I guess Dora is your working name – it doesn't sound very Latvian to me.'

The girl dropped her gaze to her knees. 'Parents must not know what I do.'

Collins waited, watching the girl expectantly.

'My name is Aspazia.'

'Do you and your parents get on well?'

'We did. They will be so ashamed of me now. Paul says we can never go home.' Tears welled from her eyes and trickled down her cheeks.

'We'll look after you now,' said Pascal kindly. He turned to Collins. 'You stay with her, I'm going to have a look at the bedroom.' He glanced at the Deputy Manager, who stood up, brushed the creases out of her skirt and led the way.

A uniformed constable stood guard in the corridor outside the bedroom which Bakker had occupied. He recorded the arrival of Pascal who left the Deputy Manager with him, anxious that there should be the minimum of disturbance to the scene.

Fifteen minutes later, Pascal rejoined Collins and the girl. Jane Ferrari was washing her hands in the corner of the room. She turned round as Pascal entered.

'Thanks for coming over so promptly, Doctor,' he said.

'No problem, Detective Inspector,' she replied.

Collins glanced from one to the other. Pascal realised she looked puzzled by their formality. There was a knock at the door, which opened to reveal Jimmy Tasker.

'Ah, Jimmy,' exclaimed Pascal, 'there's something I'd like you to see.'

He guided the CSI outside the room with a hand across his shoulders. A few moments later he returned alone.

'Sorry about that, Dr Ferrari. How was the medical examination?'

'All I'll tell you is that I've cleaned up Dora's wounds as best I can, for now. I need to take her to the hospital for a full examination and some tests.' She glanced at the girl, who was shivering slightly. 'I'll consult with my colleagues at the clinic about letting her have something to help with the pain and getting her on a programme.'

'There's a good chance the man who did this left a DNA sample, so I'd like you to recover it. And try to make sure she is, you know, okay. No lasting consequences,' he added quietly.

Ferrari raised an eyebrow, understanding. She turned to the girl.

'Will you come with me, please, and we'll go to the hospital.'

The girl glanced at her and then at Pascal and got to her feet carefully.

'I'll see you later, Aspazia,' said Pascal. 'We'll find you a place of refuge, and help you get home, if that's what you want.'

'Can I not stay in UK?'

'I'll talk to the Immigration people. Meantime, try not to worry. Dr Ferrari will take good care of you.' He nodded at the girl. 'Thank you.'

She shrugged.

He turned back to Jane Ferrari. 'Are her injuries consistent with a beating?' he asked.

She nodded. 'Uh-huh. And a bad one at that.'

Ferrari led the girl to the door and turned. 'I'll let you have my report in writing, as soon as possible.'

'Thanks.'

\*

Pascal and Collins returned to the police station to find a new face in the CID office. He was sitting in Walker's old seat talking to Frimley.

'New DC from Norwich, sir,' said Frimley.

'Graham Bell, sir,' said the portly man in a green hacking jacket and brown corduroy trousers whose belt cut into his corpulent belly. His head was very round, his hair thin and grey, and the skin of his face had the shiny, scrubbed look of someone who regularly exfoliated.

Pascal nodded. 'DI Pascal, and this is Acting DS Collins.'

Bell stared at her. 'I've heard of you, Sarge.'

Pascal noticed a tinge of colour in her pale cheeks.

'I gather you've had a bit of a crime spree round here,' Bell continued. 'Nice juicy murder and a missing schoolgirl.'

His eyes remained on Collins as he spoke.

'Didn't you used to work in HQ?'

'Yes,' she replied.

Pascal turned back to Collins. 'Alison, how do you feel about bringing Graham here up to speed on the Julia Fox and David Ellis cases?'

'Okay, sir.'

Pascal could sense an atmosphere between the two of them, but neither seemed about to enlighten him. He looked from one to the other then left the room. He closed the door of his office behind him, sat down and picked up the telephone.

In the main office, as Collins took her seat on Bell's right, he tossed a peanut into his mouth.

'What's the story with the Mis-Per?' he asked.

Collins brought him up to date on the search for Julia Fox.

'So what's our next move, Sarge? Search the area?'

'I think so. We've spoken to everyone the girl might know, including school friends and relatives. The Press Conference hasn't produced any results that led anywhere. There have been no sightings of Julia since Easter Day.'

'You said her suitcase was missing?'

'Yes. It makes me think this is a runaway rather than an abduction.'

'Also the fact that if she's seen any newspaper or local TV news programme since the PC, she'll know we're looking for her. What does the fact that she hasn't been in touch tell us? That she's staying away wilfully, or she's now in a situation where she can't get home,' he said, answering his own question. 'She could be dead.'

Collins frowned. 'You're a cheerful soul.'

'It could be worse,' he said, looking at her meaningfully.

'I'm sorry about your friend at HQ,' she said.

He stood up. 'I think you're a good copper,' he said quietly, 'but that doesn't mean I've changed my mind about you as a person. You got Freddie fired and that makes you a flaky colleague to have around.'

The spots of colour had reappeared on Collins's cheeks. 'Freddie could have been charged with attempted rape,' she hissed. 'Getting fired for gross misconduct was a let-off.'

'He's still out of a job, months later,' replied Bell, 'and I still don't believe that tosh about his trying to rape you. If you'd had evidence, you would have gone to court.'

'There wasn't enough. He didn't succeed, but only because we were interrupted.'

Bell looked at her askance. 'Interrupted? By whom? Or what? You never said anything about this before.'

Collins suddenly looked flustered. 'I – I can't say.'

Bell stared at her. 'What the hell does that mean? Why not?'

'I was asked not to by – by the person who found Freddie with his hand up my skirt.'

'If there was a witness, which seems to be what you're saying, I'm even more curious why Freddie wasn't charged with rape.'

'Because when we went to the CPS, they decided there was insufficient evidence to make the charge stick, and advised the... ACC to deal with the matter in the way he later did.'

Bell studied her expression. 'The ACC was involved? A bit far up the chain to be dealing with an HR matter... unless,' he added pensively, 'unless he was the witness in question?'

Collins's cheeks began to flush. 'I can't talk about that.'

'Okay,' said Bell. 'But if I've understood this, my mate Freddie was found in the stationery cupboard with his hand up your skirt by the Assistant Chief Constable. He was not prosecuted for attempted rape or sexual assault, or even common assault, because the CPS considered there wasn't sufficient evidence, and finally, the ACC had him sacked for sexual harassment amounting to gross misconduct. Am I right?' He leaned forward on the desk. 'It's important to me because I feel nervous working alongside someone I've suspected of lying when it suits her, never knowing if I'd be her next victim.'

Collins stared at him furiously, drawing a deep breath as she fought to keep the anger out of her demeanour.

'I'll say this just once, and you'd better believe it: Freddie got less than he deserved, and I never lied to anyone, despite the fact that having to describe what he did was about the most unpleasant thing I've ever had to do. Now let's get on and put the matter behind us.'

Bell pressed his lips together, saying nothing. Then he nodded and sat down. 'Do we know any more about the boat?'

Collins sat as well and allowed her thoughts to focus on the cases in hand.

'No. I thought it might have gone round to Yarmouth to refuel and re-supply but the Yarmouth Harbourmaster's office says they had nothing of that description in on Good Friday.'

'Have you had a word with Coastwatch?'

'No,' she replied.

'I'll ring them to be sure, then the Dutch Maréchaussée,' said Bell. He pulled a small notebook from the inside pocket of his jacket and thumbed through the pages until he found the number he wanted. He spoke to the Coastwatch organisation, volunteers who had taken over one of the ancient functions of the Coastguard service, keeping a watch over beach and sea and recording sightings of any passing vessel.

He hung up and shook his head. 'No signs of any gin palaces by Coastwatch.'

Moments later, he was talking to someone in Holland in fluent Dutch, after his little notebook yielded yet another telephone number. He kept pulling open his workstation drawers and riffling through them while he spoke.

Collins thought it was a nervous thing.

After Bell hung up he simply shook his head.

'Very organised, our colleagues in the Dutch Royal Constabulary. They've no record of a gin-palace leaving any of the usual Dutch ports within twenty-four hours either side of the time one was seen in Hartley.'

'Might that not simply mean that they left from a more unusual port?'

'It might well. I've asked my pal to let me know the names and idents of any gin-palaces which arrived back in Holland over the following two days.'

Suddenly he looked round the room before checking the drawers of the filing cabinet near him.

'You looking for something particular?' asked Collins.

'Chocolate digestives. You don't seem to have any.'

'No.'

'Don't suppose there're any ginger nuts either?'

'No.'

Bell stood up suddenly. 'Well, somebody had better go and get them. Is there a shop in Breydon that sells biscuits?'

'There's a supermarket in the High Street. Out the door, go straight across the road to the shops,' replied Collins. 'Surely you're not going out to buy biscuits?'

'Can't work without them.'

She shrugged and grinned reluctantly. His apparent addiction amused her.

'I'll phone the hospital while you're out, see if there's any change in David Ellis's condition.'

# Chapter 10

Pascal's phone rang. He was alone, in the office. He picked up the call.

'CID. DI Pascal.'

'George? It's Jane.'

Her voice sounded just a bit breathless. It had him frantically searching his memory for women he knew called Jane.

'Uh, hello,' he said, still at a loss to place the name.

The woman giggled. 'Oh, George, don't tell me you've forgotten me already?'

He took the phone away from his ear and peered at it as if the answer he sought might be there, somehow. He replaced it against his cheek.

'No, no, of course I remember you.' Who the hell was she? Something nudged at the edges of his mind. He should know. It wasn't as if he knew a lot of women socially. Well, none, lately. That must mean this one was a professional contact. He stared at the wall beyond which was the CID general office. No, it was not Collins. Then who the hell?

'You remember when we leaned across the autopsy table, our heads almost touching while I peeled back the flesh of the corpse lying between us?'

Lightning struck.

'Dr Ferrari, I presume.'

'But of course, Detective Inspector. Do you prefer formal?'

'I'm sorry.'

'You didn't remember me, did you?'

'No, to be truthful.'

She laughed gently again. 'Never mind. I was just enjoying myself. You're the kind of man I think I could enjoy myself with, a lot.'

'Uh, thanks. I think.' Pascal could feel the beginnings of a blush and cleared his throat. 'I take it there was more to your phone call than a desire to confuse me?'

'Absolutely,' she said, her voice losing its contrived softness and resuming her usual professional tone. 'I have the toxicology reports on Sara Martin. Want to discuss them over lunch?'

'Can't you just tell me?'

She dropped back into breathless mode. 'Oh, George, don't you want to see me across a table again?'

'Not if it's your autopsy table.'

'A restaurant table! I'll pay.'

'Okay,' he said, glancing at his watch which showed it was around the time he would normally have lunch. 'Where?'

She suggested a place and rang off.

Frimley walked past his office with a large bag.

Pascal glanced up. 'What've you got there, Douglas?'

'CCTV tapes, sir. I wanted to look for the white van, but I thought I'd get all those of the town centre going back a week or two.'

'What are you looking for on those?'

'I know it's a long shot, but Jared Martin's story about his wife going out regularly to – well – to have sex made me wonder.'

'Come in and sit down and tell me what you have wondered,' urged Pascal.

Frimley dumped the bag on Pascal's desk and sat on the broken chair. Pascal looked inside the bag and saw a preponderance of videotapes and a few digital versatile discs, each labelled carefully with the location of the camera, the time and date.

Pascal sat down and looked as if he was about to say something and stopped himself.

Frimley raised his eyebrows. 'Were you—'

Pascal nodded as if acknowledging a good guess. 'You're a mind-reader, Douglas. I was just going to say you look like a man who could use a coffee after all that exertion, and there you were, beating me to it. Mine's white without.'

Frimley chewed the inside of his cheek for a moment before getting up and fetching them both drinks from the machine at the end of the corridor.

'So what was your idea, with all this lot?' Pascal asked, waving at the bag.

'I just wondered where Mrs Martin would go, and I figured the town centre.'

'Think she was hanging around in the red light district?'

Frimley shook his head. 'I didn't get the impression that was her style, coming from her background. I figured she would have had some place to go. I mean, even if she was visiting men in hotel rooms, she'd need somewhere to go in between times, like a bar or something.'

Pascal was nodding. 'Seems reasonable.' A thought struck him. 'Does the name *Kittens* mean anything to you?'

Frimley shook his head again. 'No sir. What is it?'

'The girl who was beaten up at the Weston Arms, she was a prostitute mostly working in a club called *Kittens*. She said there were a lot of girls, living in a big house with lots of rooms.'

'Like a hotel?'

'Yes. Or something of that sort.'

Frimley sighed. 'Don't immediately know of anywhere that fits the bill.'

'Alison and Graham are too new here to be familiar with local stuff,' Pascal said, almost to himself. He stood up and came round his desk. 'Let's go into the hive of industry known as the CID office and see what we can do. Good idea, Douglas.'

'Thank you sir,' said Frimley, surprised, grabbing the bag and following the DI next door.

Pascal asked Collins to arrange for some more staff to study the CCTV footage with Bell and herself, looking for either the white van or any sign of Sara Martin. Bell stared at the heap of tapes and DVDs.

'Anywhere particular you'd like us to start, sir?' he asked, brushing biscuit crumbs off his shirt.

'Heard of a club called *Kittens?*'

Bell shook his head.

'There's *The Kitty Klub,'* said Collins.

Pascal shrugged. 'Why not start with that. Such a similar name.' He frowned. 'It is, isn't it? Similar. Would you open a place with a name similar to another in the same line of business – roughly. If *Kittens* is a brothel, I suppose it still counts as part of the "Leisure Sector".'

'You'd be worried people might get the two confused.'

Pascal stared at her. 'Mmm. Unless, of course, it didn't matter. If, for instance, they were one and the same?'

'I'll start there, sir,' she said.

'Me, too,' said Bell.

'What about us, sir?' asked Frimley.

'Well, I don't know about you, but I have a luncheon appointment.'

*

Monday morning had begun well for Jared Martin. Very early, he checked out of the small commercial hotel in Southend, where he'd spent the night, and drove to Ashford in Kent where he abandoned his car and went through the formalities to board the Eurostar for Paris. By mid-morning, he was in a taxi from the Gare du Nord to Charles de Gaulle airport.

In Breydon, Danny Bakker received a phone call from Willem van Ruys, giving him details of the flight booking made by Martin. Fortunately, since the amalgamation of Air France and KLM, the Royal Dutch Airline, flights to Aruba from Paris transited via Amsterdam. There were direct flights to Amsterdam from the local airport, and Bakker bought a ticket in the expectation of being able to intercept Martin in the transit lounge.

*

Jane Ferrari was wearing a startling red silk skirt, a black chiffon blouse, and a pair of black high-heeled shoes when she walked into the restaurant a few minutes after Pascal sat down at the table she'd booked. He was surprised to see that, without the cap she wore in the autopsy room, she had black hair which fell, casually elegant, across her shoulders. Her lips were painted to match her skirt. The effect, along with her tanned skin, was very "fairground fortune-teller". Pascal couldn't help but stare as she weaved her way through the tables. When he could drag his eyes from her swaying hips he found she was smiling at him as she sat facing him.

A waiter arrived and presented them with menus. Pascal waited until he'd gone.

'You have the tox reports?' he asked.

'George,' she said, 'it's lunchtime. Enjoy this moment. You don't want to hear about the chemical contents of Mrs Martin's body until after you've eaten.'

'I *do* have a murder enquiry to conduct.'

'You still have to eat, George. Now, are you having a starter?'

There was no persuading her to talk about work. Every attempt seemed to amuse her, and Pascal eventually gave in and enjoyed the meal. At the end of it, they sat back while the table was cleared of empty plates and coffee placed in front of them.

'Any time soon, Jane,' he prompted.

She smiled again, ruefully.

'Ah, George, you have too few tracks in your mind. Very difficult to drag you out of the professional one into anything else.'

He rested his elbows on the table and his chin on his interlaced fingers. 'Why do you want me dragged out of the professional track, and into what other?'

'I can't think, George,' she said, copying his pose. She grinned. 'Okay, what you want to know is that Mrs Martin contained a lot of cocaine hydrochloride, and a small quantity of semen.'

'Ah. Any DNA?'

'Of course there was, George. Semen contains plenty of it.'

'Anything useful?' he asked patiently.

'You'll like this: there's a trace on the national DNA database which matches.'

He gazed at her. She smiled back.

'I'm having to drag this out of you bit by bit, aren't I?' he muttered.

'Let me enjoy my moment, George. It's such a pleasure keeping you on tenterhooks as long as I can.'

He folded his arms and waited.

'Gordon Clifford,' she said, quietly, so other diners would not overhear..

Pascal frowned. 'Am I likely to know that name?'

'Depends how well you know the members of the old Police Authority.'

He stared at her, his eyes widening.

'Councillor Clifford, last Chairman of it?'

'Shh! The same.'

'What was he doing on the database?'

'Six years ago, before he joined the county council, he was charged after being picked up for kerb crawling. For some reason, the CPS didn't pursue the case. Somehow, the Press missed the story, or maybe the Editor of the paper is in the same Lodge as Councillor Clifford, whatever, but the story was never publicised and Clifford was elected to the council two years later, and became chairman of the PA.'

Pascal absorbed the information silently. 'And now we know that he had sexual intercourse with Sara Martin shortly before her death?'

'Yes. It's difficult to say how long before, but probably within a couple of hours.'

'Stone the crows!' muttered Pascal. 'Well, I'd better be off. I've got to pay a call on the councillor. Better tell the DCI what I'm planning, first, in case he wants to practise ducking and weaving.'

She smiled. 'Don't you want another coffee, George?'

He smiled at her. 'You knew I'd have to go as soon as you told me that.'

She nodded. 'I knew – but I hoped, maybe…'

He looked at her as a woman for once. She was attractive, without doubt.

'I suppose…I suppose you wouldn't like to perhaps have dinner together one evening?' he asked her.

'In my surgical greens or something a little more comfortable?'

'I'd like to get to know Jane, rather than Dr Ferrari, if you don't mind,' he said.

'Saturday?'

He nodded. 'That would be fine, work permitting.' He looked at her levelly. 'You know I might have to cancel at short notice if the need arises?'

She sighed. 'I know. Don't forget, I get called out, too.'

'Then if we both accept these risks, I shall look forward to Saturday.'

'Would you like to come to my place? I'll cook something up for us. Ever tried oysters?'

'No.'

'Well, there might be one or two new experiences in line,' she said, grinning. 'I'll give you a ring.'

'Yes, please,' said Pascal standing up. He began to pat his pockets.

'You will have to get over this forgetfulness, George, and start keeping some of your salary about your person.

But not now: I said I'd buy lunch. You get off and do what you have to. Good luck with the councillor.'

He walked back to the police station feeling unusually light on his feet and with his lips fixed in a smile. He told himself he must concentrate on the job, instead of behaving like forty-two going on eighteen.

*

An hour later, sitting beside Collins, he was gazing at the imposing façade of Gordon Clifford's Georgian house. He climbed out of the car onto the pavement and waited for her to walk round the vehicle until she was beside him, gazing up at the regular symmetry of the windows, arranged either side of the front door with its shell-like arch.

With a glance at her, Pascal strode forward, up the three steps to the entrance and rang the bell. After a moment, someone could be seen approaching through the obscured glass in the door. A tall, middle-aged woman opened it and looked down on him.

'Yes?' Her gaze was as cold as her tone of voice.

Pascal pulled his ID card from his pocket and introduced himself and Collins.

'We'd like to talk to Councillor Clifford.'

'Why?'

Pascal looked at her from under his eyebrows. 'That's between him and us, don't you think? Who are you?'

'Mrs Kenright. Councillor Clifford's house-keeper.'

'May we come in?' he asked.

She stood back from the door. 'He's in his study. Follow me please.'

She led the way down the hall to a room on the left, on whose door she knocked.

A man's voice responded. 'Come!'

She opened the door and stood just inside. 'Detective Inspector Pascal and Detective Sergeant Collins to see you, sir,' she said before withdrawing and allowing the police officers to enter.

The walls of the room were lined with tall, walnut display cabinets and book cases. Glass cases on top of them contained the mounted remains of game birds and small animals. Clifford's desk was a sturdy antique wooden structure with a roll top and leather inlaid writing surface. The councillor sat in a wooden swivel chair beside the desk and waved them to two simple Windsor-backed chairs he obviously kept for his visitors.

'What can I do for you, Mr Pascal? Council business is it?'

'No, Mr Clifford. We're making enquiries into the murder of Sara Martin.'

Clifford raised his eyebrows. 'And how does that involve me?'

'It appears that you had sex with her an hour or two before she was killed.'

Clifford stared at him, his face flushing. 'What do you mean, "it appears"?'

'Your semen was still in her vagina when the post mortem took place.'

Clifford glanced at Collins as if reluctant to discuss such matters in front of a woman. 'How do you know it's mine?'

'You're on the database, sir. Arising from a kerb-crawling incident six years ago.'

Clifford scowled. 'I thought that was all over and done with. Case of mistaken identity.'

'I'm sure you had your defence ready, though, of course, in the event it wasn't needed.'

'It was a mistake!' He looked down at his hands. 'I was under a lot of stress at the time. It was a difference of opinion with the Leader of the Council. '

'Six years ago you weren't a member of the Council, sir.'

'We were business rivals at the time, and he was still Leader. He was the one who later persuaded me to stand for election.'

'I'm surprised you didn't challenge the evidence in court, sir. However, that incident doesn't concern us now. I would like to know about the evening you had sex with Sara Martin.'

'I've not had sex with anyone called Sara Martin,' he said, not meeting Pascal's eyes.

Collins leaned forward. 'Have you been to *The Kitty Klub*, Councillor Clifford?'

He smiled thinly. 'I'm not quite young enough to appreciate the joys of night-clubs. I'm seventy-three.'

'Okay,' said Pascal, 'so if you don't use *The Kitty Klub*, and you don't know anyone named Sara Martin, would you tell us with whom you had sex last Friday, and where?'

Clifford looked as if he was about to protest again, then thought better of it. 'Am I going to be arrested and charged with anything?'

'Not at the moment,' replied Pascal.

'It was a tart called Viv,' said Clifford, still not meeting Pascal's gaze.

Collins withdrew the photograph of Sara Martin from her handbag. 'Was this her?'

Clifford studied the picture for a few seconds, then nodded. 'That's Viv,' he confirmed.

Pascal cast a significant glance at Collins. 'And where did the event take place?' asked Pascal.

Clifford looked into his eyes and shook his head. 'You're saying that the woman I know as Viv was really someone called Sara Martin?'

'That's Sara Martin's photograph you've just identified. Now where did you have sex with her?'

'I can't tell you that, Detective-Inspector. Too many people involved whose reputations would suffer.'

'Apart from sex, what else goes on in this place?' asked Collins.

'I really don't know,' Clifford declared. He turned towards the desk and leaned on his elbows. 'It's a possibility that one or two people might be using drugs – but I don't know for certain. *I* don't have anything to do with them.'

'So, it's a place where there's drugs and sex and… rock'n'roll? Sounds like a night club to me,' said Collins.

'Well it isn't – not like *The Kitty Klub*, anyway.'

Pascal leaned forwards. 'Was it at *Kittens?*'

Clifford looked up. 'You know about that place?'

'I know it's a brothel.'

'It's a private members' club.'

'Where sex is on the menu, and the girls are foreign imports with new heroin habits.'

Clifford looked down at his hands. 'Yes,' he whispered. He looked up again. 'That's where I had sex with that woman.' He nodded towards the photograph. 'But I didn't pay anything.'

'Is *Kittens* open every night?'

Clifford nodded.

'Is *Kittens* part of *The Kitty Klub?*'

Pascal glanced at Collins, not waiting for Clifford's confirmation. 'Right, Councillor. I want you to come back to the police station with us and sign a statement to that effect.'

Clifford stood up. 'You don't expect me to admit in writing that I fucked a tart, do you?' he demanded indignantly.

'I'll settle for a simple statement that you're a member of this "private members' club" called *Kittens*, and that it's part of *The Kitty Klub.*'

Clifford shook his head. 'You can't make me do that! They'd kill me if they found out – and they would find out,' he added. 'I'm not the only member in a position to keep them informed of what goes on at the police station.'

Pascal tried not to let his surprise show. 'Who'll have you killed?' he asked. 'Who runs *Kittens?*'

Collins spoke. 'If we know who, we could protect you from him – or is it a woman?'

Clifford glanced at her. 'No, he's a man.' He stared at Pascal.

'DS Collins is right, sir. Tell us who to protect you from and we'll see it's done.'

'You promise?'

Pascal nodded and waited.

Clifford looked down at the desk. 'His name's Derrick Jackson. He runs *Kittens.'*

'The same Derrick Jackson who runs *The Kitty Klub?'*

Clifford nodded. That's his legitimate business. *Kittens* is in the back of it, through a concealed door which is always guarded whenever the club's operating.'

Collins asked, 'Where are the girls kept when they're not working?'

'Deej has an old guesthouse, no longer functioning as such. In Columbine Road.'

Pascal glanced at Collins. She shrugged. He felt there was little more that Clifford was going to tell them at the moment, but he was pleased with the information they'd obtained.

'Right, Councillor. Get your coat, and we'll go down to the nick, get your statement and set the witness protection process going.'

Clifford stood up, his shoulders drooping. 'Will I have to give evidence?'

'You might. It depends on whether a defence advocate would agree to accept your statement without taking the opportunity to cross-examine you. Always assuming we get Jackson into court, of course, and that's down to what evidence there is against him, and the CPS.'

Collins led the way to the car where Clifford was put into the back seat. Pascal saw Mrs Kenright watching them through the doorway as they drove away.

\*

Jared Martin would have described his mood as 'quietly confident'. He had completed the Paris to Amsterdam sector of his flight to the Caribbean without incident. He had an hour to wait in Schiphol airport for his onward journey. His suitcase would be transferred directly to the Aruba plane while he stayed in the transit lounge and had a coffee.

As he drained the cup, he examined the crowd over the rim. For a moment, he thought he saw Sara, but when he looked again, it was just a woman who looked like her. In his own way, he had loved his wife and in his quieter moments, grieved for her.

Another figure caught his eye. A man in a security guard's jacket, with an identity tag. For a moment, Martin thought it was Danny Bakker, but reckoned it was the same psychological trick that made him think he kept seeing his wife at the limit of his peripheral vision. The man stopped and scanned the people. Martin got a better look at his face as the man's head turned towards him and realised it was indeed Bakker – or his identical twin brother.

Martin felt cold fear in his heart, and forced himself to remain seated, pretending to drink coffee, which allowed him to obscure most of his face. Bakker looked past him, then turned and moved away. Martin realised he was sweating, whilst at the same time he desperately wanted a pee. His hand shook as he replaced the cup in the saucer, making it rattle enough for the person sitting on the next bar stool to glance up quickly. Martin got up and hurriedly went in the opposite direction from the one taken by Bakker, until he found a toilet. Inside, there were three urinals, one being used, the two next to it available.

I'll use a cubicle, he thought, but when he looked both were occupied. He stood in front of the left-hand urinal and released the pressure in his bladder. The man at the right-hand position turned, washed his hands in the basin, and after drying them, left the room.

A moment later, the door opened again behind him. As he was zipping up his fly, he felt something cold and hard press into his neck.

'Hello, Mr Martin,' whispered Bakker in his ear, 'do you have my money?'

Martin swivelled his eyes as far as he could to see his assailant, but the gun barrel made it impossible to turn his head. The gongs prefacing an announcement on the public-address system burst onto his eardrums as his flight was called.

Behind him, he heard the rattle of a cubicle door latch being slid back. In a reckless moment, while Bakker's attention was diverted to the man emerging from the toilet compartment, Martin stamped hard on his instep and ran for the door. In the main concourse, Martin saw a security policeman and hurriedly told him there was a man with a gun in the men's room, then headed for the gate from which his flight was leaving without a backward glance.

*

Danny Bakker emerged from the men's room at Schiphol to find a pair of security police pointing guns at him. Fortunately, there were many passengers milling around on the concourse, and a large Malaccan woman with three small children cavorting around her was passing, unaware of the drama. Bakker grabbed her, drawing his pistol and holding it to her head.

She screamed, and her children screamed too. The police didn't dare shoot, and Bakker managed to lose himself in the crowd, later releasing his hostage. After that, he'd had an uncomfortable twelve hours, during which he'd stolen a car and driven to the coast, to a place where he knew a RIB, a rigid-hulled inflatable boat, was stored, normally used for diving and the occasional run across the North Sea to Norfolk loaded with drugs.

He'd checked there was enough fuel and, under cover of darkness, slipped away from the Dutch coast, programming the GPS for Norfolk. The fast little boat covered the distance in less than five hours, coming to rest on one of the flat beaches of north-east Norfolk just as dawn was breaking behind it. He figured it would be easier to keep a low profile in Norfolk until the hue and cry in Holland died down.

His options were reducing. He assumed that Martin had probably caught his flight. Mr van Ruys still wanted his money. He decided that Derrick Jackson must be made to make up the shortfall, especially if he wanted to keep his supply lines open. He must surely recognise, thought Bakker, that he would probably be next on van Ruys's hit-list if he didn't pay. He walked inland from the beach until he found a road. There was no traffic on it and he set off, hoping to hitch a lift.

*

Bell put down the telephone and looked up at Pascal who was sipping office coffee from a cardboard cup while leaning against the door frame.

'That was my contact in the Maréchaussée. Danny Bakker was at Schiphol.'

Pascal stood up straight and moved closer to the workstations where Bell and Collins sat.

'Yes? Have they got him?'

'No.'

The hopeful little grin disappeared from Pascal's face.

'He had a gun. Took a woman hostage in the concourse and got away from the security guards. They think there's a chance he's on his way back to the UK. A car was stolen from the airport car-park and found on the coast. There's a little bay with an old boatshed where a RIB is normally kept. They think it's used for drugs runs over here, and it's not there now.'

Pascal thought for a moment. 'Get onto the control room and have the police helicopter search the coast for the RIB.'

'Right, sir,' said Bell, picking up his telephone again.

Pascal turned to Collins. 'Any news from the hospital?'

'No, sir.'

Bell spoke. 'I was thinking, sir, about the premises search. I'll have a word with the Field Intelligence Officer and see if anything jogs his memory. He might have snouts that are useful.'

'Good idea, Graham. Alison, do you want to ring round and see if anyone has any knowledge of a RIB run from Holland.'

'Right, sir.'

Leaving Collins to deal with Clifford, Pascal went upstairs to the CID offices. He knocked on DCI Steel's door and went in.

'George!' said Steel, looking up from a file on his desk and waving Pascal to a chair. 'How's it all going?'

'Councillor Clifford is downstairs, sir.'

'Oh? What's he want?' said Steel, frowning and getting to his feet.

'Uh, he's giving us a statement, and he's in considerable fear for his safety as a result. And so am I. I've promised him protection.'

Steel sat down again, but he still looked worried.

'You'd better explain what's going on,' he said. 'Help yourself to a coffee.'

Pascal poured two cups of the DCI's excellent coffee and brought him up to date on the investigations while they sipped it.

'So the murder investigation seems to be leading us towards this place called *Kittens*,' he concluded. 'I'll be going for a warrant to search the premises soon.'

'Only "soon", George?'

'There's a few more enquiries we have to make before we go in.'

'Such as what?'

'We know very little about Derrick Jackson; I'd like to find the place where he keeps the girls and raid that at the same time as we do *The Kitty Klub* and *Kittens*. I also want to talk to Jared Martin again.'

Steel nodded. 'Okay, okay, George. You decide when; just let me know before you go in.'

'Yes sir,' replied Pascal, treating his boss's words as an opportunity to get back to work. He drained the cup, got to his feet and placed it and its saucer on the DCI's window-ledge. 'I'll be off then, sir.'

'Uh yes, okay then, George.'

Pascal closed the door firmly behind him and went along the corridor and peered in at the CID office. Frimley and Bell were studying CCTV footage. Frimley glanced up as he looked in.

'Here you are, sir,' he said, holding out a videotape. 'It's one of the cameras covering the town centre.'

'What's on it?'

'The white van. Not much of a shot, but the index mark was readable, and the van was heading towards the bridge across the river at the old port. I'm checking a camera down there, but there aren't so many since the port stopped trading.'

'Let me know if you find out where it's gone.'

'Right, sir.'

Bell looked up. 'I've had a contact from the Maréchaussée about Danny Bakker.'

'The bloke who beats up women?'

'The very one. He's known to them. Few convictions, mostly in his younger days. Lately, they think he's been employed by a Dutch businessman, about whom they know very little. They're looking into it.'

'Good. I want to know what's happened to Jared Martin. He's never at home. Will you look into that, please, Graham.'

'Yes sir,' said Bell, tipping the last custard cream out of a packet. 'I'm becoming a right little missing persons bureau.'

'You do it so well, Graham,' said Pascal. He smiled and rolled his eyes, then returned to his own office. DC Frimley entered ten minutes later. Pascal looked up from behind his desk.

'Ah, Douglas, the very man.'

Frimley looked at him askance, recognising the performance. He dropped two videotapes on Pascal's desk.

'I'll just go and fetch us some coffee, shall I sir?'

'That's really good of you, Douglas.'

'No problem, sir. You can buy me one tomorrow.'

'Hmm.'

'Would you like to take a look at the top one of the tapes while I'm getting the drinks.'

'Okay,' said Pascal, picking up the tape and loading it into his video player. By the time Frimley returned, he was scanning through the grainy images on fast forward.

Frimley put down the cups and picked up the remote controller.

'Do you mind, sir?'

He stopped the tape and rewound it to where he'd set it, then pressed Play.

Pascal watched the images for a minute in silence.

'Where is this, and when?

'This is outside *The Kitty Klub* a week ago. Specifically, last Tuesday.'

The grainy image, from one of Breydon's town centre security cameras, showed people entering and leaving, past the large imposing figure of Ernest Miller, at nine-thirty in the evening. A woman approached him. He took her arm and led her inside the building. Frimley stopped the tape.

'Sara Martin, I believe, sir.'

Pascal recognised her from the photograph supplied by Jared Martin. He sucked in his breath.

'She doesn't look bad for forty,' he said with grudging admiration.

Frimley regarded him askance again. 'No, sir.'

'She looks no more than about twenty or twenty-five.'

Sara Martin was wearing a short black skirt, and a transparent pink blouse, her finely shaped legs terminating in small feet inside strappy sandals. She wore a pendant necklace and matching earrings which glinted in the club's lights.

Pascal turned to study Frimley. 'Do you suppose *The Kitty Klub* would have anything helpful, like their own CCTV tapes?'

'They might, I'd have to ask, but it might put them on notice.'

'Hmm, yes. Best leave it a while. If we raid the place, we might be able to pick up their tapes. Intel will have a field day spotting the punters using *Kittens*.' Pascal rubbed his chin. 'Any chance we might pick up Sara on the way out of the building and follow her home? I'd like to know where she was living. This was taken after she left Martin, wasn't it?'

'Yes. This was three days before she was killed on the Friday of Easter week.'

Frimley ran the tape forward until it was nearly at the end. Suddenly, he stopped it and wound back a few seconds.

'Sir! It's John.'

Pascal leaned forward to where Frimley pointed. It was obviously Walker, when he ran the tape again, emerging from the club's portal onto the pavement and turned towards Old Market Square and his home. It was the briefest of glimpses, only a few seconds long, but the image was good enough clearly to identify the policeman.

'Bloody hell!' muttered Pascal quietly.

Frimley rolled the tape further on. Just before the end, both men were rewarded for their diligence when Sara Martin stepped out of the club and walked off in the same direction Walker had. The tape stopped.

Pascal chewed his cheek. 'Got any tapes from Old Market Square?'

'Probably,' said Frimley. 'Seem to have a full set in the office. Now we know when and where to look, it shouldn't take too long to find them.'

'Don't worry about John,' said Pascal, 'I'll go and talk to him later. It's her: where was she living?'

## CHAPTER 11

A phone call to say that David Ellis's condition had worsened and the doctors were very worried, prompted Collins to visit the hospital.

'Do you want to come?' she asked Bell, who was crunching on a ginger nut.

He belched quietly, spraying a few crumbs down his shirt front. 'Yes. I don't suppose it's necessary, but it'll give me some idea of what I'm expected to break my balls over.'

He did not give Collins the impression of a man who would "break his balls" over anything, but she felt the need to visit David Ellis, and Bell might as well come along.

They arrived at the hospital to find Marion Ellis still at her son's bedside, a book open in front of her, and David himself connected by tubes from his mouth to a ventilator which steadily and regularly pumped air into his lungs. His head was heavily bandaged.

Collins stood beside Marion Ellis. 'How is he?'

The woman looked up at her, streaks of mascara below her eyes clear evidence of recent tears. 'He's been having trouble breathing. There was a time during the night when I thought I'd lost him. They had to take him to the operating theatre for an emergency...' She broke off, sobbing. Collins passed her a paper handkerchief from a box at the side of the room. Marion Ellis dabbed her eyes and blew her nose.

'I'm sorry. They said his brain was bleeding.' She looked up at Collins with fear in her eyes. 'That's a haemorrhage, isn't it?'

Collins nodded. 'I believe so.'

'Anyway, when he came back, they put him on the ventilator, and he's been quiet ever since.'

Collins nodded. Bell was on the opposite side of the bed. He glanced across at Collins.

'Has the lad's clothing been taken for analysis?' He answered his own question by opening the bedside cabinet and wardrobe cupboard, both on his side of the room. 'Well, well. They're all still here.' He turned to Collins and raised his eyebrows.

She felt stupid. Worse, Bell would know how stupid and unprofessional she was. She could feel the blood rushing to her cheeks. She turned to Marion Ellis.

'We're going to have to take David's clothing for examination, in case there's anything they can tell us.'

Marion Ellis nodded and shrugged.

As Bell put the last of the clothing carefully into an evidence bag, a doctor came into the room. He was a few years older than Collins, she guessed, and had a stethoscope in the left-hand pocket of his white coat. He glanced unsmilingly at the three people beside the bed before moving close to David and fitting the stethoscope to his ears. Easing the bedclothes out of the way, he listened at various points on the young man's chest. Putting the instrument back in his pocket when he'd finished, he leaned over, pulled David's eyelids open, and shone a small penlight into them. He looked up at Marion Ellis and smiled reassuringly.

'His lungs sound clear of any fluid – that's a good thing. One eye still has a blown pupil, but I think it's better than yesterday.'

'Does that mean he's getting better?' she asked.

He thought for a moment. 'He doesn't seem to be getting worse. The business with the ventilator might indicate otherwise, but David's breathing difficulty may well be only temporary while his brain sorts itself out. We'll be sending him for another scan just to check.' He smiled again. 'David's young and fit. It's too soon to think of giving up hope.'

'How much is he likely to remember when he wakes up?' asked Collins.

The doctor turned to her. 'Are you a relative?'

She identified herself and Bell.

'I don't know for certain,' said the doctor. 'It's quite usual for a patient to be unable to remember events just before the trauma, maybe as far back as a couple of days. Usually, their memory improves with time, but there are no guarantees.'

Collins nodded, her lips pressed tightly together.

Bell had been packing David's clothes into hospital plastic bags.

'Right then,' he said, 'we'd better get this lot off to the lab.'

Collins nodded.

'We'll keep in touch, Mrs Ellis,' she said.

The woman nodded. The doctor watched as Collins and Bell left.

\*

Jared Martin stared out of the window beyond the leading edge of the Airbus's wing at the tiny island of Aruba below. He was nearly safe now. The aircraft was entering short finals, the undercarriage hydraulics whirring until the wheels locked firmly into position with a solid clunk which made the floor vibrate. He pressed his feet hard against the footrest built in to the seat in front as the air brakes bit into the thick steamy atmosphere and caused his body to push against the seat restraint.

Lights blazed from the terminal building of Queen Beatrix International Airport. It was five to nine but, he reminded himself, night fell swiftly and early in these latitudes. The plane banked and turned to begin its final descent onto the runway. Ten minutes later, Martin was walking along the passageway from the aircraft into the arrivals terminal with a spring in his step. The heat of the Caribbean evening warmed his bones.

It was a long hike to Aruba Immigration controls in the centre of the terminal. These were the last obstacle. He had all the correct paperwork, and even an Aruban bank account, which had cost him a lot, but was now showing a healthy balance of US dollars, sufficient to set him up and keep him in considerable comfort. With any luck, Abel Scarman, his contact on the island, would be waiting for him outside the customs controls.

He joined one of the queues for the immigration offic-ers and found himself face to face with an attractive wom-an who reminded him somewhat of Sara.

*

A week since he had been sent home, effectively on 'gar-dening leave', John Walker was, figuratively, climbing the walls of his small apartment. Since his last visit to *The Kitty Klub*, he'd hardly been outside. He wore only a T-shirt and shorts. Previous days' clothing cluttered the floor, and the whole place, he acknowledged, could do with a clean. He just didn't feel like it. He lay slumped on his old sofa, star-ing at the cold remains of a cup of coffee, balanced precar-iously on the arm, thinking that he should do something, but couldn't find the energy. He dragged on a cigarette. It had been his last one, and he couldn't afford another pack. Three weeks to payday, and he had to eat.

He felt tears prick his eyes. It was so *bloody* unfair! At heart, he was a good copper, he knew. His parents had been so proud of him when he joined up: they would be horrified if they could see him now. And ashamed. If he thought about it long enough, he experienced an ache in his chest, just above his heart.

There was a knock at the door. He waited until it was repeated before getting wearily to his feet and peering through the spy-hole into the communal hallway. It was Pascal. Walker brushed the moisture from his eyes and opened the door, standing back to let him in.

'How are you, John?' asked Pascal when Walker had cleared old newspapers off an armchair for him.

Walker shrugged. 'Okay.'

Pascal seemed uncertain of how to proceed. Walker stepped into the silence.

'How's things going at work? Any further forward with the missing girl?'

Pascal interlaced his fingers. 'We've probably got a lead on her, but I'm not sure yet. More to the point, we've a murdered woman.'

'Saw a piece in the paper about her,' said Walker. He narrowed his eyes in the effort to remember. 'Sara somebody. Can't remember.'

'Hmm. Nasty business – her killer tried to set fire to her after he bumped her off.'

'Any ideas who did it? Irate husband? Boyfriend?'

'Don't think so,' said Pascal, 'though her estranged husband seems to have disappeared. He's got no previous, and, while he still has to be ruled out as a suspect, I think there are more promising fish in the sea.'

'Who?'

'There seems to be a psychopathic Dutchman in the area.'

Walker shrugged. He knew of no Dutchmen, psychopathic or otherwise, in or out of the area.

Pascal continued. 'What you may not know is that Sara Martin was, we believe, working as a prostitute at a sort of private club-cum-bordello in town.'

Walker stared. It was all he could do to remain deadpan. He had a shrewd notion Pascal meant *Kittens*. There was nothing else he knew of resembling that description in Breydon. Pascal was watching him, not particularly closely, but Walker knew he'd notice any reaction – it was automatic with anyone used to interviewing.

'Oh,' he said, as noncommittally as possible. 'Not much further forward, then.'

'I don't know if you'd call it progress, but you'll recall our murder victim's home was subjected to an arson attack last week. They lifted prints from the scene which aren't on our database.' He studied Walker's face.

Walker felt the colour draining from his cheeks and knew Pascal would have seen it. He licked his lips.

'You all right, John?' asked Pascal, 'you look as if you've seen a ghost.'

Walker swallowed. 'I'm okay. Any ideas where the husband's gone?'

'Not yet. We're more interested in the fact that the fingerprint found at the fire matches one found at the murder scene and more found in a hotel room where a young girl, a prostitute, was beaten up rather badly. The fingerprint is not the missing husband's, so we think it might belong to the alleged psychopathic Dutchman.'

Walker had recovered control of himself. 'Want a drink? There's some coffee.' He needed time to think.

'That would be welcome.'

Walker smacked his forehead with the palm of a hand. 'There's no milk,' he said. 'Haven't been down to the shop.'

Pascal stood up. 'No matter. Come on, get dressed and we'll go and get some in town. You can do a bit of shopping while we're there.'

Walker shook his head. 'I – I can't do that... today.'

Pascal looked at him sadly. 'Look, you can tell me to mind my own business, but don't forget I saw the Attachment Order. Have you any money to live on to the end of the month?'

Walker turned away. 'Sure. I'll be fine.'

'John, this is just between us. I'm speaking to you as a friend. We've been working together for a few years now. You've got to face things. It's not like you to run away from a challenge. Now, do you need some cash? It's three weeks to payday, and you can't live on air.'

Walker felt unworthy. His eyes filled with the tears of self-pity and he could not bring himself to face Pascal, nor even to speak. He slowly nodded his head.

Behind him, Pascal spoke again. 'There's two hundred quid there. It should see you through to the end of the month. Make sure you spend it on food.'

Walker looked down. The emphasis Pascal had placed on food suggested that he knew there were other things which might be bought with it. Pascal had placed a small heap of twenty-pound notes on the arm of the sofa. He reached for a facial tissue and blew his nose, folding up the tissue and disposing of it quickly before Pascal could see the blood on it.

'Thanks, sir,' he said, speaking with difficulty because of the lump on his throat. 'I'll pay you back.'

'Sometime, John, sometime.' Pascal hesitated. 'Well, come on, let's get that coffee.'

'It'll have to be a quick one, sir, I have an appointment at the Job Centre.'

He slipped into a pair of trousers and picked up the cash.

'That's a bit premature, isn't it, John?' said Pascal.

'You think so? You think they'll have me back?' Walker opened the door and let Pascal precede him onto the landing. 'I don't,' he added, checking the door had locked securely behind them.

'Never say die, John,' advised Pascal, on the stairs.

Walker followed him without replying. Once Pascal knew the truth, he felt sure he'd be the first to show him the door, if not the inside of a cell in the custody suite. The coffee would be welcome, thought Walker, but then there was a little unofficial investigation he wanted to make.

He sipped his coffee. Pascal had bought them large mugs of rich, dark Italian blend, and they were sitting in the window, peering out at shoppers. The strong aroma even found its way past his damaged olfactory sensors so he could appreciate it.

'So what's the plan with *The Kitty Klub*?' he asked.

Pascal breathed in the steam from his mug and sipped. 'I think we'll have to go in and have a look round, sooner or later,' replied Pascal. 'See if we can't find this brothel, and talk to the owner, Derrick Jackson.'

Walker nodded.

Pascal drained his cup and stood up. 'Well, must be off. You stay and finish your drink.' He leaned down. 'And I shouldn't be in a hurry to come back to work. It'll only remind Jimmy that he hasn't suspended you yet.'

Walker looked down at the table-top and shook his head. Raising his eyes, he watched Pascal walk through the doorway, out into the street.

For a moment, it had been like old times, talking over a case with his friend, then Pascal had had to drop that last thought on him, like a bucketful of cold water. Still it wasn't as bad as it had been earlier. He still had Pascal's two hundred quid in his pocket. He sipped his coffee and found himself staring at a girl who surely should have been in school. He wasn't the only one taking an interest: behind her, another man, in his late twenties, wearing sunglasses despite the day's not being particularly bright, was watching her. The girl was smoking a cigarette and gazing at a window display of music compact discs. She had a bag, so full it wouldn't close, and Walker was sure the reason was a school blazer jammed inside it.

A pantomime began to take place. The young man took an MP3 player from his pocket and began to walk towards the girl, fumbling it in his hands, and finally dropping it quite close to her, its fall only checked at the last minute by the earphone wire. As he bent to pick it up, he almost collided with her. She turned and stared at him.

There was some conversation, during which the girl seemed to be showing him how to use the machine. He nodded a lot. When he seemed to have grasped the matter, they both looked at the CDs in the window and talked more. The girl eventually pointed to a couple, and they disappeared inside the shop.

Moments later, they emerged, the man clutching a paper bag bearing the shop's logo. When the girl turned to him and reached for it, he held the bag just out of her reach. She tried again and he teased her again. They spoke to each other, after which he gave her the bag and they walked off down the street together, his arm round her shoulders.

It was, thought Walker, a very smooth operation. He felt slightly envious of the man, and wondered if Derrick had any stock-in-trade that could pass for school-age. First things first, he thought, and finished his drink. He slid off the stool and set off down the road towards a small supermarket.

\*

Jared Martin exulted. He'd been admitted to Aruba, albeit on a temporary basis, but he had little doubt there'd be no difficulty converting that to permanent permission to stay after a few months. He collected his meagre baggage and went in search of Abel Scarman.

The concourse was awash with people of every colour and nationality. Martin expected Scarman to be waving a piece of cardboard with his name on it, near the exit from the baggage hall, but though there were many such bits of cardboard, none bore his name. Martin's elation began to evaporate. Where was he?

Scarman had acted as his agent for several years, quietly seeking out a suitable property for him to buy following his 'retirement' from the UK. There'd never been a reason to doubt Scarman, and he was prepared to think that the man was simply running late. Martin sauntered over to a bar-café and ordered a Bud. It was not his favourite beer, but his mouth was dry and he needed a long drink. He kept his eyes scanning the crowd. It was several months since he'd last met the man when they'd been searching for a suitable property.

A tall black woman, elegantly clad in a green and gold silk wrap, watched him for a time. She checked his appearance against the photograph she'd been given by the Superintendent at the police station that morning. Sure she had the right man, she tore the photograph up into small pieces and dropped them in a waste bin. Glancing up, she caught his eyes on her and smiled. She made her way unhurriedly towards him.

'Want a taxi, sir?' she asked, in the island's lilting accent.

Martin drained the bottle, gazing at her appreciatively as he did so. 'Uh, no, thanks. Someone's supposed to be meeting me.'

She looked around at the crowd and sat beside him at the bar. 'Oh, okay. Mind if I sit here?'

'No, not at all.'

The barman hovered and she ordered fruit juice. When the drink arrived, it was decorated with orange slices, cherries and an umbrella. Ice tinkled against the glass and drops of moisture on the outside were coalescing into tiny rivers dripping onto the counter mat.

She sipped, holding the umbrella aside, then put the glass down, picked up a slice of orange in finely manicured fingers and sucked the juice out. Martin noticed how her full lips glistened, red and luscious. He had another look round for Scarman, but couldn't see him.

'Doesn't look as if my friend is coming,' he said. 'I may have need of your services after all.'

'Sure.' She concentrated on her drink. Martin caught the barman's eye and ordered another Bud.

'So what're you doing here?' she asked. 'On holiday?'

'No. I've bought a property on the island. Come to live here.'

'You've been to Aruba before?'

'I came here about six months ago and my friend took me round. I saw this place, and as luck would have it a few months after I went home he contacted me and told me it had come on the market.'

'You never actually got to look round it yourself?'

'No, but after he wrote to me, I went on line to the realtor's website, and they had one of those walk-through movies and 360-degree panoramas, so it was nearly as good.'

'But you've not seen it in person yet?'

'No. I was hoping my friend would be meeting me and take me to it. I'm not sure I could find it again alone.'

She studied him for a moment before seeming to make up her mind.

'Okay. I'll take you. I don't usually go anywhere alone with men – some of you are dangerous.' She grinned to take the sting out of her words. He thought it was amusing that she had been deciding whether he qualified to be accepted as a fare while he had been deciding whether to hire her or wait a bit longer for Scarman.

He nodded. 'I haven't been dangerous for quite some time.'

She looked at him askance. 'Oh, really?' She grinned.

He smiled briefly. 'My wife would have confirmed it.'

Serena looked around again. 'Where is she?'

He looked down at the table-top. 'She – she's dead. She was killed a fortnight ago.'

Serena's eyes widened. 'Oh, you poor man. She can't have been very old.'

'She was forty.'

'What happened?'

He shrugged. 'Don't know. The police haven't found her killer.' And so far, he hasn't found me, he added mentally.

She rested a hand on his arm. 'That's terrible. I'm so sorry. Had you been married long?'

'Fifteen years. In Britain these days, that qualifies for a long service medal.'

She smiled sympathetically. 'Do you have any children?'

'No. We decided not to. It was a joint decision.'

She nodded again.

'There's just one thing I need to do,' he said, 'and that's buy a local mobile phone, if there's someone round here selling them.'

'Follow me.' She led the way to a mobile phone shop on the concourse where he bought a pre-payment instrument, then they went outside to find her cab in the airport taxi rank. Sitting beside her, with the interior light on, she turned to him. She offered to help him test it, by dialling her own mobile number from it. She cancelled the call when she heard her own phone's ringtone, satisfied that she would now have the new phone's number.

'So, where am I taking you?'

He dragged a realtor's property flyer out of his inside pocket and gave her the address. She looked at the photograph in the centre of the page, showing a handsome villa set in neatly-kept grounds, with a serpentine-shaped swimming pool. It didn't accord with the address written under it, to the best of her recollection.

'This is your friend's place?'

He shook his head, smiling. 'No, no. I own it. I've come to live here.'

She studied his face. 'You want me to take you to that address?' she asked, tapping the paper.

'Yes.'

She started the engine.

She shrugged slightly. 'Okay.' She smiled. 'By the way, my name is Serena.'

'Jared,' he said.

She drove out of the airport onto a reasonably good stretch of road.

Her passenger seemed nervous, but maybe, she thought, it was just the result of a long flight and a strange country. However, there was definitely something wrong. The photograph of the villa did not accord with the address on the flyer: the villa was well-known on the island. It was just to the north of Oranjestad, between the capital and the beautiful and tourist-filled north-west of the island.

The address beneath the photograph was in the south-east, where the land was wind-blown and scrubby.

'You said a friend helped you buy this place?' she asked.

'Abel Scarman. I understand he's helped several people find homes on the island. I was introduced to him by one of his satisfied customers, and I must say, he seems to have been very helpful.'

She was quiet. The description of Scarman did not accord in her mind with the devious conman being held in the cells at Police HQ in Oranjestad. Putting Scarman and the flyer together, it was obvious that Martin had been the victim of a scam. She headed south-eastwards away from the capital. The road soon deteriorated.

Twenty minutes later she pulled up at the address he'd given her. Martin climbed out of the car, leaning against it, looking bewildered. Serena stood on the other side of the vehicle and regarded in silence the property and the effect the sight of it was having on Martin.

He turned to her, puzzled. 'I don't understand, Serena. This isn't the place in the picture.'

The headlamps of her car shone into the scrub which covered the stony path to the building they were parked outside and had taken over any garden the place might once have had. Moonlight revealed the building itself, what there was of it. A small, boxy structure, covered for the most part in ancient corrugated iron, whose coating of cream paint was flaking. One of the curved sections which made up the roof had collapsed inside. There were just two windows either side of a door which hung crazily from one hinge. Both of them were broken. An old curtain flapped through the hole in one of them. There was no pool, and the sea was miles away.

'This is the address on the flyer,' she said, 'but I agree, it isn't the villa in the picture.'

Martin dropped his hands and looked round, across the car roof. He was devastated.

'But it's not the house I saw six months ago, the one I paid so much for.'

She shrugged. 'The villa in the picture isn't for sale.'

'How do you know? Do you know it?'

'Yes. Everyone knows it. It's owned by the British government, and used as a base when British diplomats visited the island from Curaçao.'

'Let me guess,' he said when she finished, 'in between times, it's empty. Plenty of opportunity for someone to get past whatever security there is and make a movie and panoramic picture?'

She nodded. 'I guess so.'

'But Scarman?' She saw the implication sink in as his expression changed. 'I'll have him arrested! I need to see the police.'

She interlaced her fingers. 'As it's late, the police are likely to be out rounding up the drunks. Let me take you to a hotel for the night. I'll pick you up in the morning and take you to Police HQ myself. How's that?'

He stared at the ruin he had apparently bought for half a million dollars and nodded silently. They got back in the car and she drove him back to Oranjestad.

\*

Wednesday lunchtime, when *The Kitty Klub's* bar was open for business, Walker went in, intending to see Derrick. Ernest was keeper of the door, and there was something in the way he looked at Walker which rang an alarm bell. It was almost conspiratorial. He frowned as he walked across the room to the bar. He felt in his pocket for cash. He'd spent seventy-five pounds on food, stocking up on essentials to last three weeks. It would be more famine than feast, still, but he intended to buy fresh vegetables as well as he needed them. He had enough small change to afford even *The Kitty Klub's* prices for a whisky.

The barman saw him coming. Same sort of expression as Ernest's. The frown remained on Walker's face.

'Scotch and water, please,' he said.

'Coming up, sir.'

'Derrick about?'

The barman glanced over his shoulder from the optic where he held a glass for its shot of spirit.

'Think so, sir. Shall I ask him to come down?'

Walker nodded, noticing the barman shove the glass up against the spring a second time. He put it on the counter between them and slid a jug of water next to it. Walker put a five pound note down, but the barman waved it away.

'It's all right, sir. Mr Jackson has explained the arrangement you have with him. All your drinks are on the house, Mr Walker.'

Walker stared at him for a moment, then down at the glass. It forced him to consider the full implication behind Derrick's offer. Acceptance of this drink would mark the first small step on a journey he wasn't sure he wanted to take. He looked at the fiver. It wasn't his, he acknowledged. At the moment *nothing* was his: his liabilities far outweighed his assets. He chewed his lip. If he bought a drink with somebody else's money, would that make it *his* drink? Not really. If he simply took the drink, it would be a gift: more *his* than if he paid for it with Pascal's fiver. But if he accepted the drink, he would be forever compromised. The barman was watching him with a faint smile on his lips.

'Anything wrong, Mr Walker?' he asked. 'Whisky okay for you?'

Walker glanced up at the barman's face, and lost the argument with himself. He poured a tablespoonful of water into the glass and picked it up.

'No, it's just fine.' He swallowed half of the golden liquid, feeling it burn his throat. Perhaps it was the devil's mark, which would stay with him until the Witchfinder found it and cut it out.

The barman turned to the telephone, but at that moment, Derrick Jackson appeared round the end of the bar, smiling.

'Ah, John. Good to see you. Shall we go to my office?'
He glanced at the whisky. 'Bring your drink. Would you
like it topped up?' He nodded to the barman who put another shot in the glass.

Jackson was close enough now to put his hand round
Walker's shoulders and guide him gently through a door
marked 'Private' which opened onto a short passageway.
He led Walker through a door labelled 'Office' and waved
him to a seat while going round the old wooden desk to
the ancient swivel chair. The room smelled of smoke and
booze, thought Walker. The old carpet was badly stained,
and the whole place seemed seedy. He checked the seat
before sitting on it.

Jackson was still smiling. 'Well, have you something to
tell me?'

Walker wondered what he could say that wouldn't
amount to much, yet be enough to make Jackson think he
was getting something for his money.

'There was an arson attack on Viv's home.'

Jackson seemed to be waiting for more. He nodded encouragingly. 'Yes?'

'They found some fingerprints at the scene they could-
n't identify, but think they belong to the arsonist.'

Jackson nodded again and looked expectantly at Walker.

'They found the same prints in a hotel room where a
tart had been beaten up, and at the scene of Viv's murder.
They think it might be the same bloke. They'll be checking
with Interpol and their direct links with the Amsterdam
police.'

Jackson pursed his lips. 'They don't know whose prints
they are?'

'Not that they've told me.' Walker had to be careful: he
didn't want the fact of his *de facto* suspension to come out.

'Any connection with this place or me?' asked Jackson.

'Not that I've heard.' Walker finished the scotch. It was
making his head spin.

'And you'd tell me, wouldn't you, John?'

Walker sat with his head bowed, looking up at Jackson under his brows. Slowly he nodded. 'Yes. Actually,' he added quietly, his eyes fixed on the glass, 'The DI did mention that they might be getting a warrant for this place.'

Jackson stared at him and half rose from his chair. 'Why? What do they think they'll find?'

Walker looked up, his face drawn and haggard. '*Kittens.*'

'They know about *Kittens?*'

'He doesn't tell me everything,' said Walker.

Jackson looked askance at him. 'So they *do* know about *Kittens.*'

'I think so.'

'When?' demanded Jackson. 'When are they coming? How long have I got to clean the place up?'

'I don't know,' said Walker. 'My guess is if it hasn't happened yet, they'll be taking a few days to watch the place.'

'So I've got a bit of time?'

'Yes, but you need to take care they don't see the girls coming and going.'

'Fuck!'

Walker shrugged.

Jackson continued. 'But we're talking, what? Days? A week? How long? You must know.'

'My guess is a few days. A week at most. I *don't* know.'

Jackson studied him for a few moments then seemed to relax.

'Well done.' He opened the bottom drawer of the left-hand pedestal and rummaged through the stuff in it until he found what he was looking for, a small wrap of cocaine. 'Here you are, John. Tide you over. See you Friday for the party?' he asked conversationally.

'Yes,' said Walker. 'Thanks.' He looked up. 'Do you know who killed Viv?'

Jackson found a small handbag mirror under the rubbish on the desk top and placed it in front of Walker. 'I'm sure you can find a better use for your nice crisp fiver than buying scotch with it.'

He stood up as Walker began to use the edge of the note to crush the lumps out of the drug and line it up on the glass.

'Of course not. You wouldn't expect me to say otherwise, would you – you being a copper and all? She wasn't like the other girls, you know. She used coke which isn't quite so useful to me as if she'd been using heroin. Mainly, her husband seems not to have passed on my last payment to my suppliers.'

Walker stared at him. 'Is that what he did?'

'He cleaned the cash to make it untraceable. Only he seems not to have paid for the last consignment. I, for one, am very annoyed with him. Viv's death was probably to encourage him to pay up.'

'Christ!' exclaimed Walker.

'Pop in this evening if you want one of the girls,' Jackson invited, unconcerned by the complicity in murder at which he'd hinted.

Walker felt a familiar tightening in his groin, but shook his head. Sufficient unto the day... he thought.

'I'll think about it.'

Jackson walked round the desk, directing his glance at the line of cocaine. 'I'll have a bit more snort for you as well.'

He left the room as Walker rolled up the fiver, put one end of the tube up his nose and leaned forward until the other was at the start of the line.

# CHAPTER 12

Nothing much had changed in Julia Fox's miserable existence. She was given heroin as often as she wanted it, and her tolerance to the drug was growing. Paul Unwin continued with her sexual education, and she was made to engage in lesbian sex with the other new girls. She was told some of the punters liked it. When she was good, she was rewarded with extra heroin.

Unwin was beginning to think she was ready to be put to work at *Kittens*. Jackson wasn't so sure. The two men met in the lounge of 83 Columbine Road.

'Let me show you, boss,' Unwin said. 'I'll get her cleaned up and bring her down, and she can practise on you as if you were a punter.'

Jackson got himself a small scotch from a cupboard normally kept locked.

'Okay. Go and get her.'

Unwin nodded and left the room.

Fifteen minutes later, he returned with Julia Fox, looking very different from when she'd arrived. Appearing to be blonde and tanned, her face made up and her hair tidy, she entered the room holding Unwin's hand. Jackson was sitting in an old armchair, watching her. Unwin had dressed her young, as he'd expected, giving her the appearance of a voluptuous young teen, or even pre-teen. Jackson had not had sex for some time and found her appearance was stimulating. She smiled at him as she released Unwin's hand and tottered towards him on four-inch spike heels. Jackson smiled back.

I'm going to enjoy this for once, he thought.

He rarely took one of the working girls, since there was always the risk of disease, once they'd been with a few punters. Some of the men who came to *Kittens* were none too clean, but this girl was fresh and still intact.

She began by standing beside his chair, and putting a hand round Jackson's neck. Jackson nodded dismissal at Unwin, across the room, and let his own hand slide up the girl's legs. Ten minutes later, he pulled her head away from his wilting erection and got to his feet. She stood quietly beside his chair.

'Remember to keep smiling. The punters like it if they think you're enjoying yourself.' He fastened his trousers. 'And also remember,' he added, 'it's their enjoyment that counts, not yours. You just fuck them as quickly as possible and make yourself available to the next.'

'Yes, Mr Jackson,' she said.

'Good girl. You should use a working name rather than use your real one, just in case anyone knows your family.'

She stood up. 'Yes, Mr Jackson.'

He nodded towards the door. 'Go and find Paul and tell him I think you've earned a little extra fix.'

'Thanks, Mr Jackson.'

He patted her rump as she walked past him to the door. Unwin was waiting just outside when she opened it. He stepped inside the room.

'Everything okay, boss?'

'Fine. Give her a little extra. And give her the working name of Fiona. I like that. I think we should organise the auction of her cherry on Friday.'

'Okay, boss,' said Unwin.

*

'Problem, boss?'

Derrick Jackson looked up at Ernest, his face ruddy with anger. 'I've been told we're probably going to be raided in the next few days.'

'Raided? By the police? What for?'

Jackson walked round behind his desk and sat in the creaky swivel chair.

'They're looking for *Kittens*.'

Miller chewed his cheek. 'How about we move the operation out of here?' he suggested.

Jackson stared at him. 'Where to?'

Miller's brow creased with the effort of thought. 'I know it might seem barmy, boss, but what about Clifford's place?'

Jackson scoffed but Miller was undeterred.

'It's a big enough house to work in,' he continued, 'and Clifford can hardly complain. And who'd think of the former Chairman of the Police Authority giving house-room to a bunch of tarts?'

Jackson's eyes narrowed as he considered Miller's idea. He liked it, he decided.

'Okay, Ernest, organise it, a-sap. Get him to take care of the housekeeper. Don't want her talking to the police.'

*

Julia felt remote from it all. All feeling, physical and emotional, was gone. She'd given up crying after the first week when it got her nowhere. Her parents hadn't been near her, nor the police. She'd been taken and put into her present condition and there'd been no apparent fuss. She supposed that when Paul had hurriedly arranged to have her hair bleached and her skin tanned it was for 'business' reasons.

She was allowed, for the first time, to eat in a dining room with nine other girls, four of them, like her, new. The other five were relatively old hands, in experience if not in age: most were still in their teens or early twenties. One of these seemed very sick, her skin pale and since they'd sat down, she'd broken out in a sweat and was hugging herself.

Julia looked at the girl sitting next to her. 'What's wrong with her?' she asked.

Her neighbour shrugged. 'She pregnant. Having bit of a bad time with baby.'

'Should she be doing this?'

The girl turned to her. 'Of course. What else she good for?'

'Where are you from?' asked Julia, noting her companion's accent.

'Latvia, me. Them – ' she pointed ' – from Estonia and Lithuania.'

'What are you doing here? Were you a prostitute in Latvia?'

The girl scowled at her and tapped her chest with her fist. 'I not a prostitute! I came here to study at college. They promise me if I do this, I can earn enough to cover costs.'

'But you're not studying.'

'I still working to cover bill for getting here.' The girl looked down at her lap. 'Going to take quite a while before I can go do what I came to do.'

Julia shrugged. She hadn't so far thought of escaping.

At first, she'd thought it would be just a matter of time before the door to her room would burst open and her mother or father would be standing there, looking relieved at having found her. Even rescue by the police wouldn't have been too bad. By the time it had slowly dawned on her that nobody was going to save her, she was already being enslaved by the heroin, and didn't want to miss her next fix – and that meant staying put.

For a moment, when Sara had come to her room, she'd thought she was going to be rescued, but that hope had been short-lived, when it quickly became apparent that Sara was like all the rest. Julia wondered where she was: she hadn't seen her around for some time. She realised she was finding it difficult to keep track of what day it was and how long she'd been held.

She'd heard Jackson talk about auctioning her off on Friday. The thought almost made her cry, but other voices in her head told her she had to lose her virginity some time. She wondered how David was, surprised that she hadn't thought much about him at all since she'd been taken.

He of all people, she thought miserably, might have raised a fuss about her absence.

\*

'He's not at home,' Miller announced later.

'Who isn't?' asked Jackson.

'Clifford. Housekeeper says the police called earlier and took him with them.'

Jackson pursed his lips. 'Better move the operation now.'

'Where to, if we can't use Clifford's place?'

'Who says we can't? He's not there to object is he. Take the girls over there. Make sure they take everything from Columbine Road. Paul can burn anything they leave. I'll sort Clifford out if he complains – when he gets home.'

'Okay, boss.'

Jackson frowned. 'They've had him a long time. Wonder what they're doing with him?'

'You don't think he'll grass on us, do you?' asked Miller.

'Not if he knows what's good for him. Still, maybe we should be prepared.'

\*

Jared Martin's house seemed unoccupied, the boarding still in place over the doors and ground-floor windows. Collins parked outside and they stood by the gate wondering how to get in.

'Let's try round the back,' said Pascal, taking one of the powerful torches they kept in the car and passing another to Collins. He led the way to the service road which gave access to the rear of the house. The gate opened easily and they walked through the overgrown garden to the rear of the house.

'Not exactly keen gardeners, the Martins,' he observed, 'unless, of course, he's not been around to do anything with the weeds.'

They found the cellar door.

'Looks like this is open,' Pascal said, shining his torch beam on the lock and bending down until he could peer at it closely. 'Scratches round the keyhole. Wonder if it's been picked.' He pushed the door open with his elbow and led the way into the house.

The place was cold and the air felt damp, still smelling of the fire.

'Up the stairs, I expect.' He led them past a gas meter up to the hall and kitchen.

They stood in the hall, gazing at the wreckage caused by the fire. It was clear that nobody had attempted a clear up since the fire service and CSIs left.

'Nobody home, I guess,' Pascal said. He turned and stared through the open doorway to Jared Martin's office.

'Everything still seems to be here,' he said. 'Wonder why the CSI didn't take the computer.'

Collins stepped past him into the room, pulling on a pair of latex gloves. She took a quick look round.

'There's a laptop and a desktop here. How about we take them with us – after all, if Jared Martin is a missing person, we'd be justified in examining them.'

Pascal shrugged, also gloving his hands. 'Can't see it doing any harm. Is there anything else lying around that might be useful? Especially any clues where he's gone.'

Collins searched through the papers on Martin's desk. She picked up the Air France brochure from where Bakker had left it.

'There's this, but it's got pages missing.'

Pascal was eyeing the telephone. He listened for a dialling tone but the instrument was dead.

'No luck with that. Which pages?' he asked, tapping the brochure.

She scanned the list of contents, showing regions and page numbers.

'The Caribbean.'

'That ties in with the information the Aruban police gave us, and the people at Heathrow. Anything interesting on the computers?'

'The power's off, so I can't look at the desktop machine. I'm wary of trying the laptop in case it's programmed to wipe the data. Need to get it to forensics; they can get in without risking damage.'

Pascal considered the point. 'Maybe we'd better take the laptop and ask Jimmy Tasker to come in and give the place a thorough once-over. He can pick up the desktop machine.'

'I'll get on to him as soon as we're outside.'

She picked up the laptop computer. Giving the room a last quick visual examination, she followed Pascal out towards the cellar stairs. Pascal waited for her to go through the door ahead of him.

Phut!

A hole appeared in the wall plaster close to his head. He turned and saw a man crouching on the staircase, pointing a silenced pistol at him.

Pascal let out a yell. 'Run!'

It seemed to disconcert the shooter long enough for him to dive through the door and slam it closed behind him. A turn-bolt on the inside allowed him to lock it, before hastening to follow Collins down the stairs.

Another shot blasted through the door panel, splinters flying off and lodging in Pascal's head and face. He didn't feel a thing in what was nothing more than an undignified dash to safety, the adrenaline pumping round his system. Collins was waiting at the door. He gestured to her impatiently.

'Get a move on! Don't wait for me,' he shouted, following her towards the gate.

Out of sight of the house, Pascal found his phone as he ran and summoned an Armed Response Vehicle with its crew of firearms-trained officers. By the time they'd run to the end of High Ridge Avenue, they were out of breath and blood was running down Pascal's neck and staining his suit. Collins took one look and phoned for an ambulance.

At the end of the street, he set Collins to watch the front of the house, and himself the rear, in the hope that they'd spot the shooter if he tried to leave. Sirens sounded in the distance, switching off as the ARV approached. It had a full crew of four officers, heavily protected with body armour. They donned helmets as they climbed out of the car close to Pascal. The vehicle commander approached.

'What's the situation, sir?'

Pascal was finding speech increasingly difficult as the adrenalin began to wear off. Collins explained while an ambulance made its way along the Avenue towards them. She beckoned it on quickly – more to get it out of the line of fire than because Pascal needed urgent treatment.

By the time Sergeant Donnelly of the Armed Response Team was in possession of the details, a paramedic had taken stock of Pascal's injuries and led him into the back of the ambulance. A second ARV was summoned, and Donnelly left one man to watch the front of the house, while leading the other two towards the back garden gate. Donnelly returned after posting his men in positions from which they could watch the house without exposing themselves to the armed man.

The CAD room had despatched another patrol car which arrived a few minutes ahead of the second ARV. The ambulance crew insisted that Pascal be taken into the A&E unit at the district hospital.

'Just stick some plasters on, or a bit of bandage or whatever,' he pleaded, but the paramedic was unmoved.

'I'll come with you, sir,' said Collins. 'In any case, we won't be able to pick up our car until the road is declared safe. It's right in the line of sight from the house.'

A new figure appeared at the ambulance's doors. Pascal raised his eyebrows.

'Hello, sir.'

DCI Steel looked concerned. 'Heard you'd been shot, George. Got over here as fast as I could. "Officer down", and all that. How are you?'

'Fine, sir,' Pascal replied through gritted teeth, 'but they're insisting I go into A&E before they let me get back here.' He nodded at the grinning paramedic.

'Very sensible,' said Steel. 'Go and get mollycoddled by some pretty nurses. I'll stay here and sort things out with the ART.'

It was not as reassuring to Pascal as Steel probably intended, but there was no escape.

Collins, still clutching Martin's laptop, sat next to the paramedic while Pascal was made to lie down on the stretcher on the other side of the vehicle.

What followed, after they reached the hospital, was, for Pascal, a painful hour until a houseman cheerfully began removing the splinters from the side of his head and face. Far too cheerful for Pascal's liking, but he kept the thought to himself. The young man injected anaesthetic in a number of places and waited for it to kick in.

I'm in danger of becoming one of those grumpy old men, Pascal thought. He glanced at Collins, sitting demurely against the side curtain of the cubicle into which he had been wheeled. She was achingly beautiful, he thought, mentally shaking his head. While the cheerful doctor pulled the wooden splinters from his face, he found himself thinking about his forthcoming date with Jane Ferrari. Someone he couldn't see seemed to speak to Collins. Pascal found himself becoming disorientated. Sounds were suddenly less coherent so he couldn't hear things clearly. It must be the bloody anaesthetic, he told himself. Collins had left.

The houseman suddenly stood back, looking over Pascal's head, then with a nod and a valedictory smile, he moved out of Pascal's field of view, his place taken a moment later by Jane Ferrari. She was wearing her green scrubs and was masked, but he recognised her eyes, and the concern in them.

'Jane,' he muttered, but it sounded unintelligible even to him.

'Just lie still, George. You've had a lot of anaesthetic, so you won't be feeling quite the thing, but I assure you, it's better than the feeling you'd get if we pulled this forest out of your head *without* it.'

He felt quite relaxed and almost fell asleep while she worked on him.

'George,' she said quietly when she finished.

He opened his eyes.

'About Saturday: you won't be feeling up to it,' she said, 'so can we postpone our dinner date? I think you should take a couple of day's sick-leave anyway,' she added.

He felt disappointed by the delay, realising suddenly that he had been looking forward to their... he supposed "date" was the appropriate term. But as for taking sick-leave... He attempted a shrug, which was not easy in his horizontal position, and anyway tugged at the wounds in his neck. Perhaps, he thought grudgingly, she was right. Another thing: he searched her face for clues as to what she meant by "it". His head was beginning to ache and the thoughts to swirl around like clouds on a stormy day. What "it" would he not be up for? Or, what "it" up for which he would not be? The words were muddled in his head. He'd have to eat and drink between now and then... so what else... ? He felt a warm rush of blood as a possibility occurred to him and shut his eyes.

When he opened them again, Ferrari had gone. It took a couple of hours before his face began to feel less numb.

It was similar to the way feeling gradually returned to lips or cheek after a dental anaesthetic, but on a grander scale. And as the numbness wore off, he felt the pain. He felt air move as someone entered the cubicle behind him. He opened his eyes and saw that Collins was back, looking almost cheerful. She stood beside the trolley.

'What's happening?' he asked her.

She must have deciphered his slurred speech. 'They say David Ellis has come off the ventilator. They think he's on the mend and coming out of the coma.'

'Some good news!' said Pascal. 'Once I can talk properly, we could go and have a word. See what he remembers.'

She gazed at him, straight-faced. 'I'm sorry, sir, were you trying to say something?'

'Don't try that! My speech is getting clearer all the time. Five minutes and we'll go.'

She shook her head, her expression innocent. 'Pardon? The doctors say you should have some time off to heal. Nobody said that interviewing witnesses had a convalescent effect.'

He scowled, or would have if the muscles of his face had been working cohesively.

'Tell you what, how would you like a cup of coffee?' she asked.

She was plainly going to ignore him for a while longer, so he reluctantly agreed.

'I think the machine only takes fifty-pence coins. Have you got any, sir?' she asked.

When he tried to feel in his hip pocket, she smiled, leaned over and stopped his hand.

'Only joking, sir. Wait here and I'll get the drinks.'

He lay back, the simple movement proving to involve more effort than he'd realised. He lifted his left hand experimentally and found he could touch his face. He felt dressings here and there. His flesh was sticky, whether with blood or something the doctors had put on. He wished he had a mirror.

Collins came back bearing coffee. She had thoughtfully put a drinking straw in one cardboard mug and slipped a hand under his head until he could suck some of the coffee into his mouth, which he realised was suddenly dry. He felt the hot liquid course through him and met her gaze as he sipped. There was concern in her eyes, but not too much. She was just a colleague, not a lover. He thought of Ferrari again. Darker and marginally less perfect in appearance than Collins, but he didn't think she'd break if he touched her, whereas his Detective Sergeant's beauty was as delicate as fine porcelain, and possibly just as fragile.

He wondered how Steel was getting on with the Armed Response Teams.

Collins laid his head back gently against the pillow when he'd finished drinking and watched as his eyes closed and he fell into a light sleep. It was one effect of coming down off an adrenaline high. She waited a while but he showed no signs of waking, so taking the laptop, she went up to the intensive care unit where David Ellis was slowly waking.

*

Pascal did not relish one day's incarceration, let alone two, when he woke up in his own bed on Friday morning. He'd agreed to take a day's sick leave, under protest, and asked Collins to tell Steel, but the prospect of a day spent in his own company chafed and around mid-morning proved too much. He decided to pay another visit to Walker.

John Walker lay on his bed feeling hungry and cold and miserable. His hair was growing lank and greasy and he needed a shave. From time to time, he shivered, despite the outside air temperature being around 20 degrees. There was a knock at the door. He pushed himself to his feet and opened it. Pascal was on the landing outside, his face covered with dressings over the wounds caused by the splinters.

'Come in, sir.' He led the way and indicated a chair. 'Help yourself. Want coffee?'

Pascal shook his head. 'Just a quick social call, John, to see how you were.'

'As you can see, I'm fine. What happened to you?'

Pascal looked round the room. Discarded clothing lay on the floor. Used dishes and plates which had the appearance of having been unwashed for several days were carelessly stacked in a corner. The room smelled of stale, sour sweat which made Pascal wrinkle his nose.

Pascal explained how he'd almost been shot. 'I feel like the Invisible Man, swathed in bandages,' he grumbled. 'They told me to take the day off and you know how difficult it is to argue when you're stuffed full of anaesthetic.'

Walker, who knew all too well how he felt when his nose was stuffed full of anaesthetic, nodded. 'Any news on my suspension?'

'I had a word with our illustrious leader yesterday, before this happened.' He pointed at his face. 'It seems he's passed the paperwork in your case on to Professional Standards, so no doubt you'll be hearing from them in the near future.' Pascal glanced round again, his gaze finishing up on Walker. 'I'd say your suspension is imminent.'

Walker shrugged. 'I guessed as much.'

'We got a replacement for you: fellow called Graham Bell from Norwich.'

Walker nodded. 'Yeah, I think I remember him. Fat geezer? Head the size and shape of a football?'

'Yes, that describes him. Anyway, John,' Pascal added, 'This might be the last time I can visit you until after Professional Standards has finished poking its nose in. Once you're suspended you'll only be allowed to talk to them.'

'Okay, sir. I understand. Got any leads in the missing girl case?'

Pascal looked at him while he considered how much to say. 'We think there's a place in town where girls are kept and forced into prostitution. We're trying to find out where, then we'll search the place.'

Walker kept his gaze lowered..

'Do you think the girl's there?'

'The girl?'

'Julia Fox. The one reported missing.'

Pascal considered. 'I don't know. Certainly, she was not a prostitute before she went missing. Hard to see why she would suddenly change.'

'Well, suppose... just suppose, she was made to take heroin until she had a habit, then made to work as a prostitute?' Walker knew he was talking too much. It was an opportunity to cleanse his conscience and he was taking it, in the guise of putting constructive suggestions to Pascal. Having started, it was difficult to know where to stop.

'I'd have thought by now that she'd have been spotted by Vice and at least had a caution,' he said mildly,

'Only if she was on the streets,' said Walker.

'Surely, no pimp would keep his girls off the streets? If they're off the street they're not earning.'

'Pimp? No: but – perhaps the bloke running them is very discreet, and only supplies the girls to regular customers whom he knows?' Walker could feel himself blush at the thought of how close this was to the truth.

'Maybe,' said Pascal, his bottom lip jutting in a sign of incredulity. 'But is there a place in Breydon or around, where he could do that?'

Walker didn't answer at once. He wondered whether he should answer at all, but a few moments' thought made him see that he was doomed anyway. Once Professional Standards got their teeth in him, they would inevitably find out where his money had gone, and he would be reported to the CPS. At least if he gave Pascal the information he wanted now, the girl – all the girls – would be rescued sooner. It might count in his favour.

'There's the private members club behind *The Kitty Klub*,' he said.

'Obviously, we know about that,' said Pascal blandly.

'Right,' said Walker.

'Nowhere else that you can think of?' Pascal grinned. 'I only ask you, John, because a young fellow like you is likely to be an expert on the hot-spots for debauchery. Far too old myself,' he added.

'Of course, sir,' said Walker, managing to grin. 'I suppose if I were still on the job, I'd recommend raiding *Kittens*.'

'I shall bear your tip in mind, if we run out of ideas ourselves.'

Pascal got to his feet.

'Well, must dash. Villains to nick, you know.' He stood close to Walker and stared into his eyes, smelling his sour breath. 'You're looking a bit rough, John. I'd go and get some help.'

He turned and let himself out, glad of the fresh air, and headed back to the office, via *The Kitty Klub*. He wanted another look at the exterior of the building. He figured he should have a word with the Field Intelligence Officer himself, find out what was known about the place and Derrick Jackson, and what wasn't. Something was bothering him, and he couldn't figure out what.

The FIO didn't have any information about *Kittens*, though he had a fairly recent photograph of Derrick Jackson. Pascal took some copies back to his team.

# CHAPTER 13

Friday evening. Julia and the other girls, including the pregnant one, were taken in Ernest Miller's van, still pungent with the smell of bleach, from Gordon Clifford's house, to which they had all suddenly been moved, to *Kittens*.

The girls were ushered into the small door at the rear of the premises. The ones who'd been there before were taken straight through into the changing rooms while the new girls were shown around by Ernest Miller. The tour covered the bedrooms, bathrooms, and concluded in the changing room, where the girls could tidy themselves up between punters. Finally, Miller surveyed them.

'Except for Fiona, here,' he said, pointing at Julia, 'you're going in there, now – ' he pointed at the door to the main room ' – and the rules are that don't get another hit until Mr Jackson says so. You'll be watched, and I can tell you he never approves another hit until you've serviced at least half a dozen.' He allowed his glance to range over them. 'You shouldn't have any trouble tonight. There's a stag party coming in, and they will all want to prove their manliness. The more obliging you are, the more favourably Mr Jackson is going to look on you when you want another fix.' He turned and pointed to a table by the door, on which stood a box. 'Condoms over there. Make sure you use 'em. The *only* person you go bareback with is Mr Jackson himself.' He opened the door, and signalled to the girls that they should go through into the other room. As Julia began to follow them, he took her arm and held her back.

She didn't like the smile on his face.

'Not you, girl,' he said. 'You come with me.'

Since Miller had mentioned another hit, Julia had begun to feel the need. He grabbed a handful of condoms from the box by the door and led her along the corridor to a bedroom.

He pointed at the bed. 'Sit down and wait,' he told her.

He left her alone.

A few minutes later, a middle-aged man she'd not seen before came in and looked at her unsmilingly. She wondered briefly what her virginity had cost him.

She remembered to smile while he covered her with his hairy torso and finally thrust past her hymen with an uncaring heave before finishing. She was glad it had been so quick. There had not been as much pain as she'd expected.

Afterwards, Ernest took her into the main room. The place was full of men, varying in age from twenties to seventies. She looked from one to another, wondering who she'd be fucking next. One of the young men, who seemed to be the focus of their attentions, was grabbed by a couple of his mates and propelled towards her.

'Here, love,' said one the two holding the arms of the man in the middle, 'this is the one getting married on Saturday, so teach him a couple of tricks to surprise his wife with.'

She smiled and nodded. 'Are you both coming too?' she asked.

'You don't mind?' asked the man.

She saw Jackson a couple of yards to her right and raised her voice slightly to make sure he heard.

'The more the merrier, I always say.'

The big man stared at her, his mouth open for a moment. She could smell the beer on their clothes and the one in the middle seemed to be not very focussed. His friend turned to the others in the room.

'You hear that, guys, this one wants us all.'

Julia expelled a breath. What had she let herself in for? She swallowed and led the men, two more joining the original three, into the bedroom area.

Jackson, she noticed, was smiling approvingly, and that was all that mattered.

The 'stag' was given the 'honour' of having her first. He was fairly gentle with her and probably because of his inebriation, or maybe the fact of having an audience, he took quite a long time. Meanwhile, she was obliged to use her mouth on the one who'd been doing all the talking. Thereafter, she lost count as one after another took their place in the queue. She'd put the condoms on the bed sheet and told them all to use them when they fucked her, but she couldn't always check and when all five men had exhausted themselves, there were still a couple of unused prophylactics on the sheet. She couldn't remember how many there had been to start with.

They left her, and she slid off the bed. She was in pain with bruises in her groin and round her mouth. After the first, the other four hadn't cared much whether they hurt her. She picked up the unused condoms, and made her way to the changing room to clean herself before going back into the main room. The need for another fix was that much greater now. The clientele had changed, with most of the stag party having left *Kittens* while she'd been busy.

She glanced hopefully at Jackson. He smiled but waggled a finger at her as he came over.

'I hope you're being a good girl. The man who had you first was pleased, anyway. Just be careful – we don't want you catching a baby, or a disease,' he said. 'I had to let the last girl who used the name Fiona go because we couldn't use her here any more. She was pregnant and diseased. She works the streets now. Let that be a warning to keep yourself clean and never forget the condoms.'

'Except with you, Mr Miller said.'

'I've had a vasectomy, so if you end up pregnant I can prove it won't be mine.'

'Can I have another hit now, Mr Jackson?' she asked.

'You've only done five. Go over there and give that chap what he wants.' Jackson pointed at the tall, dark-haired, jaded rake who was crouching pensively over a glass of whisky, staring at nothing in particular.

\*

Walker had decided to use his new privileges at *Kittens*. He might figuratively only have four pence in his pocket, with another party due next week, but a succession of empty days meant he was in desperate need of the sort of distractions he found in the club.

Miller had been taking a turn on the door, and nodded him through with a conspiratorial wink. Inside, Jackson smiled when he saw him, and laid out a line of coke. With the crystals lining his nose, he looked round the room.

'Fancy anyone in particular, John?' asked Jackson by his side.

Walker pointed at one as the cocaine kicked in. She smiled at Walker, and led him through into the bedrooms. The girl had a few rough edges, but she was new, and he figured Derrick would see them rubbed off in the next few weeks. But she was a nice change from the ones who'd been round the block a few times, he thought. They were kind of more hungry, keener to please.

The girl smiled a lot, didn't say much, and performed efficiently enough. Her few words were spoken in a strange accent, and he wondered where she came from. She smiled and remained politely silent when he asked her, and after they returned to the main room, she simply moved on to someone else.

He did his second line of coke then. He felt amazingly good and virile. Ernest put a fresh glass of scotch in front of him, and after a while, another of the new girls came over. Walker was dimly aware that Jackson was watching him closely and wondered why. The girl's accent was local. He studied her for a moment. She looked like a teenager, blonde, with clear, tanned skin, nice breasts thrusting against a thin, low-cut lacy top, and a black miniskirt that looked like suede. Sexy, bare legs, and black strappy sandals with four-inch heels.

She was little more communicative than the previous girl. She handled him well, took him into one of the bedrooms fitted out with beds and washbasins, and allowed him to fuck her. Her smile had remained fixed throughout. He didn't want to know what Derrick did to make the girls so compliant, but it was certainly one reason he kept returning. He had pulled his trousers back on while she watched him from the bed, her legs still spread and her skirt flipped up to reveal her nakedness. Almost, he was tempted to go back for seconds, but he doubted he could get it up again so soon. Later, perhaps.

Then she surprised him. Her smile suddenly vanished, he saw her stomach convulse and she made a dash for the washbasin, where she was sick. At another time, outside the club, he would have done something to help, perhaps take her to hospital, but inside *Kittens*, she was Derrick's problem. He'd be livid if anyone interfered with his property – and that included the girls. Walker knew he ran an exclusive stable. It was part of the attraction of the club – you knew the girls hadn't been working the streets between party-nights. So he'd left her, throwing up into the basin, mentioning the matter to Jackson when he got outside.

Jackson got Ernest to go and see her a few minutes later and give her another hit of heroin.

*

'Where's Jared Martin?' Pascal wondered aloud. 'He wasn't home when his house was set on fire, and hasn't surfaced since.'

Collins shrugged. 'Don't know, sir.'

'I fancy another look round his house. There's something odd going on there.'

It was Saturday morning. Pascal had not slept well after his day's sick leave. His face was still dotted with dressings and he was rubbing his eyes as he entered the CID office and found Collins concentrating on something she was doing on her computer. He moved to stand behind her.

'What have you got there, Alison?' he asked, studying the monitor which bore small icons representing men, women, homes, factories, cars and telephones, with a myriad of lines joining them.

'It's a bit of software I got into at Police HQ,' she said. 'You hope it will reveal a connection which was not apparent before. Let me show you.'

Pascal dragged the chair from the unused workstation round the end of the unit so he could watch her screen more comfortably.

'Let's take our psychopathic Dutchman for instance,' she began. 'He left a thumbprint at both the murder scene, on Sara Martin's car, and at her home, on the letterbox. When he half-killed Aspazia at the Weston Arms, having had to book in with his passport and therefore his proper name, Danny Bakker, he left more fingerprints, allowing us to be sure he was chief suspect for both the arson and the murder.'

As she spoke, she moved the cursor around her screen, pointing at different symbols which illustrated the points she was making.

'Here's another example,' she continued. 'We know Ernest Miller owns a white van, which he keeps at the back of *The Kitty Klub*.'

'Yes.'

'Well, if someone else was reported as driving the same white van, then it would establish a connection between that person and Miller, and indirect connections with Jackson and *The Kitty Klub*.'

'I think I see,' said Pascal.

'A real example is the connection established between Miller and Paul, thanks to Dora/Aspazia. She identifies Paul with the drugs and pimping, Jackson, *The Kitty Klub*, and *Kittens*. We can now surmise reasonably that all these things are connected, and it seems that Derrick Jackson is the focus.'

Pascal glanced at her then back at the screen. He tapped a cartoon male identified by the letters JW.

'Is that our John?' he asked.

'I'm afraid so. He's got to be treated as suspect for now, since we know he uses *The Kitty Klub*. I think there's a good chance he uses *Kittens,* too.'

Pascal nodded, reviewing in his mind what he might have told Walker when he visited him.

'I think we've got enough information to go for a warrant on the club and *Kittens*. I don't suppose your nifty little program contains any clues to the whereabouts of our missing schoolgirl? I'm getting really worried about her.'

Collins shook her head, making her ponytail swing across her neck. 'Not at the moment. But I agree: there's absolutely no information come in about her, despite the Press conference. It's very worrying. Graham's out chatting to his contacts. Hope something will turn up soon.'

'Me too,' Pascal nodded. 'Have we obtained the plans of the building?'

Collins nodded, reaching round onto Bell's desk for them.

'You can see all the rooms here,' she said, pointing.

'Not identified by purpose,' muttered Pascal.

'No,' she agreed, tracing the rooms out with a long fingernail. 'These look like the main rooms of *The Kitty Klub,* though. There's the bar. Behind the bar there's quite a large room, and the end wall has one door through it into this whole suite of rooms behind.'

There was a central corridor leading from the door, with small rooms to the right and a doorway on the left which led into another large room.

'It doesn't take much imagination to see these as bedrooms on the right and some sort of club room on the left,' said Pascal.

He pulled at his lower lip for a few moments.

'We've seen John Walker coming out of *The Kitty Klub* on tape, and he's mentioned *Kittens* to me by name, so he obviously knows about it. I suppose the obvious thing will be to talk to him about it.' He glanced at his watch. 'Maybe tomorrow.'

'I've a bit more to do with this software, if you don't mind, sir.' She was already making small changes to the pattern on the screen.

'I hope it solves the case, Alison,' said Pascal.

The telephone in his office began to ring. He crossed the corridor and answered it.

'Pascal.'

He listened intently and made some notes before hanging up and returning to the CID office.

'That phone call, DS Collins, was from our colleagues at Heathrow Airport. They trawl passenger lists routinely, and guess what.'

'What?' she asked, allowing him his thunder.

'Jared Martin has gone to Aruba, which, they tell me, is in the exotically-named Netherlands Antilles, a cough and a spit from the coast of South America.'

'Sounds like the sort of place you'd go if you were doing a bunk.'

'Or trying to keep out of someone's reach... Like Danny Bakker's.'

They both absorbed the information silently for a moment or two.

'What does your chart show us about him?' asked Pascal.

Collins looked at the screen. 'Not much,' she said. 'He and Sara Martin jointly owned 17 High Ridge Avenue. Danny Bakker attempted to burn the house and, we think, killed Sara.'

'Why?' asked Pascal. 'Why would Bakker kill Sara and attempt to set light to the Martin's home? You don't just do something like that for no good reason.'

'What did, or does, Martin do for a living?' Collins asked.

Pascal stared at her. 'He's a financial advisor.'

'So might he have been into money laundering?'

Pascal thumped the table. 'Of course! Well,' he continued more calmly, 'it's a good idea. Very possible. Does your chart thing give any clues as to who he might have been laundering money for?'

'No,' she replied, 'sorry.'

'Can you look into Martin's business dealings, and see if there's anything to support the money laundering theory, and if so who he does it for. Who was paying whom, and for what.'

'Can we get a warrant to search Martin's house on the basis of our suspicions?' she asked.

The phone in Pascal's office rang again. He went and answered it. Collins, curious, leaned on the frame of his open door. She saw his eyebrows arch in surprise, and he fixed his gaze on her as if willing her to hear what he was being told. He slowly sank into his chair and beckoned her into the room, towards the other one.

'Well, it's funny that you should ask,' he said into the phone, 'but we have our suspicions that Jared Martin might have some involvement with money laundering. We're not sure who he's doing it for, but there might be a Dutch connection, since we think a Dutchman killed his wife and set fire to his house.'

He listened again, nodding and grunting from time to time. 'No, not enough proof to go to court with.'

Collins found the one-sided nature of the conversation very frustrating.

'Not enough for extradition either,' Pascal said into the phone, 'but of course, if the Aruban authorities wanted to expel him, deport him back to Britain, I'm sure we'd be delighted to provide a taxi service from the airport back here to the nick.'

He reached for scrap paper and a pen. Reading upside down, Collins guessed he was writing down an international telephone number.

He hung up at last and smiled.

'It's like buses, isn't it! You wait for ages, then two come along at once.'

She guessed he was talking about the phone calls.

'Good news, sir?'

'Jared Martin is in Aruba, as we've just been told. He's under surveillance because the police picked up a known con-man called Abel Scarman – what an unlovely name – who is, as they put it delicately, helping them with their enquiries.'

He clasped his fingers.

'Anyway, he's apparently told them about Martin, whom he met on an earlier visit to the island and decided to target. Martin was looking for a nice new property, and Scarman offered to help him buy the British Consul's official residence.'

'Did the British Consul know this?'

'No. It's not his to sell, anyway. Scarman went through the process of setting up a website that looked like a realtor's, and even included video footage from inside the house. Not difficult when it's only used a few times a year.'

'And Martin was persuaded to buy it?'

'Martin was persuaded to wire Scarman half a million dollars to buy it for him.'

'And what happened?'

'Well, it's a common practice of hustlers to make sure that if someone pays a lot of money to them, they get something. That way, there isn't the same legal comeback.'

She frowned, puzzled.

'Suppose you were a book collector, and I said I could get my hands on a rare copy of the Lindisfarne Gospels, not in a hard cover. Even showed you something that looked like them. You hand over your ten million or whatever they'd be worth and I hand you a book – a publisher's remainder paperback on the subject of the Lindisfarne Gospels. In law, you've agreed to pay ten million for a paperback book. It would be stupid, but you got what you paid for. Contract agreed and fulfilled.'

'So Scarman did buy a property with a few dollars of Martin's money?'

'He did. Forwarded the deeds in impressive pink ribbon, but they were the deeds of a run-down plantation-worker's shack. Scarman pockets nearly half a million dollars, and Martin is the owner of a ruin.'

She chewed her cheek, trying not to laugh. Martin's misfortunes amounted to a bad case of *schadenfreude*.

'You know,' Collins said, 'if the half-million had been embezzled, that could explain why Bakker seems to have been after him.'

'If Martin was supposed to be laundering money between someone here and someone... in Holland – Bakker's employer – for goods or services supplied...' said Pascal, thinking aloud.

'We know there are links, albeit tenuous in some places, between Martin and Bakker, Bakker and Sara Martin, Sara and Gordon Clifford, and Clifford and Derrick Jackson's clubs.'

'Tenuous is the word!'

'Yes, well, Jackson is supplying girls. We know from Aspazia that many are from the Baltic states, and they are forced into heroin habits.'

Pascal nodded. 'Jackson has to get his girls and drugs from somewhere – someone! – and Holland has a reputation for both.' He smiled at her. 'Do you know? I think we might have just solved this lot, the murder, the abduction, drugs, prostitutes... I might even buy us all a drink on the way home this evening.' He glanced at her, deadpan. 'A coke or a tomato juice or something, of course.'

She stared at him, amused, and shook her head. 'I realise what a signal honour that is, sir, but I'm seeing someone as soon as I get away from here. Thanks all the same.'

Pascal seemed surprised. She smiled and went back to her office. He watched her go, reminded of the fact that, though his forthcoming dinner date with Jane Ferrari wasn't far off, it seemed far too long to wait. He wanted to see her now and share his exultation.

*

If some of those entering *The Kitty Klub* seemed a bit old to be enjoying that kind of entertainment, thought John Walker on Monday night, at least nobody seemed to have raised the matter publicly. Perhaps, because the older customers were hardly seen once they were inside. Ernest stood surreptitiously on guard near the hidden door to *Kittens*, taking the additional cost of admission from the men who came to enjoy its services.

Walker approached him nervously, knowing that he had insufficient cash for the usual charge, and was relieved when Ernest merely winked at him and waved him past. The knowing way Derrick Jackson and his employees grinned and winked at him was frightening: they were treating him as a brother-in-arms, on their side of the legal fence, where he'd never really been.

Jackson saw him and waved him over to the small bar where he spent most party nights.

'Everything all right, John?' asked the big blond man.

Walker nodded.

Jackson placed a glass of whisky in front of him. 'Don't look so miserable, then. After all, you just moved up the scale a bit.'

Walker took a large mouthful of the liquor. 'What do you mean?'

'One thing you'll realise, if you haven't already, is that coppers are the least of our worries. Don't wish to cause offence, but let me just say, you're well out of it.'

Walker drank again. 'I'm not "out of it".'

Jackson grunted. 'You will be. You're not the only friend I have in the force, you know.'

'Meaning?'

'Meaning I can tell your fortune to some extent. What I can't tell doesn't really matter.' He reached under the counter and pulled out a small mirror, blade and a drinking straw. From his pocket, he took a small plastic bag filled with white crystals. 'Let's start as we mean to go on, eh. You help yourself to this, and I'll line you up one of the new girls.'

Walker felt embarrassed at the suggestion that he could be bought for a line of coke and a prostitute. Deep down in his mind, he knew it was true, and hated the fact. Jackson had left him to take the drug and now reappeared with the same tanned and blonde girl he'd had on Wednesday night, with the Norfolk accent. She waited until he'd dusted the surplus crystals from around his nostrils, then smiled at him.

'Hi, I'm Fiona. Would you like to fuck?' She smiled and ran a finger down hr skirt and over her pudendum.

He drained his glass, watching her over its rim. Below her short skirt, she was bare-legged, and wore four-inch high heeled shoes. He felt the pleasant ache in his groin which presaged an erection and figured it was time to put the girl's availability to use.

'Okay, lead me to paradise, or at least a little room with a bed.'

She smiled briefly, turned and led the way through the door to the private bedrooms. Walker saw Jackson watching, still with the same little knowing grin. Something in his mind tried to drag him back from the abyss, but he set it firmly aside.

In the room, Fiona sat on the bed and wriggled until she was in the middle of the mattress. She spread her legs apart and leaned back on her elbows.

'How do you want me?' she asked.

Her position was very inviting, very arousing.

Walker grinned. 'Just the way you are.'

He shed his shoes, trousers and jacket and climbed between her legs, pushing her skirt out of the way. Suddenly, his need was urgent. He didn't stop to remove her thong – simply pulling it to one side while she expertly rolled a condom on him – before plunging into her.

Afterwards, he rolled to one side, removed the condom and threw it in a waste bin, while she took the opportunity to cover herself. It had been good again. Maybe in a minute or two, he might be able to do it a second time. Hell, she probably was expert at giving men erections.

He turned his head to look at her. She was watching him carefully.

'Can you get me hard again?' he asked.

'I can try,' she replied.

She shuffled down the bed and he felt her fingers, then her lips engulf him. Nearly twenty minutes passed before her ministrations could be said to have borne fruit. She pulled her thong off and rolled another condom on him before holding up her skirt, straddling his thighs and impaling herself on him. She bounced up and down and worked her internal muscles for another quarter of an hour, while leaning forward to let him handle her breasts under her blouse. He was beginning to worry that he might not be able to come when thankfully, he felt the tightening in his testicles which preceded his orgasm, and moments later, filled the condom.

She lifted herself off him, found her thong where she'd dropped it beside the bed, and straightened her blouse. Walker took the condom off. She took it from him carefully and dropped it in the bin.

'Where are you from?' he asked.

'Where would you like me to be from?'

'Your accent sounds local.'

He saw a flush appear under her makeup, which suggested to him that he was correct.

'I might be.'

He studied her appearance, and tried to imagine her without the makeup.

'Is Fiona your real name?'

She shrugged. 'Does it matter?'

'Are you seventeen?'

She stared at him, swallowed, nodded slowly. 'How old would you like me to be?'

With the sex out of the way, Walker was beginning to think again. There'd been the school photograph of Julia Fox, taken not long ago. He hadn't paid it much attention, and she was a brunette while Fiona was blonde. On the other hand, women could change their appearance nearly as often as their handbags. She was the right age and height, and she was local. 'Fiona' was probably not this girl's real name, he reasoned. He began to feel alarmed. If Fiona was Julia, and she found out he was a copper – even if he wasn't exactly on the strength – there would be hell to pay.

Unless he kept his mouth shut.

The consequences of telling Pascal his suspicions were frightening: he would be certain to discover the extent of Walker's complicity, and that would be that. He would undoubtedly go to jail, and he didn't think he'd survive well in prison.

He was probably already lost, he thought, studying the girl who was sitting on the edge of the bed, presumably anxious to move on to her next customers.

'What are you using?' he asked her suddenly.

She turned to him. 'Heroin.'

'Injecting?'

'Of course.'

'How long?'

She stared at him suspiciously. 'Why do you want to know?'

He shrugged. 'If it's not long, you could be helped to get off it. There are treatment centres.'

'You're using coke. Why don't you get off it if it's so easy?' she asked him.

'Did you use smack before you came here?' he asked her, ignoring her attempt to turn the subject, 'because my guess is, they got you hooked on it to make you do what you do. I started using a long time ago, and nobody made me. There's more hope for you.'

She looked at him silently. Her eyes were yellowish, the pupils tiny. He sighed.

'If you can keep me in smack, I'll fuck you as much as you like. I'll come and live with you,' she added.

He shook his head. 'No. Can't do that, but I could help you get off the stuff.'

'How?'

'I've got... contacts. Rehab clinics.'

'Yeah? And what do you get out of it?'

He couldn't answer the question in any way which she'd believe.

'Nothing,' he muttered.

'You must think I'm stupid,' she said scornfully, 'and I don't care if you tell Mr Jackson I said that.'

Walker watched her check her face in the mirror and make adjustments to her appearance before leaving the room. He dressed himself and used the toilet before following her.

Jackson was waiting for him.

'Everything all right?' he asked.

Walker shrugged. 'Fine.'

Jackson studied him while laying out another line of cocaine on the mirror on the counter. 'Girl all right? Do what you wanted?'

'Yes. Thanks,' said Walker.

'You seem a bit depressed, old boy,' said Jackson, 'here you are: see if this brightens up your life.' He held out another drinking straw.

Walker looked at it, glanced at the white powder, then back up into Jackson's eyes. He could handle another snort of coke, no worries, but he thought of the girl and what she'd said. The remains of his last snort must still have been sloshing round in his brain because suddenly he shook his head.

'No thanks, Derrick. Some other time, maybe.'

Jackson studied him from under his brows.

'Not thinking of going straight on me, are you, John?'

'I don't think I could now, do you?'

Jackson thought for a moment then grinned, shaking his head. 'No. I think you're well and truly in the bag. Have another drink. Cheap at twice the price.'

Walker realised he wasn't talking about the cost of whisky

## CHAPTER 14

DC Graham Bell sat in the back seat of a big police Volvo estate. Two uniformed constables sat in front of him, both wearing stab vests and all the accoutrements of the modern police officer on night patrol. They were parked in a narrow road which led off the main east-west route through Breydon into the heart of the main shopping area.

Diagonally opposite was the large block which housed *The Kitty Klub*. More directly opposite was Wickham Street, the dead-end service road running down the side of the club building.

They were keeping a watch on the club premises, with a view to following anyone who left, in the hope of finding out where the girls they were fairly sure worked there lived.

Sometime after two a.m. on Saturday morning, Bell's eyes started to close. He shook himself awake and rummaged in the bag on the empty seat beside him, produced a small thermos flask, and poured coffee into the cap. He rummaged further, in search of biscuits, but found only an empty wrapper. Two hundred yards away, the lights of a 24-hour supermarket illuminated the pavement. He stared at the club. There were no signs of activity. He tried to decide whether he could risk a dash to the shop. He drank his coffee but the hunger for biscuits or something else to eat would not go away. It was the same every time he did surveillance: somehow, whatever supplies he took with him, at some point they would all be consumed and he would want more.

He refilled his cup from the flask and sipped the drink. He glanced again at the dashboard clock and at the street entrance of *The Kitty Klub*. A sound filled the air, but it was only one of the customised vehicles the council used to sweep the pavements. It came round the corner ahead of him and trundled past his car towards the shopping centre behind him. After it was gone, the quiet of the night returned. His stomach rumbled.

'Sod it!' he muttered. 'I'm just popping out to that supermarket,' he told the other two. 'Shan't be a minute.'

The one in the left-hand seat glanced round. 'You'd best shift your arse, Graham. If anyone does come out, we might have to move quickly.'

Bell peered through the sodium-lit night and opened his door.

He climbed stiffly out of the car, pulling his trousers up by the belt, over his belly and walked quickly towards the supermarket. Inside, he hurried to the shelf where they kept pre-packed sandwiches, grabbing three packs bearing *Reduced* labels, having reached their sell-by date, and two packets of chocolate biscuits.

As he stepped outside again, he glanced along the street towards the Volvo, in time to see headlamps appear at the end of Wickham Street, and Miller's white van turn right, heading westwards.

'Shit!' Bell muttered, running. The Volvo's engine fired up and the car began edging forward as he grabbed the door handle and flung himself inside. By the time he sat up, the van was almost out of sight.

'Told you to be quick, Graham, old son,' said the front-seat passenger in a voice lacking in sympathy. 'It's Sod's Law that the minute you bugger off on a bit of private business, the shit hits the fan.'

'Thank you,' said Bell. 'I'll know who to come to next time I want advice. Now, don't lose 'em!'

'We haven't lost him yet. Hold on!'

Bell had only enough time to grab the handle over the door before the big car swung round a corner and entered

Columbine Road in time to see the van stop outside a dilapidated-looking former guest house.

Miller got out of the van and went up to the front door, letting himself in with a key. He reappeared a few minutes later, got back in the van and moved off. The Volvo, some four hundred yards behind followed it steadily. After a couple of miles, it turned into the driveway of a large old house. They stopped the Volvo short of the gates and Bell got out.

Leaving the uniformed officers in the car, he advanced cautiously until he could see up the drive. The rear doors of the van were open, and around a dozen girls were climbing out. A smile of satisfaction curled his lips. He noted the address and went back to the car. They waited to see what would happen next.

Twenty minutes passed with only the sound of the turned-down police radio breaking the silence in the car. Bell found a new packet of chocolate digestives, which he opened and began munching. The driver looked round.

'Hope you're not going to leave crumbs in the car, Graham.'

Bell scowled at him, feeling a build-up of gas in his colon, and squeezed the cheeks of his bottom together in order to prevent its escape into the vehicle. The pressure proved too great and with a gentle and lengthy hiss, the malodorous fruits of his digestive processes filled the air with an eye-watering stench. A moment later, both driver and front-seat passenger stared at each other, shook their heads, then turned to glare accusingly at him, before turning back and opening the car's windows.

Moments later, the van emerged from the drive.

The police waited until he had driven to the end of the street before going after him. Bell was twitching with concern that they wouldn't lose their target.

'Relax, Graham. You're in the care of professionals now,' said the observer. He called Control and began a running commentary on their direction.

'Ask Control to let us have the helicopter,' Bell told him.

The observer stopped his commentary and looked round at him, frowning.

'Have you no faith in us, *Detective* Constable? *We* know what we're doing, you know, and the chopper costs the Force hundreds every minute it's in the air.'

His hand rose automatically and gripped the handle above his door as the driver swung the big car round a tight corner.

'We're here,' the driver interjected. He pulled up sharply, some way back from the van, which had turned up the drive into the garden of a house. Bell glanced at his watch. Almost half-past two in the morning. He jotted down the address in his notebook, guessing that Pascal would want to hit all the addresses simultaneously. When he had done, he looked up at the two officers in the front seats and grinned twistedly.

'Um. I don't suppose you'd mind if we hang around here for a while, just in case they come out?'

The driver turned in his seat to look at Bell over his shoulder. 'How long is "a while" likely to be?'

Bell shrugged. 'An hour? Two?'

The driver and his partner looked at each other before the former turned back to Bell. 'How about thirty minutes? I mean, our activity log is looking a bit thin, and if all it says, when we get back to the nick, is *sat around waiting for a while,* Sergeant Henslow is going to be a bit curious, like. He'll suspect us of wasting police time.'

'You could always tell him you were helping CID with their enquiries.'

The driver regarded him askance for a moment.

'Okay then. Just thirty minutes. We'll try to keep the sergeant off our back – and yours.'

'Oh, for fuck's sake!' muttered Bell as he slumped into his seat. 'All right then. Make it an hour."

'Forty-five minutes, Graham,' said the driver, "but if you fart again, you'll be chucked out onto the pavement.'

*

Jared Martin woke up when there was a knock on his hotel bedroom door. Sunlight blasted through the bedroom window. He was in a typical room containing a double bed, a dressing-table-cum-chest of drawers, a chair and a coffee table. He stood up and ran his hand through his hair. He was still wearing the clothes he'd arrived in. His suitcase was in a corner of the room and appeared to be untouched. He opened the door and found Serena in the corridor.

She had abandoned the fabulous ethnic silks of the previous evening for a fairly unexceptional cream linen mannish-style jacket and trouser suit. He thought she looked very elegant.

'Are you feeling more awake now?' she asked as he closed the door behind her and pointed her at the chair. He sat on the bed.

He nodded. 'Yes, thanks. Thank you for looking after me.'

She shrugged.

'Have you thought about what happened to your property?' Serena asked.

He shook his head. 'No. I must have been tricked by the man I trusted to act as my agent.'

She sat at the table across from him, nodding. 'It seems very likely. Did you give him a lot of money?'

'Yes. More than I can afford to lose. It was my retirement home – or supposed to be.'

'You planned on staying on Aruba for the rest of your life?'

He grinned wryly. 'If you'll have me. Would you like some tea?'

She eyed the small kettle and packets of dehydrated flavourings. 'I'd be surprised if you found tea among that lot. We tend to drink coffee here.'

He searched through the sachets and grinned ruefully. 'I think you're right.'

'Let's go and find a café which sells tea. I prefer it, too, but then I'm not typical.'

He glanced at her and nodded briefly. 'I can see that.'

She smiled at him. 'I doubt that.' She waved her hand at his rumpled clothes. 'Did you want to change or clean your teeth or anything?'

He caught sight of himself in the mirror. 'Do you mind waiting while I make myself presentable?'

'Okay. I'll wait downstairs in the lobby.'

Half an hour later, they sat on tubular metal chairs either side of a circular metal table outside a pavement café.

She sipped her tea and gazed at him over the rim of her mug. 'I'd have thought, if an Englishman was going to retire to the Caribbean, he would have gone to one of the ones with British traditions, like St Kitts or Tobago, rather than a Dutch one.'

'I – I suppose it seems more logical.'

'So why come here?'

'I wanted to make a really fresh start.'

She sipped again and raised an eyebrow. 'You're not hiding from anyone, are you? Or wanted by the police?'

For a moment, he glanced down at the table-top. 'No, no! I told you, my wife was recently murdered, and I want to put distance, both physically and emotionally, between that and my future.'

She nodded and emptied her mug. 'Do you know what the main industry on this island is, Mr Martin?'

He stared at her. 'I suppose it's sugar cane and bananas and stuff.' He frowned. 'How do you know my name?'

She smiled, unconcerned by his sudden suspicion. 'It was on the deeds to your property which you showed me last night. The sugar cane industry has gone. Once the slaves were freed, there was no-one to work the fields. Not helped by the falling world price of sugar, which was the last nail in most plantations' coffins.'

'Oh, I see.'

'Is it a problem if I know you are Jared Martin, from England, hoping to remain in Aruba?'

'No, of course not,' he said quickly, his eyes flicking away from hers.

He drank the last of his tea and put the mug down. 'I suppose if I really do own that tin shack, I'd better go back and see what work has to be done to at least make it habitable.'

'What will you do about the man who was your agent?'

'I don't know. Probably nothing.'

She seemed surprised. 'I know this isn't England, but we *do* have a police force here, and if you've been defrauded of your money, that's a crime. You should really report it.'

He clasped his hands and shook his head.

'I don't want to make any difficulties before I've been on the island five minutes.'

'But you said it was a lot of money.'

'Yes, but — '

'Surely you can't afford *not* to involve them?'

He shrugged, not knowing what to say. If he went to the police, it would bring him to their attention, and there was always a risk that news of his presence on the island might leak out. If he didn't report the loss, it would seem suspicious, and Serena would be only the first to wonder why, and how he could afford to write off what amounted to nearly half a million dollars. That sort of information travelled fast, and would probably get back to the police eventually anyway.

He tried to smile reassuringly. 'Maybe in a few days, when I've found my way around... '

She studied his face for a moment. 'Would you like me to take you back to your... shack?'

'Yes please. The sooner I get started on it the sooner it will be done.'

She rose elegantly to her feet, waiting for him to join her, then led the way to her car.

The windswept ruin that was his new home seemed nearer than it had the night before. They left the car at the gate and walked up the overgrown path to the building. He had to push hard to open the door, but at last it opened on screeching hinges. There was a flurry of movement which suggested animals were using the place as a squat, and indeed the floor was covered with evidence of their presence.

'Watch for snakes,' Serena reminded him helpfully.

Whatever had been there had gone into deep cover. Martin and Serena stepped gingerly into the living space. Old furniture stood there, broken and crooked. An ancient, deep stone sink stood on bricks against one wall, but there was no sign of any plumbing. A rusty bucket under the outlet gave him a clue that water supply and waste management was going to be crude, to say the least. He could, however, get the place fixed, but it was obvious he would need to live elsewhere while he did.

'I suppose I need to find a builder who can sort the place out,' he said at last. 'Can you recommend one?'

'I think we need to go into town.'

*

Despite his overnight activities providing little opportunity for sleep, Graham Bell appeared in the CID office not long after Pascal arrived. It was obvious to everyone that he was, to use an old phrase, big with news.

Pascal was standing in the main office, leaning against the wall beside the door. Frimley and Collins were sitting at their respective workstations when he arrived, a faint miasma betraying his unwashed status.

'What's afoot, Graham?' asked Pascal.

Bell told him what his efforts had yielded the previous night.

'I have the two addresses the van visited,' he concluded, 'and interestingly, one of them could well have been used to house the girls.'

'What makes you think that?'

'According to Sergeant Henslow, 83 Columbine Road used to be a guest house, but it ceased trading a couple of years ago. He thought it was a private house these days.'

Pascal looked at the other address, and glanced up. 'Are you sure about this one, Graham?'

Bell nodded. 'Why?'

'It's Councillor Clifford's home.'

'But he's not there,' said Collins. 'Probation have found him somewhere to stay until after we've finished with Jackson or his trial is over.'

Pascal chewed his cheek. 'So what is Ernest Miller doing driving his van round there and parking in Clifford's drive as if he owned the place?'

'Was Miller the only person in the van?' asked Collins.

Bell smiled wolfishly. 'No. I saw Miller open the rear doors and about a dozen young women got out and went into the house.'

'I'm thinking we should be including Councillor Clifford's home in the search warrants,' said Collins.

'Without a doubt,' said Pascal. 'I wonder if he knows? Must be time to have another chat with him!' He made up his mind. 'Okay. Let's go for it. Alison, you and Graham can prepare the warrants and go down to the court. We'll plan on executing the warrants on Saturday. It'll take until then to plan everything.'

*

A haggard-looking Sergeant Claude Henslow shook his head for the third time. Frimley tried again.

'Surely there's a way of getting a few more officers together?'

'A few?' demanded Henslow. 'A few? A *few* I could do, but you want to search the home of the last Police Authority Chairman, a former guest house and a bloody great night-club *on a Saturday?*' His voice rose.

Frimley shrugged. 'We really need to hit all three at the same time. Can we get any help in from anywhere else?'

Henslow thumped his forehead with the heel of his hands. 'No can do! Let me explain one more time: on Saturdays, the cells are full from Friday night's boozers and brawlers, and everyone I can spare is enjoying a morning off before going into the city to police a home game at Carrow Road in the afternoon – an activity for which we are paid, and can't therefore give up lightly.'

'Is that your last word, Sarge?'

'Yes!'

'You're condemning a lot of drugged-up young women to another night of sexual slavery.'

'I just don't have the staff.'

'How about after the footie?' suggested Frimley, not wanting to give in before exploring all possibilities.

Henslow chewed his lip while he considered the matter.

At last, he nodded. 'Yes. Okay, yes. You organise things for around seven Saturday evening. That'll give the boys and girls time to have their refs after the match, and there'll be a few hours left before the end of their shift.' He scowled at Frimley. 'It's not as if they'd have anything else to do, like paperwork.'

Frimley smiled at him without responding.

*

Pascal had sent Bell home after his sleepless night, when he'd found him slumped over his workstation, so deeply asleep his last chocolate digestive had fallen from his fingers and now rested, sticky-side down, on the carpet. He was back in the office before any of the others on Thursday and answered Collins' phone when it rang.

He listened without speaking, then put the instrument down and shuffled back to his own chair where he absent-mindedly picked up a chocolate biscuit from which he'd already taken a bite. He shoved the rest into his mouth and brushed the crumbs off his keyboard. Half an hour later he heard the click of Collins' heels and Frimley's softer foot-falls in the corridor. They entered the room smiling at something and went to their places.

Frimley was bringing them both up to speed on the proposed raids when the door at the end of the corridor opened and Pascal's foot-steps could be heard. He appeared in the doorway.

'Morning, sir,' said Collins.

'Morning!' he said. 'Any coffee about?' He looked at her as he spoke.

'Only in the machine at the end of the corridor, sir,' she said.

He patted his pockets. 'Um. Right. I'll get some later.' He turned to Frimley. 'Okay, Douglas, are we sorted out with bodies for Saturday?'

'I've arranged with Sergeant Henslow for uniforms to be available at seven p.m. to do the raids,' said Frimley.

Pascal rubbed his hands happily. 'Excellent. Would have preferred a dawn raid rather than evening, but needs must, eh, Douglas?' The smile fell from his face when he recalled that Saturday evening he'd been hoping to spend with Doctor Jane.

'Indeed they must, when driven by you, sir.'

Pascal glanced at him askance for a moment. Was that a suggestion that he was standing *in locum tenens* for the Devil? He grinned and was about to turn away to go to his own room when Bell spoke up.

'An anonymous call came in on DS Collins's phone, sir.'

They all looked at him.

'When?' asked Pascal.

'Earlier this morning. Half an hour or so ago.'

'What was it about?'

'It was a man. Just said that in his opinion, Julia Fox was working at *Kittens* as a tart.'

Collins angled her head to one side. 'He used the name of the girl and the name of the club?'

'Yes.'

She turned to Pascal. 'Must be one of the punters. Or one of the people who works there.'

Pascal stared at her. 'Someone who knows her. Or recognised her from the photo in the paper.'

'Member of the family? Male friend?' She turned to Bell. 'Did the voice sound old or young?'

Bell considered. 'Somewhere in between, I'd say.'

Collins thought some more. 'And the call came through to your telephone?'

Bell shrugged. 'Well, actually to yours, but you weren't here.'

'Was it a switchboard call or a direct-dialled one?'

Bell looked flustered. '*I* don't know. How'm I supposed to know that?'

'Because our switchboard is a bit more old-fashioned than the one in Norwich: when a call comes through the operator, the ring pattern is ring-pause-ring-pause. Direct dialled calls ring like a normal call, ring-ring-pause, ring-ring-pause.'

Pascal stared at her, slight amusement in his gaze.

Bell screwed up his face. 'Normal ring.'

'Try 1471,' suggested Pascal.

Collins shrugged. 'Won't work, sir, dialling out is on different lines from the incoming calls. It's done so we can always make calls out even when the incoming lines are choked with traffic.'

'Bugger!'

'It points to someone who knows our telephone extensions,' Collins observed. 'Mine, anyway.'

'That should narrow the field,' muttered Bell.

She arched an eyebrow at his ironic tone.

'Grab a coffee and come into my office, Alison,' said Pascal. 'Here,' he added, holding out a pound. 'That should cover a couple of cups.'

'Sir.'

Five minutes later she joined him and closed the door in response to his request.

'Sit down, Alison.' He waited until she had curled herself into the broken chair. Her colour was slightly raised as if she expected a telling-off. He hitched one leg onto the desk, making it obvious that it wasn't that sort of meeting.

'I need to tell you something I'd rather didn't go beyond this room.'

She waited, her grey eyes fixed on his.

He cleared his throat. 'John – DC Walker – is suspended, following the start of an investigation by Professional standards. You know that, I expect?'

'Yes, but I don't know why.'

He told her what he knew of Walker's debt problem. 'Obviously, being that much in hock makes him a liability to the job; he's far too vulnerable, and whilst I've never before had any doubts about John's loyalty in the past, I've got to tell you, I have now.'

'I know we have him on tape, visiting *The Kitty Klub,*' she said.

'Yes. In addition to that, I'm pretty certain he's using cocaine.'

'The sniffs, and blood on his hankies?'

'You noticed too.'

'I admit I wondered.'

Pascal circled round the desk and sat behind it, picking up the coffee she'd brought him.

'The thing is, John knows about *Kittens* and probably goes there. It's my guess that he was our anonymous caller.'

'Which would mean he'd seen and recognised Julia, and knew she was working as a prostitute.'

Pascal looked at her, his expression grim. 'At least,' he said.

She arched her eyebrow. 'Meaning that it's possible he used her services.'

'Hopefully before he recognised her and not afterwards.'

She sipped her drink.

'But why phone us?'

'Because at heart,' Pascal replied, 'he's not a bad man. I expect his conscience wouldn't let him ignore what he suspected.'

# CHAPTER 15

It was after half-past six on Saturday evening when Pascal entered the briefing room. It was filling up, some officers grumbling about being brought in on their rest days, some talking about the football match they'd seen. The local team was hovering dangerously near the relegation zone, and there were not many more matches to play when they might pull their irons out of the fire.

The room fell silent as Pascal stood in front of the big whiteboard containing photographs of Jackson, David Ellis, Sara Martin and Julia Fox, together with copies of the plans of the properties.

'Two weeks ago,' he began, 'a 17-year-old girl called Julia Fox was reported missing. On the same day, a young man of the same age, David Ellis, was found badly injured and in a coma which earlier today he was still in.' He pointed to the school photographs of Julia and David. 'Also earlier today, we had an anonymous phone call earlier in which a man's voice told us that Julia Fox was working as a prostitute at a private members' club some of you may have heard of, called *Kittens*.'

There was some subdued sniggering from one rear corner of the room.

'Yes, well! I didn't say I thought anyone here would be a member – I hope and expect that nobody is, considering what goes on there.'

The room fell silent again. The faces of the people listening to him were eager and interested, he noticed.

'For some reason we don't yet know, the girls, who appear to be eastern European, brought here on the pretext of non-existent jobs, were moved from premises in Columbine Road, which is one of three addresses where we're executing warrants this evening, to the home of a County Councillor you should all have heard of, as he's the last chairman of the Police Authority – Councillor Gordon Clifford. We need to talk to him about another matter as well.' He glanced at his watch and compared it with the wall clock.

'Don't forget, one of the girls we expect to be Julia Fox, and at present, we believe they've all been put into prostitution unwillingly. Probably a combination of drugs, rape, blackmail and simple bullying has been used to do this. We're not aware that any girl has committed offences, so please treat them as victims, not suspects.' He turned to Collins who took his place at the end of the room.

'The object is to arrest everybody at Clifford's house and bring them here for questioning, and also to examine each of the locations for evidence of any crime,' she said. 'There will be three teams, led by uniformed sergeants. A CID officer will be at each of the locations. Are there any questions?'

One or two practical matters were raised and dealt with. By the time the briefing had finished, there was an air of eager anticipation in the room. They began filing out to the minibuses being used to convey them to the target addresses.

Collins drove Pascal to Clifford's. Out of sight of the house, they stopped and Pascal asked the sergeant in the minibus behind them to send four officers ahead to make a stealthy approach to the rear of the premises. After the officers sent behind the house reported themselves in position, Collins drove ahead of the minibus to Clifford's front door. Pascal went up the steps with Collins behind him and rang the bell. The door was opened by the Councillor's housekeeper.

'Mrs Kenwright, Detective Inspector Pascal, Breydon CID. I have a warrant to search these premises on suspicion that they are being used as a brothel.'

The woman's mouth gaped. Pascal took the opportunity to enter the hallway past her, followed by the Collins and the other police officers.

'You aren't serious?' she demanded at last.

Pascal held out the warrant without speaking.

'The Councillor's not here!' she cried.

'We know.'

As soon as the search began, pandemonium began to break out. Officers began to bring girls downstairs, most of whom were in a state of considerable undress. Pascal stopped them in the hallway.

'Get these girls covered up, will you, we're not running a peep show for curious neighbours.'

Blankets were fetched and wrapped round the girls. Pascal and Collins studied their faces as they appeared. They were led into the minibus where uniformed female officers kept control while they were ferried to the police station. Neither Pascal nor Collins recognised Julia Fox among the girls.

As the search wound down, a sergeant appeared from one of the downstairs rooms

'Anything found?' asked Pascal.

He shrugged. 'Nothing of great interest, sir. There's a computer back there which we'll take for examination, and a few books that look to have fairly explicit content, but nothing illegal.'

'No sign of Julia Fox?' asked Pascal.

The sergeant shook his head. 'No, sir. We haven't seen her either.'

'Right. I'll leave this to your men to finish off. DS Collins and I will visit Columbine Road.'

The sergeant nodded.

In the car, Pascal suggested to Collins that she might drive past *The Kitty Klub* on the way, so they could see how Frimley was coping.

*

Frimley had in fact been coping well. The team of uniformed constables led by their sergeant had followed him into the premises where he had served the search warrant on Ernest Miller. Frimley was slightly surprised when Miller made no objection to the search, but figured, at the time, that it was simply because Miller knew there was no point, faced with a court order. Activities on the dance floor were brought to a halt and the police took the names and addresses of those present before letting them go.

Jackson emerged from his office and stood beside Frimley while the search progressed. A drugs dog was brought in and at first had shown signs of interest in parts of the dancing and drinking areas, and a few small finds of discarded cannabis were made. The search had then widened, entering the area behind the bar, where the dog had quickly headed for an area behind the curtained wall. The handler had pulled the curtain aside to reveal a door. The dog had barked excitedly and the handler pushed the door open.

Beyond was a corridor. On the left was the main room of *Kittens*, whilst on the right were several small bedrooms.

To Frimley's surprise, but not the handler's, the dog quietened and seemed to lose interest as soon as it went through the door.

Pascal and Collins arrived in time to follow the others through into what Pascal guessed was *Kittens*, and take a look around. Jackson stood beside Frimley, his expression grim but unconcerned, as if sure the search would yield nothing.

Pascal drew Frimley aside. 'No luck?' he asked quietly.

Frimley shook his head. 'Not yet, sir.'

Pascal pursed his lips. 'Don't miss Jackson's office,' he said.

'No sir.'

It was becoming apparent that the place had been cleaned of all traces of the girls and drugs, apart from those wraps discarded by the punters whose interest had extended only as far as *The Kitty Klub*. The handler led the dog from *Kittens* back into the legitimate area, and Frimley pointed him at the door leading to Jackson's office.

Jackson himself was standing beside Frimley watching the dog, when it suddenly ran to his desk, and tried tugging at the handle of a pedestal drawer. The handler opened it and a moment later stepped back with two small deal bags containing a white crystalline substance.

He held it out to Frimley. 'Cocaine, I reckon, Douglas.'

'Lovely job,' Frimley congratulated him, bending to fondle the dog's ears. 'Good boy!'

The handler gave the dog a reward from one of his pockets. Frimley turned to Jackson.

'I'm arresting you on suspicion of possessing a controlled Class A drug, Mr Jackson.'

Jackson scowled. 'I don't know how they got there. In any case, you don't know they're drugs!'

'You're only being arrested on *suspicion*, Mr Jackson. We'll carry out a field test on the contents of the deal bags back at the nick, and they will be sent for proper identification,' said Frimley.

He informed Jackson of his rights and watched him being led away to the police van. He arrested Miller on the same basis at which point Miller took a swing at him. The blow missed, but two burly constables grabbed him and half-carried him towards a second vehicle where he was locked into the cage after a tussle.

Frimley brushed his jacket with his fingers and turned to Pascal, pointing to a large plastic bag beside him. 'I've picked up the club's CCTV tapes for the past month, in case there's anything helpful on them.

'It looks as if you got two of the biggest fishes.' Pascal scratched his head. 'I have a feeling there's another one... Paul somebody.' He glanced at Collins. 'Didn't our Latvian friend tell us what a good pal he'd been to all the girls, getting them hooked on heroin and showing them how to be prostitutes?'

Collins nodded.

'No sign of him,' reported Frimley. 'There was nothing much going on here, and all of it apparently legal.'

'No matter. Check they have all the right licences, and keep them at the nick until we've had a word.'

'Yes, sir.'

'We're going to carry on over to our third target. As soon as you can wrap this up, will you go back to the nick and start to process the girls. They should have someone from Immigration down there, medical staff, the works.'

'Right, sir.'

After one last look round the scene, Pascal and Collins returned to the car.

*

Walker was feeling 'stir crazy'. He found his old anorak on the floor near the door, pushed his feet into his trainers and let himself out into the fading light of evening. Not consciously heading anywhere in particular, his feet carried him towards Breydon's nightlife. People, most a decade younger than him, in their teens and early twenties, were beginning to drift from pubs towards the centre of the town's night-life. He leaned on a safety rail at the edge of the pavement and watched. Two girls, scantily dressed and apparently badly inebriated, staggered along the road, leaning against each other and giggling loudly. He saw them clock him, and moments later, they collapsed in a heap, gasping and hooting with laughter. Their unbalanced efforts to stand up resulted in one girl's skirt riding above her waist, revealing her panty-less state, while the boobs of the other spilled out of her low-cut top almost into his hands.

'Whoops!' said the girl with enhanced boobs, and giggled in his face while she took her time covering up. 'How d'you like them, mister? Cost me three grand they did.'

He smiled at her and nodded. Her friend leaned on the other side of the rail next to him and smiled slackly.

'I think I've got a scratch on me arse,' she told him, alcohol fumes souring her breath in his face. 'How would you like to lick it better?'

He regarded her wryly. 'Depends how much you'd charge,' he said.

The grin disappeared from the girl's face and she scowled at him.

'I'm not a fucking prostitute!'

He moved away from the fumes. 'Really? I thought you were one half of a double-act.'

She turned angrily to her friend. 'Oy, Nic, 'e's saying we're on the game!'

Nic had finished securing her wayward enhancements and grinned at him.

'Well, you can have me for forty quid, nice bloke like you,' she said cheekily.

'The going rate is twenty for newcomers,' he said. 'I'd expect both of you for forty.' He turned to the panty-less one. 'And that *would* make you a pair of fucking prostitutes,' he added.

'Fuck you! I don't want yer money. And I don't want you – not when there's better-looking blokes, and younger, who don't insult me.'

'They insult you every time you allow them to have sex with you,' said Walker. He stood up. 'You should be going home. I expect it'll be back to school tomorrow.'

They stared at him as he walked away.

'Who's he fuckin' think he is!' he heard one of them say as he moved in the direction of *The Kitty Klub* and *Kittens*.

He wondered that himself, he thought. He'd always wanted to join the police; he'd been a good copper, too, until he'd been introduced to Derrick's girls and then cocaine. It wasn't just that he was now able to get both things free, it was from the first time he'd bought a line and paid for sex with a girl who might have been underage. She'd almost certainly been under the influence of a drug, and heroin was the likeliest candidate. His career was over, he knew, and he wondered what would become of him.

He became aware of the crowd outside *The Kitty Klub*. Seeing the police vans, he realised the raid Pascal had hinted at was taking place, and wondered whether Jackson had cleaned the place up. A noise behind him made him turn round. The two girls, accompanied now by two fit-looking young men, were a dozen yards from him. As he faced them, they stopped.

'You insulted my girl,' said one man.

'And mine,' said the other.

They approached him, watched by the girls. Walker sensed the danger as the men closed in on him from either side. He caught sight of a Stanley knife in the hand of one. While he was watching that, the other man grabbed him. He was very strong, Walker discovered. Almost at once, the other man's arm flashed out and he felt a punch in his lower abdomen. He began to struggle to free his arms, but the man with the knife struck him several more times, on his chest, arms and thighs.

He cried out for help, but the crowd watching events along the street were making too much noise to hear him. He felt no pain, but became aware of warm wetness running down his legs. He vaguely worried that he might have pissed himself, and realised he was having trouble seeing anything. One more stroke of the knife had opened a flap of skin across his forehead and blood was pouring over his eyes. Both his hands were still being held, and he couldn't wipe it away.

Vaguely, he heard a shout, and was suddenly released. He slid to the ground and passed out.

*

Somebody had taken the trouble to erect a couple of floodlights on stands outside 83 Columbine Road, but no amount of lighting would make the place look other than what it was: a dismal, run-down ex-guesthouse. The short front garden was unkempt, and paintwork peeled away from the door and windows.

As Pascal and Collins arrived, it was clear there was something wrong. They joined Bell on the pavement outside. He was looking grave.

'What's the situation?' asked Pascal.

'We had to smash the door in, sir. We began the search, working from the ground-floor up.'

'And?'

'We got to the top floor. It's where the servants would have slept in the good old days. Anyway there's a narrow passageway runs the length of it along the front of the house, and leading off, towards the back, are all these doors.' Bell looked away towards the house. Pascal heard some distant shouting.

'What's that all about?' he asked.

'The place seemed to be empty, but when we reached the stairs to the attic rooms, there was this bloke, and he'd got his arm locked round the neck of one of the girls.'

'So what stopped you rescuing her?'

'He was holding a bloody-great syringe full of what he said was heroin against her jugular, threatening to let her have the lot if we got any closer.'

'Hell!'

'He dragged her along the passageway into a room. He's locked the door.'

'Surely he knows he can't get away?'

'Think he's wanting to negotiate a safe passage.'

Pascal took a moment to think.

'Did you recognise the girl, Graham?' asked Collins.

He pursed his lips. 'She was blonde, about Julia Fox's age, Sarge, but I couldn't say for certain. Looks a bit older than I expected.'

'I should think she's aged a few lifetimes in the last couple of weeks,' observed Collins dourly. She looked at him. 'She wasn't at Clifford's house. The school photo we saw wasn't this year's, and girls can change a lot between sixteen and seventeen. Including their hair-colour.'

He nodded.

She turned to Pascal. 'Do you think I could try talking to him, sir?'

'Done it before?'

'Once.'

'Okay,' he said, 'but be careful. Don't promise him anything quickly, and before you do, talk to me about it.'

'I understand, sir.' She turned to Bell. 'Can he hear us talking or do we need a phone or something?'

'He can hear.'

'Don't get closer than the end of the passageway, Alison,' Pascal admonished.

She nodded and went into the house.

At the top of the attic stairs two officers in body armour were standing. One bore the chevrons of a sergeant, the other held a matt black stubby-looking sub-machine-gun loosely against his shoulder. Collins introduced herself.

'Sergeant Dashwood and PC Richardson,' said the sergeant.

They moved aside to allow her to glance round the corner, along the passage.

'They're three doors along,' said Dashwood. 'It's been quiet for a while.'

'Any idea who they are? Their names?'

He shook his head.

'Right' she said, taking a deep breath. She peered round the corner again.

'Hello?' she called. There was a scuffling noise then silence. 'Hello? I'm Detective Sergeant Alison Collins. Can you hear me?'

She heard a man's muffled voice from behind the door. 'I hope you're someone in authority, because I need someone in authority to talk to.'

'What's your name?' she asked.

'Don't you know?'

'No.' She glanced at the sergeant and constable who were listening politely. 'We thought the place was empty. That's why we broke the front door down.'

'Well, you were wrong. We were here.'

'Who's the girl with you?'

'Who do you want her to be? Her name's Fiona.'

'Oh, yes,' said Collins, 'but what would her mother call her?'

She heard the sound of low voices.

'Jules,' said the man.

'And you are?'

There was silence for a moment. Collins prompted him. 'Are you Derrick?'

'Derrick? No I bloody-well am not.'

'But you know Derrick?'

'Might do. Look, I'm getting fed up with this. I want out.'

'We want you out as well, Derrick.'

'I am *not* Derrick!' he insisted.

'Well, I might just have to call you Derrick until we've asked him who you are. I'm sure he'll be happy to tell us. He's helping us with our enquiries, as we say, right now.'

The voice was suspicious. 'What do you mean, "helping you with your enquiries"?'

'He's telling us stuff. You don't expect me to tell you what he's saying do you?'

'He won't tell you nothing!'

'Hang on to that thought, Derrick.'

He swore loudly behind the door. 'My name's Paul. Shut up calling me Derrick.'

'Okay, Paul; listen to me,' she said. 'We want you to put that syringe down without hurting Jules, and come out of the room slowly.'

He laughed harshly. 'You think I'm stupid? While I've got the girl and the syringe, you do as I say. And I want a car and free passage to Holland.'

Collins chewed her lip while she thought.

'Did you hear me, detective sergeant?'

'Yes, Paul, I heard you. I was just wondering how long you were going to keep Jules with you?'

'Long enough!'

'That would have to be a long, long time, Paul,' she told him.

'Why?'

'Well, obviously, you won't kill her, because that would be destroying your meal ticket. I bet you don't have a job, do you Paul? All your income derives from the working girls? You'll be needing her to work for you, won't you? And some time, Paul, you're going to have to sleep.'

There was no response. Collins waited patiently, figuring he was weighing the odds.

'I'll kill her if you don't let me go.'

Collins chewed her lip.

'Once you do that, Paul, we'll have no reason to wait out here. We'll have to come and get you.'

'I mean it. I want out.'

'And I want to know that Jules is still alive and well. Let her speak to me.'

She heard his voice, low and urgent, but couldn't make out the words. Then, suddenly, the girl called out.

'Please... do as he says.'

'Jules? Is that your name?' asked Collins.

'Julia.'

'Julia Fox?'

Paul's voice interrupted. 'So, she's alive and well – for now. Now, move away and let us out.'

Collins thought a moment. 'Paul? Are you listening?'

He grunted.

'I need to arrange that with the area commander. He's the one who can order his people to back off. It'll take a few minutes. I'll see what I can do.'

'Yeah. Ten minutes, then.'

'Okay.'

She glanced at her wristwatch, then at Dashwood and Richardson, putting her finger to her lips. She edged back away from the passage and went back down the stairs to where Pascal waited at the bottom. She took his arm and led him away from the staircase into one of the empty bedrooms.

'What are you thinking, Alison?' he asked quietly.

'I think we should pull back and see if I can persuade him out of the room. Put some marksmen round the plot on the periphery, and take him out if they can get a clear shot.'

'Think we'd get that past the CC?' he asked, referring to the Chief Constable, who would be involved following any discharge of a police firearm.

'That syringe he's got is tantamount to a knife or gun. It will kill her just as surely if, as he says, it's loaded with a massive dose of heroin. We'd be acting in defence of her life, but unless we can get the girl away from him, we won't be able to warn him because the minute we do, he's likely to go for it.'

Pascal considered the options. 'Let's get Sergeant Dashwood down here. I think I need to discuss this with him.'

*

More than a week had passed since Danny Bakker escaped from Jared Martin's house by the skin of his teeth. He'd followed Pascal and Collins down the cellar steps and was in time to see them run out of the gate at the bottom of the garden into the service road. He'd figured them for police from what they said and did in Martin's study, and realised that to go after them would be asking for trouble. Accordingly, he'd set off in the opposite direction and been gone before the ARVs had arrived, slipping away between the houses.

Once clear of the area he found himself on top of the topographical feature which had given High Ridge Avenue its name, overlooking the town. He cursed as he realised that he'd left his briefcase in the house, but there was no way he could go back for it now. He'd laid low for the next week, in a Bed & Breakfast outside the town, but by the following Saturday evening decided he had to risk going to see Derrick Jackson who must be made to pay again for the drugs supplied by Mr van Ruys.

He pulled his leather jacket around him to make sure the silenced Sig Sauer tucked into his trouser belt wasn't visible and walked into town through the recreation ground. A few people were walking their dogs or simply enjoying a stroll. Others sat on benches and admired the view. Nobody seemed to be paying him particular attention. He turned up his collar and tried to be as inconspicuous as possible.

The walk into town took half an hour. He reached the centre and saw that *The Kitty Klub* was surrounded by police vehicles. Officers in reflective, high-visibility yellow tunics and body armour stood guard on the premises, and it was obvious some big operation was taking place.

Bakker stared at a shop window, using its reflective qualities to survey the scene without appearing to look. It was a fair guess, he concluded, that Derrick Jackson was not available. How was he to get the money for Mr van Ruys, before he found himself being picked up by other men like him, in van Ruys's employ, and probably torn limb from limb? He felt sweat begin to soak into his collar, and moisten the palms of his hands.

Bakker was someone who enjoyed his own company, most of the time. Occasionally, he needed a woman: they provided the only relief he ever seemed to get. They were like hire-cars: he used them and finished with them. Maintenance and repair was a matter for their owners. Ever since he had accidentally broken the neck of the first girl he'd ever really enjoyed, who'd been not much above fourteen at the time, he'd learned how to pull his punches. One day, he knew, he would ride another girl to death, feeling her spasm around him in the final twitches of her body.

The pressure to do this was increasing daily, and never more so than when he had spent a lot of time under stress.

Perhaps, he thought, there might be time... He would go to the house in Columbine Road, where he had first set eyes on Jared Martin's wife at an upstairs window and seen that she wasn't the only woman on the premises. He could have fucked her while killing her to see if the sensations were as energising as with that first girl – except that he didn't like to mix business with pleasure: his business was to kill her, not to enjoy her. It could have made him careless. He might have left too many forensic clues behind.

He strolled casually past the road leading to *The Kitty Klub* and headed for Columbine Road. As soon as it came into view, he saw more police all over the place and realised the girls would not be there..

So where were they? Had the police mopped up all of Derrick Jackson's operation? What was left to do? The only options open to him were to follow Jared Martin to Aruba, which would be expensive and tedious, or he could go to ground in Holland. Maybe make contact with van Ruys and find out what he thought they should do.

He was scared of few people, but van Ruys was one who frightened him to death. Admitting to failure would easily amount to a death sentence, unless he could persuade the powerful Dutchman that he was more use alive.

How to get to Amsterdam? Flying was not really a possibility, because of the higher levels of security involved. Go by sea? The rigid inflatable boat in which he'd arrived would be gone: if the police hadn't found it, it would have floated off the beach at the next high tide. He could steal another boat, but inevitably it wouldn't be a fast RIB and there'd be a hue and cry, and for the hours it would take an inevitably slower craft to sail across the North Sea, he would be vulnerable to discovery.

Or there was the ferry. Passenger and car ferries sailed several times a day from Harwich to the Hook, with several hundred passengers on board. If he assumed that the

Customs and Immigration checks were perfunctory, as they should be between member states of the European Union, he stood a good chance of getting back to Holland – better than going by air, when there were many fewer passengers, and a greater chance of being spotted. Better to be one in five hundred than one in fifty. He simply needed a car for the journey to Harwich.

*

Dashwood joined Pascal and Collins in the first-floor bedroom. Collins explained her idea to him.

Pascal listened. 'How long have we got?'

She glanced at her watch. 'Four minutes, just about.'

'Can you set up in that time?' Pascal asked Dashwood.

The sergeant nodded, already talking quietly into his radio. He deployed his armed officers out of sight, except for Richardson. He climbed inside a wardrobe standing under the attic stairs, leaving the door open a crack.

Collins drew Dashwood's attention. 'Sarge, I'll go up to the landing, to tell him it's all clear. I'll try and get him to come out, with the girl, and keep ahead of him, ensuring he can keep me in sight. I want him watching me, paying me as much attention as possible. until we get down here.'

Pascal frowned. 'Sounds risky.'

She returned his look. 'I'm a police officer like any other. We all have to take risks occasionally. I can look after myself.'

Pascal shook his head. 'It's too dangerous. You could get hurt.'

'I have my stab vest on.' She pulled open a couple of buttons on her blouse to reveal the white light-weight Kevlar garment beneath it. 'I won't let him get near me.'

Pascal wavered, then made up his mind. She was right: he was being blinded by his old-fashioned gallantry. Keeping women safe from harm to which he would expose any male officer was no longer something he could do without risking accusations of discrimination from those same women. It still went against the grain with him, but he could think of no valid reason why she shouldn't do what she proposed.

Pascal nodded. 'Okay. Go ahead.'

With Richardson in position, Dashwood followed Collins up the attic stairs, keeping back out of sight when they reached the top. She moved forward and stood in the centre of the passageway.

'Paul? I'm back. Is everything all right, Paul?'

There was a rustling sound then he spoke. His voice was strained.

'You've fixed me a car?'

'Yes.'

'Then why can't I see it?'

'It's at the front of the house, you can only see the back.'

'How do I know it's there?'

'Why would I lie? You hold all the cards. Everyone has done as you wanted, and backed off. If you come out of the room, you'll see I'm alone. Just follow me downstairs and you can go.'

She heard a key turn in the lock and the door inched open until she could see the man's face. He pushed an arm through the gap, holding a small handbag-sized mirror, and used it to scan the corridor behind him, where he couldn't see directly. He edged the door further open and pulled Julia's head against his chest. It took Collins a few moments to recognise her. Unwin held a long syringe full of brown liquid so that the inch-long needle was pressed against the girl's throat. A few drops of blood showed that he'd pressed too hard a time or two. Julia's head was turned away from him, straining to escape the needle, but his grip on her was strong. Collins saw the way the angle of her neck made the tendon at one side of her throat stretch the girl's flesh against which the needle was being held.

She stood still and watched. The man pushed the girl, stumbling and sobbing, ahead of him, two paces and stopped.

'Right,' he said, 'you go backwards down them steps. Slowly.'

Collins held up a hand. 'If you want me to walk downstairs backwards, I'll do it, but do you mind if I take my shoes off? I don't want to fall.'

Paul shrugged. He watched as Collins made something of a performance of the process, bending while she eased off her low-heeled shoes. Unwin watched her.

'Throw them in the corner,' he told her, pointing at the spot furthest from the stairs. She tossed them.

'All right?' she asked him, taking hold of the handrail.

'Yeah. And – and no tricks!' he said.

She figured he must watch a lot of old movies. No-one used *that* line did they? She stepped cautiously backwards. It was no part of her plan to fall down the stairs. As she went, Unwin, holding the girl tightly, shuffled up to the corner from where he could watch Collins's progress. At the bottom of the stairs, she waited. Man and girl came down the top two steps. He paused and indicated to Collins that she should move. He waited until she had gone round the newel post and back along the first-floor landing before he came down the remaining stairs, careful to keep out of her reach.

She passed the door of the bedroom opposite the wardrobe, and continued to move slowly backwards, watching Unwin's hand on the syringe. Unwin reached the wardrobe. Only another two paces were needed to bring him into the line of fire – Collins could see the glint of light reflecting on the twin prongs of Richardson's Taser.

Suddenly, the constable sneezed.

Paul, who'd been watching Collins as she'd intended, spun round as Richardson tried to scramble out of the wardrobe.

Collins watched in horror as Julia screamed and tried to pull away from Unwin.

Richardson no longer had a clear shot as Unwin jammed the needle of the syringe hard into Julia Fox's throat.

Behind him, the door of a bedroom opened, Dashwood emerged behind Unwin and shot him with his Taser.

Unwin fell to the floor writhing, the girl falling away and in front of him. She tried to stagger to her feet. Pascal rushed forward and gathered her into his arms.

Richardson, face beetroot red, stood beside the wardrobe, looking down at Unwin as Dashwood cuffed him. Collins reached the girl, and held her tight to stop her moving and accidentally making the situation worse. The syringe, empty, dangled from her neck, still impaling her.

Collins breathed a sigh of relief. 'Look! The needle: it went right through.'

Being careful not to touch the plunger, Pascal helped Collins keep the girl still. It was obvious that when Unwin had rammed the plunger home, the needle had been pushed completely through Julia's neck, in at the side, and out at the front, next to her stretched tendon. When he'd pressed the plunger, the lethal solution inside and squirted out, staining the front of her dress and the wall next to Richardson's hiding-place.

'Medic!' shouted Pascal down the stairs.

Collins spoke into Julia's ear. 'You're safe now. The heroin didn't go in. Just keep still until we get the syringe removed from your neck.'

There was no sign of a paramedic, so Collins took careful hold of the syringe and pulled it out.

The girl blinked at her. Suddenly her eyes rolled up and she went limp in Pascal's arms. He lowered her gently to the floor.

Collins checked her pulse and found it was strong. She was breathing without difficulty.

'Medic!' Pascal shouted again.

The girl's eyed flickered open. She stared at Collins and Pascal.

'Are you Julia Fox?' asked Collins.

The girl looked at her through wary eyes. She nodded.

Collins smiled. 'That's good. We've been looking for you. We have to get a doctor to you, and we'll tell your parents you're safe.'

Julia shook her head.

'I can't go back to them,' she told him through clenched teeth.

'Why?'

'They don't know... what I've been doing.' Julia looked round and saw Unwin, who was being helped to his feet by PC Richardson, anxious to make amends. 'What are you doing with Paul?'

'I'm afraid that he'll probably be going to prison for a very long time for what he did to you and the other girls.'

Julia's hands shook and she chewed her lip. 'But you can't. He's... he'll...'

'He won't be doing anything to any of you from now on,' said Collins reassuringly.' As she was speaking, two yellow-jacketed paramedics appeared at last and approached them.

'You took your time,' Pascal complained. He indicated Julia. 'She's had a needle-full of heroin stuck in her neck.'

'Bloody hell! Okay, mate, we'll deal with it,' said the first paramedic.

Pascal glanced round at Collins, who had moved along the landing. 'I think you get the privilege,' he said, grinning and nodding at the handcuffed man.

Collins faced him.

'What's your full name, Paul?'

'Paul Unwin,' he muttered.

'I'm arresting you, Paul Unwin, on suspicion of supplying controlled drugs, and for wrongful arrest and false imprisonment of Julia and the other girls who've been kept here, and on suspicion of conspiring with others to facilitate the unlawful immigration of those girls. There will probably be more charges of rape and living off immoral earnings to follow, but I think we've enough to be going on with.'

She administered the statutory caution then asked Richardson to escort Unwin to Breydon police station. When she turned round, it was to find Sergeant Dashwood holding out her shoes.

'Thank you,' she said.

'You did really well, DS Collins,' he said, adding, wryly, 'better than my man.'

'I'll bet he didn't count on the inside of the wardrobe being dusty, Sarge. it was an oversight any of us could have made.'

'It doesn't make your performance any less brave and resourceful. It'll go in my report.' With a nod to Pascal, who was smiling behind her, Dashwood followed Richardson and Unwin down to the police vans waiting in the street.

She turned to look at Pascal as he grinned at her and tapped the side of his nose with a forefinger.

'Well done, Alison,' he said, 'now let's see how Julia is.'

The paramedics appeared with Julia at the front door of the house and led her gently to the ambulance. Pascal reminded them that Julia's heroin-stained clothes would be needed for forensics. He rang Jane Ferrari, in her capacity as Police Surgeon, and told her the situation.

She was of the view that Julia should spend one night at least in hospital. Collins went with her in the ambulance, while Pascal phoned her parents to let them know the good news.

*

It was a late start the next day, after the long night. Pascal had only just arrived in his office on Sunday morning when his telephone rang. He scowled at it. Surely by now everyone knew he wasn't at his best until he'd had at least one cup of coffee, and preferably more. He picked up the receiver.

'Pascal.'

'Hello, George.'

He recognised Julian Steel's voice. 'Morning, sir.'

'I just thought I'd let you know, I'm on my way to see all of you.'

The DCI hung up without waiting for a response. Pascal stared at the phone as he hung up, then went across the corridor into the CID office. Only Collins was in there.

'Where are the others?' he asked her.

'Not in yet, sir.'

'Umm. Well, there's just going to be you and me to greet our revered DCI when he gets here.'

She lifted her gaze away from the monitor screen. 'What's he want?'

'Not sure. Probably wants to congratulate us on a job well done. He's good at speeches like that.'

Her eyes focussed over his right shoulder. Pascal turned. Julian Steel was just emerging from Pascal's office, turning and seeing him.

'Ah, there you are George.' He looked round the general office and smiled briefly at Collins.

'Everyone else out, George?'

'Working late, sir.'

'Ah.'

Pascal didn't like the look in Steel's eye. It was shifty, as if he had something to say that no-one would take pleasure in. The DCI cleared his throat.

'I'm afraid I have some bad news,' he said.

Pascal frowned. Usually anything serious would have been mentioned to him in advance of his team being told. He and Collins waited.

'Detective Constable John Walker was admitted to hospital last night, suffering from multiple knife wounds,' Steel said. He looked at both members of his audience in turn. 'I'm afraid he lost too much blood from too many wounds.' Collins' lips parted and her eyes widened.

'He was pronounced dead at fourteen minutes to midnight.'

Steel had to pause while he swallowed. His lips were pale. 'It took some time to identify him, which is why we weren't informed of his identity until half an hour ago.'

He sat down, as if making the announcement had taken away all his energy. Pascal stared, initially at Steel. then into the distance, while he absorbed the news. Then he, too, sat down.

'Any idea how it happened?'

Steel looked up. 'No. You'd better get your skates on and find out.'

'Yes, sir. What about the murder and the abduction? There's only four of us. From what you're saying, this is another murder. I could do with more people.'

'Of course,' Steel nodded. 'I'll ask Norwich if they can spare us some additional personnel. The second murder on our patch in – what? – two weeks? It's beginning to sound like a crime-wave, in Breydon terms.'

'I'm sure you're right, sir,' said Pascal. 'Where was DC Walker found?'

Steel stared at him. 'I – I'm sorry. I forgot to ask.'

'Don't worry, sir, we'll begin at the hospital. Come on, Alison.'

They left Steel dealing with an obvious sense of shock.

# CHAPTER 16

Walker's body had been moved to the morgue before they arrived. It lay on a trolley, covered by a sheet. Pascal and Collins were shown in by one of the mortuary assistants who silently left them alone after lifting the sheet away from Walker's face.

Neither police officer spoke for a while. The bloody gash across Walker's forehead was quite visible. Pascal peeled the remainder of the sheet away, so he could see the other wounds to the body. The flesh of one leg was stained below a puncture wound in the groin, evidence that a copious flow of blood had run down into his shoes. Walker's flesh was pale grey-blue.

Collins had to remind herself he could no longer feel the cold air of the morgue or hear the echoes of water dripping from unseen taps. Pascal's voice, breaking the silence, startled her.

'Poor sod.' He looked up from Walker's wrecked face and gazed at her. 'We were mates, more or less,' he said. 'Went back a long way. He joined the service just after me, in the early nineties. We were DCs together.'

He looked away. 'That's the trouble with this job. You don't have many friends. It wrecks marriages, upsets other relationships: it's a shit job!'

He stuck his bottom lip out in an expression of stubbornness.

'And the worst of it is, the chances of finding out who did this are about the same as coming up on the national lottery.' He turned and glared. 'The great British public wants us when they've been burgled or mugged, and then when somebody sets about a copper, they all somehow see nothing.'

'We've still to find out where he died,' said Collins. 'Come on sir, I think we'd better go and ask some questions in A&E.'

She took his arm, but waited patiently while he carefully covered the body once more. Then he turned and led the way to the lifts.

In A&E, the registrar consulted the notes made by the team who'd been on duty when Walker had been admitted.

'He was half on the pavement, half on the road, not far from *The Kitty Klub*. About a couple of hundred yards away. It's a nightclub,' he added by way of explanation.

'We know,' said Pascal.

'The ambulance was there in seven and a half minutes.'

Pascal glanced at him.

'But you still didn't manage to save him.'

'No, Mr Pascal. I'm sorry. The team did all they could but one of the stab wounds had opened his femoral artery, and he bled out. Bad facial wound, too – head wounds always tend to be heavy bleeders.'

'Yeah, yeah.' There was too much talk of blood – not that he was squeamish, but why keep on about it! 'Is that what killed him?'

The registrar nodded. 'Basically, yes. And the blood loss was the result of multiple knife wounds – I'd say a small, sharp one. We get people in here every weekend and sometimes more often who've been cut with one of those. The law restricts the sale of long-bladed knives, but you only need a half-inch of blade to kill someone if you know where to strike. The sort of knives used by handymen and carpenters are a popular weapon of choice. The post mortem will confirm, but for my money, that's what was used on him.'

Pascal nodded. There was nothing more to be gleaned from the morgue.

'While we're here, let's go and see how David Ellis is doing. You never know – it might be good news. We need some after this.'

Collins nodded and they made their way up in the lift to the Intensive Care Unit of the hospital.

Marion Ellis looked up as they opened the door and came towards the bed containing her son.

Collins held out her ID card to remind the woman who she was, and identified Pascal to her.

'How is he?' he asked, looking at the pale, sleeping figure in front of them.

Mrs Ellis put down her knitting and gazed at David. She sighed.

'They say he's coming out of the coma. They took him off the ventilator a few hours ago.' Her eyes met Collins'. 'They say it's a good sign. He's been breathing by himself most of today.' She glanced at the monitor screens. 'Apparently, they can tell from those that he's slowly waking up.'

'That's good to hear. We urgently need to talk to him about what happened.'

The woman looked at Pascal's face. 'What happened to you?' she asked.

'Just a few cuts. I'm okay,' he said.

'Any news about Julia Fox?'

Pascal looked at her. 'We found her yesterday evening.'

Mrs Ellis gripped her fingers together. 'Oh! That's wonderful! Is she all right?'

Pascal glanced briefly at Collins. 'As well as can be expected. She'll need time to get over it. She's had a terrible experience.'

Marion Ellis nodded. 'Oh, yes.' She hesitated. 'Do you know what happened to her?'

'We've a pretty good idea,' Collins replied, 'but it wouldn't be helpful to our investigation if we were to speculate publicly. We'll know more soon, we hope.'

'I'm going to post a constable outside this room from now on until David wakes up,' Pascal told her.

She looked alarmed. 'He – he's not in any danger is he?'

'I don't know that he is,' he replied, 'but I don't know that he isn't, either. Whoever hit him left him for dead, and that person may still be in the area, worried that David could identify him. So, I'm trying not to take chances.'

She nodded. 'Thank you.' She turned to her son and took his hand gently in hers. 'He's my only child. I've probably lost my job by being here every day, but I don't care. I love him so much.'

'Jobs can always be replaced, sons and daughters can't,' he said.

Marion Ellis smiled at him through unshed tears. 'That's right.'

Pascal and Collins left the room and made their way back to the car.

'I need coffee,' he said as he climbed into the passenger seat beside Collins. 'There's too much bleedin' tragedy in life sometimes!' he growled.

She glanced at him out of the corner of her eye as she started the engine. His face was set in a mask of anger and frustration.

'How well did you know John, sir?' she asked when they were seated in a nearby coffee bar.

There were not many customers at that hour of the day. They sat at a small table in the angle between a side wall and the front plate-glass window. He stared out into the street.

'I wouldn't say we were exactly mates,' he said, 'but we occasionally went for a drink together.' He glanced at her. 'That was about the long and the short of it.'

'Did he have girlfriends?'

He glanced at her again. 'Is this an interview?'

She smiled. 'Just trying to find out what I never had time to learn about him.'

'He did from time to time,' said Pascal.

She glanced at him quickly to see that he was lost in thought.

'I mean he was single, not exactly on the breadline...' his voice tailed off.

She glanced at him again. 'Makes his whopping debt seem all the more curious.'

Pascal chewed his lip. 'Drugs and girls, I guess.'

Pascal and Collins got back in their car and she drove them out of town, past High Ridge Avenue, up onto the road leading to the cliff edge. A few minutes later, she parked where they could look down on the activity below.

'You know,' Collins said when she'd switched off the engine, 'John must have been killed while we were a hundred yards away, searching the club.'

Pascal chewed on his lip. He'd been deep in thought since leaving the hospital. He glanced at her sideways. 'I wish you hadn't said that, Alison. It's bad enough that he's been killed without thinking we might have been able to save him, if we'd known he was there.'

He lapsed into silence again.

Collins spoke again eventually. 'We have a murdered woman, who has connections with *The Kitty Klub;* we know, or at least strongly suspect, that there is a covert operation, called *Kittens* attached to *The Kitty Klub* which involves drugs and prostitution.' She counted her points off on her fingers. 'We know that girls are being brought into the country from the Baltic states, and put into prostitution by those who brought them. We have Julia Fox, abducted, and put into prostitution with them.' She twisted in her seat. 'And now we have a copper murdered not far from *The Kitty Klub*. Everything seems to connect to this place.'

Pascal looked at her without speaking for a moment.

' I last saw John the day before he was killed.'

She stared at him. 'You went to see him?'

Pascal glanced down briefly. 'Well, he's alone. *Was* alone. I wanted to be sure he was all right.'

'So what happened?'

'He talked to me about *Kittens.*'

She raised her eyebrows in enquiry.

'I hadn't told him the name of the place. But he knew it. We found out the name from the Latvian girl, Aspazia or whoever, and John wasn't with us at the time. But he knew about *Kittens*.' He stared out through slitted eyes at the rooftops below. 'And he was killed nearly outside it. Well, outside *The Kitty Klub,* and that amounts to the same thing. And I'm prepared to put money on the theory that he was getting his drugs from there.' He glanced round at her. 'Aspazia was attacked as far as we know by a Dutchman, Danny Bakker. Does that connect him with the clubs?'

Collins nodded.

He thought for a moment. 'Most likely, he's an enforcer. Doing the strong-arm stuff for... ' He shrugged. 'Who knows? Derrick Jackson?'

'Wouldn't he use a local person, if he wanted someone killed?'

'Yes, I reckon so. And anyway, why would *he* want to bump off Sara Martin? Wasn't she an asset?'

Collins looked at him askance. 'I suppose that's one way of putting it,' she said. 'I take it that you mean she was one of the women working the clients of *Kittens*. By all appearances, she worked the older ones.'

He glanced at her wryly. 'I take it your evidence is Councillor Clifford?'

She nodded, lips pursed.

'Might she have been bumped off because of him? She recognised him, and threatened to go to the papers if he didn't pay her a bit more?'

Pascal thought about it for a moment. 'Would Councillor Clifford have the knowledge and wherewithal to organise her murder? Would he care enough to want to do it? Blokes of his age caught out shagging younger women might be an object of admiration. You know there's still a double standard in society. A 40-year-old man shagging an 80-year-old woman would be disgusting. The other way round somehow isn't.'

'And it still doesn't answer the question about Danny Bakker.'

'No.' He turned to her. 'And Jared Martin is in Aruba. We don't seem to have enough evidence to seek his extradition.'

'We have yet to interview Derrick Jackson,' she reminded him. 'He might be useful.'

Pascal rolled his eyes. 'Don't remind me! The Custody Suite is brim-full of young women until recently engaged in the sex trade, a few men who controlled them, and a Councillor who used their services. Claude must be run ragged. Better get back there.'

At Breydon Police Station, Pascal had barely sat down in his office when his DCI brought in a man and a woman he didn't recognise.

'Ah, George,' began Steel, 'glad I caught you. This is DS Stonor and DC Kidder. They've been sent over by HQ to join our team.'

'Thank you, sir.' Pascal turned to the man and shook his hand. 'DI George Pascal.'

'Frank Kidder, sir, and this is my boss.' He nodded at the woman. She held out her hand. Pascal, who realised that he'd wrongly assumed the man was of the higher rank, managed to cover his gaff and smiled at DS Stonor. She responded to his smile with an appraising stare.

'Rachel Stonor, sir. We're here to take on the John Walker murder.'

Pascal nodded. She was tall, thin and angular. Shining black hair was held securely in a bun. She looked about thirty and was wearing a red, tailored linen suit. She wore thin, circular, gold-rimmed glasses through which she studied him, and high-heeled black shoes. Pascal noticed there were no rings on her fingers, no sign of jewellery anywhere about her. She was attractive in an ascetic sort of way.

'Good,' he said. 'I'll let you have a note of what little we have so far.'

She nodded. 'Of course. We prefer our own office, sir. Frank and I work as a team.'

She looked round at the clutter in his and wrinkled her nose. She had slightly uneven teeth, he noticed, only really white in the middle, as if that was the only place she cleaned.

'There's one workstation available in the CID office,' he said, pointing across the corridor. 'You can both try to share it.'

Stonor shook her head, watching him from under her dark eyebrows.

'I don't think that'll work,' she said, glancing at Steel.

'Work out your accommodation needs with DI Pascal,' said Steel, neatly placing the responsibility on Pascal's shoulders. 'I'll be off. Keep me informed of events, George.' He smiled at the newcomers. 'Good to see you both.'

After he'd gone, Kidder went through into the CID office at Stonor's suggestion, leaving her alone with Pascal.

She closed the door and turned to him. 'I would really like my own office, sir. I'll share one with Frank, if it helps.'

'My DS sits in the CID office because it helps to be in the same room as the DCs.'

'My point exactly, sir,' said Stonor. 'DS Collins is in the same office as *her* DCs; I want to be in an office with mine.'

'We don't have the space, sergeant. The best I can offer is to get an additional workstation put in, and the spare one in there already moved across to make a pair in place of the filing cabinets behind the door, which we'll move to the opposite corner, behind Bell.'

'But sir—!'

Pascal shrugged. 'Best I can do, DS Stonor.'

She studied him through her gold-rims.

'Very well, sir.'

'You'll be needing this, I think,' he said to her.

He passed her a manila folder. It had Walker's name on the outside, and the fact that his murder was the subject matter, while the content at present amounted to one piece of scrap paper on which the details of the original call were noted. Stonor read it, then looked up.

'I thought you'd have undertaken some preliminary investigative work, sir. After all, he was your DC.' Her voice was heavy with disapprobation.

'We've been very busy, and simply haven't had time to type out the report on what we've done so far. We've only just got back from the morgue.'

'I see, sir,' she said, putting the folder down. 'What did you find out?'

Pascal explained the latest thinking on how Walker had died. 'Subject to change at the PM, of course, if they find anything else.'

She nodded. 'Thank you, sir. I'll make a note and put it in the file.' She picked up the phone. 'Now I'll just get on to HR and sort out the furniture and workstations.'

'Perhaps you'd like to use the phone in the other room,' he said, and it wasn't a suggestion. 'I have to do some telephoning of my own.'

She stared at him, but released the telephone. 'Very well, sir. No doubt I shall be experiencing for myself the duties and requirements placed on a DI in the not too distant future.'

'You're up for promotion?'

'Yes.'

'There are some vacancies in Suffolk,' he said.

Stonor pursed her lips and stared at him unblinkingly through her circular lenses.

'I do hope, Detective Inspector Pascal, that was not an attempt at sarcasm? I never sink to the use of sarcasm myself, nor do I respond to it favourably,' she told him, before turning on her heel.

He picked up the phone, still staring at the doorway after she'd left.

He dialled, and was put through to Jane Ferrari at the hospital.

'Hello, George,' she said after he'd identified himself, her voice sinking to a seductive purr. 'What can I do for you? '

He squared his jaw determinedly. 'Uh, I'm sorry Jane, but I think I need to ask if we can postpone dinner again. We pulled in a lot of people last night and I'm likely to spend the rest of today interviewing them.'

'Oh,' she said.

He thought she sounded disappointed.

'I hope this isn't inconveniencing you too much,' he said. 'Besides, my face is still a mess. Another day might make all the difference.'

'Don't worry about that, George,' she said, and her voice had changed, as if she was muffling it from anyone around her. 'A few scars on a man can make him appear all the more romantic. Swashbuckling. Errol Flynn.'

Pascal coughed nervously. 'I – uh – I'm not quite in the Errol Flynn bracket,' he muttered.

'Oh! Come now, George! I'm sure if I present you with a chandelier, you won't be able to resist swinging on it.'

He coughed again, glancing towards the door to make sure he wasn't being overheard. 'Sorry. Got to go. Villains to catch, suspects to interview. You know how it is.'

'Just what I said, George: a swashbuckler.'

He hung up and sat back, staring at the telephone which seemed suddenly to have become extremely warm. He pushed his hair back and tried to get his thoughts back on                                                        business.

## CHAPTER 17

The ground floor of Breydon Central Police Station was divided into three main areas: the smallest was the 'front office', or public enquiry desk; behind it was the next largest area, occupied by the shift-working uniformed officers. The largest amount of floor space was given over to the Custody Suite, where prisoners were brought in under arrest and presented to the Custody Sergeant whose authorisation for detention was needed before a suspect could be held for questioning.

The Custody Suite itself was further subdivided into four corridors arranged in a star, or panoptic, shape which allowed the Sergeant and anyone else at the centre to oversee each. They were the main reception and waiting area, where prisoners were queued before seeing the Sergeant, a corridor containing private interview rooms where solicitors could consult privately with their clients, another corridor containing interview rooms fitted out with audio and video recording equipment where formal interviews took place.

The fourth area was a corridor lined with cells. At the far end of it was a special interview suite, which seemed positively homely after the harsh lighting and screwed-down facilities of the ordinary interview rooms. The 'soft' room was furnished with comfortable armchairs and a coffee table, which had a few magazines spread out on it. In one corner was a tiny sink and a kettle for making tea and coffee. The 'soft' room was also equipped with audio and video recording devices, but these were more discreet than those up the corridor. The 'soft' suite was for interviewing children and victims of domestic abuse and rape.

The cell corridor contained twelve cells, one of them a 'tank', designed to hold many people for a short period of time. When Pascal arrived, wanting to interview Derrick Jackson, the tank was full of girls. There was a gabble of conversations in a language Pascal didn't recognise, audible through the door. He approached the Custody Desk, where a harassed-looking Sergeant Claude Henslow was speaking very patiently down the telephone before staring at it and hanging up. He saw Pascal.

'What? I'm busy. Coffee Machine's over there.'

Pascal blinked as if in pain. 'Claude, how can you think I'm only here for the coffee?'

'I haven't got time to think, with all this lot cluttering the place up.'

Pascal looked round. The overall impression was of bedlam. Everyone seemed to be shouting at once. 'I see you've stamped your authority on the assembled multitude, Claude.'

Henslow glared at him. 'What do you want, George? I'm a bit busy this morning, on account of *somebody* arranging to bring in half the tarts in Breydon just as it's my turn in Custody.'

'Surely there's more than half, Claude?'

Henslow regarded him through narrowed eyes. 'Just what *do* you want? I have to find another blessed Latvian interpreter or two.' He indicated the phone with a nod of his head.

'I want to interview Derrick Jackson, one of the town's leading entrepreneurs, and friend of people in high places – like the Police Authority.'

Henslow stared at him. 'Who, for God's sake?'

'The last Chairman. He was our guest earlier. Gone somewhere safe now.'

Henslow frowned at him. 'How do you mean, safe?'

'Somewhere the mates he's grassed up won't find him easily.'

Henslow stared. 'You mean he's a *witness*?'

'For the prosecution,' said Pascal. 'Which is why he's been taken somewhere safe.'

'Witness protection?'

'Quite. Even I do not know what they've done with him, and as long as he turns up in court when required, I don't care.'

Pascal smiled at Henslow, his head tilted sideways.

'Meantime, can I have Mr Jackson?'

'Of course, you can, George,' said Henslow in a tone of voice which indicated that their brief moment of togetherness was over. 'Why didn't you say so? Would you like someone with you to take notes? As everyone else is busy, I'd volunteer to do it myself, but as you can see – *I still haven't found all the interpreters I need!*' He allowed his frayed temper to show.

Pascal smiled with exaggerated gratitude. 'Thank you Claude. Which room shall I use?'

'Any that isn't in use. Bell and Frimley are using two rooms so there should be a couple spare, unless any of my PCs has grabbed one to interview one of the shoplifters who were brought in overnight.'

Pascal shook his head. 'Ah, the impetuosity of youth, eh, Claude?'

Henslow shoved the Custody Record for Derrick Jackson in front of Pascal and jabbed it with his finger. 'Sign here – and no rough stuff. I want him back in good condition.'

'Claude, anything for you! You know how careful I am with the merchandise.'

Pascal signed the record, taking formal charge of the prisoner's welfare during the interview, and went to get Jackson from his cell.

*

'We have footage from your own CCTV cameras that show you taking people through a doorway in the back wall of *The Kitty Klub*. Where were you taking them?' Pascal asked.

'There's a part of the building which you've seen, containing a few bedrooms for any guests who want to stay the night,' Jackson said. 'Sometimes, they prefer to do that if they've had a drink too much,' he added unctuously.

'You're right when you say I've seen that part of the building. I saw the bedrooms, as you call them. What colour were the bed sheets on that occasion, Mr Jackson?'

'I'm sure I don't remember.'

'Do you remember what fabric they were made from?'

'Sorry, no. The sheets are changed daily. I don't tell the room maids what sheets to put on the beds.'

'What is on the ceiling above the beds?'

'Mirrors.'

'Why do you have mirrors on the ceiling above the beds?'

'So people can see themselves in them.' Jackson turned to his solicitor. 'Really, I don't see the significance of this.'

'Neither do I, Mr Jackson,' said the lawyer, turning to Pascal. 'There's no offence of having mirrors above your bed, Detective Sergeant. Can we move on?'

'Does anyone use drugs – heroin or cocaine or the like – in either *The Kitty Klub* or *Kittens*?'

'It's possible. We try to stop people bringing drugs onto the premises, but I suppose inevitably, some gets through our checks.'

'Have you ever seen anyone snorting coke, or taking heroin by any means?'

'No.'

'Are you aware that during the execution of the search warrant yesterday on your club premises, we used drug detector dogs?'

'Yes.'

'Were you able to watch the dogs at work in *The Kitty Klub?*'

'Most of the time.'

'Were you present when two small bags containing a white crystalline powder, which reacted positively to our field test for a class A drug, and which are now being analysed properly by the Forensic Science Service, were found in the bottom drawer of the desk in your office?'

Jackson hesitated for a second. 'Yes.'

'Are you able to tell us what the bags contained and account for their presence in your desk?'

'No.'

'Did you watch the dog which approached the hidden door into *Kittens?*'

'You seem determined to read something into the fact that the entrance to *Kittens* is curtained off. But that's all it is... '

Pascal allowed himself the faintest of grins. 'But did you see the dog approach it?'

'Yes.'

'How did it behave?'

Jackson glanced at the solicitor, who shrugged. 'It barked.'

'Yes. It's how the dogs are trained to react to the presence of drugs.

'I suppose so.'

'What happened next, Mr Jackson?'

It was Jackson's turn to smile. 'They took the dog through... the door.'

'You saw this?'

'Yes.'

'Did you follow the dog handler into *Kittens?*'

He nodded. 'Yes. You were there.'

'It's for the benefit of the tape, Mr Jackson,' Pascal explained. 'I suppose the dog darted about, straight to where the drugs were?'

Jackson shook his head, smugly. 'No. As a matter of fact, the dog seemed to run round in circles for a while before sitting at its handler's feet. No barking, no excitement.'

'Why do you think that would be, after all the earlier excitement outside the door?'

Jackson raised a cynical eyebrow. 'How should I know? I'm not a dog trainer.'

Pascal sat back for a moment and studied Jackson.

'Turning now to other matters. Do you know a woman by the name of — '

'A moment, Detective Sergeant, please,' interrupted the lawyer.

'Yes sir?'

'Perhaps you could explain the significance of the dog's behaviour.'

Pascal considered whether to answer for a few moments, deciding eventually that there was probably no harm in doing so.

'That particular animal has an excellent track record for detecting quite small amounts of heroin and cocaine. Barking and excited behaviour are what the dog does to tell its handler that it has caught the scent of one or other of these drugs. If the dog is still and silent when it's working, it either hasn't got a scent, or it is totally immersed in the scent.'

'But why doesn't it register excitement if surrounded by the scent of drugs?'

'Because their scent doesn't stand out from the surroundings. At the door to *Kittens*, it barks because the scent is coming through the door, but once beyond the door the whole establishment stinks of the drugs to the dog.' Pascal sat back. 'If a woman wearing perfume walks past you, you tend to notice it. If you pass that same woman in a room which is entirely soused in the same perfume, you wouldn't notice hers against the background. Not a perfect analogy but the best I can do at short notice.'

The solicitor seemed satisfied and sat back, crossing his legs and resting his document wallet on his knees to support his notepad.

'To move on,' Pascal continued, 'Did you know Sara Rebecca Martin?'

Jackson's eyes flicked downwards for an instant. 'No.'

'How about a prostitute calling herself Viv, or Vivien?'

Again the downward flick of the eyes. His hands gripped each other across his stomach. He shook his head.

'No.'

'Her husband said she regularly went to see a man friend. She called him Deej. That's you, isn't it? Derrick Jackson? D.J.? Deej?'

'I have no idea. I don't know a Viv.'

'Do you know a local councillor called Gordon Clifford?'

Jackson's interlocked fingers were squeezing each other. Another downward flick of the eyes before looking up and meeting Pascal's steady gaze.

'Possibly. I'm a businessman, running one of the larger leisure activities in Breydon.'

Pascal held a hand up. 'Before you go further, please bear in mind that we have the CCTV tapes.'

Jackson stared at him for a second before dropping his gaze to the table top again.

'I was going to say, it's possible that we've met.'

'How well do you know him?'

'Hardly at all.'

'It's a bit unusual to entrust your valuable stock-in-trade to someone you hardly know isn't it?'

Jackson managed to wrinkle his smooth forehead into an attitude of puzzlement.

'I don't know what you mean.'

'And have you ever had dealings with Danny Bakker, a Dutch national?'

'No!'

It was a swift response and to Pascal's ears, failed to ring true.

'How about a Latvian girl who came over here to take up secretarial work, she thought, and finished up by being forcibly hooked on heroin and made to work as a prostitute in *Kittens* and in Danny Bakker's bedroom?'

'I don't know any Latvian girls!' Jackson cried, his self-control reaching breaking point. 'I don't know Danny Bakker! I don't know Viv or Sara!'

'But you know Sara *is* Viv, don't you?' demanded Pascal, leaning forward until his head was within inches of Jackson, who, he noted with satisfaction, had broken out into a sweat.

Jackson's hands were now beating his knees and his feet were constantly moving. 'Sara is Viv? Yes?'

'And you know that Sara is dead, killed by Bakker, and I want to know why.'

Jackson lifted his head so Pascal could see his eyes, suddenly full of fear. He shook his head.

'No! No, no!'

The lawyer shifted uncomfortably in his seat. 'Detective Inspector Pascal! Please stop harassing my client!' he demanded.

Pascal kept his eyes on Jackson. 'I think you're lying,' he said. 'We shall know soon enough when we've finished interviewing everyone.' He nodded towards the door. 'There's about forty potential witnesses against you out there. With their help, we'll see you put away for life, and there'll be no reduction in sentence because you co-operated. This is your last opportunity to get in first. My colleagues are already interviewing the others, and as soon as they tell me you've been incriminated, your chance is blown. Or will you bet on them not mentioning your part in all this? Do you think they'll take the rap for you?'

He stood up and turned to the officer sitting beside the tape recorder.

'Right. Interview terminated—'

'Wait,' said Jackson quietly.

Pascal sat down.

'I'm waiting.'

The solicitor leaned forward. 'You don't have to incriminate yourself, Mr Jackson.'

Jackson turned to look at him and slowly, sadly, shook his head. Then he turned back to Pascal.

*

Alison Collins crossed one long leg elegantly over the other and gazed sympathetically at Julia Fox. The girl was rubbing her arms as if cold in the warm single-bedded side ward. She was wearing a hospital gown, her clothes having been taken for forensic examination. Andrew and Cathy Fox, her parents, sat at the opposite side of the bed from Collins.

'Look, if you don't feel like talking,' Collins began gently, 'let me tell you what I think happened and you can tell me if I'm right.'

Julia nodded.

'On the Saturday before Easter Sunday, you had a disagreement with your parents about spending the weekend camping with your boyfriend, David Ellis. How am I doing?'

'Okay.'

Collins continued, hoping the girl would contribute more. 'And then you left home. You took a suitcase full of clothes, so you were obviously going somewhere. Where?'

Collins's tone was gentle, seeking to reassure the girl that she was safe. She was shocked when Julia's eyes closed briefly and a moment later tears oozed from them and rolled down her cheeks. Julia made no sound, and Collins felt a chord of sympathy within her. She waited patiently, turning to reach a box of tissues and place it within Julia's reach.

When at last she spoke, Julia's voice was soft, her speech interrupted by sobs. 'I thought my Godmother was my friend. I went to stay with her and Jared.'

Collins stiffened at the name. 'Do you mean Jared Martin?'

Julia nodded, dabbing her face with a tissue and finally blowing her nose.

'So your Godmother – was that Sara Martin?'

Julia nodded again, and frowned. 'You know her – them?'

It was Collins's turn to nod. 'Has nobody told you? I'm sorry to have to say that Sara Martin is dead – murdered – and Jared Martin has disappeared – we think he's in the Caribbean.'

Cathy Fox, on the other side of the bed, covered her mouth with a hand and forced back a cry. Collins glanced at her and shook her head briefly, discouraging her from interrupting.

Julia had folded her arms across her stomach and now rocked back and forth in her chair, her eyes again closed while tears flowed.

When she opened them again, they were dull, uninterested. Collins waited.

'I thought she was my friend,' repeated Julia. 'We used to send emails to each other, and meet up in chat-rooms on the internet. When I had the fight with my parents, I decided to go and see her – I mean, it's not as if she lived on the far side of the moon or anything: it's just a bus ride.'

'So you turned up on their doorstep out of the blue?'

'I'd sent Sara an email to say I was coming, but she hadn't seen it. Anyway, she didn't seem to mind. She said we could go to this club she knew. We got dressed up – it was fun. During the evening, we met the bloke who owns it, and he bought me a drink.'

She stopped, a look of confusion on her face.

'What happened then?' prompted Collins.

'I – I don't remember. The next thing I do remember, I was in a tiny room, with just a bed, a washbasin… and a bucket,' she added, dropping her gaze. 'Derrick and another man started… messing… around with me. I couldn't stop it. They found out...' She hesitated, glancing at her parents. 'They found out I was a virgin.'

'Did they rape you?'

Julia shook her head. 'No. They said they could auction off my virginity. I didn't know what they meant at first.' She screwed up her face. 'You've got to understand: I didn't want them doing this! I just couldn't stop them.'

Collins rested a hand on Julia's arm, comfortingly. 'It's not your fault. You'd been drugged, I expect. Something in the drink Derrick Jackson gave you.' She waited a moment before continuing. 'Who was the other man?'

'Paul.' Julia glanced round at her parents and seemed to make up her mind about something. She turned back to Collins and shrugged. 'He made me take heroin and taught me how to – to fuck punters.' She shivered and pulled the bed sheets closer.

Cathy Fox was biting her hand. Her husband was looking pole-axed. Tears streamed down his cheeks.

'Did Paul have sex with you too?' Collins asked, concentrating on the girl.

'Every time he shot more heroin into me, he'd do something. He never actually had sex with me, but he did other stuff. Eventually, I didn't care.'

Collins nodded. 'Did you think about escaping?'

'I couldn't. The door was locked, and besides, they'd taken photographs of me and said they'd send them to my parents if I gave them any trouble. So...' She sobbed. 'So... I let them do what they wanted,' she added in a whisper.

Cathy Fox reached forward and touched her daughter's arm.

Julia turned to her. 'I'm sorry, mum,' she said.

Cathy leaned forward and hugged her.

Collins waited a moment until Cathy sat down again.

'So Paul in effect taught you to have sex with men and got you used to heroin?' she asked.

Julia nodded.

'Did you then begin to work in *Kittens?*'

'Me and the other girls.'

'What's *Kittens?*' asked Andrew.

Collins glanced at him. 'A high class bordello.'

He blenched. 'Oh, God!'

Collins turned back to Julia, worried that her present co-operative streak might disappear if the need for more heroin became too much to bear.

'Do you know any of the men you saw there?'

'Not really. Some came more than once.' She blushed suddenly. 'I mean to the club.'

Collins smiled. 'But none of them stand out in your mind?'

'No.' She hesitated. 'Well, there was the first bloke, the one who bid the highest. Then there was a bloke I had a couple of times – a couple of visits. He was tall and fairly good-looking. I remember wondering why he went there.' She stared at nothing in particular, looking deep in reflection. Beside her, Cathy Fox was silently weeping, and her husband had put a comforting arm round her shoulders.

'Did he have sex with you?' Collins continued.

'Oh, yeah. He was a coke-head, probably felt on top of the world. He fucked me all right.' She lifted her gaze to Collins'. 'Talked about re-hab. Said he had contacts. Seemed bothered that we were fucking, but not so bothered he didn't.'

'Do you know his name?'

'He never told me... but the boss called him John. I thought he called him that because he was a punter – you know, a john.'

Collins nodded. 'Yes. The boss: that was Derrick?'

For the first time, Julia's expression grew wary. 'Yes. What'll happen if he finds out I've told you?'

'If he's the man back at the police station currently talking to DS Pascal, he'll be facing years inside. It could be life, because we think he's involved in Sara's murder.'

Julia's eyes widened briefly before resuming their life-less appearance.

'But what if he doesn't? He'll come after me, or Paul will.'

'Paul is also currently helping us with our enquiries at the police station – not least because of his attempted murder of you with the heroin syringe, which he'll go down for. But he's also looking at multiple rape, prostitution and drug-dealing charges.'

'And what's going to happen to me and the other girls?'

'You've not gone far down the road to addiction – none of the girls has – so getting you off the drug should-n't be too difficult. There are programmes and clinics which will help you do that,'

'What about... prostitution?'

Collins grinned. 'In one of those vagaries of the law, soliciting on the street, running a brothel, living on immor-al earnings, are all illegal. Prostitution itself isn't. You can be a prostitute legally, but almost every activity you'd nor-mally have to engage in to be one is illegal. I don't under-stand the thinking of the politicians, but fortunately I don't have to. As far as we can tell, none of the girls has solicit-ed, there's no evidence any of you took money for sex, and you only ever worked in *Kittens,* not on the street. I think you were all there against your will.'

Julia was silent a moment. 'So nothing's going to hap-pen to me?'

'No. Nor the other girls. But we'd like you to give evi-dence in court.'

She went on quickly, seeing fear cross Julia's face. 'It'll be a long time before that happens, and you won't be needed if Jackson admits his part.' She stood up. 'In the meantime, you only have to concentrate on getting well.'

She stopped when Julia frowned.

'What?'

The girl looked at her parents. 'Why didn't you come looking for me? And why didn't David?'

Collins replied. 'Your parents had no idea where you were. There was a big hunt for you, your picture was in the local papers and on TV. David – ah! you probably don't know about David?'

'No, what?'

'Sometime in the middle of the night between Maundy Thursday and Good Friday, he was struck on the head with a piece of iron pipe on the quayside at Hartley-over-Sands. He was seriously ill, in a coma from which he's only just emerged.'

Julia stared at her. 'So that's why he didn't come…'

'He couldn't.'

'Is he all right now?'

'I think so. Still very bandaged up. It'll be a while before his skull heals properly.' She grinned. 'Would you like to see him?'

Julia's eyes widened. 'He's here?' She chewed her lip. 'If he knows what I've been doing, he… he won't want to see me.'

'That's not what he said when I saw him earlier. You were the first person he asked for.'

Julia shook her head. 'Can I go to him?'

'I think so. Slip your shoes on and I'll take you.'

Julia got out of the bed. She was still shivering. Her mother stood up as if to come with her, but Julia shook her head.

'I'll come back, mum. I promise.'

Julia followed Collins along the corridor. At the door of David Ellis's room, she let the girl go in ahead of her. Marion Ellis was in her customary place, beside her son's bed. They both turned as the door opened. David's head was heavily bandaged, but it was slightly raised on a pillow, and his eyes sought out Julia's as she crossed the room nervously to the side of his bed.

'Hi, David,' said Julia softly. 'I'm glad you're all right.'

'Julia!' He reached out until he found her hand. 'Thank God they found you.'

'Julia!' exclaimed Marion. 'Oh, how glad I am to see you!'

She hugged the girl briefly before walking round the bed towards the door. For a moment she stood beside Collins watching the reunion, then both women stepped outside. Collins stood where she could see the two teenagers. Mrs Ellis fumbled in her bag for a paper tissue, mopped her eyes and blew her nose.

'Just about the first thing he said when he came round was where was Julia and what had happened to her,' she said. 'I told him she'd been missing since he'd been attacked. He's been very miserable, thinking he let her down.'

Collins watched as, in the room, after they had spoken for a while, Julia very carefully sat on the edge of the bed, leaned down and kissed David, while his arm went round her waist to hold her there

.

# CHAPTER 18

The last Chairman of the Police Authority looked round the interview room, his roving gaze hesitating on the statutory notices about his rights under the Police and Criminal Evidence Act, before moving on.

He'd been produced for interview by the witness protection people and brought into the police station through the staff entrance. The Custody area had been cleared while he was led into an interview room.

His solicitor sat silently beside him. The door opened to admit a fat police officer in plain clothes, his round, moon-like face seeming to wobble on his shoulders. Behind him, a constable in uniform brought a new pair of interview tapes and took his place beside the tape recorder. In a corner of the room, near the ceiling, the red tally-lamp on a video camera was evidence that the video tape was already running.

After the preliminaries, when Bell introduced himself and got them all to record their presence for the benefit of the tape, Clifford sat back, a sour expression on his face and waited for the inevitable.

Bell leaned forward. 'Now, then, Councillor Clifford, how long have you been fucking women at *Kittens?*'

Clifford's breath caught in his throat. He coughed and swallowed. 'That's an insolent question, Mr Bell,' he protested.

'A reasonable one, though, Councillor, given that we know for a fact you had sex with Sara Martin, whom you knew as Vivien or Viv, an hour or two before she was killed. Murdered. So this is serious stuff, and I'm not mucking about. Now answer the question.'

For a moment, Clifford looked as if he was about to continue his protest, then the wind seemed to leave his sails and he sagged forward, his elbows propped on the table between them.

'Since my wife died fourteen years ago.'

'And what put you on to the place?'

'Derrick Jackson proposed a business investment. He wanted me to put money into the development of *The Kitty Klub,* in return for which, I'd have free access to the premises and use of the facilities.'

Bell's eyebrows shot up. 'The facilities?'

'In those days, before *Kittens,* it was a few drinks at the bar. A few working girls used to come in and some of them were very attractive. Derrick saw some pecuniary advantage in kitting out the rooms beyond the main club for the girls to use, in exchange for a percentage. Very quickly, he became the one taking the money on the door, so to speak, and the paymaster for the girls. At first it was a mutual arrangement, but then, I suppose, he became greedy, and started taking the biggest cut of the punters' money. Then the girls threatened to walk out. They could have, too, except that Paul Unwin came on the scene. He'd been a pimp for several of the girls, and wasn't very pleased with what Derrick had done, effectively cutting him out of the revenue stream. So Derrick made him, like, head wrangler, keeping the girls in order. It was Unwin who had the idea of getting the girls dependent on heroin to keep them in order. Some of them were already on the stuff anyway.'

He paused and reached for a plastic cup of water put there for him.

'When did Jackson begin importing girls from the Baltic states?' asked Bell.

'About a year or eighteen months ago,' Clifford replied.

'Do you know how often he would bring them in, and in what numbers?'

'No. Not really. Every few months, he'd tell us there was a new crop – that's what he called them, a new crop. And there would be a Friday night party when we got first crack at them.'

'Are you suggesting they were virgins?'

Clifford shook his head and waved his hands in a negative gesture. 'No. Well, some were, and he'd auction off the right to be first with them. The others, Paul simply trained.'

'Trained?'

'You see, the first girls had been on the game anyway, but the imports were told they were being brought here to fill respectable posts, like secretaries and translators.'

'But illegally? As illegal immigrants?'

Clifford shrugged. 'It wasn't as if they were taking jobs away from British people or living on benefits.'

'How often has your home been used by the prostitutes for their business?'

'Never.'

Bell considered telling him what the police had found when they raided the place but decided not to.

'What's the extent of your financial stake in *The Kitty Klub* and *Kittens*?'

Clifford looked down at the table-top. 'I'm not sure.'

'Do you declare it to the Revenue? Do you declare it on the Register of Members' Interests at the Council?'

Clifford looked up at him derisorily. 'It's not the sort of thing you'd normally mention to other people.'

'Do you use drugs, Councillor Clifford?'

'I take a number of prescribed medicines for blood pressure and cholesterol. And my GP gives me *Cialis* if I ask.'

Bell leaned closer. 'Don't get cute with me, Councillor. Do you do coke or heroin, or Ecstasy or dope, or anything else in schedule three of the Misuse of Drugs Act?'

Clifford moved his head away and sat back in his bolted-down chair. 'N-not as a rule.'

'Had you taken *Cialis* the night you had sex with Sara Martin?'

'What business is that of yours?' demanded Clifford.

'I conclude you must have since she was found to contain your ejaculate.'

The solicitor sitting beside Clifford leaned forward. 'What is your point, Detective Constable? As Councillor Clifford has said, what business is it of yours whether or not he had taken *Cialis* that night?'

Bell looked at him through narrowed eyes. 'Intention.' He turned toward Clifford again. '*Cialis* is like *Viagra*. You need to take it in advance, so it has time to work. Let me put the question another way: did you go out that Friday night with a view to having sex?'

'That was the point, the purpose of going to Derrick's Friday night parties.'

'How much say do you have in the running of *The Kitty Klub* and *Kittens*?'

'Derrick ran everything.'

'Will he agree, if that question is put to him? If I ask him if you had any say in the running of the organisation, he'll admit to running everything?'

'I don't know what he'd do.'

'Might he not agree with you? Might he say that you had some control over the business affairs of the clubs?'

Clifford clasped his hands and looked down at them, held in his lap. 'He might,' he muttered.

Bell leaned forward again and spoke softly. 'Might he say it in the witness box?'

The solicitor shook his head. 'Mr Clifford cannot possibly know what someone else may or may not say in the witness box.'

Bell nodded, keeping his eyes on Clifford. 'You're right of course... but the idea of Jackson giving evidence against your client might give Councillor Clifford here a few sleepless nights.'

'Is there a question in there, Constable?'

'No, sir, just an observation.' Bell turned his gaze on the solicitor. 'Personally, if I were in your client's shoes, former Chairman of the Police Authority, member of the County Council, pillar of the community and long-serving member of his Parish Council, I'd be scared shitless that Derrick Jackson would try to offload as much responsibility as he could onto my shoulders. I mean, we're looking at a probable murder charge and life imprisonment.' He turned back to Clifford. 'If I was Jackson, I'd be desperate to let somebody else take the rap for that. Who better than the man who's had a financial finger in the pie for, what, fifteen years?'

'I believe I need to talk with my client privately, Detective Constable.'

'Very well sir. Ten minutes enough? Would you like tea or coffee, gentlemen? I'm going to have one. Could be a long day. Constable, please suspend the interview, and we'll leave these two alone.'

Out in the corridor a few minutes later, Bell found Frimley, also on a break from his interview with Paul Unwin. Bell filled him in on the information Clifford had imparted concerning Unwin.

'He's a really nasty piece of work,' said Frimley.

'Which of them isn't?' said Bell. 'Any idea what came out of Pascal's interview of Jackson?'

Frimley shrugged. 'They're still in there,' he said, nodding towards Interview Room One. 'Been there for hours.'

'Reckon he must be stonewalling like mad, or spilling the beans,' said Bell.

'See if there's a clue on the CCTV.'

Bell followed Frimley into the CCTV monitoring suite, where a civilian employee was making sure the recorders didn't exceed the capacity of the recorders and that the microphones and all the cameras, two to each interview room, were working properly. They asked her to put the sound from Interview Room One on the speaker, and the pictures on the largest monitor, where a close-up of Jackson's face was superimposed in a corner of the screen, over a wide shot of the whole room, showing everyone present. They heard Pascal's voice.

'So it was because Jared Martin had not paid the money you gave him for laundering to the Dutch that they sent Danny Bakker over to extract it?'

'Yes,' Jackson replied.

'And was he successful?'

'No. Martin said he didn't have the money and was unable to pay.'

'Why, if you'd already given him what you owed the Dutch?'

'I don't know.'

'What did Bakker intend to do about it?'

'He said he wanted to figure out a means to encourage Martin to pay. I think Bakker will do everything he can to keep on the right side of Mr van Ruys.'

'Van Ruys is Bakker's Dutch employer?'

Jackson scowled as if realising he'd volunteered information unnecessarily. 'Yes.'

'So van Ruys supplies your drugs?'

'No comment.'

'How did Bakker intend to encourage Martin to pay?'

'I don't know.'

'There's a connection between Bakker and Sara Martin, and between Bakker and you. We know what your connection with him was, but what was hers?'

Jackson looked away before dragging his eyes back to meet Pascal's. 'Maybe she fucked him.'

'When?'

'I don't know. That Sunday?'

'She left the club with him that evening. It's on CCTV. Where'd they go?'

'I don't know.'

'Do your working girls often go off the club premises with clients?'

'No. And they're more Paul's girls than mine.'

'You only need to be shown to have control of one of them to face a charge of living off immoral earnings and procuring girls to work as prostitutes. I think we can manage that, but by all means tell me how far Unwin is involved.'

In the CCTV monitoring room, Bell's coffee was nearly cold.

'Ah, well, back to our revered former PA Chairman.'

He and Frimley left the control suite and headed towards their respective interview rooms.

*

Collins left Julia in the care of Jane Ferrari and her parents. The process of weaning the girl off heroin was under way. When she arrived at Breydon police station, she found Frimley and Pascal in the latter's office going through one of the CCTV recordings uplifted during the raid.

'What's that?' she asked.

Frimley told her. 'Taken the day Sara Martin disappeared,' he said.

She perched on the edge of Pascal's desk as he pressed Play.

*The Kitty Klub* was undoubtedly popular, Collins thought, watching the flocks of young, scantily-clad girls clustering round the bar, taking gulps of attractively-coloured drinks from bottles. They were at the centre of a group of young men in sharp suits consuming lagers. There were no faces she recognised in the crowd and Frimley must have thought so too, as he fast-forwarded the tape, until the time-stamp at the bottom of the frame showed half an hour had passed.

At mid-evening, Sara Martin came into shot, nodding at the bar tender as she passed out of view again.

'There she goes!' exclaimed Frimley, pointing at the hidden doorway to *Kittens*, out of focus in the top right of the screen. He replayed the recording and Collins watched carefully so Sara Martin could be identified, passing through the curtains in the far wall.

'Now we need to see her come out,' said Pascal.

Frimley fast-forwarded the tape a time or two until quick movement in the top right of the frame made him stop and rewind a few seconds.

Three men emerged through the curtain. They disappeared from view for a few seconds before re-entering the frame close to the camera covering the bar. They bought drinks, and were apparently in a jovial mood.

'Anybody recognise them?' asked Pascal.

The three detectives were so intent on trying to recognise the features of the men that Collins almost missed another movement of the curtain in the top right corner of the pictures.

'Someone else has just come out,' she said.

A moment later, Sara Martin and a man who looked to be in his late twenties walked through the shot.

'Who's he?' demanded Pascal.

Frimley stared at the young man and stopped the tape while he went to his desk in the other room, returning with the photograph of Danny Bakker which the Dutch had sent.

'Him, unless I miss my guess,' he said.

Pascal nodded. 'What time of night was this?' He peered at the timecode on the screen. 'Nearly midnight. And six hours or so later, Sara Martin was found dead. We need to find him.'

*

Pascal went to the Crime Scene Investigator's office. He was still feeling the euphoric effects of the interview sessions the previous day. He sipped coffee and stared at an empty half-bottle whose label stated it had once held whisky. Jimmy Tasker, the CSI who'd worked on many of his current crime scenes was holding it up in an evidence bag.

'Whisky is not the last fluid it held, DS Pascal.'

Pascal leaned back until the chair behind his desk creaked in protest. 'I'm sure at this point I'm supposed to look astonished and ask what did it last hold, Jimmy.'

'That would be playing the game, George,' Tasker nodded. 'It was petrol. 95-ron unleaded as sold on forecourts everywhere.'

'Such as was used to set the fire at Jared Martin's?'

'Yes,' replied Tasker, but added, 'Also as used to set fire to Sara Martin and the car she was found in.'

Pascal tipped his head to the side slightly. 'That car stank of petrol. Are you saying it could have been as small an amount as what that bottle holds?'

Tasker nodded. 'You don't need much, and the vapour expands with the heat. Sara Martin should have been totally incinerated, if only the cliff hadn't fallen on the car and cut off the oxygen supply.'

Pascal nodded. 'And where was this bottle found?'

'In a briefcase in Jared Martin's bedroom.'

Pascal pursed his lips. 'Surely it wasn't his?'

'No. The room had been searched earlier, immediately after the fire, but after the shooting incident involving you, it was searched again – obviously, since there was a gunman hiding out in the place when you got there.' Pascal nodded. 'That was when we realised the briefcase hadn't been there before, and the chances are it belonged to whoever shot at you.'

'And whoever that was, he could have set the fire or killed Sara Martin or both?'

'Precisely, George.'

'Anything else you want to tell me?'

'Well, the case is covered with fingerprints, inside and out, which match the ones found on the bottle, Jared Martin's letterbox flap and in the hotel room used by Danny Bakker.' Tasker put the bottle on the desk. 'So it's elementary, my dear DI: Bakker is your murderer.'

'All right, all right! I'm the detective round here.' His eyes belied the seriousness of his tone. 'Okay, so Bakker is our *alleged* murderer.'

Tasker nodded.

'So what will he be doing now? And I still don't know *why* he killed her.'

Tasker shook his head in mock regret. 'Sorry, George, I can't do everything. You'll have to work that out for yourself.'

'Hmm.' Pascal chewed his cheek. 'Anything else in the briefcase that might be helpful to our enquiries?'

'Three SIM cards for mobile phones. A couple of passports, including what looks like Bakker's proper Dutch one, and one that seems to be Czech, which I'm pretty certain is false, but they're easy to get on the Continent.'

'Brilliant!' Pascal nodded his approval. 'Well, let me know if you find anything else interesting,' he said, getting to his feet. 'Meanwhile, I have to go and interview a few people.'

\*

Danny Bakker turned off the main Harwich road into the approach to Parkeston Quay, berth for the Harwich-Hook ferry. He would have to box clever, he knew, if he was to get past the security checks onto the ferry. They'd been beefed up since Britain had been on the receiving end of terrorist threats, and whilst it was no problem to dump the car he'd stolen in Breydon, he didn't want to have to dump the Sig Sauer: somehow, he'd have to get it past the checks.

As a foot passenger, was he more or less likely to be noticed than if he was in the vehicle? The one he'd stolen was a fairly nondescript Zafira MPV, whose owner had left the engine running while she got out to open the gates across her driveway. She would almost certainly have reported the vehicle stolen, and he didn't know if a report would automatically be circulated to ferry ports. It seemed logical. But only if he kept the Zafira could he hope to keep his pistol. Passengers went through metal detectors at ferry ports just as they did at airports these days, and that meant he needed to find another way on board.

And, of course, the port police might well be on the lookout for him. On balance, he figured he had a better chance if he dumped the Zafira and took his chance as a foot passenger, trusting that he'd simply be one face among many, and the police too distracted to recognise him.

He pulled into a car park. Until that moment, he hadn't had a chance to search the vehicle for anything useful. He twisted round and found a pair of shopping bags on the seat behind him. A pack of chocolate biscuits reminded him it had been a long time since he'd eaten anything. He opened the pack and grimaced at the sight of what the British called 'Milk Chocolate', so sweet and sickly compared to the real thing. Nevertheless, sugar would be good for the short term energy. He began eating. There were some fresh vegetables, and he found some carrots and celery.

There was a sharp knock on the side window. Cautiously, his hand on the Sig hidden between the seats, he cracked it open.

'Yes?'

The man outside was wearing a yellow hi-vis anorak with the hood covering his head, black square-framed spectacles, and a bristly moustache, greying at the tips.

'Don't fergit to buy yer parkin' ticket, mate.' He jabbed his finger towards the pay and display machine.

Bakker smiled and nodded before closing the window. Jobsworth!

He waited till the man had gone out of sight.

He bit off half a carrot and chewed it as he got out of the vehicle. The shock of the tap on the window had boosted his adrenalin. Now, taking the purloined food in one of the carrier bags, he strolled across the car park towards the passenger terminal. Crossing the railway line which ran at the rear of the terminal, he entered the building. A further complication had occurred to him on the journey down from Norfolk: he couldn't buy a ticket without his passport, and his chances of getting on board with neither were slim. He racked his brains for a means of getting aboard the ferry which stood at the quayside.

He had one more biscuit covered in awful alleged chocolate, walked into the Gents' Toilet, where he had a pee and walked across to the hand basins. The sight of his face in the mirror caused him to stop in his tracks. How long had he looked so filthy? It looked as if some of the soot in Jared Martin's hall had transferred itself to his face. He was about to wash it off when he realised that it made a good disguise.

*

Andrew and Cathy Fox followed Collins and their daughter into the 'soft' interview room at Breydon.

Andrew put his arm round Julia's shoulders.

'It's wonderful to have you back, sweetheart,' he said softly.

She stared at him without expression, one hand slipping down and rubbing her thigh under a skirt which had been supplied by Paul Unwin for 'working purposes' – it was very short.

Her father noticed. 'Are you all right?' he asked.

Julia shrugged.

Collins took one of the chairs opposite the settee, and cleared her throat.

'I'd like to ask you a few more questions, Julia,' she said.

Andrew glanced at her and nodded, moving so he and his wife could sit side by side facing Collins.

Cathy looked worried. 'Is Julia under arrest? What for? She hasn't done anything.' She turned to the girl. 'Tell her, love.'

Julia turned her bland stare on the policewoman but said nothing. In contrast with the last time they'd met, in the hospital, Julia was sullen and obviously reluctant to help them further. Collins figured it was down to the withdrawal of heroin. The girl was not far enough gone to require methadone treatment, and was merely being given a painkiller periodically to help her cope with the pain as it strove to correct for the chemical imbalance in her brain caused by the drug.

Collins explained that Julia was not under arrest and, indeed, was legally free to leave at any time, but she also strongly advised the family that the woman from The Matthew Project, the county-based organisation which tried to help people with a drugs problem, should have the opportunity to talk to them before they left.

Collins turned a couple of pages in the file on her lap, drawing out a five by three photograph of John Walker..

'Did you ever meet this man?'

Julia studied the picture briefly. 'He had me a couple of times.' She glanced up at Collins' face. 'He wasn't so bad. Careful, like.' She smiled reminiscently. It was the first sign of any emotion she had displayed. 'He was the one offered to help me get away and get off heroin.' The smile disappeared. 'Speaking of which, I could do with some.'

Cathy Fox's mouth opened in horror. 'No, Julia! You can't have any more of that stuff. It'll kill you.'

Julia turned her head slowly to look at her mother. 'You don't understand, mother. When Paul told me that heroin would be my new best friend, he was right.'

'No-o-o!' Cathy Fox wailed.

Andrew cradled his wife in his arms. 'Cathy!'

Julia stared at them both without expression, but she kept pressing her lips tightly together.

'Have you not seen the police surgeon, Julia?' asked Collins.

'Yes, but she only gave me a couple of tablets.'

Collins shrugged. 'Then I guess that's all you need. I'm going to type out a statement for you to sign.'

She got to her feet.

'Are you leaving me here with them?' asked Julia, looking at her distraught parents.

'They are your real best friends, Julia, your mum and dad. Not the stuff you're so anxious to have. Paul Unwin lied.'

She took Walker's photograph and left the room. Outside, the Matthew Project Counsellor was waiting. Collins nodded at her to go in, and made her way up to the CID office.

*

Life was not treating Danny Bakker well. The ferry on which he should have been returning to Holland was suffering from a technical fault with the ship's on-board sewage treatment system. On the plus side, it gave him time to think about alternative methods of getting on board.

He remained alert and watchful for any signs of official interest being taken in him, but saw nothing to alarm him. He stood next to the windows which gave a wide view over the quayside and the ferry moored there. A glass-sided walkway connected the terminal building with the ship and his eye was caught by movements along it. Passengers were being kept off the ship, but the job of servicing it was continuing. He watched a trolley being pushed up the slope of the walkway by a tired-looking man in the usual apparel of yellow hi-vis anorak and leggings, with stout work boots and gloves covering his extremities. He wore a woolly hat, pulled low on his brow and over his ears, and black-rimmed spectacles. The man and his trolley disappeared into the far end of the terminal building, towards the departures lounge.

A few minutes later, Bakker saw the man emerge through a side door, which came from the restricted area beyond the controls into the concourse where he stood. It gave Bakker an idea. He moved slowly, casually, after the man.

*

'Anyone seen or heard of Bakker?' asked Bell.

'So far, not a squeak,' replied Pascal. 'I suppose Douglas did send the email out to all ports?'

'I'll ask him when he gets back,' said Bell.

'Right.'

Frimley appeared with three steaming cardboard cups on a tray.

'Thanks, Douglas,' said Bell, taking one of the mugs. 'You did send out the all-ports email about Bakker, didn't you?'

'Uh, ye-es... ' He handed Pascal a mug and took his own back to his seat, scrolling through his email program. He suddenly put a hand over his mouth. 'Bugger!'

Pascal slowly closed his eyes and counted to ten. 'What, Douglas?'

'The Harwich copy's been rejected by the Postmaster.'

'Who the hell's the Postmaster?'

'It's the mail handling computer.'

'So, it's not a person?'

'No, sir. It'd be able to make intelligent decisions if it was.'

'So what's happened?'

Frimley peered at his monitor screen. 'Something wrong with the Harwich address. It's not been accepted.'

Pascal gazed at him wearily before picking up the telephone and holding it out.

'Here, see if you can get through on this.'

Frimley nodded. 'Sorry, sir,' and picked up his own telephone finally to put the Harwich port police on notice.

When the call was answered, he found difficulty in hearing the person on the other end of the phone.

'What?' He listened hard. 'Oh, my Lord!'

He glanced up at Pascal and put his hand over the microphone. 'It's bedlam, sir. They've just found one of the cleaning staff badly wounded and minus his outer clothes, in a toilet cubicle.'

'Sounds as if Bakker's already there.'

Collins came into the room.

'Much as it grieves me to deprive you of a bit of action down in Harwich, Alison,' said Pascal, 'I think you'd better stay here and get an International Arrest Warrant for Jared Martin in Aruba. I think we've enough evidence to charge him with money-laundering.' Pascal yawned. 'Poor old bugger. He's been dealt a rotten hand: first his wife gets killed, then his retirement dream is brought crashing down by a con artist in Aruba. Of course, it wasn't really his money, I guess. It's probably what Danny Bakker came looking for – or some of it is.' He shrugged. 'I suppose DS Stonor and DC Kidder are out and about on the Walker murder?'

There was no answer. Bell shrugged. 'Dunno, sir.'

'I'll have to talk to them later,' Pascal continued. 'We're going to Harwich: I'm pretty sure Bakker's there. I reckon he's trying to leave the country.'

Julian Steel cleared the path for Pascal and his team with the Essex police, who arranged for Sergeant Dashwood's ART to go with them to Harwich. It was still over an hour's drive to the port, even with the strobes and sirens, the 'blues and twos', helping to part the traffic ahead and giving them exemption from the speed limits. While Frimley drove, Pascal used the phone to talk to the officer-in-charge at Harwich, and was relieved to hear that the ferry's departure had been delayed.

'Keep it there, if you can,' Pascal pleaded.

They promised to ask the captain, but he was already behind schedule and further delay was not something he would readily agree to.

Pascal had asked Collins to send the photograph of Bakker they'd received from the Maréchaussée to Harwich so they could begin a search for the man. His next phone call was from Rachel Stonor.

'Sir, your forensic report on Jared Martin's computer files arrived. I thought it might be urgent, so I opened it.'

Pascal's lip curled cynically. 'Oh, yes? And was it?'

'I think so, sir. You know I've been familiarising myself with all our cases – '

'Uh-huh.'

' – so I'm thinking you'll be happy about this.'

'Well, go on then,' he muttered.

'Once they got past Martin's security, they found out what he's been doing. I think it explains everything.'

'Money laundering at a guess.' He said. He thought he heard a sudden indrawn breath and allowed a faint grin to curl his lips.

'Yes, he's been laundering money for Derrick Jackson, and paying large amounts to van Ruys in Holland via an offshore bank.'

'Good. DS Collins is getting an international arrest warrant for Martin now.'

There was a pause before she said, 'That would be *Acting* DS Collins, I suppose, sir?'

'It would. How are you getting on with Walker's murder?'

'We've been down to *The Kitty Klub* and spoken to various people in and around the place – not many *in* it, since the raid: mostly our people.'

'Uh-huh.'

'We've found a witness, one who called the emergency services.'

'Good. Who?'

'A member of the public who just happened to be drawn to your raid.'

'You're satisfied it was a bystander?'

'Yes, sir. He saw two young women and their blokes approach Walker. One of the blokes had a Stanley knife. They seemed to pick an argument with him, and the next thing, one had grabbed Walker and the other cut him several times with the knife.'

'Did you get descriptions?'

'Yes. Fairly good of the men, More graphic of the women, whom the witness referred to as slappers, probably with a boob-job. I reckon we'll find them. We get the impression they're regulars at the clubs.'

'Good work, Rachel – and Frank, too. Hope you get an arrest soon.'

Pascal closed the call, a satisfied grin on his face.

Frimley glanced at him.

'Good news, sir?'

Pascal told him.

'And Martin's computers have been examined and seem to prove the money laundering,' he concluded.

Pascal hung on as the car joined the London Road at Ipswich.

'I wonder... ' he said.

'What?'

'I wonder if he'd testify if we offered him immunity?'

'Against Jackson?'

'Have to talk to the CPS,' said Frimley.

Pascal began dialling again.

'I'm going to see if our friends at Harwich can get the ferry delayed so we can search it before it sails.'

Frimley glanced in the mirror.

'Our ARV's behind us.'

Pascal glanced over his shoulder at the big white Volvo keeping pace with them a few hundred yards behind. At that moment, the Norfolk Control Room called them on the radio and told them to change onto the Essex channel, which they did. Pascal announced their Callsign and presence. The Essex Control Room was aware of them, and put them on Talk-through so they could liaise directly with the Sergeant Dashwood.

Pascal suggested the ARV take the lead for the last leg of the journey along the A120 into Harwich. Frimley moved over, and the Volvo, travelling at not far short of the ton, slipped past them easily. Frimley pulled out into the outside lane and put his toe down. They took the slip road towards Harwich.

Pascal's phone rang again. This time, it was the officer-in-charge at the port, who wanted to know how much longer before they got there. Pascal told him their present estimate.

'The Captain's twitchy at being kept waiting. I think he'll want to cast off as soon as you're on board.'

'Can he do that?'

'Of course not, legally. You can arrest him for obstruction, false imprisonment and kidnapping, and insist the ship returns to port. Of course,' he added with a strong hint of cynicism, 'there's no telling whether the CPS would support the charges.'

At last they turned down the road which led to the quayside. The port police inspector was waiting for them as they climbed out of the cars below the crew gangplank, well below the covered walkway for the passengers.

The inspector showed them a Polaroid photograph, taken from the CCTV system.

'We think this is him,' he said.

The photograph showed a man in the ubiquitous bright yellow anorak worn by all the port workers, a woolly hat pulled down over his forehead, walking along the service walkway leading to the ship.

'This was taken about the time we discovered the cleaner in the toilet. They're his clothes, but it wasn't him.'

'Let's get on board,' said Pascal. The three Norfolk officers and the four from the ARV quickly climbed the service crew gangway which led up from the quay. The ship's Purser greeted them.

Pascal showed him the photograph. 'This is who we're looking for. Where is someone dressed like that going to be where he won't stand out?'

The Purser led them to the crew areas to begin their search.

\*

Danny Bakker saw the police arrive and get on board the ship. He'd had to take off the cleaner's spectacles as soon as he was past the CCTV cameras on the walkway: the lenses were just too powerful and threatened to give him a headache. As he looked over the side of the ship, he pushed the lenses out with his thumbs and watched them fall the ten or twelve metres into the water between the ship and the quay heading. As he did so, another man in the usual hi-vis anorak and sea-boots came out onto the deck and glanced at him. He jammed the spectacles back on.

'Hoi!' the man called, 'You need to get off the ship. We're about to cast off.'

Bakker waved at him in acknowledgement and shuffled off the deck into the superstructure of the vessel. He walked some way along a corridor. It was obviously crews' quarters, and not passenger accommodation. Every couple of metres was a door which he guessed was somebody's cabin. The doors were labelled with the names or ranks of occupants.

A door at the end of the corridor was unlabelled. Two ventilators, top and bottom, suggested it had a different purpose. He opened it. It was a drying room. Bright yellow wet-suits and other garments were hanging from hooks, and the floor was duck-boarded. Bakker considered staying in the room until the ship sailed, but it would mean he had no idea of what was going on. He would be like a rat in a trap. But it would be somewhere to hide in an emergency. The Sig Sauer was still firmly wedged in his trouser belt. Its presence was comforting.

He let himself out of the room, back into the corridor and began to make his way towards the front of the ship and down a deck, in the belief that most of the passenger facilities were that way. He needed to find somewhere to hide until passengers were allowed on board. Then he could dump the hi-vis jacket with its tell-tale *Harwich International Port* in the reflective strip across the back and revert to being an ordinary traveller. *Hide in plain sight* was a maxim he'd found very useful in the past. He kept careful watch for any sign of the police.

*

Detective Sergeant Rachel Stonor was making hay while Pascal was otherwise engaged. It looked as if she and Frank would wrap up the murder of John Walker fairly quickly. It was the first time she'd been allowed a large measure of autonomy, without having to report every five minutes to a DI, and the first murder in which she'd played a principle role. She was feeling exultant, and wanted to celebrate.

She looked in on Kidder, alone in the CID office.

'How's it going, Frank?' she asked, perching on the edge of the workstation, her skirt riding up her thigh.

He looked at her knee, smooth and rounded, in sheer stockings. He knew she wore stockings rather than tights, because he'd seen their tops, and beyond. He glanced into her eyes and saw the glint of lust. Kidder, at 27, was five years younger than Stonor, but that hadn't prevented them forming a physical relationship. Neither expressed affection for the other, but occasionally, like now, Stonor would feel like having sex, and Kidder was good looking, keen and vigorous.

He was all she needed. She led him into the stationery store, along the corridor.

As she lay back on plastic sacks of shredded paper, he slid one hand up the smooth nylon surface of her stockings, continuing under her skirt, while at the same time lowering his head and applying a row of kisses up the inside of the thigh. He used his other hand to pull her blouse out of her waistband, and insinuated his fingers beneath onto her firm flesh. She put one hand on the back of his head, encouraging him to move his lips up her thigh, while the other rubbed his back and found its way round to the front of his shirt, her long, slim fingers beginning to loosen the buttons and slithering over the wiry hairs on his chest.

The release of tension, ten minutes later, left her feeling warm and relaxed. In a few minutes, she would change back from Rachel-the-vamp to DS Stonor, professional police officer, until the next time she felt the need. Frank Kidder had been a godsend. He approached their occasional coupling in much the same way she did, with no wish for anything but a brief physical entanglement, after which they carried on with their professional lives. They never met outside of work, and only had sex when she felt the need, as she had on this occasion.

She pulled tissues out of her handbag and handed one to him, while using one herself and restoring her appearance.

Stonor smiled at him. 'That was another good one, Frank,' she said. She felt he deserved a compliment.

He smiled slightly. 'You can be so sexy, it's easy for me.'

She grinned. 'I know. I'm a right tart. Just don't tell anybody.'

Kidder nodded.

She led the way back to the CID office and sat opposite him. It was a sign she was back in professional mode.

'We'll be hanging around the clubs tonight, Frank, enjoying the delights of the "giddy metrolopis" of Breydon,' she said, deliberately mispronouncing. 'Enjoying – but not too much. We've to find the people who killed Walker.' She ran her hand over her flat stomach. 'I just need to go to the washroom then we can go.'

*

The police were the last things on Jared Martin's mind as Serena parked her car outside a builders' merchants.

'I have a cousin who works here,' she explained, 'he'll know a good builder.'

They got out of the car and were crossing the pavement when a marked police car uttered a quick burst of its siren and came to a halt behind them. The two front-seat occupants got out, their hands hovering near their holstered guns, and came up to Martin and his guide.

'Jared Martin?' said the first, 'Jared Dale Martin?'

Martin nodded, puzzled. 'Yes?'

'We've a warrant for your arrest.' The officer unclipped his handcuffs, turned Martin round, and pulled his wrists painfully together behind him. The cuffs snapped on. The officer spun him back round until he was facing Serena's car and pushed him face down across its roof, kicking his ankles apart.

He carried out a rub-down search before hauling Martin upright again and marching him towards the police car. At last Martin found his voice.

'But why? What have I done? I've been with this lady since I got here.'

The officer glanced at Serena, who nodded. 'The warrant's been issued through Interpol on behalf of the British police. You're accused of being involved in drugs trafficking.'

He opened the back door of the car and shoved Martin inside. Moments later they set off, leaving Serena watching from the pavement behind them. At the police station, there was no attempt to question him; he was put into a cell, the cuffs removed, and the door slammed shut. Martin sat on the bare concrete slab that was probably supposed to be a bed and felt himself shaking. Panic filled him and he felt dizziness as he hyperventilated.

He could not hold himself upright and rolled off the slab onto the stone floor. He heard himself moaning and his limbs writhed uncontrollably. At some stage, he passed out.

He regained consciousness some time later, and realised, when he tried to check the time, that his wristwatch had been removed. He was still on the floor and Serena was crouched beside him, her hand gently shaking his shoulder.

'Jared? Jared?'

He struggled to sit up and discovered that he'd soiled himself. The blind panic had receded.

'Serena! What's happened? Why am I here?'

'You've been arrested because the British Police want to talk to you about your being involved in supplying drugs. I shouldn't have thought this was likely, Jared. Tell me why they would think that?'

'I've never supplied anyone with drugs,' he said. 'I abhor them.'

Two chairs had appeared in the room while he was unconscious. Serena sat on one. Martin picked himself off the floor and sat on the other

'So, no connection in any way whatsoever with drugs like cocaine and heroin?'

'No!' He hesitated.

'You told me your wife had been murdered. That's very unusual – especially in Britain: might she have had a connection with drugs?'

He hung his head, ashamed.

'I believe she took cocaine,' he said.

'Ah!'

He looked up. 'But I had nothing to do with it. I didn't give it to her, or help her get it.'

Serena looked puzzled. 'But why would a cocaine habit get her killed?'

'I don't know!'

She watched him silently for a moment.

'The policeman outside – I asked him why you'd been arrested. He said you've been laundering money for someone.' She wrinkled her brow as if trying to remember. 'Someone called, uh, Jackson?'

'Derrick Jackson,' Martin said.

'Yes,' she said, nodding. 'Is it true?'

He looked at her while he tried to assess just how much he should tell her. He stood up and went over to the door, peering out through the flap in it to make sure no-one was listening. The action reminded him of something else. He made his way carefully back to his chair.

'I need a change of clothes,' he said, 'I – I had an accident while I was unconscious.'

She smiled sympathetically. 'I'll get you some fresh clothes when I go. They haven't given me long to visit you. There's one thing that puzzles me.'

'What?'

'Despite your being defrauded out of a lot of money, you didn't want to tell the police. Is that because the money was your profit from the laundering operation?'

He took a deep breath. 'Yes,' he almost whispered.

'For this Derrick Jackson?'

He stared at her again, hopelessly. 'Yes.'

She patted him on the shoulder. 'Okay, Jared. I've got to go now. I'll be back with some new clothes.'

The next day, Martin stood in a closed courtroom, in a clean pair of jeans and underpants, stunned, as Serena stepped out of the witness box to take her place next to the prosecutor, after giving the information he'd entrusted her with as evidence.

'Thank you for giving your evidence, Detective Hendrix,' the Judge said to Serena before turning to face the prisoner in the dock. 'The Court orders your extradition to the United Kingdom, Mr Martin.' To the two police officers behind Martin, he added, 'Take him away.' That evening, Martin was escorted onto a flight back to Amsterdam and then to his regional international airport at Norwich, sandwiched between two quiet men from the British Embassy.

He'd been stunned, not so much by the verdict or the proceedings, but by the revelation that Serena Hendrix was an undercover police officer whose job had been to discover Martin's most closely-guarded secret. In that aim, he had to admit, she had been largely successful. He tried not to think what would happen to him back in Breydon.

*

Pascal, Frimley, Bell and the other members of the search team had been led into the crew accommodation. While Bell and one of Sergeant Dashwood's team searched downwards from the Bridge, Pascal and Frimley and PC Richardson of the ART found the entrance to the engine room. A door leading off a corridor gave access onto a steel platform at the top of a staircase leading down into the bowels of the vessel. Each officer put on a set of ear defenders before descending.

Six steps down, only the wall on their right remained and they found themselves on a stairway clinging to it, while to their left the entire expanse of the brightly-lit engine-room universe opened up to their view. It was probably forty or fifty feet from deck plates to the ceiling and as broad, if not broader. Down the centre was a pair of massive diesel engines, with auxiliaries to generate electricity and power the ship's services.

'Come on, we haven't much time,' urged Pascal.

The three police officers descended by some eighty steps to the deck plates, and discovered that there was space below them, filled with pipes and valves. There was a distinctly unpleasant whiff in the air, and as they walked round the engines and stepped over more pipes, they came to a large rectangular tank, on which two fitters were working, wearing breathing apparatus which hid their features.

Pascal tapped one of them, working on top of the tank, on the ankle. The man glanced round and Pascal showed him his ID, and gestured at him to remove the mask. The man did so. His colleague looked up and removed his mask also. The first man was short and brown-skinned, possibly Filipino, whilst the second was white-skinned and middle-aged. He worked his way round the tank, stepping over the pipes which connected to it.

'What do you want, mate?' he bawled at Pascal.

'Looking for someone. Seen anybody you don't recognise?'

The man looked at him for a moment then pointed at all three policemen.

'Apart from us!' yelled Pascal. He produced the photograph of Bakker. 'Him.'

The man looked at the picture and shook his head.

Pascal shrugged. He was about to turn away when he had second thoughts. He tapped the man on the arm to attract his attention.

'Anywhere down here a man could hide?'

'Normally, mate,' the fitter shouted, 'he could hide in here — ' he indicated the tank with his thumb ' — and be guaranteed safe from discovery – until we docked, like. Then he'd be noticed.'

'Why? What's the tank?'

'It's the sewage separator. Why do you think we're wearing BA? Normally, nobody goes anywhere near this lot.' He reaffixed the face mask of his breathing apparatus and stepped nimbly back over the pipes to where he had been.

Pascal led the other two along the walkway which ran all the way round the edge of the engine room until they returned to the bottom of the stairs down which they'd come. He pointed upwards, and they began climbing. Eighty steps up, he thought as he counted through the first twenty, were going to be a lot more exhausting than eighty down. Around the fifty mark, his breath was rasping in his throat and his knees were aching. The last twenty were climbed by sheer will-power, but eventually, they found themselves back in the corridor in the midst of the crew quarters.

'Where next, sir?' asked Frimley when he'd caught his breath.

He's no fitter than I am, thought Pascal. 'We'll do these cabins and work our way up.'

They began knocking at doors and opening them, except for those which were locked. Pascal sent Frimley to find someone with a pass key, and slowly, they worked their way up the crew accommodation. Finally, they stepped out on the top deck from where Pascal watched as one of the ART officers climbed the vertical steel ladder up the exterior wall of the bridge onto its roof.

As they were watching, the Purser reappeared beside them.

'Saw you on the ship's CCTV,' he explained, seeing Pascal's puzzlement that he had known where they were. 'No luck in the engine-room?'

'No,' said Pascal lugubriously, 'but we did find something called a sewage separator, being worked on by a couple of blokes.'

'Yes, that's what's delayed sailing. We can't really go while it's not working.'

'I presume it's something to do with the toilets.'

'Separates liquids from solids, you might say. A miniature sewage farm.'

'You don't say!'

'Processes the waste to an environmentally satisfactory standard.'

'I am so glad,' muttered Pascal ironically. 'In the meantime, our man is still at large.'

'You were able to get in all the cabins in the crew's quarters?'

'Yes thanks. I'm left wondering where else he could be hidden.'

Frimley straightened up, having been peering over the rail to look down on the lower decks. 'I was wondering, sir, if Bakker might not have got out of those clothes after getting on board. Surely he only wore them while he passed the port security cameras.'

There was a beep. 'Excuse me,' said the Purser, who took a few steps away and began talking into a phone.

Pascal scratched his head. 'Quite possible. I think I would. So perhaps there's a pile of clothes somewhere, and Bakker's back in civvies?'

Frimley shrugged. 'It's possible.'

The Purser interrupted. 'The Captain is terribly keen to be off. We're nearly two hours behind schedule.'

'Please convey my apologies to the Captain, but he can't go yet. Surely he doesn't want to sail with a gunman on board?'

The Purser nodded and passed the message to the Captain. He listened a moment.

'The Captain says is there anything he or his crew can do to help?'

'If anybody sees a man behaving suspiciously, whom they don't recognise, they might tell us, but keep out of his way. He is believed to be armed and dangerous. Very,' he added.

The Purser nodded and passed the message on.

Pascal joined Frimley in staring down over the lower decks.

'I suppose,' he said, 'it would be polite to fill our DCI in. He likes to think he knows what we're doing.'

Frimley grunted and continued to watch the decks below for signs of life. Pascal called Steel and brought him up to date with events.

'Sergeant Stonor and DC Kidder are following a couple of leads on the John Walker murder,' Steel told him.

'Yes, sir. She told me earlier on the way down here.'

'Okay George. Good luck.'

Pascal finished the call and informed Frimley. 'Let's get Bakker found so we can get back home.'

'Right, sir.'

*

Bakker didn't know much about the layout of ships the size of the one he was on. Posted on the main deck were the fire plans of the ship. These were reasonably detailed charts giving a deck-by-deck view of the layout, provided for use by a fire-fighting team which might arrive on board in such an emergency.

He'd discovered that most of the superstructure above the main deck was given over to passenger accommodation, apart from one block just behind the bridge where most of the crew's cabins were located. On decks below the main deck were passenger cabins, the double-height car-decks and many of the ship's services, such as the laundry and sick bay.

At the bow, beneath the deck plates which formed the roadway for vehicles loading and unloading at that end, was a room containing anchor chains and the motors which drove the twin bow-thrusters, impellers mounted longitudinally within the keel, which were used to move the bow left or right, usually during the processes of mooring and casting off.

A similar space was at the stern of the vessel. Both these 'chain lockers', as they were described on the plan, were accessed via hatches and vertical ladders from the extreme ends of the car deck, outside the watertight doors.

Bakker figured he could find his way around if he had to after studying the plans. He figured a chain locker would be a good place to hide, but knew he would have to risk been seen on the open deck if he was to get to it. He let himself out of the crew accommodation and set off for'ard.

In a cabin below the Bridge, the First Officer had been scanning the ship's CCTV monitors. He saw Bakker appear and contacted the Purser, who was with Pascal. Meantime he used his radio to warn crew members to stay clear of the port side of the ship.

Pascal, Frimley, Bell, Richardson and Dashwood, with the Purser kept firmly in the rear, headed aft.

The Purser received another message from the First Officer, with Bakker's new position. He called softly.

'Mr Pascal!'

Pascal stopped and turned. 'Yes?'

The Purser pointed across the ship, a little forward of where they were. 'He's about there, on the port side. If you go through the doors there – ' he pointed ' – there's a passage way which cuts right across to the port side.'

'Right,' said Pascal. 'Thanks. Graham, go with Richardson through there. We'll go a bit further down this deck and cross to the Port side at the back of the accommodation, and come back up towards you.'

They moved quickly. As Pascal, Frimley and Dashwood were fifty metres short of their turning point, there was the sound of several shots being fired. They broke into a run, reaching the end of the accommodation, where the deck they were on curved round almost at the back of the vessel, just as Bakker appeared, from the other side of the ship.

'Police!' yelled Pascal. 'Stand still.'

'Drop your weapon!' commanded Dashwood.

Bakker turned, surprised by their presence, and let off two shots in their direction.

'Halt! Police! Put down your weapon!' shouted Dashwood again.

Bakker's response was another shot, which hit the officer in the chest, knocking him down. Bakker then climbed over a chain meant to deter passengers from going beyond the aft rail. Below it, a vertical metal ladder went down the rear wall of the vessel towards the roadway below.

Pascal checked that Dashwood was not seriously hurt, his Kevlar vest having absorbed the bullet. Meantime, Bell and Richardson had reached the port side ladder which Bakker had used. They took cover. Richardson risked a look over the rail. Another shot flew past his head, burying itself in the steel wall of the superstructure behind him. Pascal, on the starboard side, peered briefly over the rail, and saw Bakker climbing down the port side ladder. Beyond him, Pascal could see only the sea. Beside him, Dashwood had got to his feet. He and Pascal both peered over the rail. In the poor light, they could see Bakker clearly, but not quite what he was doing. Dashwood yelled Bakker's name, causing him to jerk his head round, gun still firmly gripped in his hand. The officer fired, and Pascal watched as Bakker fell from the ladder.

Pascal lost sight of him then as, still cautious, he raised his head enough to see all the way down to the roadway. Once it seemed safe, all the police officers crowded together, looking down at the stern of the ship. There was no cover, no sign of Bakker. Dashwood and Richardson aimed torches into the sea behind the ship.

'Look, sir,' said one, pointing his beam of light.

In the water, drifting in the slow current astern of the vessel, was the hi-vis jacket Bakker had been wearing. Frimley climbed down the ladder to the roadway. He stripped off his own jacket and trousers before jumping over the stern the two metres or so into the dark water.

'Douglas!' yelled Pascal, but it was too late to stop him.

Frimley surfaced and swam to the jacket before turning to swim towards the quay heading. Pascal hadn't noticed before but here and there – and fortuitously, quite close to Frimley – were iron ladders set into the concrete of the quay.

'Quick! Down onto the quay! Help him!' shouted Pascal.

Richardson, younger and fitter than either of the two CID officers, descended the ladder to pick up Frimley's discarded clothes. Someone on the Bridge with the benefit of CCTV must have seen what was happening. There were loud clanks and bangs as the car deck doors unlocked, and the one on the seaward side began slowly to open, allowing the officer to enter the ship. Pascal turned to Dashwood who was wincing with pain.

'You okay, Sergeant?'

'Might be a cracked rib, sir,' he replied.

'Thank God for effective body armour,' said Pascal.

'Yes. Gives us an attempted murder charge to add to the list.'

'If we catch him. Looks as if your mate's shot blew him off the ship.' He stood up. 'You two can make your way back to your car. Call up an ambulance and get yourself examined.'

'I'll be all right, sir.'

'That was an order, not a suggestion, Sergeant,' said Pascal with mock severity.

'Need to stay here with my men for the moment, sir, with respect.'

The other two members of the ART had arrived from the other end of the vessel. They gathered round Dashwood. Pascal figured he could find out what had happened to Frimley. He made his way ashore. Frimley and the jacket had been recovered and both were on the quayside. The Purser turned up with a couple of towels and Frimley dried himself off and resumed his clothes.

'You all right, Douglas?' asked Pascal as he arrived, once more out of breath.

'Yes, thanks, sir.'

Pascal nodded in approval. He looked at the others. 'Any sign of Bakker's body?'

'No, sir.' They shook their heads.

'Hmm.' Pascal would have been happier if there had been. 'We'll need to get a team of divers out in the morning to search under the ship.'

As he spoke, the distant growl of engines could be heard. They turned towards the front of the ship and saw a stream of cars driving onto the vessel through the bow doors. Foot passengers were moving along the walkway. The Captain had evidently decided that the emergency was over and he could embark his passengers and payload.

Pascal returned along the quay to where Dashwood and his team were stepping off the crew gangplank.

'You're quite sure you hit him with your shot?'

'I didn't have long to aim, sir, but 99 per cent certain.'

'Where do you think you'd have hit him?'

'Normally I'd aim for the chest, because it's the biggest target, but I might have got him in the stomach.'

'Okay, thanks. Is that ambulance on its way?'

'Yes, sir.'

Pascal returned to the small crowd around Frimley.

'Let's have a look at the jacket,' he said to Bell, who was near to it. He passed it over and Pascal checked it carefully.

'No bullet holes or blood,' he said, 'but the man who shot him said he might have hit him in the stomach.'

'I don't think he had the jacket done up, sir,' said Bell, 'so it's not conclusive.'

Pascal surveyed the scene. 'Keep the jacket for forensics. The Captain clearly wants to be on his way. It'll be dark before we could get a proper underwater search team here.' He shook his head. 'But I don't like leaving things like this.'

They went into the terminal building and were given hot drinks – drinking chocolate for Frimley, warm sweet tea for Dashwood and coffee for the rest of them – to warm them up.

'I'd suggest, sir,' said Frimley, 'that we let the ship sail but ask the Maréchaussée to give it a good going-over when it arrives in Holland. Bakker's a Dutch national, might be better to let the Dutch have first dibs at him.'

Pascal rubbed his chin thoughtfully. 'As long as we get him back for murder and attempted murder. And arson. Should see him put away for a few years.'

Half an hour later, they were in the car, heading back northwards to Breydon.

Pascal would still have preferred to see a body.

# CHAPTER 20

It was full daylight on Tuesday when Jared Martin arrived at Breydon Police Station. By this time, everyone had heard from DCI Steel of events on the ferry, and of the search by Essex police divers currently under way where the ferry had been moored the previous evening. The good news seemed to be that Danny Bakker had been shot and killed. The bad news was that his body had not been found.

DS Stonor and DC Kidder had spent their time fruitfully. The previous evening, they had arrested two men and two women matching the description of Walker's attackers. A search of their homes had already yielded the knife suspected of killing Walker, and more of the CCTV from cameras covering the area outside *The Kitty Klub* had been found to have recorded much of the incident. The camera operator had been spoken to by his manager to find out why he did not report the matter at the time. His reason was that it didn't seem much more serious than any number of fights which broke out in the area, sometimes several times a night, and by the time he had realised it was, and called the police, someone else had already done so.

The two young men were charged with conspiracy to murder Walker, and the women with aiding and abetting.

Pascal faced Martin across the table in an Interview Room, with the duty solicitor sitting beside him.

He waved three sheets of paper at Martin.

'Do you know what this is, Mr Martin?' he asked.

Martin shook his head. 'How would I?'

'It's a fax from the Aruban police.' He lifted the top sheet away and held the second page in front of him. 'These two pages are a transcript of your extradition hearing.'

'Oh,' Martin said, without much show of interest.

'So tell me about Abel Scarman.'

'He was someone I met a couple of years ago, when I was looking for a place to buy. We got on well, and he was very helpful when my intention came up in conversation.'

'When he knew what you wanted, he volunteered to help you?'

'That's right.'

'What did you give him?'

Martin looked up. 'What do you mean?'

'How much money have you paid to Scarman in the last two years?'

Martin looked down. 'Almost half a million dollars.' His voice was so low that Pascal had to ask him to repeat his answer.

'And what do you think has happened to it?'

He looked up defiantly. 'You know what happened to it.'

Pascal scanned the document in his hand. 'I gather you have a property on the island, bought for four hundred and ninety-seven thousand, five hundred dollars?'

'Yes,' said Martin.

'I gather it's worth about five thousand, no more.'

'Possibly less.'

'But you agreed to pay nearly half a million. Why was that?'

Martin clenched his jaw and spoke through gritted teeth. 'Because I was ripped off.'

'By Scarman?'

'Who else!'

Pascal leaned back and indicated to Bell that he should take over the interview.

'Where did the half-million dollars come from?' Bell asked.

'Look, if I tell you, what's in it for me?'

'We don't do deals.'

Pascal leaned forward. 'We'll talk to the CPS if you co-operate.'

Bell didn't give any sign of upset at Pascal's interruption, merely sitting back and waiting for a response.

Martin studied his face, as if trying to work out whether he could trust him.

'You promise?'

'I'll do it now, if you like.'

Martin still hesitated. 'I want to talk to my solicitor privately,' he said.

Bell formally suspended the interview and he and Pascal left the room, informing the Custody Sergeant of Martin's request to talk to his solicitor. While they waited, Pascal called the Crown Prosecution Service and explained that he wanted to use Martin to give evidence for the Crown in exchange for a lesser charge.

Martin's solicitor and DCI Steel, accompanied by a Crown Prosecutor, arrived in the Custody Suite at the same time. They met Pascal outside the interview room. While Martin's solicitor spoke to his client, Steel introduced the man beside him.

'George, this is Nick Dickens, from the CPS. As you requested.'

Pascal and Steel shook hands.

'So what's the idea, Detective Inspector?' asked Dickens.

'Let's go through here,' said Pascal, leading the way to one of the few unoccupied rooms in the Suite.

Inside, with the door shut, Pascal explained that he wanted to negotiate a deal with Martin, who would be sentenced to nothing more than community service in exchange for testifying against both Jackson.

'Jackson is the big fish,' Pascal explained. 'He's the one who sells the drugs, provides the girls, who are trafficked in from the Baltic, and probably he's to a large extent responsible for Sara Martin's murder, even if we can't actually do him for that.'

'But without people like Martin, Jackson would find it more difficult to operate,' argued Dickens.

'In my opinion,' said Pascal, 'Jackson would simply have used someone else, if Martin hadn't been willing. Jackson is the real evil, not Martin.'

Dickens pursed his lips while he thought about the matter.

'Okay,' he said at last. 'Let's put it to him. I hope he doesn't realise a community sentence is a tough option.'

'That would be up to the Judge, Mr Dickens.'

The solicitor was still in conversation with Martin when they went back to the interview room. He was about to protest at being interrupted but Martin nodded and looked at Dickens. Pascal switched on the recorder again, and introduced himself and the man from the Crown Prosecution Service.

'Why Mr Dickens is here,' Pascal began, 'is to lend his authority to a proposal I have for you.'

Martin stared at him askance. 'What proposal?'

Pascal interlocked his fingers as he leaned over the table.

*

George Pascal awarded himself a rare night off. Three days after the main investigations were completed, and much later than he'd originally intended, he had finally found the time for a social life. His one concession to the demands of work was that his mobile phone was switched on, in silent mode, tucked into his pocket. He wore his white shirt open-necked, a navy blue blazer and grey trousers. It was not, he knew, what the well-dressed man-about-town would consider wearing for one second, but it was clean.

His appointment with Jane Ferrari was the nearest thing to a date he'd been on for a long time. He'd worried what would be appropriate for him to bring along, trying to choose between flowers or a prosaic bottle of wine. He'd decided to bring both in the hope of covering all his options.

What was he expecting to get out of the evening? He refused to consider the prospect in any detail, but figured that just about anything was possible. She'd made that plain enough, one way and another. If they found they liked each-other's company, this evening might be the beginning of something new in his life. The idea of having a new long-term relationship was appealing: it was nice to have someone with whom to share thoughts and exchange opinions. Sex was great, but it was a meeting of minds that really made for ongoing togetherness.

He rang the bell.

The door opened. Pascal's mind emptied of all thought. He gazed – his eyes feasted – on Jane Ferrari, taking in everything from the brushed, wavy tresses of her dark hair, resting on her shoulder, her perfectly made-up eyes and lips, and the plain black slinky strapless silk gown which clung to her figure. The chisel-toes of shiny black high-heeled shoes peeped out under the hemline of her dress.

She smiled and glanced at the flowers and wine he held.

'George, thank you. Are those for me?'

Pascal smiled, and nodded. 'Yes.'

'Come in, then,' she said, relieving him of the gifts.

His mind still trying to get over her striking appearance, he stepped past her into the hallway of her house. Her breasts brushed his chest, while the tips of his fingers caught her thigh accidentally. The sensation that engendered, and the first molecules of her musky perfume in his nose, caused a reaction which he was glad he could hide from her by walking ahead to the door of her living room.

'George.' She stopped him before he could enter.

He half turned. 'Yes?'

'Would you mind awfully taking off your shoes. The carpet... It's new.'

He heeled them off, but glanced at hers which she showed no signs of removing. She must have understood his thoughts because she explained.

'These are new shoes, George. I bought them today, and they've never been worn outside. Do you like them?'

'Oh yes,' he said, and meant it.

She led the way into her lounge. Nat King Cole sang in the background. The room was lit by dimmed wall-lamps and candles, and furnished simply with a white sheepskin carpet and half-a-dozen large bean-bag seats scattered around the floor. A television occupied a corner, with a home theatre system under it. Bookcases filled the opposite wall, and occasional tables were located convenient to the bean-bags.

'I'll just put these in water,' she said, looking at the flowers. 'Help yourself to a CD, if you want something different. Do you want a drink?'

Pascal eased himself into one of the bean-bags. He looked up at her.

'Do you have any scotch?'

'As it's you, there's a bottle of ten-year-old Glenkinchie in the cupboard in the corner.' She pointed to a small tri-angular corner unit whose lower part was a cupboard.

'Do you want one?' he asked.

'Please,' she smiled.

As Ferrari took the flowers and wine into the kitchen, Pascal heaved himself out of the bean-bag and crossed the room to the unit, which was situated near the dining table. He found the bottle of malt whisky and two glasses and poured a shot in each, bringing one glass to his nose to sample the bouquet.

While taking his first sip, he looked at the dining table at the far end of the room, covered by a pink cloth with an embroidered edge, polished stainless-steel cutlery and gleaming glassware. Two candles burned at one side of the it.

He made his way to the kitchen door and leaned against the frame. Ferrari was snipping bits off the stems of the flowers he'd brought and was arranging them in a vase. She glanced at him.

'You found the whisky?'

'Yes.' He held out the untouched glass to her.

'Thanks,' she said, taking it from him. They touched glasses. Her finger brushed his, her brown eyes locking with his as she raised the glass to her lips and drank half its contents before she went back to the flowers.

'Is this called "starting as we mean to go on", George?' she asked him, the liquor making her voice more than usually husky.

He didn't answer her at once, but raised his own glass and drank half of the measure.

'This is called, "having an aperitif",' he said, and smiled. 'I have no plans to get drunk.'

'Nor have I,' she said, 'so I may be a while drinking the rest of this.'

He grinned.

She finished arranging the flowers and brought them through into the living room and placed them on an occasional table where they would catch the eye of anyone in the room. Pascal watched from beside a bean-bag, taking a connoisseur's pleasure in the side slit in her dress, which revealed that she was wearing stockings rather than tights, and above the slit, the curve of her behind as she leant down to position the vase.

She peered at him before straightening up. 'George! Do you like my bum?'

Pascal cleared his throat. 'Uh, yes. Since you ask.'

She grinned and came up to him. 'Good!'

She reached behind his neck and pulled his face down until she could kiss his lips. He cleared his throat again.

'Got a tickle in your throat, George?' she asked. 'I could look at it, if you want. I'm a doctor.'

He saw the glint of amusement in her eyes as she spoke. Suddenly, he knew he wanted to know more about this woman. She seemed very much on his wavelength, so far. He suspected greater depths. He opened his mouth to speak, but she laid a finger across his lips.

'I think our first course will be ready.'

'What's that?' he asked as she led the way towards the table.

'Sit there. I won't be long. *Huîtres au beurre blanc et épinards*. Oysters with butter and spinach. Sets you up for what comes later.'

He sat as she continued into the kitchen. 'You mean the main course?'

Her head appeared round the door frame. 'What else?' She disappeared back into the kitchen. Pascal smiled to himself. Jane Ferrari was fun.

\*

Ferrari slid the oysters onto the warmed leaves of spinach in their shells and coated them in the *beurre blanc* before putting them under the grill for a few seconds to warm through. She enjoyed cooking, and it gave her pleasure when others enjoyed sharing her meals with her. She glanced at the wine Pascal had brought, an estate-bottled Bordeaux, which should go well with the main course. She'd decided that she would stick to uncomplicated recipes, since she didn't know what Pascal preferred, and was simply intending to grill some fillet steak with a coating of Dijon mustard and various herbs, served with plain steamed new potatoes and vegetables.

She pulled the oysters out from under the grill and placed them on a pair of plates. She twitched the tip of her nose with amusement: what would Pascal make of the molluscs' fabled aphrodisiac qualities?

She carried the dishes through and placed them on the mats in front of them. One further trip to the kitchen was necessary in order to bring a bottle of white wine from the fridge and a corkscrew from a drawer. She held them out to Pascal.

'Would you like to open the wine?' she asked him.

He cut the foil and inserted the screw, removing the cork with a satisfying pop. She liked seeing a man opening a bottle of wine at her table. It had been a long time since the last one to do so. Pascal half-filled their glasses, something of which she approved. The Vouvray was a wine not as dry as some, and went well with the seafood.

Ferrari was perfectly well aware that oysters do not figure in the diets of many people and wondered how Pascal would tackle the job of eating them. After what seemed to be a moment's indecisiveness, he simply picked one up on his fork and ate it whole, followed by a forkful of the spinach. She followed suit, watching a trail of butter escape from his lips and run down his chin. He mopped it up. He glanced at her and, using a clean corner of his serviette, leaned across and gently wiped a drop of butter from her lips. The touch sent delicious feelings through her and caused her to catch her breath. She caught his wrist in her hands and brought his fingers to her lips. Kissing them lightly, she looked up at him, her eyes dancing with amusement.

'And after only one oyster, George! What will you do after you've eaten them all?'

'Sit around and wait for the next course, I suppose,' he replied. 'That's assuming there will be one.'

'Beef. Fillet steak.'

He nodded approvingly. 'I've always thought you'd have a string of boyfriends because of the way you look: I never knew that your culinary skills would be a further attraction.'

'I don't have a boyfriend, or even a man-friend at the moment, George.'

'Th-that's a coincidence, then, because I don't have one either. Girlfriend, woman, whatever,' he clarified.

She watched him as she slipped another oyster onto her tongue and swallowed.

'Really, George?' She knew perfectly well that he was unattached, having made discreet enquiries of some of the people who knew him before inviting him round for the meal.

'No-o-o,' he said as he watched her lips close over the mollusc. This time, she deliberately squeezed some of the melted butter down her chin. He reached across with his serviette, but she deflected his hand and reached behind his neck, pulling them towards each other until their lips met again, over the salt and pepper.

She felt a nervous qualm about what she was doing, but her reckless side was telling her to get on with it, no man would really object to a woman kissing him. She pushed her chair back and quickly moved round the table so she could sit on Pascal's lap. The kiss deepened. She felt one of his hands begin to explore her breasts, a knot of desire beginning to grow inside her. Her breathing became ragged. Their tongues were twisting together and she knew she had to do something or the situation would spiral out of control.

With great effort, she pulled herself away from him.

'Don't you want to finish the first course, George?' she asked.

'I was beginning to think you were the first course, Jane,' he replied, his voice hoarse and thick with need.

She swallowed. 'No. Oysters, then beef, then maybe you will have a choice of dessert.'

He pulled his hands away from her. She was aware of his arousal as she took the opportunity to stand up, and almost relented. Instead, she smiled at him and returned to her seat.

She drank her wine and refilled her glass. Pascal did the same, then they ate the oysters and, after them, the beef *tournedos aux herbes*, without further teasing.

He finished first and waited until she centred her knife and fork on her plate.

'Shall I take the plates into the kitchen?' he asked.

She grinned at him, the tip of her nose twitching. He'd noticed her do that when she was amused.

'I'm looking after you, George. If you want to look after me, you do it another time.'

He shrugged, and watched as she cleared the table of the used crockery and disappeared into the kitchen. Moments later, she emerged with a bowl full of red, black and blue berries in a warm vanilla syrup. She served a ladle-full of the fruits into each of the dishes and passed one over to Pascal.

She was still amused about something, he thought, feeling an answering smile on his own lips.

'What?' he asked eventually.

'I had this idea, when I offered you a choice of dessert, you might opt for the other one. You've surprised me, George.'

His smile deepened. 'I thought the real dessert was yet to come,' he said.

She pouted. 'You just wanted – as my grandmother used to say – your toffee *and* your ha'penny.'

Pascal switched the smile for a look of innocence. 'Moi?' he asked. 'I love your cooking,' he added, 'so I had to see what else was on the menu.'

She smiled at him coyly. 'You're just saying that, George,' she said in an affected Scarlett O'Hara drawl.

He shovelled the last of the fruit into his mouth, and dabbed the juice off his lips.

'I'll show you what I'm saying!' he said, standing up and taking her by the hand. He led her to the bean-bags and pushed her gently down onto one. The slit in her dress fell open gratifyingly and allowed her left leg to crook. He pulled off his blazer, took her cheeks between his hands and kissed her firmly on her yielding lips.

He gently teased her breast through the slinky-smooth material of her dress before allowing his hand to slither downward until it encountered her stocking-clad leg. As his fingers began to explore further up her thigh, she reached down and restrained his hand.

Breaking the kiss, she grinned. 'George, I have one other surprise for you.'

Pascal drew back from her. He quickly looked round the room.

'We're not live on the World-wide Web, are we?'

She giggled. 'No. No cameras or microphones this time – but another time?'

He shook his head. 'Certainly not. Some things should remain very private.'

'Then if you won't tell anyone else, I'm going to tell you a secret,' she said.

'What?'

She pulled his head towards her until her lips were an inch away from his ear. 'I'm not wearing any knickers.'

For a moment, he stared, then squeezed his eyes shut and expelled a lungful of air before opening them again. His hand moved up her thigh, beyond the slit in her dress until he was convinced she was telling the truth.

*

An hour later, Ferrari lolled against a bean-bag wearing only her shoes and stockings, and looking very relaxed and happy. Pascal leaned against another, wearing just his socks, exhausted after their second rapturous bout of love-making. She grinned at him from under her lashes.

'George, do me a favour next time and leave the socks off. They ruin your image.'

*

A week passed before Pascal could return the favour, at his home.

'So it's all sewn up then?' asked Jane Ferrari over coffee. 'You've got Jackson blaming Unwin for the drugs and girls, Unwin anxious to put the blame on Jackson as the

319

lynchpin, Martin prepared to give evidence against Jackson as well, Julia Fox prepared to identify both Jackson and Unwin as being involved in the prostitution, supplying drugs, the sex trafficking and abduction.'

'That's about the size of it, not forgetting the *former* Chairman of the Police Authority, who's going down for running a brothel. I heard today he's been removed from the Council,' said Pascal, sipping a twelve-year-old tawny port at the end of a meal which had taken him about an hour to prepare and cook, but which had apparently gone down extremely well with the woman – the *very attractive* woman – sitting opposite him in a classic Little Black Dress. 'But we didn't get Danny Bakker, who killed Sara Martin. At least, we *might* have shot him, he *might* have drowned in the sea at Harwich, but the fact is, we don't have a body.'

She nodded, then smiled and rested her chin on her hands, her elbows on the table as she leaned towards him.

'Do you feel the necessity for a body, George?'

He copied her position, leaning towards her, the light of the candles on the table illuminating both their faces. 'Yes – but not just *any* body, you understand.'

'I should hope not,' she murmured, her slender fingers reaching across the gap to follow the lines of his face, all the while holding his attention with the light of encouragement in her warm, brown eyes.

THE END

# ABOUT THE AUTHOR

Peter Holdroyd lives in the county of Norfolk, eastern England, with his wife of more than 40 years. Although he has written short stories for more than 50 years, mostly for his own satisfaction (though some have been published and other turned into screenplays), he only began writing novels after he retired from gainful employment in 2003.

Peter and Dee have a son and married daughter, and two beautiful granddaughters, currently closing in on their teenage years.

www.ingramcontent.com/pod-product-compliance
Lightning Source LLC
Chambersburg PA
CBHW030018180626
46810CB00001B/102